THE ELMINSTER SERIES

ELMINSTER'S Daughter

ED GREENWOOD

Wizards
OF THE COAST™

The Elminster Series
ELMINSTER'S DAUGHTER
©2004 Wizards of the Coast, Inc.

Distributed in the United States by Holtzbrinck Publishing. Distributed in Canada by Fenn Ltd.

Distributed to the hobby, toy, and comic trade in the United States and Canada by regional distributors.

Distributed worldwide by Wizards of the Coast, Inc. and regional distributors.

Cover art by J.P. Targete
Map by Jack Fred
Interior Art by Stephen Daniele
Original Hardcover First Printing: May 2004
First Paperback Printing: June 2005
Library of Congress Catalog Card Number: 2004116914

9 8 7 6 5 4 3 2 1

ISBN-10: 0-7869-3768-8
ISBN-13: 978-0-7869-3768-4
620-88775000-001-EN

U.S., CANADA,
ASIA, PACIFIC, & LATIN AMERICA
Wizards of the Coast, Inc.
P.O. Box 707
Renton, WA 98057-0707
+1-800-324-6496

EUROPEAN HEADQUARTERS
Hasbro UK Ltd
Caswell Way
Newport, Gwent NP9 0YH
GREAT BRITAIN
Please keep this address for your records

Visit our web site at www.wizards.com

FORGOTTEN REALMS®

Novels by Ed Greenwood

Sedit qui timuit ne non succederet

This one's for Brenna.
A daughter lost, not by me...but by us all.

nihil amori iniuriam est

A salute and thanks to the lore lords who have come to love Cormyr, and the work they have done on it, including Eric Boyd, Grant Christie, Tom Costa, George Krashos, and Bryon Wischstadt—and of course Troy Denning, Jeff Grubb, Eric Haddock, and Steven Schend.

Sons, sons—always you boast of what your tall sons will do, with their sharp new wits and sharper new swords!

Remember, O Prince, that you have also daughters! You're not the first man, great or low, to forget the shes he's sired, but mark this wisdom, Lord (not mine, but from the pen of a loremaster who was dust before dragons were ever driven from this land): The sages who turn the pages of history have a word for men who overlook their daughters . . . and that word is "fools."

Astramas Revendimar,
Court Sage of Cormyr
Letters To A Man To Be King
Year of the Smiling Flame

MARSEMBER

1. Dagohnlar House
2. Haelithtorntowers
3. Thundaerlyn Hall
4. Indur's Warehouses, overlying the Maranthar Undercellars
5. Mistwind Towers
6. The Lightless Lamp

One

A MURDEROUS MEETING OF MERCHANTS

A wizard, a merchant, a lord among merchants—I see no shortage of fools here.

The character Turst Sharptongue
in Scene the First
of the play *Windbag of Waterdeep*
by Tholdomor "the Wise" Rammarask
first performed in the Year of the Harp

It was a moonfleet night, the silvery Orb of Selûne scudding amid racing tatters of glowing cloud high above the proud spires of Waterdeep. Wizards in their towers and grim guards on battlements alike stared up and shivered, each thinking how small he was against the uncaring, speeding fire of the gods.

Far fewer merchants bothered to lift their gazes above the coins and goods—or softer temptations—under their hands at that hour, for such is the way of merchants. Hundreds were snoring, exhausted by the rigors of the day, but many were still awake and embracing—even if the hands of most of them were wrapped only around swiftly emptying tankards.

There were no tankards, no embraces, and no soft temptations in a certain shuttered upper room overlooking Jembril Street in Trades Ward. Instead, it held a cold, bare minimum of furniture—a table and six high-backed chairs—and an even colder company of men.

Six merchants sat in those chairs on this chill night in the early spring of the Year of Rogue Dragons, staring stonily at each other. The glittering glances of five of them suggested that the health of the sixth man, who sat alone at one end of the table, would not continue to flourish for more than a few breaths longer had it not been for the presence of the two impassive bodyguards who stood watchfully by his chair, cocked and loaded hand-crossbows held ready and free hands hovering near sword-hilts.

That sixth man said something, slowly and bitingly.

Outside, in the night, a shadow moved. An unseen witness to the merchants' meeting leaned closer to the only gap in the shutters across the windows of that upper room. Clinging head-downward to the carved stone harpy roof-truss nearest to the shutter, the shadow sacrificed as much balance as she dared, and strained to hear. Her slender arms were already quivering in the struggle to keep herself from plunging to the dark, cobbled street below.

"There are really no more excuses left to you, sirs," the man who sat apart told the others, smirking. "I *will* have my coins this night—or the deeds to your shops."

"But—" one of the men burst out, and then bit off whatever else he'd been going to say and looked helplessly down at the bare table before him, face dark with anger.

"So you'll ruin us, Caethur?" the next man man asked, his voice trembling. "You'd rather turn us out onto the streets than bleed us for another season? When you could set your hook at a higher rate, grant us more time, and keep us in debt forever, paying you all our days and yielding you far more coin than our stones are worth?"

Secure in the strength of the two murderous bodyguards at his back, Caethur leaned forward with a widening—and not very nice—smile on his face and replied triumphantly, "Yes."

He leaned back in his chair, very much at his ease, steepled his hands, and murmured over the resulting line of fingertips, "It will give me great pleasure, Hammuras, to ruin you. And you too, Nael. And especially you, Kamburan."

He moved his eyes in his motionless, smiling face to the other pair of seated merchants and added with a sigh, "Yet it almost pains me to visit the same fate upon you two gentlesirs. Why, I'd almost be inclined to give you that extra season Hammuras speaks of, if, say, something happened to still Kamburan's oversharp tongue forever. Why—"

One of that last pair of merchants slapped his hand down on the table. "*No*, Caethur. You'll not turn us to savaging each other whilst you gloat. We'll sink or stand together."

The other merchant of the two nodded balefully.

Caethur gave them both a brittle smile, wiggling his ring-bedecked fingers so the gem-studded gold bands adorning them flashed in the lamplight like glasses of the new vintage Waterdhavian nobles had dubbed "sparkling stars," and said airily, "*Well*, then, we've come to that moment, sirs, when the wagging of tongues must give way to making good, one way or another. Kamburan, why don't you begin?"

Reluctantly, the white-bearded merchant reached a hand into the breast of his flame-silk overtunic and drew forth—slowly and carefully, as two crossbows lifted warningly—a glossy-polished wooden coffer only a shade larger than his palm. Wordlessly he flipped it open, displaying the frozen fire of the line of gems within for all to see. Seven beljurils, sea-green and shimmering, their flash-fires building.

Kamburan set the coffer gently on the table and slid it toward Caethur.

Halfway to the moneylender it stopped. Caethur lifted a finger, and one of his guards stepped smoothly forward to close the coffer and slide it the rest of the way down the table. The moneylender made no move to touch it.

"We should have gone to Mirt," Hammuras muttered.

Caethur gave the spice dealer a shark-like grin. "Life is filled with 'should-haves,' isn't it, Hammuras? *I* should have chosen to deal with more astute and harder-working tradesmen and never come to this regrettable salvaging of scraps from the wrack of what should have been five flourishing businesses."

"None of that!" Nael snarled. "You know as well as the rest of us that times have been hard! The beasts from the sea, a season's shipping shattered, wars in Amn and Tethyr and the fall in trade with both those lands. . . ."

Caethur spread his hands and lifted his eyebrows at the same time, to ask mildly, "And did not every merchant of Waterdeep face these troubles? Yet—behold—they're not *all* here, sitting around this table. Only you five." Turning his gaze to Hammuras, he held out a beckoning hand.

Grimly, the spice merchant produced a small coffer of his own, displayed the rubies it held, and slid it along the table.

It stopped within reach of the moneylender, but Caethur made no move to take it up. Instead, he turned his expectant gaze to Nael.

Who sat as still as stone and as pale as snow-marble.

"Well?" Caethur asked softly, into a silence that was suddenly very deep and yet as singingly tight as a drawn bowstring.

Nael swallowed, lifted his chin, swallowed again, then said, "I've brought neither gems nor my deed here with me, but—"

Without waiting for a signal, one of the crossbowmen fired, and Aldurl Nael's left eye was suddenly a bloody profusion of sprouting wood and flight-feathers. The brass-merchant reeled in his seat, head flopping back and mouth gaping, and did not move again. Crimson rivulets of blood spilled from his mouth, seeking the floor.

"—but how unfortunate," Caethur said mildly, finishing Nael's sentence for him. "For Nael, and for all of you. After all, we can't have any witnesses to such wanton butchery, can we?"

The other guard calmly fired his crossbow, and Hammuras died.

As the three surviving merchants shouted and surged desperately to their feet, both guards tossed their spent crossbows aside and plucked cushions off a shelf affixed to the back of Caethur's chair. Four more hand-crossbows gleamed in the lamplight, loaded and ready. Coolly the guards snatched them up—and used them.

Kamburan groaned for a surprising long time, but the rest of the room was still in but a breath or two.

"The bolts my men use, by the way," the moneylender told the corpses conversationally, "are tipped with brain-burn, to keep prying Watchful Order mages from learning anything of our meeting—and how you happened to so carelessly end up wearing war-darts in your faces. After all, we wouldn't want to start one more irresponsible city fashion, would we?"

Caethur rose from his chair, nodded to his two guards, and waved a hand at the gem-coffers on the table. "When you're done stripping the bodies of *all* deeds and coins and suchlike, bring those."

As he strode to the door and slipped out, he took something from a belt-pouch. It looked like a beast's claw: a grip-bar studded with a row of little daggers. When Caethur closed his hand around the bar, the blades protruded from between his fingers like a row of sheathed talons. With his other hand, the moneylender drew a belt dagger and used it to cautiously flick away the sheaths that covered every blade of the claw. Something dark and wet glistened on each razor-sharp point.

Thrusting the dagger through a belt-loop and putting the venomed claw behind his back, Caethur waited, humming a jaunty tune softly under his breath.

When his two laden bodyguards came to the door, he gave them a frown as he blocked their way and pointed back into the room.

"You've missed something," he said sharply.

His bodyguards gave him astonished and displeased looks but whirled to look at the dead merchants; the moneylender was not a master to be crossed.

The moment they turned Caethur took a swift step, slashed them both across the backs of their necks with his claw, and sprang away to avoid the thrashing spasms he knew would follow.

The guards were young and strong. After they stiffened with identical grunts of astonished agony, they managed to whirl toward their master, glaring, and claw at the air wildly for some seconds ere the venom stilled their limbs, and sent them toppling into the long dark chill of oblivion.

Caethur applied another knife, this one slaked liberally with brain-burn, to both of the men he'd just slain, and calmly set about collecting everything of value in the room full of corpses. After all, brain-burn was expensive . . . and after word got around of this night's deaths, the hiring-price of guards agreeing to work for him was bound to go up sharply.

Still, the cost of just one man informing the Lords of Waterdeep of his deeds would be much higher. Kamburan's cloak, still draped over the back of his chair, was unstained, and when bundled around Caethur's takings, served well as a carry-sack. He drew his own cloak around him with not a hair out of place nor any change in his easy half-smile at all.

It wasn't the first time Caethur the moneylender had walked away alone from a room full of dead men. Such things were, after all, a regrettable but all-too-often inevitable feature of his profession.

*   *   *   *   *

Outside, the shadow moved, swinging up and away from the shutter, seeking the edge of the roof. A booted foot slipped, a curse blazed sudden and bright in a mind that kept its dangling body coldly silent—and with a sudden surge of effort, the shadow gained the roof and scrambled away.

*   *   *   *   *

As soon as he entered the portal, he felt it: a disturbance in the flow of the Weave, straight ahead. Someone or something was casting a spell on his intended destination or had laid a trap of enchantment on it already. Only those like himself, highly attuned to the Weave, could feel it—and move to avoid whatever danger was waiting.

Chuckling soundlessly, the archmage stepped aside, moving through the drifting blue nothingness to emerge elsewhere, from a portal linked to neither the one he'd entered nor the imperiled one it reached.

*   *   *   *   *

Narnra crouched in the lee of a large but crumbling chimney, wincing at the burning ache in her shoulder. She'd torn something inside, it seemed. Something small, thank the gods.

Ah, yes, the watching, all-seeing gods. She glanced up, and thought another silent curse upon the enthusiastically devout idiots who enspelled the Plinth to glow so brightly by night. Thieves don't welcome beacons that illuminate their working world well.

And a thief was what Narnra Shalace was. That had been her profession since her mother's mysterious death and the rush of neighbors, clients, and Waterdhavians she'd never laid eyes on before to snatch all they could of what had belonged to her mother. Only frantic flight had kept a frightened and furious Narnra from being taken herself, doubtless to be sold as a slave by whichever noble had set his men to chasing her.

Everyone knew there were laws in Waterdeep that touched nobles and many more that—somehow—did not. Moreover, noble and rich merchant families had ships and wagons in plenty and outlying lands beyond Waterdeep's laws to travel to, where anything or anyone could be taken.

Leaving a suddenly coinless, bereft Narnra Shalace hunted through the alleys and rooftops. So she'd become what she was being treated as—one more thief scratching to survive in a city that was not kind to thieves.

So here she was, aching and scheming on a decaying rooftop in Trades Ward. A lonely young lass, fairly nimble in her leaps and tumblings but not particularly beautiful, with her slender, long-limbed build, her hacked-off dark hair, blackfire eyes, and beak of a nose. "The Silken Shadow," she billed herself, but still she saw men smirk when she uttered that title in the dingy, nameless taverns near the docks where odd stolen items could be sold for a few coppers—and no questions.

The winter had been hard. If it hadn't been for chimneys like this one, the cold would have taken her before the first snows—and one had to fight for the warmest rooftop spots in Waterdeep.

As it was, Narnra spent much time hungry these days. Hungry and angry. Fear was with her at every waking moment, keeping her glancing behind her and knowing it was largely in vain. She could not help but be uncomfortably aware of how skilled other thieves in this city were . . . to say nothing of the Watch and the Watchful Order and the Masked Lords alone knew how many powerful wizards. She was a match for none of them and not even a laughable challenge to most.

To come to their notice—save as a passing amusement— would be to die.

So here she crouched, desperate for coins to buy food for her belly and all too apt, these days, to fall into rages.

Rage is something a thief who expects to live to see the dawn can ill afford.

She sighed soundlessly. Oh, she was lithe and acrobatic enough to prowl the rooftops, but not comely enough to seek the warm and easier coin—hers if she could dance unclad inside festhalls. No, she was just one more lonely outlander scrambling to make a dishonest living on the streets of Waterdeep. Scrambling because she lacked the weapons of a noble name or a shop of her own to make forging a dishonest living comparatively easy.

Scowling, Narnra drew forth the purse she'd snatched earlier in that street fight in Dock Ward. A gang of thieves, that must have been, to set upon two merchants that way, and she'd raced in and plucked their prize, so they'd be looking for her. . . .

All for three gold coins—mismatched, from as many cities, but all heavy and true metal—six silvers, four coppers, and a claim-token to a lockbox somewhere in Faerûn that she knew not. Well, they would have to serve her.

From inside the top of her boot she drew a larger yet lighter purse, drew open its throat-thong with two fingers, checked that the cloak was laid beside her in just the right position, and shifted herself a fingerlength closer to the edge of the roof, ducking low.

So far as she could tell, the moneylender had no more guards left. He was wearing some sort of daggerclaw, shielded from idle eyes by a cloak he was carrying draped over that arm, but he moved like a man wary and alone. He'd hastened through Lathin's Cut to reach the High Road, and there waited in the first deep doorway for a Watch patrol to pass, and fallen in close behind it. He looked like any respectable merchant caught in the wrong part of the city late at night and trying to wend his way safely home.

If he was going to avoid the scrutiny of the standing Watchpost ahead, where the great roads met, he would have to turn aside just below her, in only a few paces more. His gaze flicked upward, and Narnra held her breath and kept very still, hoping she looked like a rooftop gargoyle. Caethur strode on, slowing and stepping wide so as to look around the corner, then drawing in toward it, to duck around close to the wall.

Delicately, the Silken Shadow spilled her paltry handful coins down from above, to flash before his nose and bounce and roll. The moneylender froze rather than darting into a wild run back and away, peered at a rolling gold coin, and—looked up.

To meet the handful of sand from her larger purse, followed by a shadow that leaped down at him with spread hands clutching the cloak in front of her like a streaming shield.

Caethur the moneylender had time to gape but no breath for a shout ere she slammed into him, smashing him to the street. She felt something in him break and crumple as she rode him mercilessly, their bodies bouncing on the cobbles together. By then she had the cloak tight around his head, one knee atop the arm that bore the claw, and a hand free to backhand him across the throat, as hard as she could.

That quelled the dazed beginnings of his groans and left him sprawled and limp. Narnra cut his well-worn belt with a slash from her best knife, snatched away the belt-satchel—heavy with deeds, coins, and coffers—and was up and gone, leaving her sacrificed coins and stolen cloak behind.

Yet swift as she was, she was not quite swift enough. There was a shout from up the street and the flash and flicker of Watch torches turning.

Grimly the Silken Shadow sprinted for her life, seeking the shop just ahead that had an outside staircase.

You'd think I'd be somewhere grander than this, she thought savagely for perhaps the ten thousand and forty-sixth time, if my father truly was a great wizard and my mother a dragon. Where's my high station, my wealth, and my power? Why can't I hurl spells or turn into a dragon?

* * * * *

The old cook whirled around. "*Hah!* Caught ye! Boy, d'ye still want to have yer hire here, come dawn?"

The greasy kitchen lad froze, a basket of discarded cuttings and rotten leavings clutched to his stained apron, and gave Phaerorn a look of utter astonishment. "Hey?"

The cook stumped forward on his wooden leg, hefting his well-used cleaver in one stubby-fingered, hairy hand, and asked softly, "And now ye give me 'hey,' do ye? Fond of your nose, are ye?"

The rising cleaver gleamed menacingly, and Naviskurr realized the depths of his error. "Ah, *no*, Master Phaerorn, sir—ah, that is, yes, I am, but I meant no harm; truly, and—and—"

As the old cook advanced, the boy's voice rose in a terrified squeak as that shining steel rose coldly to touch his nose, "—and before all the gods I swear I know not what I've done to offend what'd I do wrong sorry sorry *what* lord?"

"Huh," Phaerorn said in disgust. "This is the spine they send me, these days. *This* is the eloquence of the young who'll shine so bright an' save us all."

He turned away—then spun so swiftly and smoothly that Naviskurr shrieked, pointed with his cleaver at the three baskets the lad had already set down, and growled, "How many times have I told ye *nothing* is to be set against that door, lad? Nothing!"

Naviskurr looked, blinked, set down the fourth basket where he stood, and hastily went to shift the three offending ones, grumbling, "Sorry, Master Phaerorn, sir . . . but 'tis no more than an old door. We never open it, never use it . . ."

He dragged the baskets aside and straightened with a grunt to regard the nail-studded old door here in the dingiest corner of the Rain Bird Rooming House kitchens. Peeling blue paint on rough, wide planks, adorned with an admittedly impressive relief carving: a long, flowing face of a beak-nosed, bearded man that Naviskurr had privately dubbed "The Stunned Old Wizard."

Naviskurr scowled at its perpetual sly smile. "So why

must we keep everything clear of it, anyway?"

The carving flickered, glowing with a light that had never been there before—and even before the scullery knave could stagger back or cry the fear kindling in him, the face seemed to thrust forward, *out* of the door!

It was attached, Naviskurr saw as he gulped and scrambled away, waving vainly at Master Phaerorn, to a swift-striding man—a hawk-nosed, bearded, long-haired old man in none-too-clean robes. The man *flowed* out of the closed door, leaving it carving-adorned and unchanged in his wake.

Merry blue-gray eyes darted a glance at the gaping kitchen lad from under dark brows and gave him a wink ere turning to favor old Phaerorn with a nod, a wave, and the words, "Thy son's working out just fine in Suzail, Forn, and looking likely to be wedded by full spring, if he's not careful!"

The old cook's jaw dropped, his eyes widened with delight—and the briskly walking visitor was gone, a curved pipe floating along in his wake like some sort of patient snake.

"Wha—wha—who . . ." Naviskurr gabbled.

Master Phaerorn folded his arms across his chest, gave his scullery knave a wide grin, and said triumphantly, "*That's* why we keep that door clear, lad. Yer Mystra-loving, world-blasting archmages don't look kindly to stepping knee-deep in kitchen slops, look ye!"

"Uh . . ." Naviskurr blinked, swallowed, and asked weakly, "Mystra? Archmage? Who *was* he?"

"Just an old friend of mine," Phaerorn said briskly, turning back to his sizzling spits. "No one ye'd know. His name's Elminster."

With a chuckle he turned the roasts, waiting for the storm of questions to come.

Instead, to his ears came a soft, rather wet thump. After stirring thickening gravy and licking the steaming wooden spoon consideringly, Phaerorn turned to see just how the lazy lad had made such a sound—and discovered Naviskurr sprawled across all four baskets of slops. His least promising scullion yet was staring sightlessly at the skillet-bedecked rafters. He'd fainted.

Phaerorn sighed and flicked his spoon at the lad. Perhaps a few drops of hot gravy would revive him. Or perhaps not. Ah, the mighty valor of the young. . . .

* * * * *

Her mother's apprentices had been lying to her, of course. They must have been. Yet they'd been angry and taunting her, not watching their words . . . and they'd acted later as if they shouldn't have told her what they had. One had tried to make her think they'd been drunk and uttered nonsense, but the others had tried to use drink on her to find out exactly what they'd said and she'd remembered.

Crouching on a rotten and unsuitable rooftop that would send tiles clattering down right in front of the Watch if she dared to move, Narnra thought up some furious curses at the scudding moon.

She'd been over these memories more times than she could count and knew—*knew*—that Goraun and the other apprentice gemcutters had been telling the truth, or thought they were. It had taken her a year of careful probing to make sure they literally meant Maerjanthra Shalace the sorceress, better known to all Waterdeep as Lady Maerjanthra of the Gems, jeweler to the nobility, was a dragon with scales and wings and not merely the sort of "dragon" that meant a bad-tempered, powerful woman who was to be feared.

Which powerful wizard? They'd never told her that.

"Three gold," came a voice from below as another Watch officer joined the others peering about the alley. The two who were halfway up the stair that led to Narnra turned at something in his voice and asked gruffly, "So?"

"Well, so he was lured, right enough. But our victim's Caethur the moneylender."

There was a general growl of disgust. "Pity the thief didn't slay him," one of the others said. "Or did he?"

"Oh, he'll live, though it might be long years, if ever, before he has much of a voice again. But unless Clutchcoins knows who did him—and will tell us—I think Waterdeep's best served if we—"

"Exactly," an older, deeper voice agreed. "I'm sure there's something that needs our urgent attention going on over River Gate way, about now. Help Caethur to the Watchpost, and see if he feels like making us all wiser. I'll be deeply unsurprised if he does not."

* * * * *

The bearded old man ignored the grand entry stair and its flanking stone pillars, striding instead up a flight of steps set into the mossy side of a rock garden that rose to the right of the sprawling stone magnificence of Mirt's Mansion. Through a bower of dappled moonlight he moved unchallenged to a small stone arch bridge that joined the rising shoulder of Mount Waterdeep that held the moneylender's gardens to an upper balcony of Mirt's fortified house.

Halfway across that span the air seemed to sparkle, and he was suddenly facing a silent woman in a clinging, flowing gown . . . a gown of pale moonglow, to match the tatters streaming across the sky overhead.

Elminster smiled and bowed his head in greeting. "Fair even, Ieiridauna. Are Mirt and Asper at home?"

Smiling silently, the watchghost nodded and stretched one long and shapely arm back to point at the door behind her. Then she drifted forward tentatively to touch the Old Mage's cheek with her other hand. Elminster took a slow step to meet her.

The soft brush of her fingertips chilled him deeply as it stole a little life-force, but Elminster turned his head to kiss those icy fingers, then clasped Ieiridauna gently against him.

Her breath was like a icy thread of glacier-wind, and her

shoulders and breast seem to grow more solid the longer he embraced her, but suddenly his encircling arm was empty, and the watch-ghost was past him, weepingly softly and saying into his ear, "Too kind, great lord, too kind! You must not give me too much."

Elminster turned and said softly, "Lady, 'tis my hope that you abide in Faerûn for at least an age to come, to bear witness and whisper wisdom—and the life is mine to give."

The watchghost shook her head and knelt to him, her head and shoulders silvery-solid but the rest of her mere shiftings in the night air. "You do me too much honor, Lord Chosen."

Elminster chuckled. "Ah, ye'll have me blushing yet, lass!" He struck a mock-heroic pose, pulled a face at her, then winked, waved, and went to the door. Ieiridauna's gentle sobs followed him.

The plain dark door opened before his hand could touch it, and a bristle-moustached face peered out of deeper darkness at him. "Seducing my watchghost again, El? Is there no end to your lecherousness?"

Elminster spread serene hands. " 'Twould seem not, Lord Walrus. Nor my meddlesome curiosity, when it comes to the affairs of others—such as the overly rich of Waterdeep."

Mirt grunted and beckoned him inside. "This had *better* be good—ye interrupted us in the midst of Asper dancing."

"Ah!" Elminster said quickly, as they stepped between two motionless helmed horrors, into a lamplit bedchamber dominated by a massive many-pillared bed. "Pray continue!"

Mirt's lady love unfolded herself from a seemingly impossible pose. She'd been balanced on her shoulders on the bed, head looking back down its length as her legs arched over her to clutch a gem between her toes and dangle it in front of her own nose. She tucked her legs back in one graceful movement, tossing the gem upward in a sparkling of reflected glows, caught it deftly, and said firmly, "Later. I'll hear fewer lewd comments this way. What befalls?"

"Ye'll pull something, doing that," the Old Mage commented, watching Asper flip herself forward and to one side in a deft, sinuous movement to end up reclining along the edge of the bed facing him.

She twinkled a fond smile at him. "Indeed: the undivided attention of a moneylender and a Chosen of Mystra. Drink some of yon wine and speak."

Elminster raised his eyebrows, held out his hand, and a decanter lifted itself from a forest of its fellows atop a tall, ornately carved greatchest and drifted into his grasp.

"No wonder mages are such drunkards," Mirt muttered. "Why, if I could do that . . ."

"You'd never have to get out of bed at all," Asper murmured sweetly. "El?"

"I come from Cormyr," the Old Mage replied, uncorking and sniffing appraisingly at the mouth of the bottle. "Where coins in profusion enough that they'd best be described as 'huge heaps of wealth' are being spent on a secretive campaign to overthrow the Obarskyrs and put a new king on Cormyr's throne."

"So what else is new?" Mirt grunted. "Our so-called nobles spend in like manner here, seeking to learn who each hidden Lord is, so they can have us murdered and bribe those who're left to choose them to step into our shoes. They never seem to reflect that they'll be setting themselves up to be murdered in turn, but then nobles are rarely swift-witted enough to get dressed without help." He held out his hand. "Are ye going to drink that or just pose with it?"

Elminster swigged, sighed appreciatively, said, "Nice fire, that!" and handed the old moneylender the bottle. "Well," he continued, strolling to the bed to pluck up the palm-sized gem from Asper's fingers and idly stroke one of her long, slender legs with it, "These coins are coming from deep pockets somewhere here in Waterdeep. Whose, I know not—nor even to whom precisely they roll when they reach the Forest Kingdom, but I abide in hope that ye . . ."

Asper smiled. "Will find out for you, lord? Of course."

Mirt grunted agreement and passed the bottle back to Elminster.

It was almost empty, of course.

* * * * *

Tirelessly, the tattered clouds chased each other across the sky, so many silver wraiths fleeing a deeper darkness. From the battlements and windows and guardposts atop Mount Waterdeep, watching men shivered and looked away. Breath curling like gusting frost in the chill night air, each reflected some melancholy variation on the thought that there'd be nights like this long after he was dead, just as there had been nights like this long before his birthing.

Unwarmed by such cheery thinking, each man clutched his cloak or nightrobe tighter around himself, shook his head, and tried to call to mind more pleasant things.

* * * * *

Elminster lifted his head to regard the rushing, ragged clouds. So many flames of silver in the moonlight in a silent, raging hurry to be elsewhere.

"On a moonfleet night like this," he murmured, "anything can happen—and all too often does."

He ducked through a narrow, noisome arch into the dung and refuse choked run of an alley.

A dead-end alley. The shadow overhead frowned at that and stole forward over a shallow roof-peak like creeping smoke.

Those cursed merchants had come light-coined to their fateful meeting, all of them. Oh, the satchel she'd cached where none but her would ever find it was full of bright gems and deeds that made her the owner of three buildings—in Castle Ward, yet!—but her lure-coins were gone, and she'd only three coppers left between her and starvation. And now this muttering old man comes blundering along right under her best hiding-place . . .

He didn't look the sort to carry much coin—but then, she didn't need much. A handful of gold to replace what she'd lost, but a handful *now*.

Across soft moss on old silver-worn wood shingles, Narnra crept to the ruins of an old bell-spire that perched above the midpoint of the alley, just as the old man passed below. . . .

She had neither coins nor cloak, but he didn't look like much. Only fools and drunkards walked weaponless by night in these alleys. Another handful of sand, a good kick when she came down on him, then away while he was still groaning.

Across the next rooftop she went, almost to the end of the alley now. In a moment he'd see there was no way out and curse and turn. Narnra dug out a handful of sand, checked the blackened blade in the sheath at her wrist, leaned over the edge of the roof, and gasped, "Oh, *yes!*"

That voice should make any man look up—and did. Her handful of sand followed it, at just the right moment. There was a hasty scrabbling from below—gods, he was away to the blind back wall like the wind!—and Narnra leaped.

He was too fast, despite slipping on slimy debris under-foot, and she landed catlike on stinking broken things, missing him entirely. He must have had his eyes shut when she threw the sand for they were gleaming calmly enough in her direction now!

With a soft, wordless snarl Narnra drew her knife and came at him in a rush, bounding and springing from side to side as she came, hoping he'd slip in the trash. He was still barehanded, and chuckling now, low and deep, like a delighted madman.

Furiously, the Silken Shadow slashed at the old man with her steel fang, crosswise as she dodged, so that he couldn't grapple her or surprise her with some stab of his own. She wasn't afraid of any lunge at her—in all this heaped and tangled refuse, he'd go flat on his face!—but surely there was more to this old fool than mere witless wandering, and . . .

He stalked toward her, for all the world as if she was the cornered prey and he the hunting cat, and in a sudden flowering of fear Narnra thrust her blade deep into him, pulling it up hard to gut him open.

It was like stabbing smoke. He was there to her knuckles but *not* there to the steel of her blade.

With the soft beginnings of a curse Narnra sprang back from one long-fingered reaching hand and sprinted away, slipping and stumbling in the rotting refuse. Blue eyes blazed eagerly at her from beneath dark brows, a nose to outthrust her own, and a white beard. Yet for all his years, he was taller, leaner, and a *lot* faster than he'd looked, and—the air before her started to glow.

Oh, Watching Gods, a *wizard!*

Narnra ducked and spun aside, hoping to avoid whatever the magic was, and ran in earnest now, just trying to get out of the alley. This had all been a mista—

Something dark and tentacled rose out of the refuse and shadows along the wall ahead of her, reaching forth to bar her path and to gather her in. Something with many fell, glistening eyes, that slid greasily about in a loosely slumping, slimy body as it hissed and burbled and came for her.

A fancy for her eyes spun by the wizard's spell, it must be! No slithering tentacled thing had been in the narrow alley when the old man had walked along it, she—

A cold, wet tentacle slapped around Narnra's wrist.

She screamed involuntarily and slashed at it furiously, tugging and turning away as she did so, to keep another four or six tentacles from reaching her. Dark stickiness spurted as she sobbed and hacked, sawing and pulling desperately this way and that . . . then something gave way, and she was free, crashing and rolling through dung, filthy water, and slimy rotting things.

The old man's voice was as deep as his chuckle. "Behold, a thief steals her greatest treasure: her life."

Furiously, Narnra found her feet and spun around, panting. The monster was gone as if it had never been—but the alleyway seemed changed. The way out was nowhere to be seen, and it now seemed a round pit of old crumbling walls and garbage, eerie in the soft moonlight streaked by the racing silver clouds overhead.

The old man was standing near one stretch of wall, his hands still empty. "Go home, lass. Leave stealing things to fools, and find another life. I tried your way and had my fun, but . . . there are better ways. Go home."

"I have no home," Narnra spat at him. "They stole it, merchants of Waterdeep. They stole it all."

He took one slow step forward, and she brought her knife up to menace him in one trembling hand.

"You tell me to go," she snarled fearfully, "and yet hide the way from me! What jest is this, wizard?"

The old man frowned. "Ah, that spell does take some that way. Stand still."

He lifted a hand, muttered something, and pointed at her. Desperately Narnra tried to duck away, but there was nowhere to hide, nowhere to run. . . .

The air glowed a different hue, and a tingling sensation spilled over her. She glared at him helplessly, feeling weak and empty with terror, and . . .

The feeling passed, but the alley still seemed a walled-in cage. The wizard made a sudden, curt sound of surprise and strode toward her. Narnra scrambled back, slamming against a rough stone wall almost immediately. "Keep away from me!" she cried. "I'll—I'll scream for the Watch!"

She knew what a ridiculous threat that was even as she uttered it, but he neither sneered nor laughed. Instead, he said quietly, "Lady of the night, turn your knife-hand over, so I may see your knuckles."

Narnra glared at him, then, curious, did so. Her tumble in the refuse had scratched the back of her hand, and she was bleeding freely. She reached her hand toward her mouth to suck the blood away, but the wizard snapped, "*Be still!*"

His voice was like thunder, the air around her suddenly

afire. Magic again, freezing her limbs utterly! She—he was going to—she couldn't—

Her eyes could yet move, and she could still breathe. Something was burning close before her, a flame rising where there'd been none. The blood on her hand was blazing with cold, silent fire.

Narnra stared at it helplessly. It burned nothing but yet burned. She could see her dirt-smeared hand and her glistening blood through that flame, and there was no pain.

The wizard stood before her now, staring at the same thing she was. Slowly, under their shared scrutiny, the flickering flame faded away.

Helplessly Narnra lifted her gaze to his. He was smiling. "Well," he said, in a rich, whimsical voice. "Well, well."

She stared at him, spell-frozen, unable to speak. The mage shook a small purse out of his sleeve—it looked like a palm-sized pea-pod but was made of some sort of dark and scaly hide and hung at the end of its own intricate lace-link chain—thrust it open with his thumb, and spilled seven gold coins into his palm. As deftly as any tavern juggler he flicked them into a neat stack and placed it delicately atop her bleeding hand.

"Fare ye well, lady," he said gently, gave her a kindly smile, and turned away—and walked through the wall.

Narnra Shalace stared at where he'd vanished, blinking unbelievingly at the solid, unbroken stones. All she could hear was her own racing breath, all she could feel was the cold weight of coins, the faintly tickling trickle of blood beneath them, and the solid feel of her own knife, still in her hand.

It had all been so sudden, so unbelievable, so . . .

That flame, whatever it had been, had surprised him. It had come from his spell but from her, too. He'd given her coins instead of death. Coins, as if she were a beggar or a pleasure-lass . . . or a successful thief. A stack of more gold than she could have dared hope to gain from one old man. And in a wink of an eye he was—gone, right through that wall, and she was . . .

She was able to move again, a little, and the walls of the alley seemed to *move*, around her, straightening and shifting.

Desperately, Narnra stared at where the wizard had vanished through the wall, marking just which heap of refuse was at that spot. She could move her other hand now, as slowly as a feather falling on a windless day. She reached up, took the coins, and was almost surprised to find them every bit as solid and heavy as they'd seemed. She put them into a pouch, her movements still slow but quickening with every breath, and saw that the alley around was once more long and narrow, coming to a blind end here and curving slightly as it stretched back out to the street there.

She went to the place where the wizard had vanished and cautiously extended her knife at the wall. It plunged into the stone as if through empty air. Wonderingly she leaned forward, her arm following it.

This could be the worst sort of death if the stone closed around her. Suspicious, insulted—who *was* this old wizard to lecture her and pity her and give her a beggar-offering of coins?—and yet, yes, fascinated, Narnra Shalace stepped forward into darkness.

Two

A FINE NIGHT FOR REVELRY

Those who hope to survive adventures are advised to pick their own forays, rather than striding blindly into someone else's schemes—and another someone's trouble. For trouble thus found has an almost inevitable way of being freely shared.

Seldreene Ammath of Suzail
Married to a Merchant
Year of the Serpent

It was dark, and smelled of damp stone, old earth, and the faint reek of garbage receding behind her. The Silken Shadow went forward cautiously, keeping low, as careful of her balance in this unseen footing as if she'd been on a crumbling roof.

There was a singing in the air in front of her, a singing that built swiftly into a shrieking as she advanced—a tumult she somehow knew she heard more than the world around her would. A sickening, shuddering feeling was growing inside her, too. It faltered when she drew back but surged anew when she stepped forward again.

Narnra kept the knife ready in her hand, wondering what sort of fool she was being, and peered ahead, seeking any glimmer of light.

Obligingly, radiance suddenly flowered before her, quite close, blossoming as swiftly as the flaring of any new-lit torch. It was a deep, rich blue light, a glow of magic mightier than anything she'd ever seen before. As she watched, it raced along in straight paths, outlining an archway where the white-bearded wizard stood.

Narnra promptly went to fingertips and knees on the stones then slid forward onto her belly as quietly as she could—and was barely down and motionless when the mage turned and peered in her direction.

Nodding as if satisfied—had he seen her or not?—he turned and stepped through the glowing arch—and the singing and shuddering within her ceased, as sharply as if severed by an axe-blow.

Narnra lifted her head, listening intently, but all was dark and silent except for the archway. As she stared at it, the radiance pulsed, flickered, and started to fade.

In a trice she was on her feet and running to it, swerving aside at the last moment to keep out of sight of anyone looking out of the arch. Its center was dark, and the Silken Shadow crawled the last few feet like a lizard in a purposeful hurry and peered around its edge, chin almost brushing the floor—to find herself looking at more dark nothingness.

The light was definitely dimmer than before. Narnra bit her lip then rose and stepped forward through the archway. If the wizard had a hidden lair right under Trades Ward, she had to know about it. All about it.

Another step into silent darkness, then another. At her third stride, the darkness vanished, and she was standing in more deep blue radiance, blueness swirling like mist on all sides and falling endlessly past. Narnra fell with it, yet stood upright and unmoving on an unseen floor, pausing uncertainly. Whirling around, she could see no hint of whence she'd come, only a blue void that . . . that . . .

She was suddenly drenched with sweat, more afraid than she'd ever been in her life. Where was she? Which way was forward? With great care she pivoted back until she was facing, she hoped, in exactly the direction she'd been facing while advancing . . . and went on.

Two steps later, darkness returned, and the damp. Yet the smell was different, somehow. The tang of the sea was strong, but there was also old rotting, like a swamp—a smell her nose had known in Waterdeep only when the harbor was being dragged. She stood in another narrow stone passage, and there were distant echoes ahead. Someone—no, a lot of someones—were talking. Chattering and laughing, like a merchants' revel. She was somewhere large, with unseen stone chambers opening out from her passage.

Under the City of the Dead? Deep beneath the drovers' streets nigh the River Gate? Or—somewhere else entirely, far from Waterdeep?

Another step brought her into blue light once more—a faint, fading glow. Narnra spun around and beheld an archway like the one she'd stepped through to get here. She stepped back into it, walked freely for a few strides then shrugged, turned around, and went back to the arch.

This time its glow was almost gone. She peered at the radiance narrowly and positioned herself exactly in the center of the arch. When the glow failed utterly, Narnra stepped forward—slamming her knee hard into what was now a solid stone wall.

She was trapped here, wherever here was, and suddenly enraged at herself for being so easily lured. She slapped the unseen wall in front of her, beat her fist on it with a snarl, drew a deep, tremulous breath, and spun again. She had no choice now but to go on.

Towards the revelry. In the wake of the wizard who'd so casually defeated her.

He knew how to make this magic of archways work, so

she'd either have to find her own way out or find him and
. . . and what? Beg?

Growling soundlessly, Narnra hefted her knife in her
hand and prowled forward. Old, worn stone blocks were
under her soft boots, sea-breezes ghosted around her ankles,
and the first glimmers of light could be seen ahead.

This was looking less and less like Waterdeep.

Oh Mask and Tymora, aid me now.

* * * * *

Elminster cast three illusory disguises, one atop the next,
saving his shapechange in case it became necessary to fly or
swim out of this gathering in haste. The company he'd be
keeping in a moment would be neither savory nor safe.

He was taller, now, in his outermost seeming, and scarred,
with the jet-black hair of the older branch of the Cormaerils.
He selected a tiny token from a belt-pouch, murmured a
word over it—and was suddenly holding a scabbarded sword
in his hands. A needle-slender blade of the sort favored by
many at court in Suzail, mirror-bright, its ornately swept
and curved basket hilt studded with small, glossy-smooth
sapphires like so many ever-curious eyes.

Strapping it on, he strode across a dark, pillared hall,
where rotten barrels moldered and rats scurried in the dim-
ness, and up an old, worn flight of steps. The Marsemban
harbor-stink grew stronger with the faint light ahead. Quite
suddenly, he was in a better-lit yet still gloom-shadowed
room where grim guards stood watching a throng of laughing, drinking, loudly talking people, who were sporting
under lamplight in a much larger chamber beyond.

Elminster sighed inwardly. Revelry was the same everywhere, and he'd managed to enjoy it for the first thousand
years or so . . . but no more. Too much noise, too much
pretence and sneering and nasty rumors—and too many
wonderstruck lovely young things, all hope and excitement
and bright laughter, who lived now only in his memory, gone

in their countless legions to graves. He'd even helped to put a few of them there.

Yet he strode on, not hesitating for a moment. Meddling and stepping into distasteful danger was, after all, what Elminsters did.

Threading his way through the guards with the purposeful stride of a man who has every right to be present and considers himself greater in rank than all others, he advanced—and was two long strides from the archway that opened into noise and full lamplight when the challenge came.

Blades suddenly slid out to bar his path and rise up behind him. "Down steel," he ordered curtly.

The swords menacing him moved not a fingerwidth.

"And who are you," an unpleasant voice hissed from the other end of one of them, "to be giving us orders? Or coming up from cellars we searched *very* thoroughly?"

The tall, scarred man with the jet-black hair and the grand rapier at his hip turned his head coldly. "My name is Cormaeril, my lineage noble, and my patience limited. Who are *you* to be stopping me?"

"You're older than the other Cormaerils," a different voice observed coldly from behind another sword.

"Easy, now! They said they hoped some of the older branches would make an appearance," a third voice said hastily. "Some Cormaerils were out of the realm long before the order of exile, with no chance to make claims nor set affairs in order. Let him pass—there's only the one of him."

"Have you any magic on you?" the first voice demanded.

"Of course," the scarred newcomer replied icily. "But no spells up my sleeves nor things I can hurl doom with, if that's what you fear."

Reluctantly, the blades drew back, and Elminster was aware of a lot of armed men drifting disappointedly away into the far corners of the room again. There wasn't going to be the fun of watching a little bloodletting after all.

The scarred Cormaeril glanced all around to make sure no covert blades were within reach, gave the grim bladesmen a wordless nod, and stepped out into the revelry.

*   *   *   *   *

The Silken Shadow reached into the bodice of her leathers and drew forth the black cloth hood she'd made several seasons ago but so rarely used. It made her look like some child playing at being hangman, with its eyeholes and ragged edge, but it covered the pale flash of her skin in dim light and might hide her femininity for a few moments from an inattentive observer. Which was most folk, really.

Narnra pulled it on, sheathed her knife, and flexed the too-long-clenched fingers that had held it. She stretched like a lazy cat and hunched down to the floor to smell and listen.

Yes, this smelled different than Waterdeep, somehow. More dead things in the water but fewer taints of spilled strange cargoes from afar.

Revels meant servants, or guards, or people peering in at the fun from around the edges—or all three. She'd have to be very careful as she went on from here.

Why, gods bless me, *how* unusual for a thief . . .

*   *   *   *   *

"So which noble family are you part of?" the masked merchant half-shouted through the chattering din, wine sloshing in the warhelm-sized metal goblet he clutched in both hands.

The cold-eyed warrior in worn and much-patched leather armor eyed him sourly and replied, "None of them. The benevolent Obarskyrs have exiled many more folk than our precious nobles. Most of us lowborn were hurled out by personal proclamation—because they couldn't get us with their blades or nooses before we scampered."

"Oh?" the tipsy merchant leaned forward to peer at the warrior more closely. "So what'd you do?"

"Wounded Duke Bhereu for dallying with my sister. Cut him good and proper and gave him a limp that lasted through two seasons of high-coin healers. I'd've had his life, too, if he hadn't had a dozen bodyguards within shout. Cursed Obarskyrs can't even go out rutting without help!"

Elminster swayed around the warrior's elbow and edged past in the press of bodies.

"Ho for the conspiracy!" someone bellowed across the crowd—again. Several other someones took up the cry, as they had done on several previous occasions. "The Rightful Conspiracy!"

"A new king, a new hope!" someone else bawled.

"Aye! Let Cormyr rise again!"

Elminster felt like rolling his eyes. How many centuries had he heard these same cries, now? 'Twas as if the Forest Kingdom had a set script all would-be rebels and traitors came and consulted, perhaps under the watchful eyes of the scribes and Master Scrollkeeper at the Royal Court.

"And why are *you* here?" the warrior asked. Elminster stiffened then turned slowly, his face cold and haughty—to discover that the question had been directed at the merchant and not the tall, scarred noble sidling past.

"Money," the red-faced merchant replied promptly, punctuating this emphatic declaration with a belch. "They want some of mine now to buy blades and hireswords in Westgate and such but promise me contracts and trade-hires enough to make it back ten times over, once their king's on the throne. Haven't said who that'll be yet, 'course"—he belched again—"but I don' really care." He waved a dismissive hand, his goblet spilling a line of wine drops floorward, and added, "All the same anyway, they are. 'S'just that we'll be on the take with the new one, 'stead of shut outside the gates, lookin' in at all the lovely coins and whisper-deals."

The warrior caught Elminster's eye and snapped, "What're you listening to, high'n'mighty?"

"Overloose tongues," Elminster grunted, "if the War Wizards are listening or there're any Highknights lurking amongst us. I'm a little uneasy that this—" He waved at the merriment all around. "—might be a way to gather us all together so we can be slaughtered without them having to take the trouble to chase us all down."

The warrior nodded grimly. "Such thoughts have crossed my mind, too. You're noble, right?"

"Noble by birth, nameless by nature," Elminster told him with a smile. "Call me: Nameless Cormaeril."

The warrior grinned. "Aha! Some of your kin are here." He waved his hand at the thickest part of the crowd. "Over yonder, somewhere."

The merchant swayed toward Elminster. "W-well met, grand sir. I'm Imbur Waendlar, I am, and am . . . am . . . delighted to make your acquaintance. Should you ever have need of—ahem—coffins, or strongchests, or splendid greatchests to grace the finest of chambers, I'm your man. Best work and best price in all Suzail, wares to fit the needs of one so noble as yourself! Why, let me—"

Elminster and the warrior exchanged winks and grins. "Drunk as a bear drowning in honey," the duke-whittling warrior muttered, "but still manages his pitch. Gods bless stubborn merchants."

Master Waendlar blinked at him. "I cry: 'stubborn'? I cannot help but know I heard you say 'stubborn,' sir. Know you that you are mistaken, for a stubborn merchant is one who cannot turn with the times, shift with the deals, and so keep his coins about him! Why—"

Elminster and the nameless warrior sidestepped in opposite directions, leaving the merchant turning to continue his converse rather unsteadily. His disagreement was with the warrior, so he clung to that path, leaving Elminster free to move on.

Or rather, as free as two excitedly squealing ladies in very low-cut and well-filled gowns would allow.

"Gods a-mighty," someone growled, from Elminster's left,

"but if I had those, *I'd* be squealing in excitement too."

"Well, have them you can," another voice said slyly. "The price is steep, mind you, but . . ."

Elminster ducked past the luridly displayed flesh and out of hearing of more of that particular converse. A knot of men beyond was heatedly discussing the wisdom or lack of same in various "what must be done next" stratagems. Their voices were low but swift and cutting, but their words faltered as Elminster stepped almost into their midst.

"Ho, sir! This talk's private!" one of them snapped.

Elminster shrugged. "Sounds very much like what I've heard in a hundred nobles' chambers across the realm when they thought they were alone. Which leads me to think: when we plotted, we trusted in our hired wizards to keep War Wizard scrying at bay. Is anyone doing the same here, tonight?" He pointed at the goblets most of the men were holding and added, "Or checking those for poisons or concoctions to make us babble?"

The circle of men gave him sharp looks. "Did you not hear the Knight of the Mask's assurances?" the shortest man asked suspiciously. "Where were you then?"

"Yes, yes," Elminster snapped back, "but did you—any of you—actually *see* spells being cast or anything of the sort? Words are easily said; 'tis deeds I trust in."

"Well said, stranger," put in a tall, slender man whose chin bore a tiny black spike of a beard. "However, know you that *I* cast a shielding spell, if no one else did. It covers only myself and those close by, but I was not the only one here to do so. As to the rest, this isle was chosen because Purple Dragons will have to fight their way through three guardposts and across two bridges to reach it. My name, by the way, is Khornadar, most recently of Westgate. And you are—?"

"Nameless," Elminster said firmly, his gaze locked with the tall man's eyes. Familiar eyes. The semblance he'd never seen before, but the man wearing it he'd met in what was presumably his real shape a few summers back. "Nameless Cormaeril."

·

There were dark chuckles, and someone said, "Be welcome, then—as long as you're not like young Thorntower yonder, who spent too long a heated time telling us that only the nobility understand Cormyr and so only nobles—the *right* nobles, mind, such as, well, surprise: himself—could take the throne or command any effort to remove the Obarskyrs from it. He even cited as proof of this the superb job our rightful betters have done guiding the realm thus far!"

Elminster snorted. "Who is this puppy?"

"The one with his nose buried in Tharmoraera's bosom," another man in the circle said in dry tones, pointing. "You'll notice he finds lowborn flesh quite suitable for his purposes."

"Well, that's the definition of a noble, isn't it?" someone else grunted then added hastily, "Ah, no offense meant, lord."

Elminster chuckled. "None taken. Living by wits and the sword in back streets across Faerûn strips away any arrogance of birth right swiftly . . . or such has been my experience, anyway." He looked back at the tall man—the minor Red Wizard Thauvas Zlorn, he was sure, in quite a good magical disguise—and asked, "So why now? This 'Rightful Conspiracy,' I mean? There've been exiles and others who hated the Obarskyrs for centuries and plenty of Sembians happy to toss coin to all malcontents in Cormyr, in hopes of gaining something in return, but: Westgate? I've met others here, from farther afield, too. Why now?"

The man calling himself Khornadar smiled coldly and bent forward, pitching his voice low. So did the others, and Elminster found the circle of plotters rejoined, with himself part of it.

"Well, Nameless," the disguised Red Wizard purred, "folk with wits are backing us. This revel's a master-stroke, making fools and rich alike excited to be part of something secretive and important and bringing them together to shield those really behind it. We get to know each other by sight and forge a few little friendships on the side, so everyone feels they benefit . . . thus far, all good. Dangerous, yes, but all treason's dangerous, no Obarskyr finds welcome here in Marsember, and we outlanders have easy sailing and other reasons to be here."

Head nodded around the circle. "A boy too young to walk or talk wears Cormyr's crown while a rutting bitch of a Regent settles scores in his name, many loyal nobles are angry or afraid, shadow-sorcerers blast things at will up in the Stonelands—Purple Dragons included—while the whole realm tries to rebuild and feed itself. Behold: weakness. The time's right, or better than it's ever been in my lifetime."

Heads nodded around the circle, and Khornadar went on. "Now look around you. One more decadent revel in rotting Marsember, yes, but see who's here: the usual seacaptains, pleasure-lasses, and throne-hating Marsembans, but also exiled nobles like yourself; a few sons of nobility still welcome in the realm who're disgusted at what the Obarskyrs have done and allowed; ambitious merchants; and outlanders like me who see gain in a stronger, fairer Cormyr. Behold both the chance and its willing takers."

The disguised Red Wizard waved his goblet. It was empty, Elminster noticed.

"So why're we all risking our necks to be here? Exiled nobles want their lands, wealth, and influence back and see a way to reclaim it all. Marsembans burn to snatch back their independence. I've seen a few folk from Arabel here who desire the same. Sembians ache to seize lands in eastern Cormyr or desire goods they can make quick coin on. That same reason draws most of the merchants of Suzail who are here this night."

Khornadar thrust his face still farther forward and lowered his voice to a mutter. "But what of me? Earlier conspiracies invited hireswords and wizards to work violence for promised rewards, but I've been offered no such clear prize—and therefore fear treachery less from masked and anonymous men who want me to help overthrow the hated

Obarskyrs but not live to claim what I've been promised. Why am I here?"

He smiled. "Well, I see Cormyr as a storehouse of magic—War Wizard magic—that I, who am no threat to anyone right now, can use to become powerful without years of toadying to cruel mages in return for spell-scraps reluctantly tossed my way. This room holds quite a few like me. Our very numbers, plus War Wizards scrambling to seize magic for themselves once the Obarskyrs are dead, *and* the fear and hatred commoners of Cormyr hold for those same oh-so-benevolent War Wizards—a lot of farmers will put daggers or pitchforks through every wizard they see!—will keep us from forming any collective threat. The wise ones will snatch what magic they can and get out."

Elminster frowned. "Were I one of the hidden masters of this Rightful Conspiracy, I wouldn't want any wizard here unless I believed I or my fellow Secret Masters had magic enough to smash them down . . . or we'll all be dying to trade a baby king for a ruthless wizard, no?"

The disguised Red Wizard nodded. "Which is why I believe there *is* a great wizard somewhere behind this, one who intends to make any new king his puppet. He can then rule Cormyr without any of the dangers of reigning—after all, this Caladnei and her bedmate Laspeera very much do so now, strolling along the path old Vangerdahast paved for them. All it costs them is a few spells to keep the Dowager Queen and the Steel Regent in mind-thrall! Why, our hidden mage could even fund a few of the intrepid wayfarers of that Society of Stalwart Adventurers club in Suzail to find him spells and long-lost riches in other lands, too!"

Thay would be your "great wizard," young Thauvas, Elminster thought, and Cormyr would then swiftly become a farflung western tharch—and, just as you say, a base for reaching out to other cities and lands. Keeping any hint of this from his face, El nodded, stroked his chin thoughtfully as he frowned, and said, "Gods, this is why I've never thought about joining any rebellion until now. All this scheming and thinking about what others are thinking hurts my head!"

There were nods and chuckles from the circle of faces around him. Elminster was aware of the close and thoughtful scrutiny the false Khornadar was now giving him. Quickly he called to mind the faces of two Cormaerils he knew—one of them Jhaunadyl, sitting up warm-eyed in her bed after their lovemaking. . . .

The Red Wizard's probe was as fierce as it was sudden, but rather than let it shatter against his mind-shield, Elminster let it slide in and spun a welter of mental images for Thauvas to see, leaving Jhaunadyl's laughter and outreaching arms to the fore.

The wizard stiffened and reared back his head in disgust. Ah, yes, rampant incest among decadent nobles. Another man might have eagerly looked for more memories of even warmer moments, but many Red Wizards regarded women as little more than cattle and intimacy without domination as hardly worth the time spent on dalliance. Young Zlorn was evidently one such.

It takes great strength of will to maintain such a probe, let alone steer the invaded mind to certain thoughts and memories, and the false Khornadar was gone from Elminster's thoughts as swiftly as he'd come, looking pale and tired as he stepped back in the circle. Someone noticed the trembling of his goblet.

"Art well, mage of Westgate?"

"I—yes. Merely tired," Khornadar replied curtly.

"More wine?"

"Nay, that would be the worst thing. I must sit and listen for a time, letting others do the talking!"

The circle moved confusedly toward a pillar that was apparently encircled by a stone seat, and several of its members took the opportunity to drift away into the throng—where dancing had now broken out in earnest, imperiling several platters of savory tarts being taken around the crowded dance-floor by uncomfortable-looking, weatherbeaten-faced men who were obviously unused to serving food forth.

Elminster ducked under a platter that was well on its way floor-wards—only to see it rescued in his wake by a whooping merchant whose fat quivering chins boasted trembling chinlets of their own—and turned from that impressive sight to find himself face to face with a stunningly beautiful woman in a shimmering gown adorned with gilded badges. Or rather—El dragged his eyes with some difficulty away from an impish smile, swirling dark hair, and darkly knowing eyes—the same badge, repeated over and over in gold thread upon blue-green and clinging shimmerweave. A seashell crossed with a trident, the arms of a Marsemban house . . . Mistwind, that was it. A very old family, very private, few in number.

Regal Lady Mistwind—for this must be the heiress apparent of the house, it could be no other—gave him an even wider smile, showing just the edges of a fine row of pearly teeth, and asked sweetly, "You look like a nobleman who's tasted the world, sir. How does our hospitality here, this night, measure up?"

Well, *that* was clear invitation enough. Elminster gave her a gallant smile, a bow in the elder court style to signal that he was of a long-established house, too (though of course the Cormaerils would have been scorned in such a claim by many 'true' oldblood nobles of the realm), and the words, "Most beautiful lady, I've but begun to taste what's offered here—yet confess myself impressed thus far by any measure. Perhaps we can speak more of this later?"

Her smile broadened. "Perhaps."

She danced toward him a trifle, almost concealing the hard-eyed bodyguards swaying in time to her movements beyond both of her shoulders, and added huskily, "Your discretion speaks well of you. Lady Amrelle Mistwind gives greeting to—?"

Elminster gave her a smile. "Lord Nameless Cormaeril, at your service."

One dark brow arched. "Namelessness is a matter for scorn if there's no good reason—but you must acquaint me with your reason before I'd presume to pass judgment on it. Later, as you say."

She spun away, her slit-to-the-waist gown giving Elminster a brief glimpse of a gem-studded wyvern tattooed high on her thigh—and a complete lack of undergarments—and left Lord Nameless Cormaeril facing a scowling bodyguard . . . and feeling very warm indeed. 'Tis these damned magical disguises; they hold the heat so.

* * * * *

Narnra glided to a stop behind another pillar. The guards and servants were growing bored and hungry, and increasingly made little forays out onto the floor to snatch tarts or fancies from platters, ceasing to be so alert for unfolding trouble. Most of them seemed to have been expecting blades drawn between conspirators, anyway, rather than attacks from intruders.

Hmm. There was that tall noble again . . . tall enough to be the old wizard, yes, but of course spell-guises need not have the stature or bulk of the person using them. Yet most men disliked being shorter than they were used to being and avoided such shapes unless they had good reason to do otherwise—and time for reflection upon the matter.

There were at least three men here who were even taller, but two were hulking bodyguards who looked to have orc blood well back in their ancestry, and they kept to the darkened outer rooms, half-dozing . . . and the third claimed to be a wizard from Westgate. Would a mage disguising himself be stupid—or vain—enough to make himself into the likeness of . . . a wizard? Yet wizards *were* vain, and this shape was far younger and more handsome than the one he'd worn back in the alley. He'd acted the Old Wise One then, but—was this his true shape? He'd been awfully fast on his feet for a white-bearded dodderer, and the Silken Shadow wasn't as clumsy as all that, if she thought so herself.

The tall noble turned his head and seemed to stare right at her. Narnra froze then looked away, leaned back against her pillar, drew her dagger, and pretended to clean and pare her nails with it. Well, he wasn't coming any closer, at least.

The smell of roasted fowl tarts wafted past, and Narnra suddenly found her mouth full-watering. A moment later, her flat stomach added its own growl of protest. Narnra sighed silently, then put away her knife, stepped around the pillar, and strode out into the chattering throng toward the nearest platter. As the saying went: Swords crossed? Then we might as well shatter realms in battle!

She was a stride away when someone grabbed at the platter, and the servant holding it quickly lofted it out of reach. A tart that had been inches from Narnra's fingertips was suddenly several paces away. With a growl that matched the sound her gut was making, the Silken Shadow stalked after it.

*   *   *   *   *

With a grin, Elminster turned away. Well, well, his playmate from the alley had been far bolder than he'd given her credit for—and was now finding, as so many farmers gone to be splendid warriors had discovered before her, that there's nothing like the taste of adventure for making the belly feel yawningly empty. Of course, all too often the meal it soon received was a goodly length of sharpened steel, but there was no need to cast down her spirits warning her of that. She was in it, now, with no going back—and by the looks of her, she had realized that for herself already.

In the dim lamplight, Elminster peered about for the noble lass he'd seen dancing earlier, but she was now—perhaps wisely—nowhere to be seen. There was something about her that made him think of fathering little wizards. Ah, well . . .

Three

THE BRIGHTNESS OF THE LURE

I put out my hand, and the fish swam right into my net—as they always do. It's all in the brightness of the lure you offer.

Fzoul Chembryl, High Lord of the Zhentarim
Conquering What I Want of the World:
Words For All the Brethren to Live By
(text of speech, circulated amongst the Zhentarim)
Year of the Unstrung Harp

Some of the revelers were really drunk now. Narnra stepped around folk who were sprawled senseless, or busily being sick—some with watchful bodyguards standing over them—trying to catch sight of the old wizard, or someone who might be him.

She'd managed to snatch just one tart—with a leap that had drawn more than one appreciative eye, curse the luck—and it had been good, very good. There'd been lamb kidneys and a touch of venison in its rich gravy. The rich aftertaste rested warm and comfortingly in her mouth even now.

This couldn't be fabled Skullport, for none of these folk looked familiar, and their speech was subtly different. They seemed to be discussing rebellion against a king who was barely a king, or some such—could they really be so bold, or foolish? She had a bad feeling that a lot of royal warriors were going to charge out of doorways and arches she hadn't even found yet and slaughter everyone here—wandering thieves from Waterdeep included.

Like a wide-eyed fool, she'd stepped through some sort of magical door and right into an adventure that might slay her in short order. Gods spit, she *had* to find that old wizard!

He might have slipped away somewhere else, of course, and have nothing to do with all these drunkards. He might be rallying the force that would burst out to slay them all, even now. He might even be leading this conspiracy—though after the way he'd treated *her*, why hadn't he marched right into the center of the lamplight and enspelled everyone to quivering obedience?

Whatever that old man was up to, if Narnra Shalace was going to save Narnra Shalace's smooth but unlovely hide, she'd best scout where each cellar went and which archways led out into the open air. Twouldn't do to get trapped down here. By the smell, this place might well be below sea level, and some wall-shattering spell or sluice-gate could flood it at will. *That* would save the authorities even the chasing and shouting.

Many of the revelers seemed to be drifting away from the shoulder-jostling crowd under the lamps, now. On all sides, little groups of excitedly plotting folk were seeking this or that dark corner for privacy. Wary bodyguards were every-where, and Narnra took care not to seem *too* interested in anyone as she threaded her way along through side-arches and around pillars, seeking ramps or steps leading up.

"That's the beauty of it, you see—"

She ducked away from that merchant and his chortling, reeling-drunk friends and on into the next room.

"Ah, my lord, at *last*," a woman's voice growled, as its owner tore at the robes of a man who looked more bewildered than ardent—as three bodyguards stood in an impassive little ring around the amorous pair, facing outwards with arms folded. Narnra kept going.

Four fast-striding men were crossing the next cellar, one calling out from behind the others.

"Sorval? Is that Sorval Maethur?" The speaker sounded delighted, as he caught up to three merchants.

One turned. "Aye, I'm Sorval. And you might be—?"

"Delighted to bring you *death!*" was the snarled reply, as a dagger was plunged into a throat, a lamp was tossed into the face of one of the victim's companions, and the other fled with a terrified shout. Bubbling as he struggled to speak and spraying much blood from an opened throat, Sorval slumped to the ground. His slayer stepped back and strode unconcernedly away from the twitching corpse and the moaning man clawing at his burned eyes.

So did Narnra, steeling herself to look just as unconcerned—because any moment now, the killer was going to turn and look around for witnesses who might have to be slaughtered, too, and her life would depend on . . . *yes!*

Sorval's slayer cast her a dark glance. Narnra pointedly ignored him, murmuring aloud as if to herself, "*How* did that spell go, again?" as she kept steadily walking.

Dagger still dripping in his hand, the man hesitated briefly, glaring at her, but then decided ducking away was wiser than tackling someone unknown. A masked woman, his widening eyes told the Silken Shadow, at that.

Several groups of men were converging in a far room, lanterns glimmering in their hands . . . and those lights were bobbing upward. Narnra headed that way, striding purposefully—and letting Sorval's slayer see her dagger flash in her hand as she drew it.

She waved the fingers of her other hand over it in a flourish, hoping he'd think she was working some sort of magic, and swallowed hard. She'd seen throats slit before, but Sorval had given the world so gods-blessed *much blood* . . .

Sorval's slayer hurried in another direction, and was lost behind pillars and through archways. Narnra kept going, trying to forget Sorval's last horrible moments. Whoever he was, he hadn't . . . but enough!

She waved a hand as if to banish the memory and looked back once more. No slayer creeping back to follow her. Good.

Another amorous couple were locked together in half-seen urgency in a corner of the next chamber she crossed, and on the other side of the same room some furious men were trying to stab each other with daggers. They were too falling-down drunk to do much more than snarl incoherent threats and curses at each other, fall on their faces, roar and rage some more, and fall over again. Yes, a "Rightful Conspiracy" indeed.

Dancing was still going on here and there, though the piping and drum-thumping seemed to have stopped back behind her. The men ahead were chattering tirelessly, words flashing back and forth between them like slung stones: lots of excited speculation about how riches would come to them once "those bastard Obarskyrs were all dead."

Narnra frowned. Obarskyrs? They were the royal family of some realm way east of Waterdeep—a good, trustworthy, law-abiding place. Some place with a strange name . . . Cromyar? Cromeer? Cormeer—Cormyr, that was it!

Gods, she was halfway across the world!

Well, that'll teach you to follow wizards through glowing archways, she told herself savagely. Idiot.

Dagger in hand, Narnra joined the men climbing the stairs. No one paid her the slightest attention, as they wallowed in their own excited schemes and conclusions and get-even-richer dreams. Twice men stopped to strike dramatic poses and declaim things to their fellows, only to get shoved from below with calls of, "Move along!" and "Stand aside!" and "Don't hold up the Conspiracy!"

The steps were old, broad, and well-worn, but there were

a lot of them, in little short flights that led to landings that gave onto more little runs of worn steps. As she ascended, Narnra felt the dampness increase, and tendrils of mist started to drift in around the busy stair.

Quite suddenly, she was in a many-pillared portico, on a dock that looked at the glittering lights and darkened spires of a sizable city—across mist-wreathed waters that stank. Skiffs and lantern-hung pleasure-barges bobbed against the dock, anchored to metal struts of many rings that were nothing like the great bollards of Waterdeep Harbor. This was the sea, all right—*a* sea—but . . . oh, so different from the City of Splendors.

A stone arch bridge linked the land she stood on to a small islet crowded with rotting, leaking buildings with slate-tile roofs that sagged alarmingly and railings that were fire-brown with rust. No lamps were lit anywhere on it or on what seemed to be a second island beyond the first, where half-sunken barges lined crumbling, bird-dung-streaked wharves.

Instinctively, Narnra stepped away from the rush of chattering men proceeding over the bridge or strolling to barges where the patient faces of crewmen could be seen surveying the arrivals. Along the covered dock she went, seeking to be alone. There must be some way up to a vantage point where she could look around and see more of this new place . . . but where?

Behind her, someone fell into the water with a splash, and there were shouts of drunken merriment. Someone else on a nearby barge took advantage of the tumult to slit a throat and shove the body over the side. Narnra watched it slip headfirst beneath the inky waters without a sound.

A third someone lit a hand-lamp and hauled the drunken man roughly aboard another barge, and by its light Narnra got her first look at the water, as the man's pale robes burst up through it: peat-brown and reeking even more strongly now that it had been disturbed. She curled her lip, turned away, and froze.

At the end of the dock a quiet company of men was standing, eyeing her steadily. All of them wore dark leathers, and some held blades and capture-nets ready in their hands, others hand crossbows of the sort Narnra had seen all too many of in Waterdeep. Still others held delicate sticks of wood: wands!

It had been a wave of one of the wands that had rolled back a thick bank of mist to reveal these men—and women, too, Narnra noticed—and now they were starting purposefully forward, keeping together in a menacing band.

From behind her came more laughter, new splashings—and a shout of alarm.

There was a clang of steel aboard a drifting barge, the ring of blades crossed in anger, and a sudden cry: "Betrayed! The War Wizards are here!" That shout ended in an ugly, wet gurgle, which was followed by another clash of swords—and a scream.

One of the men striding along the dock toward Narnra had his head cocked to one side, as though listening to someone who wasn't there, and was muttering a steady stream of orders as he came.

"Horngentle, Lord Blackwinter's been seen here: arrest him. Thoaburr: one of us, the novice Beltrar Morgrin—yes, a War Wizard, everyone; keep clear!—has turned traitor and is still down-cellar . . . he mustn't live to see the morning, but take him quietly. Constal? Constal, it seems the Regal Lady Mistwind turned her nightly manhunt hither. Put a scare into her, but let her win free. Bereldyn, I'll need you to find me that wizard someone saw arriving—Khornadar of Westgate, he's calling himself, but Laspeera thinks he may be someone more powerful posing as an ambitious lackspell. He's . . ."

This flood of—gods, they looked like *Harpers*, and, *yes!* That one was wearing a little silver harp pin at his throat, and that one sported an identical pin on an eyepatch—grim folk was only paces away, now, and Narnra was standing right in their path. It just wasn't possible that they'd failed to see her, though as yet no one had aimed a handbow or drawn back a blade in menace.

The Silken Shadow stood stock-still. Whirling and running now would probably earn her swift death in a volley of quarrels. "The Cormaerils all seem to be here," she announced calmly. "Beware also Mathanter of Sembia."

She wouldn't know a Cormaeril if she fell over one, and she'd never seen or heard of this Mathanter before tonight—but he'd brought along more than a dozen fully armored bodyguards and impressed *her*.

The nearest Harper gave her a sharp look and without turning his head or taking his eyes off her asked, "Armeld?"

The man snapping orders swivelled an eye to scrutinize the masked Silken Shadow as he strode past—they were all streaming past her now, on both sides, save for the one Harper facing her—and replied, "Never seen her before. Not one of yours?"

"Remember," an earnest man in dark robes was saying on Narnra's other side to an elderly man holding two wands, "some we arrest, some we slay as quietly as possible, and some we just scare—so *don't* go blasting anyone you see! For once? Please?"

"No," the Harper said slowly, shaking his head and raising his blade. Its blackened point hung just below her breasts. Narnra swallowed and tried not to look at it again.

"I am not," she told him almost severely, "a member of this 'Rightful Conspiracy.' I abhor conspiracies." She'd heard an old, wrinkled noble matriarch dressing down a captain of the Watch once, and she tried to make her voice sound just like that old, highborn Waterdhavian's: imperious, disgusted, and somehow pitying.

The Harper's eyes flickered, and he asked quietly, "Caladnei?"

"No," Narnra told him in the same tones, not knowing what else to say, "I am not she."

"That's good," said a dry voice from behind the Harper, "considering that the last time I looked at myself in a mirror, I remained fairly certain that *I* was Caladnei."

A wryly smiling, dusky face came into view behind the Harper's shoulder. Dark eyes surveyed Narnra coolly from under startlingly dark brows. "So . . . have you a name of your own, Hooded One?"

A tingling of magic washed over Narnra before Caladnei was even finished speaking, and without thinking the thief from Waterdeep crouched tensely, as if facing battle.

"I am the Mage Royal of Cormyr," the woman behind the Harper said gently, "and that was a truth-reading spell—nothing more. My word here is law—'tis a crime to evade or deny me. Please answer fully."

Narnra trembled, eyeing the Harper's steady blade and the purposeful look in Caladnei's eyes. The Mage Royal stepped to one side, gesturing to Narnra to keep looking at her—and forcing her to take her eyes off the Harper menacing her.

Narnra sighed, drew herself up, and turned smartly to do as she was bidden. The Mage Royal wore boots and a warrior's leathers, and her long black hair was gathered behind her shoulders with a ribbon. Her belt was crowded with pouches interspersed with daggers, and she wore no proud insignia or touches of wealth.

"Look at me." That gentle voice came again, and Narnra knew what was meant. She lifted her gaze to meet Caladnei's eyes directly and found herself caught and held, staring into two dark flames.

There was a high scream, a thunder of hard-running booted feet, and another splash, but none of the trio standing at this end of the pier paid the slightest attention.

"I asked you a question. Surrender to me your full name."

"I . . . I am called Narnra. Narnra Shalace, of Waterdeep."

"Are you conspiring against the Crown of Cormyr?"

"Lady, I don't even know who the Crown of Cormyr *is*—and until you just said that to me, wasn't even certain I was in Cormyr. I—I've never been in your land before tonight."

"So how came you to be on this island?"

Narnra sighed. "Well, there was a wizard . . ." She hesitated, not knowing how best to say things. In Waterdeep, to openly admit one was a thief was to be punished regardless of what one might or might not have done.

That was when the Harper standing beside her made a queer sort of grunt—and was suddenly slamming into a distant pillar, his body aflame. Caladnei staggered and clutched at her head as if someone had shrieked in her ears, and the dock-stones under Narnra's boots rippled as if some gigantic bulk was swimming past in the solid stone, close beneath her feet. She saw stones heaving and falling all over the dock and spun around and was running hard away from her interrogators even before the ceiling above her cracked, a pillar toppled far ahead and the bridge of shouting, shoving men that linked the dock and the next island broke in a dozen places . . . and slumped into the harbor with a crash that sent walls of reeking water crashing across the dock. Narnra dived to a pillar and clung to it to keep from being washed away.

The waters were still roiling around her when blinding-bright lightning cracked through the mists, heralding many screams. Someone blew what sounded like a war-horn, and from here and there crossbow quarrels started to hum out of the night, snarling across the docks like hunting hornets.

Cursing, Narnra ran away—she knew not where, just *away*.

Small armed bands of Harpers and War Wizards were everywhere, and many of the pillars along the dock were festooned with slumped, sleeping folk in torn and now drenched finery, who'd been tied to the pillar and each other at the wrists, ankles, and throats—presumably by the Harpers who stood watchfully by.

One such challenged Narnra with a shout, gliding to intercept her with his blade held ready, but she snarled, "Caladnei sent me! Out of my way!" and he put up his steel to let her run past.

There was little dock left to her, and several Harpers watching. She had to enter one of the darkened archways. These must lead into cargo-rooms, and what urgent business could she have there? No, it must be back to the cellars she headed. Not only did she not like the look of the stinking harbor-water at all, but with so many crossbows and hurlers-of-lightning about, that way would be almost sure death. That stair to the cellars was directly in line with the bridge that was no more, so despite the fact that no water seemed to have splashed hereabouts, *this* archway would be the right one. . . .

"Hah! Another rat scurrying back to the bolt-hole!"

More than a dozen men were crowded around the stair-head, conferring—and two of them already had blades almost into her.

Narnra spun aside rather than slowing. "Caladnei's orders!" she snapped, trying for her Waterdhavian matriarch's voice. "Out of my way!"

"Armeld?" one of the men moving smoothly to bar her path called, over his shoulder.

"She was talking with the Mage Royal. Let her past, and go with her—just you two. See where she goes, what she does." Armeld turned back to the men who'd been reporting to him, and as she hurried down the stairs with her unwelcome escort hard on her heels, their voices resumed. "Dozens of nasty little stabbings and drownings—scores settled, I'd judge—a lot of sex and drunkenness, the usual cliques . . ."

"Any more wizards now that Lightning-Dolt's dead?"

"There *should* be, but . . ."

Someone cursed in the darkness below—lamps were noticeably fewer, now—and the rushing Narnra was out of earshot of the stair-head by the time those oaths—and the skirl of steel and choked-off groan that swiftly followed—had died away.

"—got clean away!" someone said suddenly, almost in Narnra's ear, as she skidded around a corner and raced toward the next flight of descending steps. "Ho!"

"Stop her!" another voice snapped. There was a heavy crash as someone stepped into the path of the two Harpers racing after her. Men bounced and rolled down the steps in a heavily thudding, cursing, and ultimately groaning bundle in her wake. Narnra dared not look to see what had befallen, but as she turned at the next landing she got a momentary glimpse of what looked like the lamplit silhouette of a man leaping over tumbling bodies on the stairs to keep after her.

She slipped in something sticky—probably blood—and almost went into a tumble herself. Slamming into the wall instead with force enough to drive away her breath, she skidded painfully along it to a gasping halt and felt for the stone rail she could not see. All was in darkness, here, though she could see the glimmer of torches bobbing somewhere far below.

"Well," a man's voice came nastily out of the nearby darkness just below her, "if they got aboard *that* skiff, they're at the bottom of one of Marsember's fabled fetid canals right now. That was the one—"

"Hold!" another man snapped. "I thought that was a corpse rolling down the stairs, but someone's panting—and so, yet lives."

"Touch left," the first voice muttered, and—as she crouched low, mastering her balance for a desperate spring—Narnra heard stealthy movements.

Light flared, below her: a soft blue magical glow arising from the pommel of a dagger held out over the center of the steps at full arm's-length by someone in dark leathers who was crowded against the wall to Narnra's left. Someone else was crouched right ahead of her against the right wall.

"A lass!" the one on the left said, sounding startled.

"In a *mask*," the other responded, in tones that made it sound like mask-wearing was the most dire crime possible in Cormyr.

"We're on the same side," Narnra snapped, sounding very much like an irritated Waterdhavian noble matriarch. "I was hurrying down here on Caladnei's orders when I slipped on these damned stairs."

"Why the mask?"

"My face is no longer very attractive, sir," she said, making her voice sound bitter. "One price of my loyal service."

"Oh. I see. Ah . . . sorry. Have you no lamp?"

"None, nor permission to use it. My orders are otherwise."

"Armeld, that'd be," the other man said disgustedly. "Always fancies himself battle-lord riding into doom-glory." He moved aside. "Pass, lady—but use the rail; it runs right through the next landing, at least. Damned luxurious warehouses these Marsemban nobles built themselves, I must say. Makes you wonder what sort of goods they stored here, eh?"

"Yes, it does. My thanks, sirs," the Silken Shadow replied cautiously and hastened past, using the rail.

* * * * *

"No, Thauvas, that's not the way," Nameless Cormaeril said pleasantly, the tip of his sword already—but only just—through the skin that had until now covered the place where the Red Wizard's throat joined the back of his jaw. "Why must you Thayans always make things so complicated? Business, all business, remember? Let me put it again, simply: I ask a few questions, and you give me a few honest answers—something you're unaccustomed to, I know, but it doesn't hurt much once you get into the habit. A little truth spills, I let you go free, and you'll have plenty of time thereafter to plot my doom . . . simple, no?"

"Idiot noble," the Red Wizard hissed, his sweating face as pale as a bleached skull. "Do you know what risk you place upon fair Cormyr by this overbold action? Or how terribly you doom yourself?"

The tall, scarred man at the other end of the grand rapier smiled. "Yes," he told Thauvas sweetly.

Behind his back, the Red Wizard finally completed the

intricate gesture he'd been tracing. "Sssardamar!" he said triumphantly—and twisted away from the sharp sword-point, shouting, "Die, fool! To *dare* to threaten a mage of Thay so! Down-country *dog!*"

Magic flared up around the man who'd called himself Khornadar of Westgate with a roar, hungry flames that thrust out at the raven-haired noble.

Who did not scream and shrivel and die but instead lost sword and dark hair and clean-shaven chin to stand smiling through the flames as a hawk-nosed, white-bearded man with busy brows, stained old robes—and even brighter fire in his hands.

"Ah, but it seems fools dare just about anything, these days, doesn't it?" he asked merrily. "Do ye know me now, Thauvas Zlorn? Do they still, in Thay—amidst all their swaggering and gleeful counting of as-yet-unhatched chickens, as they scheme to rule all Toril a dozen times over—mention the name 'Elminster' from time to time? Just to warn young wizards of the natural perils of this world?"

Blood trickled down Zlorn's throat as magic that sliced through his own as if it were mere false conjurer's fancy-feathers lifted him into the air and held him dangling there. He swallowed, managed the nigh impossible feat of growing even more pale, and fainted.

"Mystra mine," Elminster murmured disgustedly, "but they let just about anything swagger out of Thay these days, don't they?"

*   *   *   *   *

It was dark at the bottom of the stairs. The only lights were lanterns and torches moving to and fro with grim bands of searchers—humans all, men and women who bore either blades, handbows, and silver harp pins, or wands and the vacant expressions of folk listening to conversations only they could hear, raging in their heads.

Narnra paused, not sure at first which way to go. She knew

roughly what direction led to the archway—but without that wizard it was closed, and she'd probably not be able to even find its exact location. Moreover, with all the corpses and spilled blood down here, it would be a horrible thing to have all the searchers depart and leave her groping in utter darkness with the rats. Her best chance lay in somehow joining a band of searchers, being accepted as one of them, reaching the city beyond the broken bridge with them . . . and, she supposed, starting a new life. With nearly nothing in a strange realm where she'd already been marked as a possible traitor by a royal wizard.

"Thank you, merciful gods," she muttered sardonically—then stiffened as two things happened at once: she remembered the silhouette leaping down the stairs, presumably chasing her but somehow not yet upon her . . . and a Harper suddenly veered away from a passing group and thrust a flaming torch at her. "Yours," he said shortly. "Caladnei's orders."

Narnra gaped at him then numbly, because she could think of nothing else to do, took the torch. It spat pitch, as they all did, and burned with a brilliance that warmed her cheek—very real and with enough hard-nailed cloth on it to last for hours. Of course, it made her a beacon in the dark cellars . . . but really, with a Mage Royal casting spells on her, wasn't she that already?

The Silken Shadow sighed heavily, spread her hands in exasperation—for so accomplished a Waterdhavian snatch-thief, she wasn't much of a strategist, *thank* you, Holy Mask—and set off briskly through the cellars, toward where that archway had been. There was the slimmest of chances the old wizard had returned there or would do so, and she had to at least *look* or forever gnaw at herself for having failed to do so.

Her way took her through almost a dozen cellars, and she saw almost a score of sprawled corpses and many, many more huddled, sullen prisoners. The Rightful Conspiracy, it seemed, was reduced to its mysterious masters and perhaps a few fugitives who'd managed to slip away.

Yes, this was the right place, here . . . and the passage she'd arrived by would be this one, and . . .

There was a sudden cold flare of magic off to the left, through another archway—and Narnra thrust the torch as behind her as she could manage and sidled nearer to see who was casting what down here—quite away from the bands of grim searchers.

Then she stiffened once more, and turned around very slowly. *Why* had all the searchers veered away from this area as she walked between them . . . and why was there now utter silence behind her?

Her torch showed her nothing but pillars and dark emptiness.

With a sudden snarl she flung the torch as high and as far back along her trail as she could.

The ceiling was high, and the beacon whupp-whupp-whupped end over end quite vigorously, trailing sparks and flame, to bounce with a flare of fire that sank immediately down to a few fitful flames. They were quite enough, however, to show her the shapely leather-clad legs of a lone figure who'd been following her.

That person lowered one hand to point at the torch—and it rose smoothly into the air, fires quickening once more . . . and came floating upright back to Narnra. At the beginning of its journey, its flickering radiance was quite sufficient to show the Waterdhavian thief the half-smiling face of the Mage Royal of Cormyr.

Narnra swallowed and raised her hand in salute—and caught the torch in her other hand, hoping Caladnei wasn't so spiteful with her Art as to make it explode into a thief-incinerating inferno or some like doom.

The torch stayed a torch, and with a sigh of mingled relief and resignation Narnra turned back to those strange flickerings of magic.

A few paces onward she spun around again to see if Caladnei was following her. She could see nothing but shifting darkness, but a very dry voice murmured in her ear, so seemingly close that she couldn't help but jump: *A beacon indeed, Narnra Shalace of Waterdeep. Lead on, and together let us see what unfolds.*

Narnra turned her face to the unseen ceiling overhead and flung a silent curse at Mask and Tymora, hefted the torch despairingly in her hands . . . and stepped forward again.

The archway was very close now, perhaps a dozen paces ahead to her left. She held the torch as low and as far to the right as she could, walked in that direction, then crept along the wall toward the edge of the arch. Yes, she was carrying a blazing beacon—but perhaps there was light and strife enough in the cellar to keep attention away from one closer torch among many. Perhaps . . .

Going down to her knees and ducking her head as low to the cold stone floor as she could, the Silken Shadow of Waterdeep peered around the edge of the archway.

The cellar held only two men—and their magic. One was the old wizard, her only way out of all this peril. The other was a younger man who hung gabbling fearfully in midair, gripped in a glowing, swirling cloud of enchantment.

So she was caught between the slowly and carefully advancing Caladnei of Cormyr—herding her as deftly as any drover crowding oxen into a caravan-pen—and the old mage who'd so casually defeated her. No doubt the Mage Royal was walking with spells upon spells raised like shields around her . . . and the power of the old wizard was obvious.

The very air glowed and throbbed with it, a pulsing so mighty it almost hurt the ears.

"Ye could have done this the easy way, ye know," Elminster told the sweat-drenched, trembling man trembling in the air above him. "I'm a gentle tyrant and require only a few breaths of thy precious time—a hindrance in thy scheduled rush to world domination, I grant ye, yet 'twill give thee a chance to practice gloating and shouting clever jests and phrases about thy puissance to come . . . but no, Thauvas, ye had to struggle. And I thought Thayans understood the proper roles of master and slave. Ye disappoint me." His voice sharpened. "So speak. Ye are—?"

"T-Thauvas Zlorn, Red Wizard of Thay."

"*Thank* ye. So, Thauvas, ye came all the way to damp Marsember—not the nearest port of call from Thayan shores—merely to enjoy a revel with some strangers in a cellar, is that it?"

"Y-y-yes—uh—ah—I mean *no!*"

"Thy mind wavers and is troubled; bad traits for one who seeks to master wizardry." Elminster shook his head. "The day of thy becoming any sort of zulkir seems distant indeed. Ye came to join or at least scout this Rightful Conspiracy, did ye not? Or is Thay already behind it, and ye were but carrying out an assigned mission?"

Zlorn's face rippled and contorted as he fought against the horribly strong prying that stabbed into his memories and thoughts like a cook jabbing a skewer into a quacefruit. Unwillingly, his lips moved at the bidding of a second inexorable magic to blurt out the truth. "Y-y-yes."

"Yes *which*, most eloquent Thauvas? Speak loudly, for all to hear!"

Narnra froze at the old wizard's words—then spun around to look at Caladnei. The Mage Royal's face was as wryly astonished as her own.

"Yes," the Red Wizard gasped hastily, "I was assigned this task . . . many rising Red Wizards involved . . . a test for each of us . . . Sembians sponsoring this conspiracy . . . begun by exiled malcontents of Cormyr, of course . . . we of Thay are keeping hidden, as much as possible, thus far . . ."

As Elminster's fiercely tightening will penetrated thought after memory after precious secret, peeling the Thayan's mind as some folk strip an onion, layer by layer, Thauvas Zlorn began to sob forth phrases more and more freely.

"And your jovial mention of using the Stalwart Adventurers? This is part of the plot? Under way or a future effort?"

"I—I—I—'twas my own idea . . . Velmaerass very pleased . . . praised me . . ."

"I'm most warmed to hear that," Elminster said in dry tones. "He might even give ye a tharch or two, if ye're still alive by then."

Thauvas was already weeping in fear, bright lines of tears streaming down his cheeks. His teeth now began to chatter, and the Old Mage sighed, waved a hand, and said scornfully, "Sleep then—for now—and keep thy wits, such as they are. All this fainting and gabbling . . . when will these puppies learn that being a mage means facing the possible consequences *beforehand*, and weighing them, and acting mindful of their weight? Or is thinking before one goes merrily blasting off into red war left only to wise old fools, these days?"

He spun around suddenly, and an unseen, irresistible force took hold of Narnra's throat and wrists and plucked her off her feet, torch and all, before she could so much as gasp.

"And ye, little Masked One? How much did *ye* think, before ye plunged through that gate on my heels, hmm? Or are ye so young that adventure dazzles ye into plunging after it?"

Narna Shalace found herself hanging in the throbbing air, faint white mists of sheer power roiling around her, looking down at the wryly smiling, bearded face of the old wizard.

She gasped for breath, finding herself suddenly sweating all over. Was that creeping numbness around her neck and ears his magic sliding into her mind? Was she going to end up sobbing and helpless, teeth chattering, tongue not her own? Would he slay her or leave her a half-wit, ruined by his magic?"

"I—I—I—"

"Are far too upset, Lady of the Night. I've no particular desire to work spell-murder right in front of the Mage Royal of Cormyr, who would then feel a duty to do something that could only get her hurt. All I want is something that should please us all: a sharing of the truth."

Blue-gray eyes gleamed up at hers. "The truth, lass, is a precious thing. Sharp, yes, all too rare in daily use, aye . . . and therefore all too precious. Are ye willing to deal in it?"

Narnra swallowed helplessly, stared down at him, and struggled to reply.

The Old Mage gazed back up at her and asked softly, "Or is it death ye'd prefer?"

Four

TRUTHS AS SHARP AS RAZORS

Nothing wounds so deeply as unwanted, unblunted truth.

Thauloamur Reerist, Minstrel
Clever Words From A Failed Jester
Year of the Prince

"That's not much of a choice to hand me—or anyone—is it?" Narnra snapped bitterly, anger rising in her to roll back the fear . . . a little. "Do as I say, or I'll blast you to ashes or leave you forever drooling. How can you trust any 'truth' handed you under such menace?"

The old wizard shrugged. " 'Tis the same cruel choice most folk of power in this world hand to everyone else. Ye seem a bit too old, lass—especially considering the nature of thy nightly trade—to yet believe Faerûn is a fair place. If ye truly do, ye're *already* a drooling idiot, whether ye admit it or not. I simply make choices blunter and clearer than many when I'm not in the mood for wasting overmuch time on tongue-fencing or frivolity. I'm not in the mood right now. I *like* Cormyr and have seen *so* many of these idiot rebellions in the making: the 'making' always seems to involve the deaths of many good and even some innocent folk. As to how I can trust thy truths, my magic will tell me when ye lie and when ye speak true."

"And that's supposed to make me willing and obedient?" Narnra snarled.

"Nay, but a hope to survive this night should. 'Prudence,' I believe 'tis still called. Ye came back down here seeking my gate and a way home out of all this, did ye not? I'm the only way through it ye know, am I not? I'll be a trifle more willing to be helpful to someone who tried to rob and slay me in a dead-end alley not so long ago if she now tries to deal with me in at least a civil manner, will I not?"

The Waterdhavian lass drew in a deep, defeated breath. Despairing yet still furious, she sighed, took another shuddering gulp of air, and growled, "So ask your questions. I'll *try* to keep to the truth."

"Prudent," the wizard agreed calmly. "If, that is, ye wish to keep me to truth-reading and not mind-forcing ye, as I started to do to Thauvas, there. *He* learned wisdom quickly."

Narnra tossed her head. "Ask," she repeated quietly, hanging helpless in midair.

The mists around her glowed with sudden light, a flash of radiance that died away as abruptly as it had come.

Her captor turned his head quickly to look out into the darkness. "Caladnei, please just watch and listen and pretend ye're not here for a bit, eh? Vangerdahast will be *most* annoyed with me if I destroy his replacement without good cause—and ye may as well know now that thy reckless testing of my shield-spells is doomed to fail."

From the darkness came only silence, but after a long, motionless time the old bearded mage added quietly, "Thank ye."

He turned his head to look up at Narnra and asked, "Thy full, proper name, lass, is—?"

Gods, his nose is an even sharper hawk-beak than mine. Narnra looked down into those bright blue eyes— more blue than gray now, as his magic surged around them—and said steadily, "Narnra Shalace. My mother was Maerjanthra Shalace, a jeweler of Waterdeep. My father I never knew."

Bushy brows arched. "Maerjanthra, eh? I knew a Maerjanthra Shalace of Waterdeep, years back—a sorceress for hire, not a jeweler." He regarded his floating captive thoughtfully. " 'Tis not a common name. Describe her, as she is today."

Narnra let him see her fury as she spat, "A few bones, some dust, and probably a tangle of what's left of her hair—in a bonepit outside the walls of Waterdeep. She's *dead*, wizard."

The old wizard's face was unreadable. "I see. Yet in life, she had dark hair and eyes like thine?"

"Yes," Narnra said flatly, volunteering nothing more.

"How did she die?"

"I don't know. Murdered with magic, I think, but by whom, I've no idea—or they or I would be dead now."

"I see. Have ye kin?"

"No. Unless my father yet lives."

"And what know ye of him?"

The thief shrugged. "He was a man. A powerful wizard, I was told."

"By whom?"

"My mother's apprentices—gemcutters, all long fled. They were drunk when they said that."

"Mother dead, apprentices fled—where d'ye live now?"

Narnra shrugged. "The rooftops. By the warm chimneys in winter. The City of the Dead, mostly, in summer."

"Alone?"

"Alone."

"And ye earn coins enough to eat by—?"

"Stealing. As you know."

"For or with anyone?"

"Alone."

"Any friends?"

"No."

"Folk ye sell stolen things to?"

"Many."

"Name some of them."

Narnra stared into the old wizard's eyes and said evenly, "Dock Ward holds many men who ask no questions about where something came from—and take care that they know nothing about whoever's selling it. If the Watch confronts them, they always say they just found it, tossed into their yard—or window—that morning. In turn, I take care not to ask or know their names. 'Tis the accepted way of such business dealings."

The mage nodded, as if remembering things far away and long ago. "Truth rides on thy tongue well."

"So reward me."

"With?"

"My freedom. The way back."

The old wizard smiled. "High payment for a few civil answers. I'll have more before we advance so boldly into rewarding, hmm?"

Narnra shrugged again. "The power to dictate," she observed flatly, "remains yours."

The wizard below her grew a sudden grin, and from beyond the mists came a faint, swiftly suppressed sound that might have been a Mage Royal's chuckle.

"Are ye a member of any guild?"

"No."

"On any rolls?"

"No."

"Pay taxes?"

Narnra made an incredulous sound. The old wizard grinned again and asked, "D'ye know who I am?"

"No. I can see and hear that you're an old man and a powerful mage, yes, but no more."

The old wizard nodded, strolled a few paces away, spun around, and snapped, "What do ye do with thy days?"

"Steal. Sleep. Spy on folk to steal from. Steal. Sell what I've gained and use the coins to buy food. Eat. Flee the Watch. Steal some more."

"What happened to your mother's shop? House? Goods?"

"Snatched, seized, and spirited away, the moment the city knew she was dead, thank you for asking," Narnra said coldly. "Some slave-seeking noble sent his men after *me*."

The wizard nodded slowly. "I find myself unsurprised."

The mists suddenly boiled up into a gigantic, looming serpentine head, all scales and great jaws, parting to menace her—

Narnra screamed—and so did the Mage Royal.

The world burst into blinding brightness in a great roaring flood of force that swept the dragon head away and the Silken Shadow after it, tumbling end over end unseeing into—surging flows of power that caught and clung and held her, drawing her down out of roiling chaos into . . . hanging upright in midair once more.

The mists churned and whirled around her with more force than before, trailing sparks here and there, but otherwise, the cellar was much as before—except that the senseless Red Wizard now floated head-downwards.

The old wizard was standing just as before, but his gaze was now bent on the cellar entrance arch. "I *did* warn ye, Mage Royal," he said quietly. "Know ye not an illusion when ye see one?"

Narnra found that she could turn her head and did so. Caladnei was on her knees, struggling against what looked like ropes of crawling fire that held her wrists down and away from her sides, looped around her neck, and snarled around her spread knees and her ankles behind her.

"Will ye stand peaceful, and work no magic?" the old wizard demanded.

The Mage Royal of Cormyr glared up at him over the crackling flames and said flatly, "*No*."

The wizard shrugged and turned back to Narnra—and in

a chilling, throat-choking moment the dragon head loomed in front of her once more.

She knew what it was now and managed to keep from screaming but could not help staring at it, trembling, as those great jaws yawned once more. . . .

"Lass, did ye ever see anything like this before now?" the white-bearded wizard asked gently, from below.

"N-no," Narnra managed to hiss. "Take it away!"

The dragon-head dwindled and backed away from her at the same time, shrinking until it was barely larger than her own head—whereupon it became frightening all over again, seeming like the head of a great serpent watching her out of the mist, a snake that could slay her at will while she hung mage-bound.

"Have ye ever seen a living beast like this before?" the old wizard asked again, sharply. The smaller dragon-head turned this way and that, displaying itself to her as a gown-merchant's model might have done . . . then sighed back down into the mists and was gone.

"N-no," Narnra managed to say, suspicion suddenly welling up dark, hot, and choking. Was this old brute . . . ?

The mage pounced. "But?"

"But nothing," she flared, eyes blazing down at him.

"*Truth*, lass! Ye lie as badly as a wrinkled rug! Tell me truth!"

"I . . . Mother's apprentices used to tell me about dragons. That was a dragon, wasn't it?"

"How many apprentices?" the old wizard snapped. "Their names?"

"Uh, five, most of the time. Goraun, Rivrel, Jonczer, and the two younger ones, Tantheld and Silen—Rorgel, who was called 'Silent' because he almost never spoke. They . . . Rivrel's dead; knifed by someone taking things from the shop after Mother died. I think Jonczer was killed too, but I saw only a lot of blood, not his body. The others . . . disappeared. They may be dead, they may've stolen things and fled; I know not."

"Did ye ever see any of them work magic?"

"No."

"What exactly did they tell ye about dragons?"

Narnra glared at the old wizard, her suspicions even stronger now. "When they'd been drinking," she said heavily, "they'd grumble about the dirtier tasks, then wish they were rich bold adventurers and start telling tales of adventurers. Some of them had dragons in them . . . that ate folk, tore apart castles, and smashed villages flat—I'm sure you've heard better. Later, they'd always warn me I shouldn't mention anything they said to Mother."

"And did ye?"

"Did I what?"

"Ever talk about dragons, with her?"

"No. Look, sir wizard, she's *dead*. Now I've told you my name, I've told you hers, I've even babbled the names of five apprentice gemcutters—and *your* name remains a mystery to me. So what is it?"

"Elminster Aumar, though most folk know me better as 'Elminster of Shadowdale.' I'm also called the Old Mage, the Old Sage, and a lot of less polite names and titles, besides. Wiser now?"

"I've heard of Elminster the Great, the Meddler of Mystra, who did things in Waterdeep centuries ago. I guess you're named after him."

"Ye could say that, yes." The old wizard smiled thinly. "Now that we know each other somewhat better, lass, suppose ye set aside thy fury and tell me true: are ye beholden to anyone? Working with anyone? Spying for anyone? Hired out to do any task?"

"No," Narnra replied, anger flaring again. "No, no, and no again!" So he believed nothing of what she'd said, did he?

"Can't you tell truth when you hear it? Or d'ye not want to hear words that don't fit with how you've already judged me? You didn't show yon Red Wizard much kindness!"

"He deserves none, believe me."

"Hah!" Narnra snarled down from where the mists held her. "What if I *don't* believe you? Why should I? You slyly hint that I lie, and that you know a lot more about my mother than I do, and that wizards must do what wizards must do. Well, as to *that*, all I see and hear is that wizards do just as they please and cloak self-interest in a lot of grand words and hints that they're doing things important that protect all Faerûn and all of us with it! Yet do they show any proof of this?"

The smile stealing onto the Old Mage's face seemed a little sad around the edges. "What proof would ye believe, Narnra?"

"I . . . I . . ."

Elminster spread his hands. "Ye see? Rage ye have to spare, and no wonder, for I've endangered ye and scared ye, and my power lies as sharp as any blade between us. Furious ye are that I trust thee not—yet do ye trust me?"

Narnra stared down at him. "No," she whispered. "Not yet."

"Ah. Ye want to. So do I, thee. So how can we build trust between us?"

The thief floating in the mists frowned then said, "Why don't you tell me some answers to things *I* ask?"

The white-bearded wizard grinned. "As ye said to me: so ask your questions, and I'll try to keep to the truth."

Narnra managed a smile. "When did you first meet my mother, and why?"

"If Maerjanthra Shalace the sorceress is also Maerjanthra Shalace the jeweler of Waterdeep," Elminster replied, "I first met her in the ruins of a elven palace in the Sword Coast North some seventy summers ago, when she looked to be about the same age as ye are now. She was with a band of adventurers, seeking tomb-riches to plunder—something I was there to foil."

"*Seventy* winters? But that's impossible! Mother . . ."

"Told ye exactly how old she was, ever?"

"No, but . . ."

"But by her looks ye assumed she was at most twenty or thirty seasons older than ye?"

Narnra nodded and burst out, "And—and if she was a sorceress, could she have . . . *done* something to me? With magic?"

"Ah," the Old Mage said slowly, "ye begin to see the roots of my interest. Have ye ever had . . . strange dreams? Feelings of power rising in ye or running through ye? When my magic touched ye, did ye have any . . . visions? Feelings of power?"

The Silken Shadow looked down at him and shook her head. "No." Her voice was little more than a whisper. From somewhere beyond the mists came an angry crackle of fire that could only be Caladnei striving to win free or to work magic.

"Then," Elminster told her gently, "my answer must be: I know not."

Narnra drew a deep breath and asked, "So if you knew my mother so well, who was my father?"

The wizard shrugged.

The thief floated in silence for a few breaths, frowning at him, then asked, "You said 'first met' my mother. How many other times did you meet her?"

"Dozens. Scores." The Old Mage shrugged. "We dwelt together in Waterdeep, one spring, when I had some business among the nobility of thy city: the house was mine, and a dozen lady adventurers took rooms there."

"A *dozen*, with one man—a wizard? Didn't folk talk?"

Elminster cocked one eyebrow. "Talk? Waterdeep must have changed more than I'd thought."

The white-bearded man below her seemed to shimmer, and suddenly Narnra was staring at a tall, willowy, high-bosomed woman with a steely gaze and an imperious grace that transcended the ill-fitting, none-too-clean old wizard's robes that hung upon her body. "Besides, we were a house of women," a softer, huskier version of Elminster's voice replied. The mists whirled about the woman, sparks flared, Narnra blinked—and the old wizard was standing below her once more.

Narnra drew in a deep breath. "And were you a woman all the time? Did you live with your renters, or did everyone keep to their own rooms and trust in locks?"

Elminster chuckled. "Ye sound like a disapproving priest, lass. Beyond the outside doors, there *were* no locks; the rooms were shared. Men—and women—were in and out, as is the normal way of things, and there were fights, and loving . . . and though I spent much of my time in other, grander houses, wearing other—and grander, if it comes to that—shapes, I lived with those ladies, yes."

"Slept with them?" Narnra asked sharply. "One Maerjanthra Shalace in particular?"

The Old Mage smiled. "Aye, and aye. This would have been forty-and-some summers back."

"You never saw her after that?"

"Nay, our paths crossed every few years, when I came to Waterdeep for some purpose or other."

"My mother was your *mistress?*"

"No, I'd not put it that way—nor would she have done. She had her lovers, and I mine. We liked to talk and catch up on things for an evening, when the gods granted us time and chance."

Narnra glared at him. "When did you last . . . spend the night together?"

Elminster regarded her thoughtfully. " 'Twas either twenty or twenty-two years ago." A smile crossed his face. "Ye seem to be drifting into thinking I fathered ye. That cannot be."

"Oh? How so?"

"Wizards are targets all their lives, lass . . . and all too vulnerable, most of the time. Bearing a child is no light thing to one who works magic, and becoming with child unintended can be deadly—not just to the babe and its mother. Magic can twist the unborn into monsters."

"Wherefore?"

"Wherefore most mages use magic to prevent what isn't wanted or know when 'tis safe to not take such trouble."

"Were you both 'most mages'?"

"Maerjanthra was. Stronger bonds are laid on me."

"'Stronger bonds'? *What* 'stronger bonds'?"

"Mystra, the goddess I serve, decides when her Chosen shall—"

Narnra's head swam.

Chosen? Then this could only be *the* Elminster.

Worse than that: at the sound of Elminster saying the divine name *Mystra* a blue-white fury of fire seemed to burst silently in Narnra's head—a conflagration that flew apart into seven whirling stars before she could even gasp.

They spun themselves into a circle, she had the impression of a gigantic but unseen feminine *smile*, and in the heart of the circle of stars a dark and long-hidden door seemed to fall open in her mind. Through it she heard Goraun chuckling to Jonczer, "Ah, Maerj tricked the Old Bearded One *this* time! I'm going to love seeing the look on his face when he finds out! Lord High-And-Mighty Blackstaff looked sick enough for the both of them when he came to the door. Aye, that *was* him—for once the tavern-lasses told you true! Seems Maerj went to him for a spell to let her have the Old Meddler's child under his nose, so to speak, and Khelben threw her out of his tower . . . only to come to the door like a beggar half a day later, with a face as long as last winter and a scroll in his hand. He said Divine Mystra herself granted—and commanded—it!"

Seven stars flashed, and that warm, impish smile came again, a thrill that left Narnra shivering, somehow. She found herself still floating in the mists, staring grimly down at the bright blue eyes and wry, smug smile of the white-bearded wizard.

So this, after all these years of wondering, was her father.

This old, smiling worm.

Elminster the Meddler. As powerful as a winter storm and as corrupt and willful as a Lord of Waterdeep. A man she could so easily despise or hate. The man whose magic was holding her captive and testing her words even now.

The man—her gaze went reluctantly to the inverted body of the Thayan, arms dangling, eyes dark and empty—whose magic could slice into her mind like a barber's razor, whenever he desired. Whenever he suspected she was hiding something of value from him.

The Silken Shadow clenched her hands so tightly that her fingernails pierced her palms. Blood welled out—and she clenched them all the tighter.

She must say nothing of Goraun's words and hope that Khelben and the goddess Mystra went right on keeping the secret they'd so obviously kept from Elminster of Shadowdale for longer than she'd been alive.

If they did not, he might destroy her or try to keep her captive to train and command her . . . and whatever he tried to do, half Faerûn would come riding hard to take either her life or her freedom.

Narnra Shalace's days as a target would no doubt be all too short.

She'd always feared magic. All thieves do. Hated, feared, and mistrusted magic—how could any folk who lacked it not feel that way? Oh, the young gasped at its wonders when Watchful Order magists blasted things or cast illusions at festivals, but . . . all that power. If it was *ever* turned against you . . .

And another thing: were she to be transformed with a wave of Mystra's hand into a mighty mistress of magic to overmatch Elminster himself, she'd still hate such a life. Being a thief was hard, chancy work—but it was *hers*, battles fought at her choosing, skills she'd won on her own, fresh challenges she set herself, excitement and independence and . . . and what she was used to.

"You old, lying *bastard!*" she spat, the words bursting out before she thought to stop them. "You toad! You smug, lecherous spell-tyrant!"

Elminster blinked up at her. "I've heard such words before, aye, and deserved many of them—though not from someone who knows me as little as ye do, lass. I'd thought we'd stopped all this hissing and snarling for the sheer dramatic effect of thy outrage. Why so hostile now, little one?"

"If you knew," Narnra hissed, voice trembling as she fought to master it. "If you only knew!"

Bright blue eyes narrowed. "Is there something I should be learning amongst your thoughts, daughter of Maerjanthra?"

The Old Mage raised one hand, and Narnra bit her lip and cursed herself for a fool. Doom and icy despair were upon her—and she'd called them down on herself with her own rage and over-loose tongue! Mask and Tymora and Mystra, all, hear me! Aid, if I can win one small shard of mercy! Hel—

As if the gods had heard her and made immediate answer, the cellar shook, tiny sizzling bolts of lightning washed across the ceiling, clawing and spitting, and the mists fell away—just like a bedsheet on a wash-line the Silken Shadow had once sliced with her knife. The Red Wizard fell with them, crashing limp and face-first to the stone floor.

Narnra was also descending, though it felt like drifting down through something soft and thick rather than falling. She was still well off the floor when Elminster spun around to face the cellar arch—and something obligingly appeared there.

Four somethings, actually: four pillars of whirling sparks that occurred quite suddenly, out of thin air, the writhing form of Caladnei of Cormyr in their midst. Dark figures stepped out of those sparks, gesturing in unison—and the Mage Royal's fiery bonds became four tethers that held her helpless between the four newcomers. Four bald, dusky-skinned men whose heads were marked with intricate black tattoos advanced in careful unison. They wore maroon robes and much jewelry, and the eyes in their hard, ruthless faces glittered with anger—and glee.

Elminster spread his hands, fingers twitching and eyes half-closed, for all Faerûn as if he was *feeling* something invisible in the air.

"Stand aside, old fool," one of the four snapped. "You must be of the conspiracy to so leash the Mage Royal of Cormyr—but your life, like hers and that of this masked wench, is forfeit. No one mistreats a Red Wizard and lives!"

The Old Mage murmured something, still seemingly in a trance—and Thauvas Zlorn rose and advanced to meet the nearest of his newly arrived countrymen.

"My thanks for this rescue, Naerzil," he said with a widening smile. "Slay none of these, but keep them captive, for their minds hold—"

"Be silent, Zlorn," the foremost Red Wizard said coldly. "Your fate remains to be decided by those we both answer to, and your orders and suggestions are unwelcome."

"Ah. Such a pity," Thuavas Zlorn murmured, in a voice oddly unlike his own—and sprang forward to throttle his fellow Thayan.

The startled Red Wizard fell with a crash, struggling to keep iron-strong fingers from his throat and eyes. When he slapped Zlorn's arm aside, Thauvas thrust two fingers into Naerzil's nostrils and jerked the man's head back, slamming it onto the stone floor.

The fiery strand leading to Caladnei sprang away, spasming and coiling—and the other three Red Wizards dragged her away, shouting sharp, alarmed incantations.

The two men twisted and struggled on the floor, grunting and cursing—until Naerzil laughed in triumph beneath his foe, and a tattoo on his forehead erupted into blue, crawling flames. They swirled, took the shape of leaping talons, and tore at the face of Thauvas Zlorn.

Blood spurted, an eyeball burst, and the squealing Thayan arched backwards, Naerzil shoving and kicking to gain freedom. The blue flames tore at Zlorn's face and throat until he had nothing left to scream with—but even as his slayer scrambled out and away, chuckling, the dying Thayan formed a sphere with his empty hands—echoing movements that had just been made by Elminster, who was swaying dreamily in the distance—and the blue flames fell from his ravaged face to swirl within those fingers . . . then leap out like a striking serpent at the startled face of Naerzil.

Thauvas Zlorn slumped to his knees, making liquid mewing sounds of pain, but Naerzil's head blossomed into a blinding whirl of blue flames, racing around and around it in a sphere so swift-snarling that no shout, if Naerzil had tried to make one, could be heard.

The blue radiance suddenly burst into sparks and went out—and a headless body toppled to the flagstones, not far from Thauvas.

Flashes and high singing sounds were all around Elminster by then—but the looks on the faces of the Red Wizards told Narnra that they'd been expecting their spells to do much, much more than make a little light and noise.

"Who *are* you?" one of them gasped, at last, as his most powerful spell sighed into nothingness, leaving nothing but impotent lines of smoke curling up from his fingertips.

"Elminster of Shadowdale, at thy service—or rather, at the service of Thay, which land will be vastly improved by the extinction of all Red Wizards," the white-bearded wizard replied merrily. Little flames began to leap and wink between his raised, spread fingers. Between them, like a traveling jester, the Old Mage gave the quailing Thayans a wide, crooked smile.

"Hold!" one of them snapped desperately. "Harm us, and this woman dies!"

He made a beckoning motion with one hand, and the line of fire clinging to the back of it tightened. As its keening song rose into a shriek, Caladnei of Cormyr rose with it, clawing at her throat desperately, her body quivering like a plucked bowstring as the other two Red Wizards tightened their ends of the spell-bonds.

Faces pale, the Thayans glared at Elminster—who stepped swiftly in front of Narnra to shield her from them as her boots finally touched the floor.

The Silken Shadow shot a startled glance at the Old

Mage's back as she crouched, ready to spring in any direction that might seem safest, and wondered if the best thing for all Toril for her to do—though it would mean her death—would be to spring at Elminster with her best dagger drawn, and open his throat wide. The Chosen of Mystra was muttering something under his breath: a word she could not catch, but the same one, over and over.

Breathing heavily, hand stealing toward the hilt of her dagger, Narnra crouched, not knowing what to do . . . or what doom would reach out next to snatch them all.

"We'll depart this place, now," another of the Red Wizards said harshly, "with the Mage Royal our captive. Good hunting to us. You, old man, will leave us be and make no move to twist or harm our spells as we go, or she *will* die."

Elminster nodded his head. "I understand and agree," he said heavily, bowing his head in surrender.

Two of the Red Wizards gave him sneers of triumph as the third began a translocation spell—and silver-blue fire erupted behind them, with force enough to make them all stagger.

"And I," a crisp new voice said coldly, "understand my role in this little drama well enough and agree to it." Whirling blades of shining silver burst from nothingness to bite deep into three maroon-robed backs—and three Red Wizards, transfixed in mid-turn, gasped as those conjured attacks sliced through their torsos like razors. "Slaying Red Wizards is, after all, my task and my pleasure."

Spell-bonds melted away from Caladnei of Cormyr, who fell to her hands and knees, coughing weakly. Men were sprinting toward the cellar from all directions, now, and spell-glows flared here and there as War Wizards of Cormyr teleported in to join them.

Their advance was checked by a sudden wall of silver flames. Its source smiled at them through a wild tangle of unruly silver hair, standing proudly barefoot in a torn and tattered black robe. Her feet did not—quite—touch the floor but trod on air just above it.

"Well met, all," she said serenely, her surging fires forcing folk of Cormyr to fall back. "I am the Simbul, sometimes called the Witch-Queen of Aglarond."

She cast a quick glance over her shoulder, smiled, and said to Elminster, "Sorry, love. I came as swiftly as I could."

Five

DEFIANCE, AUTHORITY, AND DIVINITY

*You must not think that every third person you meet in
tavern or market is a mighty personage, who talks with
the gods nightly and overthrows empires by day. Faerûn
is in sad decline from the golden days of yore. The count is
now down to every seventh person, or even more.*

Thalamoasz Threir, Sage of Sembia
Signposts In The Gardens of Life
Year of the Prince

Snarling silver flames whirled severed halves of Red Wizards to the cellar floor and in a matter of moments melted
them to greasy smoke and then nothing at all. In the wake
of their obliberation the flames sighed, slowed, and sank to
nothingness, leaving the wild-haired woman in the tattered
black robe standing on high with a smile on her face and her
arms folded across her breast.

Narnra kept to her crouch on the cold cellar floor, wondering what fresh rending chaos of magic was going to erupt

precisely where and when. Soon, very soon. Gods above, her hair is *silver*. Truly silver—and alive, moving like a bucket of bait-worms!

"As this is the admirably law-abiding realm of Cormyr," the Queen of Aglarond observed calmly, the risen power of her magic carrying her voice through every dark and distant chamber of the cellars as her upright form drifted higher into the air, "my deeds are sure to bring protest from those whose duty includes keeping order here—despite my saving their hides. Again. May we, for once, begin these protests and remonstrations in a civilized manner, please?"

The half-ring of Harpers and War Wizards stared at her in grim, wary confusion, blades and bows and wands raised. In the far reaches of the cellars, behind them, new radiances blossomed as more mages arrived. Stalwarts of Cormyr cast quick glances at each other, stirred, and seemed about to speak . . . but for long, tense moments, as their Mage Royal winced, stretched, and found her feet, weakly waving away Elminster's proffered hand . . . no protests nor remonstrations were offered.

Then a lone man strolled almost nonchalantly forward from the line of tense Cormyreans, toward the Queen of Aglarond. He was stout and weatherbeaten of appearance, with sun-bronzed skin, shaggy sideburns, and the neatest trace of a beard squaring his chin. His eyes were either butter-hued or brown, and both his wintry brows and the copious white hair curling out at the world from the open front of his florid silk shirt—a fine garment that contrasted oddly with his worn and much-patched leather breeches and mud-spattered boots—told all eyes that he was not young and not likely to soon become any younger. His smile, however, was bright.

"Though I'm but a humble dealer in turret tops and spires, Glarasteer Rhauligan by name," he said, coming to a stop to peer up at the Simbul, "perhaps that makes me a more fitting ambassador for the Forest Kingdom than some. In the name of Cormyr, great Queen, I bid you welcome—so long as you work no violent magic against us. A few villainous and uninvited Red Wizards are one thing, but those sworn to uphold the laws of this realm are quite another. In the name of Mystra, if I may be so bold, I'd ask you not to bar passage to our Mage Royal, that she be returned safely to us." He swept one large-fingered hand out to indicate Caladnei.

The Simbul looked down at him, her silver tresses stirring and curling around her shoulders like the idly lashing tails of a lazy legion of displeased cats, and replied politely, "Very civil speech, Highknight and Harper Rhauligan, and yet plain. I thank you, and make reply: of course the Mage Royal is free to walk as she wills. Her writ holds in this place, so far as 'tis prudent to follow it."

"Ah," Rhauligan said quickly, eyeing Caladnei's slow and limping progress around the Simbul toward the cellar-mouth, "and what, in your experienced and worldly view, great Chosen and Queen, are the limits prudence places upon such obedience?"

The Witch-Queen half-smiled. "The commandments of Mystra regarding tyranny of all who work magic, which binds Chosen such as the Lord Elminster and myself; and the expectations of all good and loyal folk of Cormyr that the laws of the realm and the even-handed dispensation of justice shall be afforded to *all*, equally, and not misused by anyone in authority."

She lifted a hand. "I am *not* saying that your Royal Magician has thus far shown signs of arbitrary rulings, favoritism, or corruption—merely noting that should she do so or act in such a way as to seriously imperil the realm, it will be the duty of all staunch citizens of Cormyr to resist her, rather than to obey."

"And to disagree with you, most honored queen, would be to imperil the realm?"

The Simbul's smile grew a little. "Disagree, no; attack me, yes. To lose so many loyal War Wizards and Harpers at one stroke would seriously weaken Cormyr's ability to deal with hostile wizards—from Thay, or Sembian-hired, or hailing from any elsewhere—and with other conspiracies against the Crown better led than this so-called 'Rightful' one."

"Forgive me, great lady, but this sounds very much like the 'as long as I get my own way, things will be fine' argument of many tyrants," Rhauligan observed, in the gentlest of voices.

"So it does, sir, yet consider: we Chosen have magic enough to shatter kingdoms and the minds of all folk in them, wreaking cataclysm at will—yet we do not. We possess two things most tyrants do not: Mystra's leash upon us, and learned wisdom as to when to smite and when to bide in peace. Which is why you're yet standing and debating with me now, rather than lying dead here alongside all your fellows. If I was Szass Tam and you'd dared to query me, even politely, rest assured that you would be."

At that moment Caladnei reached Rhauligan and put a hand on his shoulder in thanks and support. Behind them both, the line of Harpers and War Wizards took a step or so closer.

In the same casual silence, Elminster strolled closer to the floating queen.

* * * * *

"They're hunting us down like hares all over the harbor right now, lord! It's ruin for us, unless you turn it to glorious victory by hurling some spell or other down into that cellar and collapsing it to crush the lot of them. Why, there're more War Wizards gathered together there—and more of Those Who Harp, too, gods take them!—than I've ever seen all in one place since the last battle against the Devil Dragon!"

"There's no need to shout and so draw attention to yourself, good Narvo," the unseen man who held the other speaking stone replied, almost gently. "Have you used the mindlink spell to talk with Englar?"

Narvo breathed deeply, as if trying to calm himself by

sheer will, and said more quietly, "No, lord. I cast it, but . . . it failed. He's either well away from Cormyr, or . . ."

"Dead. Most likely dead," was the calm reply. "I ordered him and some others to find and bring back Zlorn, so he was probably down in that cellar not long ago. What of Sanbreean? How fares he?"

"D-dead, lord, in the fighting on the docks. I saw him hurl a spell at a War Wizard and have his face blasted off in return. So I'm the only one of us left. These nobles and merchants are useless! All greed and chortling and nasty threats among themselves—and they turn and run like shrieking rabbits the moment things go wrong!"

"Ah, well," the voice from the speaking stone in Narvo's hands said faintly—so softly that the Red Wizard bent hastily forward over it to hear, his nose almost touching its cold, glossy-polished surface—"these things happen. As must— most regrettably—one more thing. *This*."

The speaking stone exploded with a roar, beheading Narvo in an instant. The Red Wizard's corpse arched upright, clawing the air spasmodically, then staggered back and sideways a few unsteady steps. Only a few, but enough. . . .

The peat-hued, reeking waters of Marsember harbor were home to a sizable collection of small, floating dead things already, but they accepted a larger addition with an almost welcoming splash.

The events of this evening had already afforded them much practice in such swift acceptances.

And in a dark and distant chamber, an orphaned speaking-stone was set gently down on a tabletop whose glossy polish rivaled its own. The man who'd put it there toyed idly with a black gem pendant at his throat and turned away to stroll to the window, hum softly up at the winking stars, and think. It was clearly time to consider his second, and far more subtle, plan.

* * * * *

In the tense, crowded cellar in Marsember, the Mage Royal of Cormyr turned to face the Simbul, keeping her balance by resting her fingertips on Rhauligan's shoulder. Lifting her pain-lined face, she locked eyes with the fabled Scourge of Thay.

Against her wild and towering beauty, Caladnei seemed young and of little account—just one more leather-clad Harper among many more menacing veterans. Long-limbed and slender, her dark brown skin almost the hue of the leathers she wore, she regarded the Witch-Queen of Aglarond with large, dark eyes—deep brown, rather than the ruby-red they became when she was angry—and said calmly, "I echo Rhauligan's welcome, but I must respectfully remind both of you, Elminster and Queen Alassra, that in this place, in the absence of Crown Princess and Regent Alusair and Dowager Queen Filfaeril, *I* am the royal law and voice of Cormyr."

"No dispute there, lass," Elminster murmured, spreading his hands—a movement that made several Harpers nervously raise handbows. Caladnei saw something of this out of the corner of one eye and whirled to give the tense line of Cormyreans a quelling 'down arms' gesture.

Turning back to the two Chosen once more, she drew herself up and said, "And in that wise, in the interests of the realm, I demand the immediate surrender of Narnra Shalace into my keeping—and the as-swift departure of you both from our land, honored Chosen, until times are more settled in Cormyr."

Gods watching over us, woman, but you have backbone and balls both, Rhauligan thought savagely, eyeing the two mighty Chosen in what might be his last moments of life. *Your reckless idiocy leaves me despairing but proud of you.*

Why, THANK you, most loyal dealer in turret tops and spires, Caladnei's thought echoed in his mind, as sharp as if she was shouting in his ear. *Permit me to BE Mage Royal and not merely carry the title around like a costume to be sneered at, hmm? I've two good reasons for this particular reckless idiocy: first, to make the point that must be made, that I happen to hold authority here and no Chosen should think their divine favor gives them sway to do as they please; and because what I've heard from and about this Narnra convinces me that she's much more than she appears—and at the very least could mind-yield a LOT of useful information about current "dark dealings" in Waterdeep. I visit your mind, Rhauligan, not to justify myself, but to give you this order: whatever happens, you are to capture this Narnra and bring her back to the most senior surviving Wizards of War, for questioning.*

Lady I am honored to serve, Rhauligan thought back quickly, *I hear and obey.*

"The woman you demand," Elminster observed gently, "is not ours to surrender. I have freed her from my own detention and will defend that freedom, according to her wishes. Moreover, if ye examine no less than six royal decrees and two binding treaties that I know of, preserved in the royal records of Cormyr, I—though not the ruler of Aglarond, I'll grant—have the freedom of the realm and a court rank, by the way, that outstrips thine own."

Caladnei regarded him expressionlessly, her eyes going darker and more red, then said calmly, "This may be so, yet my desires stand." She looked up at the infamous slayer of hundreds of Thayan wizards, still standing on air above her. "It remains my desire not to offend either of you, but I must ask: Queen of Aglarond, what is your response to these my stated desires?"

"*You* would defy *us*, child?" the Simbul asked, her voice incredulous but amused.

Elminster looked up at her, and she turned her head to regard him. They looked at each other in silence, thoughts clearly flashing between them.

"Great persons," Caladnei shapped, clear anger in her voice for the first time, "I demand that you hold no private converse but share for us all what you have to say to each other!"

"Demanding, isn't she?" Elminster remarked, not looking at the Mage Royal. "She extended us no such courtesy when giving Rhauligan his order."

"She's young, yet," the Simbul replied tolerantly. They turned their heads in unison to favor Caladnei with identical sweet smiles and—did as she'd demanded.

YOU DO WELL, TO ASK ME DIRECTLY, AND, YES, SHARING OUR CONVERSE WILL BE FOR THE BEST.

A voice that was gentle and yet thunderous rolled through the cellar, sending Cormyreans staggering back with faces going pale and hands faltering in fear. Not one of them needed to be told who that mind-voice belonged to: blue-white and bright in their minds, tinged with bursting and reforming stars of sheer power, it cried "Mystra" into every mind.

* * * * *

The chime he'd been expecting sang its eerie little song just outside the door, and Bezrar scrambled up from his littered desk. He was sweating—but then, Aumun Tholant Bezrar was always sweating. Part of it was because he was, let's grant it before the gods, fat . . . and the other reason was because someone whose daily business as an importer and wholesaler of sundry goods involved far more than the usual cartload of smuggling and of stolen goods well, such a one has a very good reason to sweat.

He fumbled aside the bar, the three chains, the two bolts—and flung the door wide. "B'gads, you're here!"

"Stand aside and let me in," Surth's cold voice snapped out of the darkness, "instead of announcing my arrival to the entire neighborhood, you incredible dolt."

Bezrar blinked, chuckled, and hastily shuffled back to make way for his partner. Surth was right, of course. Surth was always right. "Did y'bring the hoods?"

"No, of *course* I strolled across all Marsember to pay for a special order and forgot to bring them back with me!"

Malakar's voice was as thin, sour, and sarcastic as always. "You'll have to cut your own eyeholes—you *do* have some shears in this sty, don't you?"

Bezrar chuckled rather than stiffening as he would have done in the unlikely event of any other man in Marsember addressing him in this way. Surth was Surth: Malakar Surth, every cold, sinister, and icily superior inch of him. He was tall and lean where Bezrar was not and sour and sarcastic where Bezrar was jovial and cheerfully evil.

'Twas dealing in scents, wines, cordials, and drugs until the coins spilled out of your ears that did it—that and worshipping Shar. Bezrar neither liked nor understood Surth's love of cruelty, but there were times when it came in right handy—stop me vitals!—such as, well, *now*, for instance. He shook out the hood Surth handed him and held it up, preparatory to yanking it over his head.

"Sit down first," Surth advised him coldly. " 'Twould be less than amusing to see you stumbling around all this chaos putting the point of your shears through an eye—or perhaps me." Surth made the dry little snort that signified he'd uttered a joke and added, "Come *on*. The night won't last forever, you know!"

"Odd's fish, no!" Bezrar agreed enthusiastically—if in muffled tones—from within the hood. And promptly stumbled backwards to sit down in his chair with a resounding crash. Surth rolled his eyes in disgust as he watched the fat and hairy fingers of one sundry-wholesaling hand grope around among the litter of papers like a drunken spider, seeking the shears that lay ready gleaming less than a finger-length away.

His own hood was already prepared and—he jerked it down savagely and settled it with an impatient jerk—on. "*Bezrar*," he said warningly, in tones that produced the expected result: a frantic flurry of activity that sent the wholesaler's chair creaking.

"Yes, yes, aye, *yes!*" the frantically snipping wholesaler responded, ending with a triumphant, "*There!*"

"*Luminous*," Surth told him in a voice that fairly dripped sarcasm down the walls. "Now, shall we—?"

"Yes, yes, of course, b'gads!" The fat wholesaler heaved himself up like a walrus conquering a shore-rock, puffed his way toward the door—and halfway there smote his forehead, turned to pinch the lamp out and snatch up his ready-scabbarded longknife—a truly impressive specimen of the curved Marsemban fish-gutting blade—and turned back to his partner with the sudden question, "What if they're not there?"

Surth set his teeth. "Then we'll try again *another* night," he explained patiently. "*No one* swindles ten thousand in gold from Mal—from us and lives to whistle away with it."

"But . . . but what if they *are* there but are ready for us? With dark spells, say?"

Malakar Surth put his hand to the door and replied, "I have a . . . business associate who can step in, if need be."

"Eh? What kind of a 'business associate'?"

The tall, thin shadow silhouetted in the nightgloom of the doorway murmured, "Bezrar, the time for silence is come. Of my associate, let's just say, his spells are darker."

* * * * *

Narnra swallowed, or tried to, but seemed to be floating in calmness, in the midst of glory, enthralled by that great yet gentle voice. So *this* is a god. . . .

Slack-mouthed in awe, most of the War Wizards went to their knees in the cellars as the thunderous voice of their goddess rolled and echoed around them. The Harpers stood staring wide-eyed at the two Chosen, in hopes that they'd see something—however brief and fleeting—of the Mother of All Magic.

Something awakened in Narnra's mind as she crouched, trembling in awe, something that seemed to find and sort through seven blue-white stars curiously . . . then smile in an echo of the earlier smile that had washed through the Silken Shadow.

Narnra Shalace wept inwardly, frozen like stone, as Mystra regarded her personally and let new blue-white fire flood into those stars, leaving her quivering. . . .

Which was why she was the only person in the room who did not hear every syllable of Mystra's mind-voice:

AS A SMITH TESTS AND TEMPERS A BLADE, THE DESIGNS OF THE MAGES OF THAY CAN AND SHOULD BE RESISTED AT EVERY TURN—YET IT IS MY WILL THAT THAY'S INCREASED MERCANTILE SPREAD OF MAGIC CONTINUE, FOR NOW. YOU WERE RIGHT TO SLAY THESE, ALASSRA, BUT TO JOURNEY NOW TO THAY AND INDULGE IN SLAUGHTER OF OTHER RED WIZARDS WOULD BE WRONG. THEY'LL OFFER YOU SPORT IN AGLAROND ITSELF SOON ENOUGH.

A MORE IMPORTANT CONCERN IS FOR YOU, ELMINSTER, TO DEAL WITH: YOUR ONETIME PUPIL, VANGERDAHAST. HE'S NEITHER AS FEEBLE NOR AS FORGETFUL AS HE'S LED CALADNEI TO BELIEVE. MAKE SURE, EL, THAT HE'S TRULY CONSIDERED ALL IMPLICATIONS OF HIS UNFOLD-ING PLANS AND ISN'T JUST BEING SELFISH. FOR ME TO PRY WOULD BE TO RUIN HIS WORK—AND FURTHER ENDANGER CORMYR.

Most of the Cormyreans in the cellar were cowering or shaking with awe at the sheer weight and power of Mystra's presence, as her mind-voice thundered on. They were too enthralled to faint or become numbed. The mere contact made every mind alert and afire—but Mystra's last sentence was the first that made the Mage Royal of Cormyr go pale.

The greatest state secret of the realm, laid bare before all.

She swayed, feeling sick, and fought down the sudden urge to cry. After all the secrecy, innocent folk mind-blasted or slain to make them forget what they'd seen, and the tor-ment of facing nobles and War Wizards and courtiers, all hostile, before she was ready . . . all that work swept away in an instant.

Whereupon two gigantic eyes opened out of nothingness behind Elminster and the Simbul and stared right *through* them at Caladnei. RECKLESS IDIOCY, PERHAPS, BUT BRAVELY DONE, CALADNEI OF CORMYR. MOREOVER, YOUR SUSPICIONS OF NARNRA ARE WELL FOUNDED. NO SECRET CAN BE KEPT FOREVER, AND YOU HAVE SHIELDED IT—I HOPE—JUST LONG ENOUGH.

Caladnei stared into those great glowing orbs, fighting to find words as exultation rose in her, her face awash in sudden, silent tears. . . .

A lone, hooded figure in leathers sprang out of her crouch and was away like the wind, sprinting across the cellar floor as swiftly as any arrow. A few blue-white stars seemed to curl around her heels, just for an instant.

Glarasteer Rhauligan shook himself like a wet dog and burst out of his own trembling rapture at a run, slapping something into Caladnei's hands as he went.

She stared down at what she held, not comprehending what it was for a mind-whirling moment: a gleaming steel vial.

Drink, his firm, warm mind-voice came to her, along the spell-link that hadn't yet expired, *and be healed. Worry not; I carry two more.*

Only one other Harper scrambled to intercept the racing Silken Shadow. Narnra flung her last purse of sand into his face, vaulted a trembling War Wizard, and was gone up the stairs, panting for breath.

The older, stouter Rhauligan lumbered along in her wake at a slower, grimmer speed, threading a less bruising way through the enthralled crowd of Cormyreans.

Through the mind-link of tumbling stars, the amusement of a goddess crashed over them all in a vast flood, forcing most in the cellar into helpless, gasping laughter.

As they rocked and slapped thighs and shouted help-less mirth, those giant eyes winked out, Elminster and the

Simbul vanished along with all their mist-curling radiance—and the overwhelming presence of divinity was suddenly . . . gone.

Laughter died swiftly, as half-dazed War Wizards and Harpers clutched at each other for support, blinked, and sighed their various ways down from rapture. Many started swearing, and not a few bent over to brace themselves like winded soldiers and collect their wits.

"That . . . that was something," a grizzled Harper said weakly, grounding his sword. Beside him, two War Wizards turned and embraced each other, their uncontrollable shudderings slowly slackening into tremblings.

Standing alone still facing the dark emptiness that had held two Chosen and their goddess, the Royal Magician of Cormyr stood shaking and silent, clasping the vial to her breast and weeping uncontrollably.

A woman in trim dark robes slipped out of the crowd of Cormyreans and went to Caladnei. She was careful to circle around the Mage Royal so as not to startle her by clasping her from behind—but never slowed in her advance.

Without really looking up Caladnei saw a lock of hair that had recently gone white amid many tresses, and its owner's erect and graceful walk, and knew as gentle arms went around her that her comforter was Speera.

Laspeera. She wasn't sure she quite dared to call Laspeera Inthré Naerinth, the second-in-command of the War Wizards for many of Vangerdahast's years of service, by the nickname the royal family used for her. Laspeera, the lady she'd been afraid would resent and attack an unknown adventurer from Turmish, anointed out of nowhere by the increasingly difficult and much-feared old Vangerdahast . . . but who'd instead become a firm friend, remaining a loved and trusted diplomat and a cheerful tower of strength and moral guide for the War Wizards and the nobility of the realm alike.

Not for the first time, she wondered what Laspeera's true thoughts were, behind her unfailing graceful politeness. Many a courtier could act and speak one way and believe and covertly advance quite another, and far too many kings had fallen by trusting the wrong smiling face for too long.

Yet she could not stop crying, and Speera's arms were warm around her, rocking her as affectionately as an older sister might.

"One of the high points of any life, yes," Laspeera murmured, "and so of course devastating when it's over . . . but Cala, life goes on, and there'll be others—if you work to make them happen."

That jerked Caladnei upright, to stare at the older War Wizard. "Speera?" she blurted. "You called me 'Cala'!"

Laspeera winked at her. "Mystra take me," she murmured, "so I did. How presumptuous and graceless of me. My tongue must have run away with me."

She kept hold of Caladnei and so was ready to catch her when the Mage Royal collapsed into sudden, snorting laughter.

Six

A KNIFE IN EVERY HAND

There's one sure way to know ye've reached a city where
merchants rule: ye'll see a knife clutched ready in every
hand. If the merchants have gone so far as to practice the
misrule of kings, some of those hands will no longer be
attached to bodies.

Sabras "Windtrumpet" Araun
One Minstrel's Musings
Year of the Highmantle

One of the highest peaks of the Storm Horns, that great
shield-wall of mountains that defend Cormyr's western flank,
is Tharbost. "The Lord of Storms," some call it, and it glares
eternally out over Tunland, so high and wind-shrouded
that few creatures lacking wings know that the lofty tip of
its spire was broken off in dragon-battle long ago, leaving
behind a small, flat high table. A rampart of teethlike rocks
at the western lip of this lofty perch affords a little shelter
against the full raking fury of the winds, so when breezes

slacken, humans who somehow reach the summit of Tharbost might hope to stand thereon for a short time before the
tireless wind-talons pluck and whirl them down again.

Two humans were standing there now: figures that had
simply appeared there out of what minstrels were wont to
call "empty nowhere" moments before, without any fuss of
flowering magic or deadly struggles of climbing.

The wind moaned in a deadly rising, whipping the tattered black robe one of them wore up into a most immodest
flapping, but she stood unconcernedly—showing no signs
of struggling for balance or feeling the icy wind-chill—side
by side with a figure who spat out the end of his beard for
the third time and muttered a small, sharply worded magic
to keep it down.

The Simbul grinned at him. "Strange, how you worded
your cantrip to tame your beard but not my dress."

"Presume to alter the fashion statement of a woman who's
also a queen? I'm widely considered a meddling fool, Lady
Fire, but I'm not *that* much of a meddling fool."

Though the sorceress no more than smiled fondly, merry
laughter rolled around the summit, shaking Tharbost and
setting some of its rocks to singing out echoes.

THIS IS WHAT I MISS MOST ABOUT LAYING ASIDE MOR-
TALITY, Mystra told them a trifle sadly, when she'd mastered
her mirth. NO ONE TEASES *ME*.

Elminster lifted his head, grin widening—and his beard
promptly flew up into his face to forestall whatever he'd
been going to say.

NO, OLD MAGE, THAT WAS *NOT* A REQUEST FOR YOU
TO START DOING SO. HEAR AND BELIEVE. As a coda to that
emphatic statement, Elminster's beard slapped down to its
tamed position once more.

The Simbul promptly burst into laughter at his revealed
expression, so it was left to the long-suffering onetime
Prince of Athalantar to observe, "Ye cannot have snatched
us here, Divine One, just to hear us banter. Ye've more to
impart, eh?"

OF COURSE. WHENEVER POSSIBLE—ALASSRA SILVER-HAND, HEED ME TRUE!—YOU ARE TO SUBVERT RED WIZARDS RATHER THAN SLAUGHTER THEM.

The Simbul lifted an eyebrow. "'Subvert'?"

LAY DEEP-MIND SUGGESTION SPELLS TO GENTLY NUDGE THE THAYANS INTO ACTING AS I DESIRE THEM TO. SOME WILL YET HAVE TO BE SLAIN, BUT TOO MANY HAVE A CAPACITY TO CRAFT NEW MAGICS AND EXPAND MORTAL USE OF THE WEAVE, TO LOSE THEM ALL.

"I hear and obey," the Simbul said formally, bowing her head. "In truth, my . . . bloodlust when it comes to Red Wizards increasingly frightens me. I'll stay my hand and do as you command. Guide me as to the actions you want them steered into."

"I hear and obey," Elminster echoed, "and will do the same. Command and guide us."

I SHALL. THANK YOU.

The rising wind whistled around them, heard but unfelt. It whipped away their breath in long, fleeting plumes as the Chosen waited, finding themselves after some dozen plumes had raced away east still standing on the desolate mountaintop, beneath a sky of uncaring stars.

"There's more, Divine One," Elminster observed calmly, not leaving it as a question.

The rocks around them seemed to sigh. YES.

YES, THERE IS. The wind moaned higher. MOMENTS LIKE THAT MOOT IN THE CELLARS MAKE ME FEEL VERY . . . MORTAL AGAIN. UNCERTAIN. UNSETTLED.

The wind slackened, and after a moment Mystra spoke again. HOW WELL . . . IN YOUR HONEST, BLUNT JUDG-MENT, BOTH OF YOU, SPEAKING FREELY WITHOUT FEAR OF . . . REPRISAL . . . HOW AM I DOING?

Elminster and the Simbul turned their heads and traded sober glances, there in the whistling wind, and it was Elminster who spoke, his voice gentle.

"In this we are both agreed, Most Mighty," he told the empty, echoing air around him. "Considering how we two, who have wielded some measure of the power ye hold for hundreds of years longer than ye have existed, so often mess up: fine. Just fine."

*   *   *   *   *

A bobbing barge saved her. She leaped, landed hard, and skidded across its damp roof *just* slowly enough to kick up . . . and *out* . . . gaining the height she needed to cross a widening stretch of inky water and crash heels-first onto the already-battered rail of a barge littered with heaps of rusty chain, garbage, crab sink-cages, and a tangle of rotting nets—startling into cursing wakefulness the three filthy beggars sleeping thereon—and vault over its massive dragger-arm, onto the next island.

Where the Silken Shadow ducked into an alley and raced along, crouching low and coming to a cautious, creeping halt at its far end, which—as she'd correctly guessed—was also the other side of the isle. The bridge onward, to a much larger island that would give her a choice of routes toward the true shore, was only a few running paces away, but it would be guarded—and one or perhaps two warriors she could burst past, but more, or sentinels who had handbows or spells, would be quite another matter.

She crouched tensely, knowing she hadn't much time before the pursuit caught up with her. Mantle of Mystra, but she couldn't even count how many teleporting War Wizards and as-good-as-she-was-probably-better Harpers were down there—what if that Mage Royal sent them *all* after her?

Ironically, it was Glarasteer Rhauligan himself who saved her. He came bounding up to the top of the steps, puffing a little, and called an alarm to the guard, asking if he'd seen a lone lass in dark leathers and a mask running his way.

The startled guard stepped out to make reply. Narnra darted from behind him like an eager arrow and was half-way across the bridge before Rhauligan saw her and roared a warning in earnest.

A lantern glimmered as it was raised at the far end of the bridge—a simple, mist-slick stone arch—in the gloved hand of an armored guard who seemed to have brought several dozen of his fellows along with him. Narna cursed and sprang over the side of the bridge without slowing.

The water was as icy as it was filthy, and she came up clawing her way free of floating debris better not seen, and hauled herself around the bow of a barge that had been moored so long that weeds had grown themselves a curtain on its chains. Something nosed against and nibbled at her boot underwater. She kicked out in fear and revulsion, felt something solid flinch away, and clambered up out onto another dock as if all the gods themselves were clutching at her.

A guard called out to his fellows, somewhere nearby in the mist-curling darkness. Narnra cursed savagely and silently—and swarmed up the nearest crumbling wall, moments before a spearpoint came jabbing after her.

Loose, rotting shingles slipped and slid under her feet, pulling something in her thigh with a sickening jolt of pain, then she was away through an exhausting and seemingly endless labyrinth of slick rooftops, mist, more rooftops, more crumbling walls, and desperate leaps across narrow, stinking canals.

When a particularly long leap drove her breath from her and left her curled and gasping around an ornamental stone spire someone had thoughtfully carved jutting up from a roof-edge, Narnra Shalace took the time to catch her breath, rub at her leg, wince, and turn to notice two things.

At some point in her frantic flight, she'd well and truly reached the mainland, crossing several streets of what must be the city of Marsember. More importantly, the Harper who'd dared to bandy words with that fearsome Queen of Aglarond—Glar-something Rhauligan, that was his name— had followed her in her mad leaps and sprints all this way across the rooftops and was in sight of her now, jumping easily across an alley not three rooftops back!

"Mask and Tymora, aid me!" Narnra hurled that snarled prayer up at the few stars she could see glimmering through the chill, thickening mists, and ran on, kicking her leg to loosen the muscles, within, that were giving her pain. Yes, it was hurting less, but . . .

She scaled a roofpeak and slid down the far side, noting grimly just how far she'd have to leap to avoid a bone-shattering fall into the street below.

In mid-leap she had a momentary glimpse of a sleepy apprentice reaching out to fasten the shutters of his high window, seeing her, and freezing the moment he got his mouth open to gape at her—then she was past, slamming into the roof above the dumbstruck apprentice with her knees and elbows. Tiles broke and skittered away down the roof under her as she slid a little way, got her boot onto the dormer root just above the apprentice, stopped her fall, and doggedly climbed back up and over this roofpeak. As she went over, she risked a glance back over her shoulder.

There was Rhauligan, their eyes meeting for a brief, thoughtful moment ere she dropped out of view and slid down the far side of her roof toward a lower one, beyond. Belonging to a small building, it was narrow, relatively flat, and of wooden shingles streaked with thick and probably slippery moss—but it led to another steep roof, not far away, and the short distance between the two peaks gave Narnra an idea.

She could spare a dagger—*a* dagger. If she could get to that second roof in time . . .

She could, and—*thank* you, Mask and Tymora both!—the far side of this Marsemban mansion sprouted a side-wing whose lower roofpeak gave her something to stand on, below the one that looked back at the way her pursuer should be coming. And high-ranked Harper in the service of Cormyr or not—what'd the Simbul called him? "Highknight"?—he'd not chase her half so well once he'd stopped a steel fang in the face!

Rhauligan's head was suddenly there, bobbing up over the

edge of his roof—and she set her teeth, rose up, and threw her second-best belt knife as hard and as fast as she could.

It bit home and stuck, quillons-deep in . . . well, he must have slipped on a hood, or a mask. His head—if it was his head—sank down out of view, leaving the Silken Shadow to stare across at the rooftop, briefly moonlit, now, as the mists parted momentarily . . . and breathe heavily . . . and wonder if she'd just killed the man.

When the mists came back and returned the rooftops to smoke-like shadow, several long breaths later, Narnra drew in a deep, shuddering breath, turned, and went on.

* * * * *

"Starmara? Starmara, my love, are you awake?"

Her husband's voice was a throaty growl—the tone he fondly believed was some sort of irresistible amorous purr—and Starmara Dagohnlar stared drowsily at the luxurious rubyweave draperies of their bed-canopy, high overhead, and managed not to sigh.

Durexter Dagohnlar could certainly rake in the coins when she urged him on. He might be a thoroughly dishonest, ill-smelling brute and boor of a mightily successful—and widely hated—Marsemban merchant . . . but before all the gods, he was *her* thoroughly dishonest, ill-smelling brute and boor.

And there were times when beasts must be sated, no matter how distasteful the process. Sleepily Starmara shed her shimmerweave robe so he wouldn't tear it apart like he had the last one, elbowed a cushion aside so she'd be comfortable, and whispered back as alluringly as she knew how, "Awake and aching for you, my lord."

Durexter chuckled and rolled across the substantial acreage of silken sheeting between them, scattering cushions and breathing the garlic and Thayan pepper sauce she fervently wished he wouldn't douse his meat so heavily with, all over her.

"Well, now, my proud beauty—so smooth and warm and, heh-heh, *handy*—know the love of the most grasping, deceitful, law-shattering, tax-evading, and just gods-kisséd *successful* merchant in all Marsember!"

Starmara gently bit her husband's chest to keep from having to kiss the stinking mouth that was so enthusiastically delivering his usual modest little speech, as he bruisingly maneuvered himself into what he imagined was a heroic stance. She entertained a brief fantasy of just sliding right down the bed and out from under whilst he was still chest-beating and crowing his exploits, so that he'd ultimately crash down onto—nothing.

Then he was . . . he was . . .

Choking and gurgling strangely above her, awakening Starmara to the sudden apprehension that his heart might have given out at blesséd last and he was now going to slam down and crush her into the bed, suffocating her with his dead weight long before any servant could find them! Frantically, she clambered and slid toward the foot of the bed, her perfumed robe tangling—and emitted a brief shriek as Durexter toppled over suddenly onto her left elbow.

With a frantic twist and kick she freed herself and wormed past, wriggling—

Hard into an unfamiliar knee, that was clad in black leather and attached to someone who wheezed and smelled quite differently from her husband . . . and who now reached down to discover what had fetched up against him, felt it thoroughly as Starmara gave in to a sudden impulse to scream—as loudly and as throat-strippingly as she knew how—and roared, "Ho, Mal! I've found the wench! And she's—heh-heh—she's . . ."

"All right, *all* right," hissed another, vaguely familiar and much sharper man's voice. "Stop leering. Have you done strangling him yet?"

"Uh, well, he's not dead, but I thought y'said—"

"*Tie* him *up*," the thin voice snarled. "Back of neck to bedpost, so he doesn't get any ideas about escaping or fighting, then his little fingers together because no one enjoys breaking their own fingers—both on the *same side* of the bedpost rather than around behind it, mind—and leave the rest to me. I'll be finished with Haughty Lady Starmara here by then."

Head enveloped in her own silks, the wife of the most grasping, deceitful, law-shattering, tax-evading, and successful merchant in all Marsember threw herself up and over the ornately rolled scrollwork end of the bed, kicking wildly, and succeeded only in hurling herself into the cold and exceedingly efficient hands of the unseen owner of the thin voice. He threw her across her own footstool with force enough to leave her helplessly sobbing for breath and had her ankles, knees, wrists, and elbows trussed before she even had enough wind back to protest.

When she did, of course, he fed silken robe into her mouth until she choked then bound it there with the robe's belt, leaving the rest of the material across her face. He bent with a grunt—almost inaudible amid louder growls, grunts, and scufflings from the bed—and the next thing Lady Starmara Dagohnlar knew, a cold, hard, and very heavy weight was lying across her stomach and hips, and she could have no more struggled or moved than flapped her arms and flown across the Sea of Fallen Stars to that lovely house-of-baths in Westgate. The smell of moth-powder told her she was probably pinioned under her own blanket-chest.

"Done," the voice of the owner of the knee said triumphantly from the bed. "Trussed like a feasting-fowl."

"Then we'll have him down here on the floor next to his blushing lady—at least she should be blushing; just *look* at that tattoo!—and the fun can begin."

"Oh? What tattoo?"

"*Later*, Bez. Relocation of doomed merchants first, hmm?"

* * * * *

Glarasteer Rhauligan winced as he drew Narnra's razor-sharp blade out of his capture hood and one of his spread fingers inside it. He bound his sliced digit tightly with one of the strips of cloth he always kept ready in one of his belt pouches.

So his little fleeing vixen was down one dagger but bound to have at least two—and probably twice that many—more. Next time one might bite his real head and not a hasty counterfeit. The capture hood had one much enlarged eyehole now and would bear replacing when he . . .

He scrambled up, ran along the roof-gutter—thank the gods for Marsember's filthy-wet weather; it meant every house was covered with copious and sturdy troughs and spouts—and sprang onto the next roof along, rather than going over the roofpeak again to greet a second dagger.

If Tymora was with him, she'd run where he was antici-pating she would, which was—*yes!* There!

A slender hip in dark leathers hastily ducking away around the edge of another roof . . . she knew he was still on her heels—but he knew just how little city she had left to run through in that direction before the wall would hedge her in and force her to either go west and south and down to the streets . . . or turn back toward him.

Breathing easily, Glarasteer Rhauligan trotted through the mist that seemed now to be threatening to turn to a dawn rain and grinned. This was fun, and—*whoalaho!* She'd doubled back already and—a dark form spun across a street below him, just above a guard-lamp—was really putting wings to her boots!

His fierce grin widened. *Well*, now . . .

* * * * *

Durexter and Starmara Dagohnlar lay side by side on their new and softly luxurious Athkatlan carpet—trussed, furious, and helpless. Their two assailants wore black hoods and waved two of the largest gleaming-sharp Marseman long-knives the lord and lady merchant had ever seen . . . but both Dagohnlars knew very well by now who the two were.

There were merchants in Marsember more ruthless and dishonest than Lord Durexter Dagohnlar—but he took care not to have any dealings with them nor to cross them in even the smallest way. He even took small losses here and there in keeping himself too useful to them to be eliminated. There were also many Marseman merchants almost as shady in dealings as he was—but Durexter took care to keep holds over such men, so as to prevent what was happening right now: two of them coming by night to forcibly collect coins the bound couple had swindled away from them.

The fat, sweating, jovial one would be the smuggler and stolen-goods-vendor Bezrar, whose schemes were as brutish and simple as he was. The taller, thinner one was the real danger: Malakur Surth dealt in poisons and drugs, among other things, and had dealings with local priests of Shar and with certain spell-wielding outlanders—even, if the latest whispers Durexter had paid good coin for were correct, at least one Red Wizard of Thay.

Unbeknownst to Durexter, his lady lying beside him could have supplied the name of that Thayan mage, for—thanks to the private rental-chambers at a local house of beauty, and the enterprising matrons who patronized them—her sources were even more expensive and exclusive. Malakar Surth had recently entered into limited bound service with one Harnrim "Darkspells" Starangh for their mutual profit and advancement.

None of which was much warm comfort, considering that Durexter had openly and sneeringly short-coined Bezrar and Surth, laughingly directing them to "call on the gods" or "beseech the Crown" for their losses; sums set down in writing nowhere, if any of the parties involved had any wits at all, and concerned with completely unlawful business dealings. It would be long seasons of cells and roadgang-work for anyone who went yapping to the authorities.

It was, of course, Surth who spoke first. "You both know us," he said silkily, "and why we're here. We intend to leave this grand house of yours with what's owed to us—Bezrar, the rope!—and the persuasion we employ can be as gentle or as painful as you determine."

"Oh! Ah!" Bezrar responded, unbuckling his breeches. Starmara made a muffled sound that might have been a bleat of alarm or might have merely been an expression of disgust, but revealed to her from-the-floor gaze was a leather cod of weary age and condition, below a long, continuous coil of coarse rope that had been wound round and round the merchant's hips, adding noticeably to his impressive girth—which shrank rapidly as the merchant tugged, hauled on the rope, then began a ponderous imitation of a dancing-lass undulating on a pedestal at a revel, shedding coils around his feet with a clumsiness that made Surth sigh and Starmara suddenly want to laugh. This Bezrar was so much like Durexter trying to be alluring. . . .

"Your bedposts will do admirably to anchor the two ropes we have here," Surth explained casually, "as we tie the other ends to your ankles—securely, I hope—and lower you both out the window, head-first into the canal below."

Starmara no longer felt in the least like laughing.

"We'll dangle you underwater for a bit for the eels to have something to nibble on then pull you up and ask you for some money. Bez here is strong; he can haul you up many times, though of course the more angry and tired we get, the longer we'll leave you to breathe water or feed fishes. Simple enough, hmm?"

Durexter—who had not been gagged—chose that moment to disagree, loudly and profanely. Surth merely smiled, but when the lord merchant progressed to shouting, the dealer in drinkables knelt with a knee on Durexter's throat and remarked, "Bellow any more and I'll cut your tongue out. I know you can write down the whereabouts of your money—even with several broken fingers."

He looked over at Starmara, and added, "That goes for you too, Lady Dagohnlar. Scream once, and you'll get away with it—but my knife will make sure you don't scream twice . . . or ever again use that lashing tongue you're so proud of, for the rest of your life. However, ahem, short that may be. Bez and I have registered this little debt, you see—so we could seize this house in the regrettable event of your deaths and strip most of its contents before your other creditors awakened to dispute our right to do so."

He waved an airy hand, longknife flashing, and lifted his knee because Durexter had gone a rich, convulsively twisting purple. "Ah, but forgive me: I've forgotten to announce what will happen when we get tired of hauling you up to drip dirty canal-water all over this nice carpet. Assuming, of course, you don't simply remember where in this nice house your rainy-day wealth is hidden, so we your honored guests can recover our losses."

He pointed at his hooded companion with his blade. "Bez here has just taken delivery of a new longknife—show the nice Dagohnlars your knife, Bez! Aha, see!—and he wants to test its edge in *real* cutting. Now, I've recently noticed that men. . . and women, too, by the gods, come to think of it . . . have toes. Lots of them. Little appendages none of us really need. We could relieve you of them, one by one, and collect them for Ponczer down at the Firehelm to cook up for you in a nice dish. Durexter first, I think. When we're done, we'll drop you in your own cellar to bleed and give the rats something to nibble—I hate rats, don't you? Squeaking, swarming, ravenously gnawing things . . ."

Surth stood up, admired the glittering tip of his own knife, then lifted his eyebrows, looked down at Starmara as if only now remembering her, and said softly, "Ah, Lady Starmara! With your beauty, perhaps we could arrange a pleasanter punishment . . . or, on the other hand, perhaps you might unfortunately *lose* that beauty." He watched his knife gleam as he turned it, slowly, and smiled.

"By S-shar herself," Durexter whispered, as the slender

merchant bent swiftly to put his knife to Starmara's cheek, "what're you *doing*, man?"

"Hold still, dear," Malakar Surth said fondly—but unnecessarily, as Starmara had just fainted—and deftly sliced through the belt of her robe, to remove her gag. He turned his head to smile at Durexter and replied, "What am I doing, lord? 'Leering triumphantly' is the appropriate phrase, I believe."

As he felt Aumun Bezrar's rough hands at his ankles and the prickle of coarse rope, it was Lord Durexter Dagohnlar's chance to faint. Enthusiastically, he seized it.

* * * * *

She was panting, now, almost as loudly as the man so close behind her. They were both scrambling on the rooftops in the clinging mists, perhaps the length of a long wagon apart—and Rhauligan was gaining.

Narnra doubled around a buttress of vomiting gargoyles—vomiting birdnests, it seemed, and she slipped and almost fell when they suddenly erupted in black, squawking, fluttering gorcraws or the like—and silently cursed the man. He seemed to know every roof and façade and alleyway, where she did not, and twice now had almost cornered her with no place to leap to, and no safe place to climb down.

Almost, and—blast! *Again!*

At the far end of the roof she'd just landed on—one with a drenched little rooftop garden, reached through a door protected by a massive, chased iron gate that might have given an army trouble, let alone one thief armed with a few fangs and her fingernails—was . . . nothing.

A canal, with a near-impossible long leap across it to a grand mansion . . . and not the roof of that ornate turret-sprouting fortress of stone, either, but a lone dark and open window, high above the dark waters below. Narnra snatched a glance back over her shoulder and saw just what she'd expected: Rhauligan smiling grimly as he gained her rooftop, ready in a crouch for any desperate rush she might make at him . . . leaving her no place to go.

No place but the desperate fool's leap.

The Silken Shadow clenched her fists, threw back her head to gulp air, chose her path across the garden between the great tubs and barrels of dripping plants—and ran for all she was worth, gaining speed and veering at the end just enough to hurl herself up . . . up . . . high into the night, tumbling once . . . twice . . .

Glory of glories! She was going to—

Crash into the window-sill hard enough to numb her arm and shoulder or break them outright, smash all the wind from her lungs, and somersault her helplessly into the darkness beyond, to thump, bounce, and skid along on a thick, fur-like carpet.

Colored glass in two decorative side-panels shattered and sang around her as she burst them wide, to bounce and swing in her wake, and . . .

There was a great bed in the ornate room. A naked man and woman lay bound hand and foot beside each other by the foot of it—and turning from them, two dark-clad, hooded figures with curved, gleaming knives in their hands!

Winded and in pain, Narnra could do no more than twitch and writhe as she came to a halt—and black-clad bodies blotted out the light.

Steel flashed down and bit into her, so cold and sharp that she couldn't have screamed even if she'd had breath enough to do so. Narnra rolled away, or tried to, mewing in pain, as those knives bit down again and again.

Seven

INTRIGUE IS A FINE DARK WINE

*Making coins and crushing rivals is a fine day's feasting—
but the dance of intrigue that leads to such things is a fine
dark wine.*

Andratha Thunbarr
My Days As A Merchant Queen
Year of the Wandering Wyrm

"Get her! By Shar, a hired slayer! Durexter, you'll pay
for this!" Surth snarled, stabbing for all he was worth. He
promptly slipped on the bunched-up carpet for the fourth
time and fell heavily across the newcomer, leaving Bezrar no
safe place to stab.

"Not mine!" the trussed merchant cried frantically, from
the floor. "Not mine!"

"That's true," another voice roared, as someone *else*
burst through the window, sending fresh shards of glass
bouncing and singing across the bedchamber, "because
she's *mine!*"

Gasping, shuddering, and pawing feebly for her own knife, Narnra Shalace sobbed in the grip of worse pain than she'd ever felt before, searing and wet and—emptying. She was emptying out, flowing . . .

Struggling atop her, Malakar Surth set the point of his knife into the floor, drove it down hard through a gap in the tiles, and used it as a handle to drag himself off of the heaving, slithering night-slayer beneath him. Such folk often carried poisons—possibly ones he himself had supplied—and he wanted to be well away from this one before—

Glarasteer Rhauligan ducked under Bezrar's wild slash, slammed a balled fist into the fat merchant's rotund chest— above the belly and below the heart, forcing Bezrar into the wild battlecry of "Eeep!"—and ran on, slamming hard into Surth and smashing him back against the nearest wall, which happened to sport a glass-fronted wardrobe.

More singing shards rained down amid the bouncing of Surth's bruised limbs, and Rhauligan found his feet, snatched Narnra by the shoulder, and was away toward the window before the wardrobe wavered, shivered all over as Starmara Dagohnlar screamed for the fate of her finest frilled lovegowns and nightrobes, and began its ponderous but inexorable thundering topple to the floor.

Malakar Surth, head ringing and hands smarting from dozens of small cuts, got himself dazedly up onto one elbow, coughing for breath, in time to wonder why what faint light there was in the room was so swiftly disappearing . . . for all the world as if black night was coming down from above like a solid ceiling . . .

The crash of the wardrobe slamming down with force enough to snatch everyone off their feet—or in the case of the trussed Dagohnlars, into the air—was loud enough to deafen Surth, even before his head burst through the flimsy back panel of the piece with a loud splintering sound. Had the wardrobe possessed stout wooden front doors, on the other hand, he might never again have heard anything at all.

This was not a consideration he was presently in any fit condition to entertain. Wearing a rough cap of splinters, Surth's hooded head lolled and sagged to one side.

Bezrar caught a glimpse of his partner's fate as he fetched up against the window-frame and for one sickening moment thought he was going to go canal-diving right out through it.

When he found his feet again, he reeled across the room with more speed than skill, suffering a bruising punch from the second night-slayer as he rushed past—and was gone out the bedchamber door and down through the dark and silent house.

A few frightened servants peered at him through the little peep-panels in the doors of their rooms, but no one ventured forth to see what was causing all the tumult. Dagohnlar business was Dagohnlar business, and Dagohnlar privacy was Dagohnlar privacy. These rules had been made firmly clear years ago and upheld several times. It was very clearly understood that any servant who dared to intrude upon the Lord and Lady Masters before they were summoned by the gong could expect immediate dismissal—if not worse.

Ignoring the frantically pleading and squirming couple on the floor, Glarasteer Rhauligan dragged his quarry over to the window where the light was best and roughly unhooded her.

"Right, lass," he growled, shaking her, "let's be having your blades—*hilt* first, mind, and—"

Narnra Shalace threw her arms around him—and collapsed.

Rhauligan held her in one encircling arm and peered at her pale face. Blood was running freely from her mouth, her beseeching eyes were sliding into darkness . . . and the front of her leathers, where she was pressed against him, was dark and slick with her own welling blood.

* * * * *

•

The brazier spat a larger flame than before. This gout of
fire did not fade as most do, but grew and curled as it rose,
brightened, pulsed once more, and expanded into . . . a floating head. A long-bearded, thin, and human male head, that
turned to give the young wizard standing alone in the room
a sharp look.

Harnrim "Darkspells" Starangh smiled. "I am here, Lord
Tharundar, and quite alone. My meeting with Lady Ambrur
is but hours away."

"You know your orders, and have satisfied me as to your
reasons for meeting this person; why, then . . .?"

Starangh inclined his head. "I know you've many important workings active, Lord, and presume on your time only
in this one wise: my measure of the Lady Joysil Ambrur has
thus far been taken purely through hearsay—the testimony
of others. All deeds and entanglements and wealth, rather
than personality. It would help greatly to successfully
accomplish my task for you if I knew anything you can tell
me about this woman's character, ere I meet her."

The spell-spun head smiled just as thinly and coldly as
the real Tharundar, half of Faerûn away at this moment, was
wont to, and replied, "You, Harnrim, have perhaps a third of
the competence with spells that you think you do. However,
I value you very highly among my tools, because you are that
rarest of Red Wizards: one who combines youth, what are
so glibly called 'good looks,' ambition, slyness, the clever
tongue and iron self-control of a veteran diplomat, patience,
superb acting skills, and a talent for handling powerful
magic."

The spectral head drifted a little closer. "And you defer
to me and call on my wisdom where most others would be
too proud to do so. Keep yourself alive, young Starangh, and
you'll rise high indeed. As for the Lady Ambrur, tell me first
your judgment of her—briefly, for you've no need to impress
me further."

The man who was pleased to be called "Darkspells"
spread his hands in a gesture of amused bafflement. "I

believe, so far as I believe anything, that she's a bored noble utterly fascinated by intrigue and being 'in the know' and at the heart of secrets and conspiracies. In other words, she does it all for fun."

The head of flames seemed to nod slightly. "Your conclusions, so far as the wider world has been able to tell, are correct. Yet let me lay this warning beside them: There seems to me to be more to the Lady Joysil than mere money and sophisticated boredom. Intrigue is like a drug to her, yes, but . . . there's something more to her as well. . . ."

"Hidden depths?" Starangh smiled. "We all have them, Lord."

* * * * *

Rhauligan blinked in astonishment, shot swift glances across the bedchamber to make sure no stealthy foe was readying a blade to throw or some other mischief, and lowered the woman he'd been hunting gently to the floor. One of the trussed couple rolled over to watch.

Gods above, how could such a slender thing have so much blood to lose? If she was to be taken alive, there was no time left for thinking of such things!

Kneeling over her, he reached past the spreading river of dark, wet stickiness to his left boot, and drew out the steel vial he kept sheathed therein. Its bottom sported a spike for planting it ready in the ground, and he used that spike and his fingers to part her clenched teeth, ramming a knuckle into the corner of her jaw to keep it open as he bit the cork off the vial.

Under his finger, Narnra's eyes flickered. As Rhauligan spat the cork away into the gloom, they flashed open—and she twisted feebly under him, making no sound but a ragged hiss of pain. One hand lifted to strike at his face, wavered far from its target, and fell back as a groan escaped her. The Harper brought the vial down with his thumb over the end, thrust it between her teeth—and held it there, collapsing forward onto her to pin her where she lay.

The usual choking and coughing erupted almost immediately, but Narnra was too weak to do more than quiver and thrash . . . for the first few moments.

Rhauligan rode her bucking, arching body grimly through the wilder moments that followed, knowing the restless pain that such healing brought—then rolled her over with brutal efficiency and snatched out what he carried in his other boot: lengths of dark, waxed binding cord.

By the time her wrists were bound together and secured to the back of her own belt, Narnra was fully healed, and twisting with a furious energy that brought a wry smile to her captor's lips.

"None of that, lass," he told her merrily, as he spun Narnra around by the elbows and hauled her to her feet. "You're off to the Mage Royal for questioning. You can, of course, thank me for your life later."

Narnra's answer was to turn her head as sharply as she could and spit at him, kicking wildly at where she thought his nearest leg must be. She'd guessed rightly, but Glarasteer Rhauligan had suffered much worse than being kicked and spat on before and merely chuckled and shifted his stance.

"Come on, lass," he growled. "The chase is up, and Caladnei's not so bad as all tha—*auuoo!*"

Narnra sat down suddenly, thrusting out her behind into him—and the overbalanced Harper put out a foot to brace himself, brought it down on the edge of the toppled wardrobe, turned his ankle, and toppled helplessly. The Silken Shadow jerked, elbow-thrust, and twisted desperately to free herself from his grasp, and so bounced atop him but out of his hands when he crashed down onto the already-split back panel of the wardrobe.

"My *clothes!*" Starmara Dagohnlar moaned—as Narnra Shalace sprang up off the man who'd saved her life like a dark whirlwind and made for the window.

Rhauligan roared in pain and self-annoyance and rolled himself upright, ignoring the sudden cries from the floor of, "Rescue! Sir, a rescue! We're rich, we can pay! *Help* us, please!"

He was in time to see the faint rectangle of light at the window blotted out by Narnra's rushing body—then clear again. A moment later, there was a mighty splash from below.

The canal. She was going to drown herself in the gods-rotting canal.

With a growl of rising rage Glarasteer Rhauligan ran across the room, bounded once—and plunged through the window cleanly, heralding his own, mightier splash.

Durexter and Starmara Dagohnlar exchanged bewildered glances, but their bedchamber, as long moments dragged and passed, remained empty of suddenly appearing, charging and knife-waving hooded assailants . . . or any other unexpected new arrivals, either.

They regarded each other again . . . and in unspoken accord, stirred into action in unison, rolling and wriggling closer to one another.

"The gong-pull!" the lord merchant snarled, when he caught his breath. "Can you get upright and reach it?"

"I can't even *feel* my feet," his lady snapped, "and if you think I'm going to summon the servants in with the both of us mother-naked and bound like fowl for the roasting-spit . . . gods, Durr, don't you *realize*? They'd probably slit our throats with glee! Now, roll over so I can get my teeth to your wrists!"

A sudden groan from the wardrobe made them both freeze in fear. The hooded head thrusting up through splintered ruin turned groggily and groaned again.

"*Hurry*," Lord Durexter Dagohnlar snarled, knocking his forehead against his wife's in his urgency—and plunging her into a head-pain worse than she'd known for years. His breath was . . . even more fearsome.

Starmara's thoughts, as she rolled away from him and reared up, kicking her bound feet until she was sitting on the rucked and folded carpet, were murderous. For that, husband mine, you *die*. Not yet—not until we're safely next in Westgate—but you . . . you utter pig, Durr.

"*Hurry*," Lord Dagohnlar said again, almost pleading. "If we can kill Surth, we're safe. That fat fool Bezrar won't dare do anything without him. If Surth wakes and gets to us before we're free, it's us who'll be feeding the eels before dawn! So start gnawing!"

"You make me sound like a rat," Starmara hissed and started tugging with her teeth.

Wisely, Durexter did not reply.

* * * * *

The tireless wind whistled past Tharbost, whipping the Simbul's robe up nearly over her head.

THERE'S A SIMPLE CANTRIP . . .

"Highest," the Queen of Aglarond replied with a smile, tossing her hair unconcernedly, "I try never to waste magic on unimportant things. 'Tis so easy to fall into the habit of trying to steer every last little detail of Faerûn, from where shadows fall to the color of turning leaves . . . and every use of the Weave has its consequences. I care little for garments, am comfortable in this torn old thing, and what matters it if you or El see my rump? We all have one, after all."

I STAND CHASTENED, Mystra's thunder came more quietly. YOUR VIEW IS THE RIGHT ONE. NEVER HESITATE TO SAY SUCH THINGS, EITHER OF YOU, FOR I HAVE A GREAT MOUNTAIN OF MUCHNESS STILL TO LEARN.

Elminster groaned. "Don't let thy priests hear that phrase, or they'll be falling off mountainsides all over Faerûn."

Mystra's startled laughter sang around them with force enough to shatter small shards of rock from old Tharbost.

THANK YOU, OLD MAGE. I FEAR I CAN ONLY OFFER YOU POOR REPAYMENT: MORE ORDERS.

Elminster went to one knee. "Command me, Lady of Mysteries."

GET UP, OLD FRAUD [confusion] . . . AND ACCEPT, I ASK, MY APOLOGIES: YOU MEANT THAT, IN TRUTH.

"I did indeed."

Any deity has the power to bear down and open out any mortal mind like a book, to lay bare and read every last thought, feeling, and memory—but to do so in any manner but the slowest and most subtle way ruins the mind being examined.

Moreover, the Chosen of Mystra held a measure of her own power. It flared whenever She thrust into their minds, until to proceed was like staring into the sun, searing and being seared, harming both and learning nothing. So Mystra—the new Mystra—had swiftly learned not to pry beyond what thoughts and memories her Chosen willingly shared.

FORGIVE ME, EL. I'M STILL LEARNING. HEAR THEN MY WILL: YOU ARE TO ACQUAINT CALADNEI WITH VANGERDAHAST'S SCHEME AND WATCH OVER HER AS WELL AS HIM, STEERING HER IF NEED BE. I DON'T WANT TO LOSE THE WAR WIZARDS OR SEE INFIGHTING AMONGST THEM—OR THEY'LL BE JUST ONE MORE FRACTURED, HOSTILE FELLOWSHIP OF SELF-INTERESTED MAGES, LIKE THE RED WIZARDS.

ALASSRA, THOSE SAME RED WIZARDS ARE UP TO FRESH MISCHIEF IN AGLAROND. BEWARE MINDWORM MAGIC WORKING ON THOSE YOU TRUST.

The Simbul's smile was as wry as her voice as she replied, "Most Mighty, beyond present company, I trust no one. And sometimes, I'm not too sure about either of you."

Divine laughter rolled around the mountaintop again, but whereas Mystra clearly took the Queen of Aglarond's words as a jest, Elminster's fondly knowing and forgiving smile told Alassra he knew she was quite serious—and as wise as ever.

* * * * *

Malakar Surth's head rang like a bell, and hurt as much as if he was being beaten ceaselessly with one, too—a large and rusty specimen. Snarling at the pain and shaking his head in a vain bid for relief that did not come, he opened his eyes, let the slowly whirling room parade past him in all its wavering glory for an unknown time, and recalled something: he was in the Dagohnlar bedchamber.

The Dagohnlars were his sworn foes, whom he and Bezrar had just bound and threatened—and who were quite possibly still sharing the room with him . . . knowing where any number of weapons lay ready to hand, while he did not, his own knife lost somewhere in the crash that had felled him.

Even if they were not here, or armed and seeking his death even now, this was still their house, with all the guards, servants, and trained hungry dogs they could muster—while he was helpless here at the heart of it, trapped under this cursed wreck of an excuse for fine furniture—swathed in all manner of slithery silks, mind you, but still trapped—and by the light creeping through yon window, it was nearing dawn.

Nearing dawn?

Shar kiss and slap! Darkspells had ordered him to have the closed coach ready before dawn to take him to Lady Ambrur's mansion! Haelithtorntowers wasn't but three streets away from here, and the Thayan's inn another eight streets off, but . . . but . . .

With a scream of rising fear and frustration Malakar Surth kicked and beat his fists and pulled at splintered wood like a madman. Somehow he got the leg that was doubled under him and pinned by what was left of a wardrobe doorframe . . . *free*!

With a roar of fleeting, frantic triumph the hooded merchant erupted from the wreckage, trailing some splinters and wearing others, and staggered to the door he'd come in by, sparing only the briefest of glances for the cowering Dagohnlars.

Surth wrenched the door open and sprinted through it, flattening a timid maid who was standing uncertainly outside with the Lord and Lady Master's morning jug of hot spiced wine ready with two goblets on a tray.

Jug, wine, tray, and all flew high into the air on the wings of a startled shriek, ricocheting musically among the gaudy forest of cut glass orbs and brilliantstars that Starmara's prized and grotesquely gigantic "crown of candles" chandelier presented to the world beneath the vaulted ceiling overhead. As Surth ran, fell, and stumbled down the stairs at breakneck speed, these tumbling missiles descended again to favor him with various bruising greetings.

One goblet rolled underfoot and sent him crashing headfirst down a flight of stairs, into a huge, ring-handle-festooned (and thankfully copper rather than more breakable earthenware) pot of ferns. It toppled, spitting earth and fronds, and clanked along in his wake as Surth slithered down the next flight, found his feet at the bottom, and plunged helplessly into an embrace with a dazzlingly gleaming suit of Dagohnlar ancestral armor, full coat-of-plate and a head taller than he was.

It came down like a—well, like a toppling suit of armor that had been badly wired together and home to nests of mice for some seasons and therefore free to come apart and messily spew its contents in a bouncing, clanging chaos that carried the frantically cursing merchant down the last flight of stairs, windmilling his arms for balance and frightening the sleepy door-steward (who'd snatched down a vicious battleaxe to defend himself and found it so heavy that he'd almost fallen over) hastily aside.

Surth hit the inside panels of the ornate double entrance doors of Dagohnlar House still running at about thrice the speed and weight necessary to send them flying open. He tumbled helplessly down the broad, wet marble steps beyond, into Calathanter Street, and fetched up groaning on the cobbles by sliding rather greasily to a stop in something that smelled all too familiar: horse dung.

At least, Surth thought grimly, hoping his hurts were just aches and not bones helpfully shattered before the Red Wizard Darkspells could break all the rest of him with some angry spell or other, he was face *up* in the horse dung.

"S-surth? B'gads, you're alive! Did they throw yuh out?"

That voice was all too familiar. Bezrar, who must have run and abandoned him to certain death, alone in that bedchamber with two hired slayers! Bezrar, the utter dolt and complete simpleton who'd—

Strong hands (accompanied by much wheezing and breath that smelled like mint-sugar—mint-sugar?—rather than the usual old garlic and reekingly older fish) plucked Malakar Surth up from the cobbles and set him on his feet.

Malakar Surth drew breath for the rudest words his mind could find to blisteringly deliver to a certain fat merchant, in the few breaths it would take Surth to find and pluck forth Bezrar's own dagger and bury it hilt-deep and repeatedly in Bezrar's fat and stupid face . . . then blinked, gaping his mouth wide in astonishment with not a single choice word uttered.

Bezrar stood before him uncertainly shifting from best-booted foot to best-booted foot. The importer and wholesaler of sundry goods was clad in the quietest, most dignified finery Surth happened to know he owned. There was a just-as-uncertain half-smile on his face and a long, long lead-rein shared space with a coachwhip in one of his hands. The other had just opened wide the door of Surth's closed coach—which was drawn up neatly before the doors of Dagohnlar House. He blinked at it again, half-believing it would vanish and leave him staring into the hard and surly faces of an angry Watch-patrol, with some Dagohnlar servants pointing him out for immediate arrest.

The coach, however, stayed very much where it was, gleaming in the light, clinging rain Marsembans were pleased to prosaically call "pre-dawn mists" with its side-lamps lit and

Surth's best team of matched dapple-grays standing patiently in harness. Patiently, which meant they'd been fed.

Surth shook his head in disbelief, and his jaw dropped still more. Two folded bath-towels were piled neatly on the coach floor, below a seat that sported a complete, laid-out change of Surth's clothes. The very dark ruby outfit he'd intended to wear, from gloves to velvet-trimmed boots.

He turned his gaping face to Bezrar, who broke into a grin. "I did good, huh? I saw the note you left for your stablemaster, and he told me what it meant. So . . . here we are."

For the first time in his life, Malakar Surth threw his arms around a man with love in his heart and an intent to kiss.

"Ho! Hey! No time for that, or we'll be late for your 'associate.' Your horseman gave me to understand that doing that would be a *very* bad thing."

"Bezrar," Surth managed to say, as he clapped the fat merchant's arms enthusiastically and lunged past him for the towels, "I shall heap special prayers on Shar's altar on your behalf for this and—and buy you something you especially want!"

"That dancing lass at the Amorous Anchor?" Bezrar asked hopefully.

"*Two* of her! Or her and her best friend, rather, or— *luminous*, Bezrar! Just . . . luminous!"

Malakar Surth was not a man given to throwing back his head at the unseen, mist-shrouded stars and cackling wildly, but he did so now—attracting a raised eyebrow from a Watch officer turning the corner in the forefront of his patrol; a brow that lifted even higher as the thin, laughing man began to wildly tear his clothes off and fling them uncaringly behind him.

The Watch patrol eyed the open door of the coach, exchanged weary glances with each other, and in unspoken accord turned down another alley. Idiot nobles . . .

Surth was whipping the horses down Tarnsar Lane toward Chancever Street, still wildly grateful to Bezrar—

who sat grinning smugly beside him—until a dark thought struck him: how had Bezrar known just where, in Surth's very private and trap-fitted house, he kept these clothes? Or managed to reach that even more private and trap-guarded closet?

Eight

NIMBLE NAVIGATIONS IN MARSEMBER

If you'd see true villainy, look not to alleyways or dark taverns. Seek out the high and private chambers of the wealthy and the nobility, keep hidden, and watch what befalls. In matters of fell evil, practice improves performance as in all other things—and such practice is more possible than in alleys, because bored players seeking entertainment dally and dawdle before delivering their killing thrusts.

Irmar Amathander of Athkatla
Many Roads To One Ending
Year of the Bright Blade

The harbor water was no cleaner the second time around. Narnra was thankful she couldn't see all the slimy things she was disturbing as she plunged to the depths amid much evil bubbling of rotting things rolling all around her. Kicking against the bottom to start herself upward again, she drew her knees up, struggled to pass her bound arms down under her boots and up in front of her, and came gasping to the surface, just as a magnificent nearby splash announced the arrival of her pursuer.

Of course. She'd almost miss him, if ever she was out and about in Marsember by night without her doggedly pursuing Rhauligan. *Almost*. Why, every Waterdhavian thieving lass should have one.

With a sour smile on her lips from that thought, Narnra doubled up like a wriggling eel and swam for the other side of the canal. Even with her wrists bound together, Narnra found she could cleave the water quite quickly—and for all their stink, these oily canals were calmer and less crowded than where she'd learned to swim: the just-as-filthy waters around the docks of Waterdeep.

Still, she was used to clawing at the water when she wanted to hurry and using porpoise-wriggles only when trying to keep very, very quiet . . . and she was growing tired already.

Rhauligan would be up and quiet again to listen for her in another breath or two, and her most likely destination couldn't help but be rather obvious.

In one direction—through Rhauligan—the canal joined the wider tangle of fingerlike canals and slips that made up this end of Marsember's harbor. In the other, just ahead, it ended in a turn-basin choked with rotting nets, a scum of dead fish, and oily refuse. A lone barge, waterlogged and awash, was moored to a dock there. It looked as if only its mooring-chains were keeping it from sinking and that they—brown and crumbling with rust—might soon sigh and give up their task. The barge seemed to belong to a once-grand stone warehouse that looked every bit its rival in the race to become forgotten, abandoned, and utterly decrepit.

Narnra made for the lowest point of the barge rail where it was a good foot or so under water and rolled herself up onto the ancient vessel, scattering chittering rats and startling sleeping seabirds into complaining flight.

Rhauligan could hardly fail to miss *that*, but 'twasn't as if the kindly gods had left her any choice, now, had they?

Even if he was charging through the water at her now, her first task was to bide right where she was, sitting on something painful and unseen in the stinking, crab-scuttling water of this barge, and try to saw through Rhauligan's bindings with her boot-knife.

Easing her blade out without dropping and losing it was slow work. Wedging it in the rotting barge-planks took but a moment—but cutting her bindings took far too gods-bedamned long and involved a cut finger and some more cursing.

Shaking away drops of blood with a snarl, Narnra stood up and fumbled in her back pouch for the spare draw-string bag she carried—a mere scrap of leather with pierced ends gathered by a single thong—in case she ever found loot enough to need something extra to carry it away in (something that had happened exactly twice in her life thus far). Thong drawn tight, the bag made a clumsy bandage for her finger. She ran hastily along the barge toward its basin-end, where the dock looked more solid and less trash-strewn.

Behind her, blood sank like smoke into the inky water—which boiled up into a long, slender tentacle that burst forth, dripping, to stab hungrily out across the now-deserted barge . . . right in front of the furiously swimming Glarasteer Rhauligan. He glared at it and plunged right over it, snatching at the nearest mooring-chain.

His fingers closed around it at about the same time three more tentacles lanced out of the water, and his other hand closed on the hilt of one of his daggers.

One of the trio of tentacles undulated through the air over the barge, for all the world as if it could sniff and see, following the first tentacle in the direction Narnra had fled. The other two curled around to stab at Rhauligan, who decided—particularly in view of the fact that a habitual glance back over his shoulder had just shown him no less than *three* suspicious-looking bulges moving purposefully

through the waters of the canal, straight toward the barge—
that getting every inch of his well-used hide clear of the water
right *yesterday* would be the wisest thing to accomplish in
his life right now.

He let go of his dagger without drawing it and clawed
his way up onto the barge, rotten planking crumbling like
wet bread under his fingers. Tentacles were sliding boldly
up along his legs as he heaved, kicked, and rolled for all he
was worth, not caring if he ploughed through most of what
little was left of the barge with his face if it got the rest of
him out of the water.

Which was when he discovered that some of the tentacles
were rising from the water-filled depths of the barge itself . . .
a bare breath before Narnra at the far end of the ramshackle
wreck screamed enthusiastically.

Rhauligan saw her struggling like a suddenly animated
figurehead, body wavering back and forth on the prow of the
barge with tentacles spiraling around her in a small forest—
then a smaller but no less energetic forest of tentacles was
slapping across *his* face and body, dragging him down toward
the water his right cheek was already coldly kissing. . . .

With a snarl of fury he plunged his hand into the open
front of his plastered-to-his-hide silk shirt, found the tiny
trinket riding on its thong there—and tugged.

It took three wrenches before the gods-be-blasted thong
broke. By then his arm was hauling the weight of six or
more finger-thin tentacles along with it. Rhauligan fought
to raise his hand high, his eyes on the struggling thief he
was hunting. She had a knife out now and was using it with
frenzied viciousness—but there seemed to be no end to
these tentacles.

There were more rising up around him now, too, some
of them festooned with weed-clocked human bones . . . and
some bearing partial skeletons. Small wonder the warehouse
and barge were so deserted!

Rhauligan muttered the word Alusair herself had taught
him. He hated to lose this magic, one of the few things the

Crown Princess had ever given him—and with a lovely, avid kiss, too!—but on the other hand, he'd hate to lose his life, too, so . . .

He threw the trinket down the barge, snapping his wrist to spin it farther even as the clinging tentacles dragged at his arm. It bounced once and skittered into some refuse. He closed his eyes hastily.

Sudden heat warmed his face an instant later, even before the flash and the roar that sent the barge heaving upward under him . . . and the tentacles spasming into a wild and frantic dance of their own. A chaos of wriggling, flailing, *shivering* tentacles tumbled him over and erupted past him, desperately seeking . . .

Some impossible escape from the fire that was now raging along the barge, burning even underwater thanks to the magic, cooking the unseen heart of the tentacles. Rhauligan scrambled to his knees as the wet, ropelike things fell away from him by the dozens and saw Narnra half-flung off the far end of the barge.

She landed with a splash in the filth of the basin but churned the water in her haste to swim up and out of it, and in less time than it took Rhauligan to catch his breath and bound toward the dock she was ashore at the street end of the basin, running hard, if unsteadily, into the mists of approaching dawn.

Hurling hearty mental curses at the dying tentacled thing, the Harper hound raced past the burning barge after her, bursting out onto the street almost under the wheels of a handcart being trundled by a half-asleep fishmonger.

The cart promptly crashed over onto him—but thankfully was empty at this time of the morning. The man who'd been pushing it erupted in startled rage, clawing aside his ramshackle boxes in his haste to get at Rhauligan and do damage.

The Harper greeted him with a charge up from the ground that brought one balled fist in under the fishmonger's chin and thrust him off his feet to bounce halfway across the street—bowling over a Watch patrolman who with his fellows had just formed a ring of drawn swords around a dripping and furious Narnra.

The Watchman's fall allowed her to bolt through the space he'd been standing in—which meant she came sprinting out of the mists right into Rhauligan's arms.

Ducking and twisting at the last moment, she slid under his grasp—though his fingers raked a bruising trail along Narnra's slick, slimy-wet flank—and ran down the street, dodging twice as she heard his boots thundering on the cobbles right behind her.

The Watchmen were running too, blades and cudgels waving in all directions, so the first canal Narnra saw, safely on the other side of the street from the one that had erupted in tentacles, she sprang into. Rhauligan's splash fountained in the roiling aftermath of hers.

The Watchmen skidded to a stop at the edge of the churning, dock-slapping water, shook their heads, and turned away. "Report 'em as drowned—lovers' dispute gone ugly, both fell in with the fishes. Unidentified outlanders, the both of them, so retrieval not our duty. Write it down, Therry," Rhauligan heard one of them growl, as he followed Narnra's dark, wet head around a corner into a narrow side-canal. He was recalling, with ever-increasing verve, just how much he'd never liked Marsember.

Steam was curling out of various windows and hatches in the stone buildings that rose on both sides of the canal— straight up out of its waters, most of them, without jetties or perch-porches, though crumbling scars of stone here and there marked where such features had once been ere barge collisions, gnawing waves, and the claws of winter ice removed them. Rusting crane-arms festooned with the decaying remnants of ropes, pulleys, and wooden block-and-tackles jutted from some of the building walls, but to reach them from the water even the most nimble of Waterdhavian thieves would have had to fly—or had a boat much taller than any barge to clamber up.

Much of the steam roiling and eddying its way into the thickening pre-dawn mist was coming from lighted windows, for the hours of darkness are work-time to many in cities all over Faerûn who craft things or prepare things fresh. The smells borne on much of the steam told Rhauligan—whose alerted stomach rumbled enthusiastically more than once, as he swam grimly on—that many of these buildings were cook-shops and bakeries preparing for the flood of hungry morning workers who'd descend at dawn to snatch something more or less edible before hurrying to where they worked. Eel pie, Rhauligan recalled sourly, was the dish of choice for working Marsembans. Almost made one want to become an adventurer or a Purple Dragon assigned to the Stonelands, where eels were no more than a disgusting word used in bad jests.

A flood of refuse suddenly hurtled out of one lighted window, pelting down into the water around him. Rhauligan ducked his head under the filthy water just in time. Eel pie, indeed—and as such dishes used every last possible part of the slimeworms, the only trimmed parts to be discarded would be bits too diseased or rotten to be hidden by a thick, hot-spiced gravy, or devoured without immediate convulsions and collapse of diners. The same bits that were now sharing the waters under his very nose.

Gods, but I hate Marsember!

There was a splash ahead, and Rhauligan had a brief glimpse of Narnra's hand closing on a doorsill that hung over emptiness, the work of either a particularly stone-skulled builder or the remnant of a way down onto some now-vanished dock.

A moment later, the dark and dripping figure of Narnra surged out of the water like some man-sized eel, wriggling momentarily in midair as she snatched for a handhold that wasn't where she needed it to be, clinging to the outside of the back door that belonged to the sill. It sported a well-lit, steam-spewing open upper half, and by the sounds of sizzling and chopping and snatches of brief conversation coming out of that large opening, it belonged to a cookshop.

A moment later, a bucket of eel waste-trimmings took Narnra full in the face. Rhauligan didn't even have time to shape a grin before she plunged *through* the window. Gods spit, but she'd grabbed hold of the bucket in mid-fling and been pulled into the room with it! In with the cooks—and their cleavers!

He set his teeth, ducked his head down, and charged through the water, hoping he'd be there in time.

Eyes smarting from eel-guts and guck better not thought about, Narnra slithered belly-down through the door hatch, catching a glimpse of a startled, yelling cook's face on the other side of the bucket, as well as a lot of swaying candle-on-chain lanterns. Hitting the floor and sliding wetly along it, she found herself passing along a row of ovens, each sporting the behind of a stoking-lad beneath it who was shoving in kindling for all he was worth.

One stoker put a boot into her face backing up, so she plucked a scrap of wood from his pile and rammed it into his behind. He howled, halting in alarm, and she was past and rolling frantically away from the ovens to avoid the boots of the bellowing cook with the bucket as he kicked and stomped at her head and hands, his shouts turning startled heads all over the kitchen.

The nearest of those heads stared down at Narnra over a tray of fresh-made, raw eel pies. Narnra rammed one arm against an ankle and shoved at the other ankle with her other hand—and the tray and its holder toppled over her like a over-tall tree severed by a woodsman's axe, crashing into the kicking cook.

He stumbled back, almost falling, and flung his empty scraps-bucket at Narnra's head. It whanged off one waving boot of the man who'd been holding the tray—then Narnra was on her feet and sprinting hard into the midst of three fat, shrieking women and their small host of half-finished eel pies.

They lurched and scuttled in all directions, and she

darted this way and that through them, hip-slamming the last woman headfirst into a cart of dirty pots, ladles, and pans.

The crash was both deafening and spectacular, as the Silken Shadow left it behind, charging around a cutting-table toward the door out of this place, within sight at last.

Ahead, there was a serving-counter in the way. It came equipped with a grizzled, startled-looking cookshop owner frozen in the act of wiping it with a bit of dirty rag to gape at her. Narnra ran right at him, intending to veer away at the last moment.

Across the busy kitchen, on the far side of other cutting-tables, cooks were cursing. The racing thief had ignored them as being safely out of her way, but she'd reckoned without the swift-tempered and forearmed nature of most Marsembans. Cleaver after cleaver was snatched and thrown at her racing figure. Now in swift succession they crashed into bowls, other howling cooks, oven doors, and the faces of startled stoking-lads who'd just straightened up to catch sight of whatever was causing all the excitement.

One whirling blade caught Narnra on the arm, bruising rather than cutting her, and sent her reeling into the grizzled counter-cleaner, who embraced her with an incoherently wordless gabble of amazement and swiftly mounting fear.

Narnra pumped three swift punches into the stained and reeking apron covering the man's bulging belly. He spewed whatever he'd just finished eating over her racing body into the face of the first cook, who—lightened by the lack of his scraps-bucket—had managed to mount a clumsy pursuit of this destructive intruder.

Blinded and snarling in disgust, the cook reeled and elbow-skidded along a counter, spilling and scattering eel pies by the dozens . . . as the green-faced owner of the cookshop folded aside with a groan, and Narnra vaulted the counter with grace enough to freeze one of the young stokers where he stood, staring in awed lust—which got him smashed flat to the floor by a snarling Glarasteer Rhauligan.

The Harper and Highknight had already weathered almost a dozen flung pots on his own charge through the cookshop kitchen, cleavers being in suddenly short supply—but someone found one last black-bladed monster somewhere and sent it whirling with shrewd aim as Rhauligan rounded the cutting-table for his run toward the counter.

The Harper saw its deadly flicker out of the corner of his eye and flung up his arm to ward it away from his face. It bit deep into his shoulder and banged harmlessly away off his scalp rather than laying open his face or cleaving his skull in twain.

Rhauligan roared out his pain, not daring to slow, and the vomit-covered cook sagging on the counter took one look at his furious face and the streaming blood and fled, sobbing a frantic way aside.

Bleeding—again. Oh, this little hunt just gets better and better.

The Harper burst out of the cookshop door into the wet mists in time to see Narnra halfway up the wall of the building, clinging to a drainpipe. She was slipping often in the wet and going slowly as she tried to work her way past a balcony jutting out from the floor above the cookshop—but she was already well out of his reach, and he couldn't climb any faster than she could. To say nothing of whether or not any drainpipe would prove sturdy enough for the weight of two, all the way to the roof. . . .

Just inside the cookshop door, in the open space in front of the serving-counter, was a side door. It would be the way up some cramped, dark stairs to the loftier levels of this building.

Rhauligan turned and raced back inside, frightening a fresh howl of alarm from the kitchen. The side door proved to be locked, but Rhauligan carried a prybar—good as a cudgel, stouter than a sword and boasting some saw-teeth besides—sheathed to one leg, and he took out the frustrations Narnra was building in him on that door.

The defenseless wood offered little resistance, and the

Harper boiled up the stairs like a storm wind and put his shoulder to the door on the first landing.

It cracked like a thunderstroke, broke in half, and gave way inward, spilling him onto a half-asleep man and his only-slightly-more-awake wife who lay on a straw mattress on the floor. Their sons were already awake and peering out the lone, filthy window at the gloomy mists of slowly brightening dawn. They whirled, wide-eyed, as Rhauligan's stumbling boot came down on their father's stomach. The winded man sobbed for breath, flinging out his arms convulsively—one of them across his wife's throat, silencing her in the first meeping moment of an emerging scream.

"Morning!" the Harper rapped grimly, never slowing in his charge across the room. "Balcony door! 'Way in the name of the *King!*"

One boy gawked mutely, and the other, eyes shining, shot a bolt and flung wide the balcony door. Rhauligan thanked him with a fierce grin and plunged out into the mists, whirling to face the drainpipe in time to see Narnra's boot lifting *just* out of reach.

He grabbed for it anyway, knowing as he did that he was going to be about a fingerlength short. He was.

Well, he'd *almost* laid a hand on her. He slapped it onto the pipe instead and swarmed up it after her, grunting at the pain each pull stabbed into his cloven shoulder. He had to get close enough that she wouldn't have the time to turn on the rooftop and dagger his face or hands—aye, he had to be *that* close to her, or . . .

Narnra glanced down, hissed out a curse—he was close enough to almost feel her breath, as he clawed his way hastily upward—and wasted no time on trying to kick at him or deal him any wounds. Instead, she fled up the pipe like a little girl running from all the nightmares life could muster, panting and clawing with almost frenzied speed, and raced across a roof of loose and shifting tiles to spring out and down onto the roof of the next building.

She landed hard, knocking her breath from herself, and spun around on one knee to keep an eye on her pursuer as she panted to get her wind back.

Rhauligan was hauling himself up onto the roof she'd just left. Narnra snarled wordlessly, fought her way to her feet as he straightened—then thought of something and bent to her other boot to snatch another knife to hurl at him. Its sheath was empty.

Either she'd lost it during this chase, or he'd taken it while healing her. Hissing a curse at him instead, she spun around, ran, and leaped onto the next roof through the thickly rising, scented steam of someone's laundry, coming up from a skylight.

Beyond, the roof was flat, all of metal sheets sealed and patched with thick pitch, ankle-deep in slippery, bird-dung-dotted water—and . . . and Narnra found herself with nowhere she could safely leap to, on a building with wide streets on two sides, Rhauligan grimly approaching on the third, and a barge heaped high with spear-like, jagged salvage-wood on the last side that it would be sheer suicide to jump onto. She glared around at treacherous Marsember for a moment in the lightening dawn, then spun around and raced back to the open skylight.

Rhauligan was just launching himself at her over its billowing murk. Narnra sat down in her run and skidded over the edge moments before his boots crashed down through where she'd just been.

Her fall was a short one, onto stout metal poles draped with someone's damp tapestries. They gave way like a sling, dropping her down through a roaring stream of air. Chains were clanking all around her as racks of clothes hanging from them were rocked forward and back, forward and back, by levers that vanished down through the floor. By the loud, rhythmic hissing, the Silken Shadow guessed that there was a gigantic bellows in the room below, presumably being worked by the same grunting, sweating coin-slaves who were tugging on the levers and feeding the fire that was warming all this rushing air. My, but the world of laundry was an exciting place. . . .

Or certainly would be, if she didn't get out from under where Rhauligan was sure to land in the next few moments. She debated drawing her belt-dagger and plunging it through the tapestry when he landed in it . . . but no, she wasn't here to slay Harpers, just to get away from them. Yonder was a row of trap-doors that must offer access to the levels below—probably through shafts nearly dry clothes would be pushed down.

Someone shouted at her as she raced between the swinging racks of garments, and she had a glimpse of a startled old man whose bare arms were a riot of varicolored tattoos waving angrily at her. She gave him a nod and a smile and kept right on running to the trap-door at the . . . right end.

Flinging it back, she smelled hot fabric and saw light far below—and in it, neat stacks of what looked like folded cloaks or blankets. It was the work of but a moment to launch herself feet-first down to join them.

Behind her, she heard another shout followed by a grunt and a thud. That would be Rhauligan paying his respects to old Manybrands. It seemed she'd been right: the world of laundry *was* an exciting place.

Narnra plunged past a room full of all the noisy, sweating activity she'd envisaged and landed gently in a large, brightly lit room below that, toppling and scattering hot, fluffy cloaks in all directions. No one was near, and Narnra rolled enthusiastically, trying to get herself mostly dry ere she waded out to find footing and run on.

Along the way, she snatched up a cloak, shook it open in her hands—and when Rhauligan crashed down into view, she flung it over his head, managed to tug him over into a cascading fall of piled laundry to where she could get a hard knee into his blinded and muffled head, then sprang away, not daring to stay and try to smother him because enraged launderers were approaching at a run from various directions now, all shouting furious curses she couldn't tarry to hear properly. She left them closing in on the thoroughly entangled Rhauligan, sprang over some sort of sorting table where women cowered away from her behind wicker baskets . . . and found another handy, waiting door. This one was even open.

Still, she was losing count of doors she was having to blindly rush through and had long since lost her patience with being hunted all over this strange city. It was waking up now, and soon she'd be dodging frequent Watch patrols and carters in the streets and watching eyes, watching eyes everywhere. She doubted there even was such a thing as a dry rooftop to try to sleep on in Marsember, even if she knew this grim, tireless Harper was safely taken away from his hunt. Narnra was beginning to think the only way to do that was to make sure he was dead.

Well, she certainly wasn't wading back into the land of enraged launderers to see to that. Perhaps they'd take care of it for her, though she was beginning to doubt an army could stop Glarasteer Rhauligan, let alone a few angry Marsembans.

She fled down a short stair, through another door—smashing flat an unsuspecting man passing by as she crashed it open—and out into the streets, wondering when it would be prudent to slow down and walk as if she belonged here—in black leathers, aye—rather than running like a thief and catching every interested eye.

When Rhauligan was . . . yes, yes, *yes!* With a growl of anger Narnra saw two Watch patrols coming together at a street-moot ahead and dodged aside. She had to get aloft again before he saw where she went and—

Then she saw it. A street over, behind a wall of old buildings that sprouted balconies and rickety outer stairs above their shopfronts, beyond their lines of dripping clothing—imagine hanging clothes out to dry, in night-mists like this!—and water-cisterns . . . water-cisterns? Well, rainwater would almost have to be cleaner than canal-water, and a little less salty. . . .

There was a high stone wall in superb condition with trees rising behind it. Some sort of noble's walled garden, if Marsember was anything like Waterdeep. Yes, there was the row of spikes most nobles seemed to think a wall needed, atop a stretch of buttressed stone that must overtop a two-story building and run longer than six or seven of the shops nearer to her.

Narnra stopped looking at the wall and hurried to get closer to it, looking now for some way to get up onto it.

* * * * *

Durexter Dagohnlar drew himself upright with as much dignity as a naked, bound, and overly fat man can muster whilst sitting on his own bedchamber floor and fixed the Watchcaptain with a coldly disapproving gaze.

"There was no need to push past my wife and invade our home, sir," he said stiffly, as his steward hastened to cut his bonds, "no matter how many overexcited servants came running to summon you. No need at all. I—that is to say *we* " he amended hastily, catching sight of the dagger-laden look his wife was favoring him with, from behind the Watchmen, "Starmara and myself, ahem, vanquished a *very* old foe here this night—a foe who came to slay us with magic but was forced to flee. I'll not reveal his name even to War Wizards, because uttering it will awaken some *very* dangerous spells he left behind. So let's just forget th—"

"You can write it down for me, then, Lord Master Dagohnlar," the Watchcaptain said calmly, the mouth under his grizzled mustache carefully expressionless but his eyes every bit as wintry as the merchant's. "To save the strongest War Wizards in the city the time 'twill take to come and empty your mind of *everything* of interest to the security of the city . . . and adherence to *all* of our laws."

Durexter opened and closed his mouth in trapped bafflement for a few moments then said triumphantly, "I'm sorry, Watchman, but I can't write. I never learned how."

The Watchcaptain didn't bother to order his men to step forward and forcibly take Durexter Dagohnlar into custody. He was too busy rolling his eyes. His men moved forward anyway, their snorts of derision almost as loud as those from various gawking servants.

Starmara Dagohnlar, whose sidle toward the door had already ended in the firm grip of a Watchman, sighed and said loudly, "My apologies, Watchcaptain. Our enemy's spells must have affected my husband's wits."

"Indeed, Lady Dagohnlar," the officer agreed politely as Durexter was gagged with his wife's discarded nightrobe and hustled to the door. "How many decades ago did they take effect?"

*   *   *   *   *

Glarasteer Rhauligan was no longer in anything remotely resembling a good mood. He'd lost a lot of blood, was in great pain, and thanks to the needs of the Mage Royal and this little fool of a thief now lacked any swift means of quelling that. The hasty violence he'd just been forced to do to a small but enthusiastic band of launderers had done nothing to help matters, but at least he was now largely dry—thanks to a lot of formerly clean clothing that was now, unfortunately, smeared and stained with his blood—and was now sporting a bandage of sorts: a very large someone's freshly laundered bloomers tied around the wound in his shoulder.

It had all taken far too long, and if that little bitch had managed to give him the slip whilst . . .

Rhauligan reached the street, where a man lay groaning and twisting outside the laundry door, ignored him as being in no condition to have seen where Narnra Shalace had gone, and glared around in all directions. 'Twas bad enough having to hunt anyone in wet, hostile-to-the-Crown Marsember, bu—*there!*

Gods, give the girl a wall to run along, and she's happy!

The taller the better, it seemed . . . and she'd obviously managed to leap from another building onto a corner turret of the wall, because she was hurrying away from that turret now as fast as she could. Rhauligan sprinted across the street to get out of view before she looked back to see if he'd seen her.

Well, now. That was quite a wall she'd chosen. If Narnra ran all the way around it, she'd trot for nigh on a mile. Rhauligan happened to know that it kept the prying world out of an estate known as Haelithtorntowers, the abode of one Lady Joysil Ambrur.

That same wider, prying world knew the Lady Ambrur to be a wealthy Sembian merchant noble, a tall, demure, sophisticated patron of bards and singers, who was—correctly—said to pay handsomely for dancers to be enspelled to fly, so they could engage in her particular pleasure: elaborate aerial ballet dances performed as they sang for her, in her parlor.

"We Harpers, however, know rather more about Lady Joysil," Rhauligan murmured aloud, recalling Laspeera's crisp words at a certain private meeting in a tiny, little-used upper room of the palace.

"She's not from Sembia at all. Unearthing her true origins will be another of your little idle-time tasks, gentlesirs."

"That'd be task four thousand and seven, Lady," Harl had murmured, like a bored steward announcing the date and time.

"Indeed, Harl? Then you've missed three," Laspeera had replied with a smile, "or neglected to tell me of their accomplishment, more likely. Now, Lady Ambrur secretly employs her favorite visiting bards as information-gatherers. She then discreetly resells the lore they bring to traitorous nobles, local merchants, and anyone else willing to pay for it."

This practice was what had led local Harpers—including, from time to time, one Glarasteer Rhauligan—to keep watch over who visited Joysil Ambrur and to try to discover just what learning their coins to her bought them.

It was doubtful this Narnra of Waterdeep knew about Lady Ambrur. She'd probably just gone looking for a place aloft to hide and sleep and spotted the tallest wall around that wasn't bristling with vigilant Purple Dragon posts.

Rhauligan knew yon wall was quite wide enough to comfortably walk along, between its street-edge spikes and its inner plant-trough, which housed flourishing clumps of sarthe. Unless it'd been trimmed recently, the edible trailing plant spilled down clear to the grounds far below.

Narnra was running along inside the spikes, merrily trampling sarthe-stalks with each step, and Rhauligan knew he had no choice but to follow or lose track of her.

With a sigh, he chose a building he'd scaled to reach that same corner turret once or twice before and started to climb.

Caladnei and Narnra, know this: You both owe me!

Nine

A WIZARD'S PLOTTING IS NEVER DONE

*Heed me, Lord Prince: After nobles with too much time
and coin to resist working mischief, the wizards are the
ones you must watch. The schemes of mages are as tireless
as waves crashing upon a storm shore—and every bit as
destructive, too.*

Astramas Revendimar,
Court Sage of Cormyr
Letters To A Man To Be King
Year of the Smiling Flame

The central hall of Haelithtorntowers was a high, soaring,
darksome space of stone, its vaulted spire lost in the gloom
more than a hundred feet overhead. Torches had been lit
in the old braziers all around the promenade balcony that
ringed the hall, and the great hanging lamps on their chains
were left unlit and drawn up high, out of the way of the
soaring dancers.

The last few high, mournful notes of song soared into the

gloom of gathering smoke high above the torches, floating to a wistful end—and the sweating dancers descended to earth, saluting their lady patron gracefully.

There was applause from the guests seated at ease in the great reclining seats around the crescentiform high table, and their hostess rose and returned the dancers' salute with a happy smile. The performance had been memorable, the emotions evoked very real. Tears glimmered in the eyes of many guests, even those who were stifling yawns at the lateness—or rather, earliness, as dawn had quite come outside the slit windows high in the spire overhead—of the hour.

"And so, my friends," the Lady Joysil Ambrur announced with a smile, "our evening together must come to an end, as a new day awakens around us. Our time, I fear, is quite gone—and I'm sure we must all, like the dancers who have worked so hard for our pleasure, seek slumber now."

She raised one graceful arm to point east, toward the great double doors that most of her guests had entered by, hours—it almost seemed days—ago. "Your coaches have been made ready, and my servants await beyond those doors to escort you to them. You are all *most* welcome when next I open my doors for an evening of friendly converse and entertainment. Rest assured I shall send personal invitations well in advance. Now, I pray, leave me to find my own waiting bed." She yawned prettily. "See? It calls, even now."

There was a brief chorus of tittering, and the various grand ladies of Marsember and divers other cities—from the Lady Charoasze Klardynel of Selgaunt to the Lady Maezaere Thallandrith of Alaghôn—arose in a shifting of silks and shimmerweave and delzelmer to kiss the hands and cheek of their hostess and take their leave. Many and aggressive were their perfumes, especially among the newest-money merchant spouses of Marsember, who were known for their barely veiled viciousness and their often-jarring etiquette and fashion sense, but the Lady Ambrur smiled fondly upon them all and somehow—by a trick of true nobility, perhaps—

made each one feel personally welcome and special even as she hastened their departure.

One of the last beauteous ladies to leave was the bare-shouldered, emerald-gowned Lady Amantha Indesm of Suzail, who possessed both the smoldering eyes of a restless tigress and the tinkling smile of an innocent. She embraced her hostess impulsively, the tears the last dance had awakened in her still bright on her cheeks, and swept out to the waiting servants, leaving the Lady Ambrur alone with her very last guest: the Lady Nouméa Cardellith.

They both stood quite still until the doors closed behind the Lady Indesm. Nouméa said softly, "Forgive me, Lady Joysil, but a spell was just laid upon you, a spying magic, and I should break it." She raised a hand then halted, awaiting permission.

Her hostess smiled and nodded. "Please do so. Amantha is a dear friend but also a Harper spy—and is loyal to them first. She always tries this little trick, knows I cause her spells to fail . . . and we both ignore the matter."

"She's done this before? You know her purposes and yet invite her?"

"I like to clasp my foes close and look into their eyes," the Lady Ambrur replied serenely, rounding the table again to sip from her tallglass. Lifting it in a lazy salute to Nouméa, she smiled a little smile and added, "They see and hear only what I want them to, I think."

The two tall, slender ladies—Joysil the larger and older, but both bearing worldly wisdom in their eyes—regarded each other thoughtfully. There was clear liking and trust between them, though this was their first meeting, and after a silence Nouméa asked curiously, "You let me cast that shatterspell when I might have worked any magic on you. We've barely met, yet you trust me. I am honored but I must confess also curious: *why* does Joysil Ambrur trust this unknown, when true trust is almost unknown among these—forgive me—overpainted eels and vixens of Marsember?"

Joysil burst into merry laughter, all trace of weariness

gone. "They'd never forgive you for describing them so, yet your words are apt indeed: They *are* rapacious, sly eels and snapping little vixens."

Nouméa waited and when her hostess said no more asked very softly, "I mean no offense, but please let me know the reasons for your trust. You've barely met me."

"Indeed," Joysil replied just as gently, "but I know all about you."

"Oh?"

"Born Nouméa Fairbright, quite a keen-witted, spirited beauty. Attended a finishing school for daughters of the very rich in Sembia run by the Lady Calabrista. Tarried with none other than Elminster in Shadowdale after a school trip to visit his tower—and did not return to Calabrista but instead astonished a series of tutors with mastery of magic. Married Lord Elmarr Cardellith of Saerloon, a rich, ruthless Sembian merchant lord, and bore him four daughters. Survived two attempts paid for by him to have you poisoned because he wanted no girls but only sons. Escaped to Marsember and were paid to 'stay away' whilst he changed faiths and remarried in his new church, annulling your union. Now twenty-six winters old, and cynical, jaded, bitter—and bored, therefore hungry for adventure. The sort of woman the Obarskyrs are apt to regard as dangerous: one who could so easily drift into aiding rebels or illicit intrigues—then try wildly to make up for it. Lady Nouméa Cardellith, do I see you truly?"

Nouméa had gone quite pale. She swallowed slowly and deliberately, lifted her head, looked the Lady Ambrur straight in the eye, and said firmly, "Yes. Every word right, whether I like it or not. To fill in the gaps in my tale about which some have speculated: no man but Elmarr has ever touched me. Not Elminster, nor Lhaeo, nor have I entertained any affairs of the heart or lusts with anyone here or in Sembia. The extent of your knowledge can only be described as impressive, and I shall *not* ask how you came by it. Yet I am curious: Why do you bother to learn so much—about me, the Harper who just left us, and . . . everyone? I'll wager you know as much about all the rest of your just-departed guests as you do about me."

Joysil smiled again. "Knowing secrets . . . being part of the shady doings and intrigues that seem to be at the heart of what it is to be human . . . is meat and drink to me, the very wine of life. Believe me, I can live no other way. And yes, you would have won that wager."

A bell chimed, somewhere behind her chair, and she set down her glass and asked, "Does our agreement stand? You sent back the coins I offered but spoke of acceptance."

"It stands, but I need no payment. I consider you my friend."

"Even so. Our guest—just arrived, that bell tells us—is a Red Wizard of Thay. Being in attendance to protect me may well involve some personal danger and being marked as a foe henceforth by all Thayans, even if no outward unpleasantness ensues this morning."

Nouméa nodded. "Even so," she echoed. "I thought you spoke earlier of three guests."

"I did, but two of them are merely local villains, possessed of more dishonesty and empty ambition than anything else. Yet I'm pleased to have you remain with me, 'just in case.' Shall I introduce you as a student of architecture, visiting Haelithtorntowers to see its features?"

Nouméa Cardellith grinned suddenly. "Certainly. Spires and turrets I can talk glibly and emptily about for half a day. Elmarr thought almost nothing else was a fit subject to share with a woman—even *his* woman."

"See me standing unsurprised," Lady Ambrur replied in dry tones and pulled a tassel hanging by the arm of her chair.

The double doors opened at once, and her servants bowed three men into the room: two merchants trailed by a lone figure.

One Marsemban was tall, thin, and hard-faced, the other stout, a little battered-looking, and clutching a grand hat as if shredding it would somehow carry him unscathed through the meeting now unfolding. The two parted to let the third man through: a young, darkly handsome man in black and silver shimmerweave, looking every inch a capable, quietly swaggering noble of Suzail or fullblood merchant prince of one of the foremost families of Sembia.

"Be welcome, sirs," the Lady Ambrur said warmly. "We stand in privacy, here, armed with the information you've been seeking."

"Ah," the wizard said, eyes darting from Nouméa to Joysil and back again. "That is good. We are well met, Lady Ambrur and Lady—?"

"Cardellith, sir," the unfamiliar woman replied for herself. "Nouméa Cardellith, now of Marsember."

"A student of architecture," the Lady Ambrur put in gently. "Here to see every last crenellation and carving of Haelithtorntowers."

The Thayan smiled. "Architecture?"

The Lady of Haelithtorntowers smiled an almost identical smile. "And other things."

"Ah," the wizard said, and sat down in a seat without waiting for an invitation, leaving the two merchants standing uncertainly behind him.

"The merchants Aumun Tholant Bezrar and Malakar Surth," Lady Ambrur introduced them, waving them toward seats as she did so. "This is Harnrim 'Darkspells' Starangh, one of the most diplomatic Red Wizards of Thay it has ever been my pleasure to entertain."

"And have you entertained many of us, Lady?" Starangh asked softly.

The Lady Ambrur smiled again. "Yes, indeed, Darkspells. Szass and I, in particular, are old friends. Very old friends."

The Thayan sat as if frozen for an instant then said even more softly, "You must tell me about that some time. Some other time."

"Of course. When the time is right, as you say," was the silken reply.

Nouméa repressed a shiver. How soft and yet sharp with menace the words of both her hostess and the Thayan. She flicked a glance at the two Marsemban merchants and saw in their faces the same tightly masked fear as she knew her own held: not knowing all that was going on here but knowing enough to be certain everything hidden was bad. And dangerous.

Darkspells spread his hands. "Have you learned what I desire to know and offered twelve thousand in gold for?"

"Twelve thousand six hundred," the Lady Ambrur told her tallglass demurely.

"Twelve thousand six hundred, as you say," the Red Wizard agreed.

"Yes. Precisely what Vangerdahast, the retired Mage Royal of Cormyr, is 'up to' in his retirement, precisely where he is, and precisely what his magical defenses are."

Starangh smiled softly, his eyes glittering bright and hard, and purred, "If you can give me half an answer to those things, Vangerdahast will stand far closer to his doom—the doom he has so richly earned and that I shall take such delight in visiting upon him. Soon."

* * * * *

This damp, fish-stinking city wasn't Waterdeep, but at least it had walls and rooftops, and she could feel just a bit more like home.

Narnra grinned without feeling the slightest bit amused. So here she was running for her life, pursued by some sort of law-agent bent on slaying or capturing her.

Oh, yes. *Just* like home.

* * * * *

The Queen of Aglarond wrinkled her nose. "Ah, Marsember! Always damp cold stone, colder people, and the everpresent reek of dead fish and human waste. For entertainment, storms rage ashore and intrigues rage behind closed doors." She smiled. "Well, it serves one good purpose: to firmly remind me what I must never let my capital Velprintalar come within the full length of a large kingdom of resembling!"

Elminster stroked her bare shoulder then kissed the smooth flesh his fingers had been tracing. "Sorry," he told her. " 'Tis not my favorite place in all Faerûn either, but it happens to be where Caladnei bides at this moment."

The Simbul sighed. "Mystra's will be done," she murmured then turned suddenly, caught hold of his beard, and brought his lips to where she could kiss them fiercely.

As she always seemed to, she moved hungrily against him, melting into him . . .

"Take care of yourself," she whispered when they were both breathless and lack of air finally forced her to draw back. "I waited so long for you—don't leave me lonely now."

Elminster blinked at her. "Lass? Ye waited for me . . . ?"

"To notice and then to love me," she replied, eyes very dark. "For myself and not as one of Mystra's daughters."

She shaped a spell that called darkness, outlined by a sprinkling of tiny stars, out of the air in front of her. "I loved your mind for centuries before you knew who I was, Old Mage. Now I love your character, too." She made a face, and added, "Your body, however: *that* you could have taken better care of, to be sure. Old wreck."

Elminster lifted his eyebrows, held up his hands with an airy flourish, murmured a swift incantation—and melted into the shape of a tall, broad-shouldered young man of rugged good looks and raven-black hair. He gave her a sparkling grin.

She snorted, struck a breathlessly excited hands-to-mouth pose like a young lass about to swoon—and slid back out of it to wink at him. Stepping back into her darkness, the Queen of Aglarond murmured, "*My* old wreck," and was gone, taking her rift with her, stars and all.

The transformed Elminster smiled fondly at where she'd

been for a moment, shaking his head, then made a face of his own. "In those centuries of loving my mind, did she watch where my wandering body went and with whom, I wonder?"

He chuckled, shrugged, and strode down the cold, dark, and cobwebbed passage.

The damp made the spiderwebs thick, jeweled-with-droplets curtains. Elminster pushed through them unconcernedly, acquiring a marbled pattern of silken filth on his robes, and when he reached the remembered crossway, he turned left.

Cold blue fire flared in the emptiness in front of his nose immediately, but he strolled right through that ward-spell—and the next one, too.

By then a sleepy-eyed War Wizard, barefoot in her robes, was confronting him furiously. A rod that winked and glowed from half a dozen attached side-wands was cradled in her arms and aimed right at his face.

"Halt or be destroyed!" she snapped, as her fingers triggered a magic that sent bells chiming in a dozen chambers, near and far. Whatever befell now, this obviously not-so-secret passage would be swarming with War Wizards in a few minutes. Until then, 'twas her duty to prevent this stranger from—

He stepped forward, and she snarled and triggered three of the wands at once.

Their flash and roar almost blinded War Wizard Belantra, and sent her staggering back as the passage flagstones rippled under her feet in a great shockwave. In the distance, behind the broad-shouldered intruder, stones fell from the passage ceiling, amid much dust, and tumbled away.

He kept coming, as if the ravening magic hadn't touched him at all.

"*Back*, demon!" Belantra snapped, sudden fear rising inside her. No one should be able to withstand such a blast! Even if the handsome man before her was mere illusion, the magic that presented it should have been shredded, and—

One long-fingered hand grasped the tip of one of her wands, even as she furiously triggered it again. Calmly ignoring Belantra, the intruder lifted the wand so its emerald beam of flesh-melting fury was trained not at his chest, but directly into his eyes.

Bright blue those eyes shone as they met hers for a moment, winked, and dropped to examine the wand again.

"Ah, yes. I helped Vangey enspell this. Now, after all these years, he wastes it in some sort of toy 'mightywand' gonne, such as the Lantanna fashion?" The handsome intruder shook his head. "I thought I'd taught him better than that."

He looked up again, gently pushing the wand aside with one fingertip, and asked, "What might thy name be, lass?"

"I'm a War Wizard of Cormyr," Belantra snapped, "and *I'll* ask the questions here, man!"

"By all means," the broad-shouldered stranger agreed easily, taking her elbow in one hand and steering her aside so he could pass. When she whirled furiously to shove him against the wall, he turned nimbly with her as if they were dancing together, ending up behind her with her wrist in a grip she could not break. Towing her, he strode in the direction she'd come from.

"I'm here to see Caladnei," he explained, "but ye're welcome to ask all ye want while we go fetch her, eh?"

"How do you kno—the Mage Royal can see no one! She's sleeping, after a *very* long night of defending the realm."

The handsome stranger smiled. "Long indeed. I know. I helped make it so. To squeeze our doings into a shorter night might well have left her as a corpse."

"Who *are* y—*let go of me!* Let go, stop right here, and *tell me your name!*" Belantra shouted, thrusting the gonne of wands and rod into the intruder's face and preparing to spend her life in the defense of the Mage Royal.

Black eyebrows lifted. "Demanding, aren't ye? War Wizards weren't quite so shrill back in the early days, I must say. I did warn Amedahast she was shaping something that was sure to get away from her—but then, who am I to deny other mages their grand schemes and toys, when such strivings have brought us all such wonder? No, lass, *don't* try to set them all off at once—ye'll blast all this cellar right up through the grand edifice above it, shattering Caladnei to bonelessness as surely as ye do the same to thyself and everyone else within reach—including all thy fellow loyal mages ye summoned!"

The intruder pointed along the passage where robed men and women were approaching at a run, wands in hand and various glows of awakening magic flaring.

Chuckling and shaking his head, he plucked Belantra and her gonne around in front of him to serve as a shield, more or less carried her the few steps down the passage to the entrance she'd emerged from, and laid a hand on the closed iron door he found there.

Deadly magic flared and crackled around his fingers. He shook his head, broke it without seeming to do anything, and reached *through* the still-solid metal to turn the latch-handle on the inside.

Belantra's mouth dropped open in astonishment at that. Her jaw dropped still farther as the stranger's shape shifted into that of a slender old man with a white beard, bushy eyebrows, and a hawklike nose.

His grip remained every bit as iron-strong as he towed her through the doorway into the softly glow-lit bedchamber beyond—where someone was sitting up in a magnificent canopied bed facing them, eyes sharp above an unwaveringly aimed wand.

"Wh—*Elminster!*"

"The same. Nice curves, lass, but get something on over them, or I'll shortly be guilty of laying low the Royal Magician of Cormyr with a walloping head cold. Ye're coming with me."

The Mage Royal gaped at him just as her door-guardian had done—before Belantra turned to doing what she was doing just now, which was fainting dead away and slumping in the Old Mage's grasp—then stiffened, eyes blazing ruby-red, and snapped, "Certainly *not!* Who are you to be giving me orders? Or demanding anything of any War Wizard of Cormyr?"

"The orders aren't mine, lass. They come from Mystra. However, if ye'd rather *not* know what mischief Vangerda-hast is up to in the midst of thy kingdom, ye can of course refuse both the Divine One and myself and join the legions of proud fools waiting to fill up graves all over Faerûn. I leave ye free choice."

Caladnei swallowed, her magnificent throat moving while the rest of her sat on the bed like a dark brown, smooth-skinned statue. Elminster kept his eyes fixed on hers. She looked away first, muttering, "I was *trying* to get some sleep."

"A luxury seldom allowed Royal Magicians, ye'll learn," Elminster said, stepping forward to lay Belantra's limp form gently across the end of the bed. He went to a wardrobe, flung the doors wide, and rummaged, soon tossing a pair of boots back over his shoulder.

Caladnei caught them at about the time a dozen War Wizards burst into the room—and came to a confused halt as the Mage Royal of Cormyr flung up her hand in a 'stop' gesture. "Out, all of you," she said firmly. "My apologies for the upset of being summoned at such an hour for nothing. Go back to your posts."

"Mage Royal, forgive me," one of the older men said gravely, "but—"

"My mind is my own, thanks, Velvorn. I'm neither enchanted nor coerced by my guest, here. He has merely reminded me of my duty to Cormyr. Please go."

Leather breeches landed in Caladnei's lap, and a tunic struck her face a moment later. Velvorn lingered for a breath or two longer, perhaps to enjoy either the scenery or the sight of a Royal Magician catching clothes with her face, then wheeled around and started to shoo away all the War Wizards who'd crowded into the doorway to stare.

When he was done, he turned on the threshold with a clear question in his eyes—but closed the door at an imperious gesture from the Mage Royal.

Caladnei sighed. "Well, my loyal mages will certainly be able to recognize me now from any angle, with or without clothes."

Elminster turned from the wardrobe with a vest in his hands and grunted, "My apologies, lass. Sometimes haste is needful, and I didn't want to harm or humiliate dozens of War Wizards trying to get to you, a few hours hence." He shook out the vest, laid it on the bed, and turned his back. "I see ye're wise enough to keep thy hair gathered, so as to get up and about the swifter."

"I was too tired to remember to take it off," Caladnei admitted, reaching up to touch the ribbon at the back of her neck. She rose from the bed, long-limbed and slender. "No underclout?"

Elminster shrugged. "Ladies never wore them in *my* day."

Caladnei arched an eyebrow. "That tells me more about the company you kept, Lord Elminster, than it does about fashion—all those centuries ago, when you still looked at ladies."

The Old Mage chuckled, back still turned, but several underthings gently floated off a wardrobe shelf and past him. Caladnei selected one with the dry observation, "Ah, I see you know what they look like."

"I observe women still. Ladies, not so many."

The Mage Royal made a rude sound, dressed in whispering haste—a belt floated into her hand just as she found herself lacking it—and asked, "Should I take wands, expecting battle?"

"Nay. If ye should need them where we're going next, 'tis more than mere treason the realm need worry about."

Caladnei laid a tentative hand on Elminster's shoulder—then snatched it back. The Old Mage turned. "Fear ye'll catch something?"

The Mage Royal's eyes were doe-brown once more. "No," she replied. "I . . . I just wanted to touch you and live to tell the tale. Some say you're . . ."

"Afire with Mystra's power? A rotting lich whose joints crackle with sorcery? A shapeshifting, counterfeit creature who devoured the real Elminster long ago? Those're usually the most popular rumors."

Caladnei blushed, and then lifted her chin. "I've heard all of those, yes. Where are you taking me?"

"Stag Steads."

The Mage Royal arched the same eyebrow that had lifted before then turned to one of her bedposts, did something that swung aside a little curved door to reveal a cavity, drew forth two wands in a scabbard that she strapped to her forearm, and turned back to fix Elminster with a defiant look.

The Old Mage merely shrugged. "Ye must do what ye think wisest." He reached out his hand to her.

Caladnei eyed him. "The wisest thing to do now," she said calmly, "would be to flee you, not take your hand."

Elminster nodded. "True." He took a step closer and offered his hand again. With a sigh, she took it—and was instantly elsewhere.

An elsewhere that sported many leaves, dappled in the bright light of dawn. Caladnei blinked and stared all around, knowing by the view that she stood on a back porch of the hunting lodge in the heart of the King's Forest.

"How did you *do* that? No word nor gesture—"

A round door set deep into the moss-covered bank behind them burst open, and a blade thrust out through it—straight through Elminster. Twice it thrust then slashed sideways, cutting freely through the Old Mage as if he were but empty air.

"Caladnei!" The dark-haired woman behind the blade was angry. "You've *got* to stop scaring me like this! I thought this was some archwizard holding you captive, not your own clever illusion!"

"Mreen," the Mage Royal said quickly, holding up a quelling hand. "This is—"

"Oh, *gods*," the Lady Lord of Arabel gasped, her sword sinking forgotten in her hand.

Elminster had turned around to face her. "Forgotten me so soon, Mreen? And something so basic as an ironguard spell, or—ahem—mine own modifications to it?"

Flecks of gold flashed in Myrmeen Lhal's deep blue eyes as she stared back at him with more than a hint of defiant challenge in her gaze. The white lines of fresh scars crossed on her hands, and one scar adorned a cheek that had been unmarked when last the Old Mage had seen her—but her figure in her leather armor was as trim as ever. Her glossy, almost blue-black hair held no gray—but there were two lines of white at her temples, where there'd been only youthful darkness before.

"El," she said slowly, grounding her blade, "you chase trouble across Faerûn like a stormbird. I give you good greeting but with wariness: Why come you here?"

"To see the Crown Princess ye're trying to keep hidden behind thy shapely shoulders," the archmage replied, one corner of his mouth quirking into a smile that was almost hidden by his beard. "Ye should all hear this, mind, for it concerns the realm entire."

"Elminster of Shadowdale," the Steel Regent said calmly from the darkness inside the hill, "be welcome in Cormyr. Come in and unfold the bad news. Wine? Morning broth?"

"Thank ye, but—no. Ye still know how to tempt a man, lass."

Alusair Nacacia grinned. "I should *hope* so. Fall into a seat—there're plenty."

The princess was tangle-haired and barefoot, evidently just risen from slumber. She wore only a large, fluffy robe, but her sword gleamed ready in her hand. Its scabbard lay upon a round stone table beside her flagon of steaming broth. Elminster sniffed appreciatively then shook his head and sat down. His stomach promptly rumbled.

Alusair grinned again and ladled him his own flagon, as Caladnei and Myrmeen took seats around the table.

"So talk, wizard," Alusair commanded. Caladnei and Myrmeen both stiffened in apprehension, but Elminster merely chuckled.

"By the first Mystra and the second, but ye sound like thy father, lass!" He stretched, leaned back, and added gruffly, "Ye truly don't want to know what Vangey's been up to, but as Regent ye'd best know anyway, so long as ye've the sense not to tell anyone."

Alusair rolled her eyes and growled in mock anger.

Elminster gave her a grin to match her earlier ones. "Well then, to put it plainly: My onetime pupil and thy former Mage Royal is trying to complete a magical task that's very important to him, ere he dies. Ye might say he's putting the last of his life into it and is fiercely set upon it."

"And this task would be—?" the Steel Regent growled.

"None of ye three need me to remind ye that the Lords Who Sleep bide in armed slumber to guard Cormyr no longer. Well, Vangey seeks to replace them."

Alusair's eyes blazed. "With *whom?*"

"Dragons. Thy retired Royal Magician seeks to bind some great wyrms in stasis to defend the kingdom of Cormyr against any other attacking dragon, or the whelming of a rebel host, or an invading army from, say, Sembia or from the Zhentarim or some other grasping power."

Shock shone white on three female faces.

"Without *telling* us?" Alusair barked.

At the same time Myrmeen burst out, "This could imperil the realm as gravely as did the Devil Dragon!"

Caladnei swore, "Mother *Mystra!*"

Elminster smiled gravely around the table and thrust out his hand to catch hold of Alusair's blade before she could smash it down on the stone table in rage. She struggled against his strength in vain for a trembling, throat-straining moment then sat back dumbfounded.

"Magic," he explained with a wry smile, handing her

blade to her. The princess snarled and snatched it up, whirling it back to bring it shattering down on the stone—then stopped in midair, matched his smile bitterly, slid it into its sheath instead, and laid that on the table with deft and delicate care.

"So," she said, letting her breath out in a long sigh, "suppose, old meddling wizard, you tell us a little *more* about this idiocy—just so I know what to say when I go storming into Vangey's little hidden haven to tie his ears together under his chin and charge him with *treason!*"

Elminster's smile grew wider and more crooked. "Ah, the spirit that has carried Cormyr into the mess 'tis in today. *Temper*, lass, temper."

"Old Mage," Myrmeen put in calmly, "the Steel Regent is not the only one to be shocked, dismayed, upset, and furious. I believe I speak for both myself and Caladnei when I say that we, too, are on the verge of boiling over at this news. Pray grant the request of the Crown Princess: Tell us more."

Elminster nodded. "Excellent broth," he told Alusair brightly, earning another glowering growl.

He winked and said quietly, " 'Tis probably no news to inform thee that acting alone and in secrecy is the way of mages. Let me impart a reminder and a tutor's judgment. The former: Vangerdahast serves the realm first and its rulers second. The latter: Thy retired Royal Magician learned long ago, to his cost, to trust no-one."

"To his cost? *What* cost?" Caladnei asked sharply.

"His broken heart, the lives of more than a dozen nobles, both loyal and rebel, and three abiding perils to the realm," Elminster replied. "Ask him if ye'd know more—for I've more important words for ye three."

"Oh?" the Crown Princess asked icily. "There's more?"

"*Advice*, lass, advice. A warning, if ye will. To reveal Vangey's plan to others—to *anyone*, even Filfaeril—will be to risk rumor of it getting out and endangering the realm by luring wizards hither."

Myrmeen wrinkled her brow. "Dragon collectors?"

"Those who seek the spells Vangerdahast is crafting—spells they can't help but see that he *must* craft, to find success—to bind and command dragons. Some will see deeper and know that Vangey draws on the last of his life to power such spells. They will see him weak, and dying soon—perhaps sooner, if they can catch him at work and unprepared for battle. Then the realm will be theirs to plunder of magic—his caches, at least—or try to rule, through alliances with the more traitorous nobles . . . and suchlike mischief all of ye should be more than familiar with."

The three women looked back at Elminster, shock and anger gone. Their faces now held frowns of thoughtfulness. After a moment, they all started to speak at once. Before any of them could form a single whole word, they fell abruptly silent again, gesturing at each other to speak first.

It was Caladnei who did so. "As Mage Royal," she said, lips thin with determination, "I must deal with this. Mine is the duty and the skill—however slight, when set against Lord Vangerdahast's—at magecraft. This doom is mine."

"I . . . you're right, Cala," Princess Alusair said reluctantly. "Though it feels like I'm sending you to your death."

"As it happens," Elminster said brightly, setting down his nearly empty flagon, "Mystra commanded me to deal with this. Knowing both thy duties and how ye'd feel about being left out, I came to collect and bring ye along—the Mother of All Magic being of like mind."

"Well, if you're collecting women to come watch you swat Vangerdahast," the High Lady of Arabel spoke up, "I insist on coming along too. I don't want to miss seeing Old Haughty get his—and someone besides magic-crazed wizards should be present, to witness fairly and to report back to the Crown."

Alusair nodded. "Well said, Mreen. Old Mage?"

Elminster smiled. "If Myrmeen Lhal desires to come along, then so she shall, in all the safety I can provide."

Abruptly, his seat was empty. He, Caladnei, and Myrmeen were simply gone from the room.

Crown Princess Alusair Nacacia Obarskyr gaped at their empty seats then sprang to her feet, snatching up her scabbarded sword, and snarled, "Elminster? *Caladnei?*"

There was no answer but faint birdsong from outside. The Steel Regent threw back her head and let her fury pour out in a wordless roar. No chance to privately confer with Cala or Mreen, no chance for them to prepare gear or make arrangements! The scheming old *bastard!*

She smashed the nearest door open and strode out into the forest, striding hard. Her scabbard whirled back in her wake, almost slapping handsome young Lord Malask Huntinghorn across the face. He blinked, came out of his doorguard's stance, and started after the Crown Princess.

Ducking around wildly waving branches and swaying saplings, he reached a dense thicket in time to see Alusair hiss out a stream of curses he was glad he couldn't quite catch and reduce a defenseless sapling to kindling with a few furious slashes of her sword.

Throwing back her head to shake the hair out of her eyes, she strode purposefully to the *next* sapling. Malask Huntinghorn swallowed, drew in a deep breath, and performed the bravest act of his young life, thus far . . . perhaps his last brave act ever.

"Princess," he said firmly, striding forward to catch at her swordarm, "that tree deserves to live, just as you or I do. The living green heart of the realm, as Lord Alaphondar often reminds us, is its trees. I don't think you should—"

Princess Alusair spun around far more swiftly than she'd ever done when making love to him—faster than any battle-knight of the realm he'd ever seen—and pounced on the scion of House Huntinghorn, flinging her blade away to punch, kick, and claw.

Malask found himself on his back, winded and with a fierce pain in his shoulder where he'd fetched up against a tree-root—and even sharper pains erupting in his gut and ribs as the Regent of Cormyr slammed her fists home, snarling and shouting in fury.

He was suddenly very glad indeed that he'd donned full forest-leathers, codpiece in particular, to take his turn at guard—as knees and knife-edged hands thrust home, slaps made his ears ring and his face burn, and the woman he was sworn to defend thrust her nose almost into his eye and shouted, "*Defend* yourself, you great rothé, damn you! *Fight*, Malask!"

"M-my Queen, I—"

"I'm not your damn queen or *anyone's* queen, Lord Lummox! I'm a warrior who feels great need of a sparring partner, right now! *Hit* me, you great lump of cowering man-flesh!"

Malask swallowed, closed his eyes against a punch that almost closed one of them for him, and reluctantly thrust one arm up and out. She swatted it aside, bruisingly, and belted him across the nose.

"Aaargh!" he roared, eyes streaming as the pain stung him into trying to twist and roll out from under her. "Gods, you've probably *broken* it, Luse! I'll look like some sort of country straw-butt lout for the rest of my life!" He shielded his dripping nose with one hand, wincing and blinded by tears.

"Well, why not? You *are* a country straw-butt lout!"

With a roar, Malask Huntinghorn forgot all about duty, princesses, treason, royal persons, and how soft and ardent this particular royal person had felt on occasion—and lashed out with a roundhouse swing that had all of his pain and anger behind it.

There was a grunt, a sudden loss of weight atop his hip, and silence.

He blinked, swallowed, and knuckled his eyes feverishly to clear them. "Luse? *Luse?*"

"*That's* more like it," she snarled into his ear, as both of her fists struck home, low in his ribs, driving the wind right out of him. Groaning and flailing out, he punched, clawed, and punched again—and somehow found himself staggering to his feet, under a welter of blows, tearing a fluffy nightrobe clean off the Crown Princess of the realm as he spun her off-balance so as to plant a solid blow to her breast that sent her over backward to the ground, doubled up and spitting curses.

Glowering, he strode toward her, fists balled. She launched herself up and into his gut, headfirst, hurling him backward.

He greeted the ground with a crash, a snapping of ferns and dry dead branches, and a Crown Princess of the realm on his pelvis, punching at him. Malask got in an uppercut that snapped Alusair's jaw up and back, and she collapsed onto him with a groan, rocking back and forth.

"Oh, my jaw aches," she muttered, as she crawled up the body of her battered guard, both of them wincing at their bruises, and kissed him.

"Gods above, Luse," he whispered, "is this one more way of hurting me? My nose . . ."

"I'll help you forget your nose," she said huskily, finding and tugging at his laces. Malask Huntinghorn groaned and shook his head. Oh, Alusair. Ah, fortunate Cormyr . . . and lucky me, too.

Ten

SCHEMES AS BLOOD-RED AS RUBIES

Beware all schemes, O king, for such beasts have a way of shedding blood on the floors of this kingdom like poured-out sacks of rubies.

The character Malarvalo the Minstrel
in Scene the Fourth
of the play *Daggers In All Her Gowns*
by Nesper Droun of Ordulin
first performed in the Year of the Morningstar

Rhauligan was barely out of the turret when Narnra cast a glance back over her shoulder and saw him.

She gave him a glare, ran on a few paces, stopped, peered off to the left where the balconies and turrets of Haelithtorn-towers jutted closest to the wall—then took a few racing steps and launched herself between the leaf-cloaked boughs of the great trees of the mansion gardens, in a daring leap that . . .

. . . took her safely to a clinging landing on the head of

a brooding gargoyle, chin in hand, holding up one corner of a balcony.

Rhauligan hoped it was rock-solid carved stone and not of one those stonelike monsters that would suddenly move to bite and claw—probably when she was safely gone, but he was trying to land in the same spot.

Keeping his eyes on her to make sure she set no traps behind, Rhauligan trotted along the wall, looking for the right place to make his running jump.

He sighed, once.

Caladnei and Narnra, I'm keeping a tally here. And if the gods grant me more luck than any man in the kingdom has enjoyed for the last century or so, I just might live to collect it.

Rhauligan took his last two running steps with the wind in his face and launched himself into the air. The balcony was enough lower than the top of the wall that he'd been able to clearly see through the windows of the room it opened into. No one was moving therein. He'd paced off the run calmly enough, and now he'd just have to hope he'd been . . .

. . . right. He landed hard, numbing his elbows on the lichen-splotched old gargoyle and losing a lot of breath—but his first surge of angry strength took him safely up and over the intricately carved stone rail onto a balcony that seemed far too spattered with bird dung to belong to a house that held caring servants. The Harper took but an instant to safely plant his feet ere he looked up.

The long legs and trim behind of Narnra Shalace were just vanishing through an open window, high above.

As Rhauligan leaned out to peer, she slipped inside the window, favored him with the briefest of glares, and closed it behind her. Through its dung-streaked, amber-tinted glass, the Harper saw her turn its catch, latching it firmly.

So. He could either climb the outside wall—and though he was the stronger of the two of them, he was also much the heavier—to break that window and force his way in or stand here on a nice level balcony and do the same to a window or door.

Out of habit Rhauligan ducked low and turned back to peer over the balcony rail. Its gargoyles were still gargoyles, and there was no sign of guards or anyone else in the mist-beaded shade-gloom of the lush garden below.

He spun again to the door, still in his crouch. Nothing moved in the room beyond the door—which was dark and seemed to hold a lot of large, draped things . . . furniture shrouded in dust-sheets. Rhauligan's eyes narrowed. Lady Ambrur was certainly still in Marsember—or had been, yester-morning—so this couldn't be the usual nobles' practice of shutting up one house and journeying to another . . . not that current local Harper wisdom knew of Lady Joysil Ambrur having any other abode. Of course, she could be invited to some Sembian hunting lodge or Cormyrean upcountry castle at any time, but . . .

Perhaps she merely found the house too large for her daily purposes and used this part for storing the furniture she liked the least. Yes, that'd probably be it.

The door had the simplest of latches but also featured an ornate inner bar and two floorspike bolts, so Rhauligan undid a catch on his boot-heel and slid the heel off, exposing it as the hilt of a razor-sharp scriber.

A moment later, he was neatly removing the first shaped pane of glass, cut along its putty-lines, and reaching in to undo a floorspike. He had to work swiftly or Narnra would have time to descend the three levels or so from the window she'd entered to this floor and get below and past him . . . leaving him the entire gods-kissed, servant-crowded mansion to search for her in. Yes, the score was still rising . . .

Out of habit he kept casting glances back over his shoulder to make sure no one was on the wall or flying past—Why not? Some of these nobles sponsored or gave house room to apprentice mages, gaining the protection of thiefly fear of such guardians—to see him and raise the alarm . . . or just practice their skills at putting handy crossbow quarrels through intruding Harpers.

No such hazards presented themselves before Rhauligan got the doors open. Once the floorspikes were drawn up, the doors could be made to part enough to thrust his prybar between them, lifting the latch and thrusting the inside bar up and out of its sockets.

He had the door open swiftly enough to dart one hand out to deflect the falling bar from a crash down onto the floor—nice polished emeraldstone tiles, alternating in diamond-shapes with white marble—into a thudding impact with the nearest draped wardrobe or whatever it was and a fairly quiet tumble down the cloth to the floor.

The Harper restored the bar to its rightful place, sheathed his prybar, and advanced cautiously into the dark, quiet room. A mouse scurried from under one shrouded thing to under another, but otherwise . . . nothing moved but the dust. He was leaving a faint trail through it, he knew, and soon found the piled-up extra end of a too-large dust-sheet to wipe his boots on.

The room was large, and opened onto the next chamber of the mansion through a great tapestry-filled arch rather than doors. Rhauligan listened at the wall of cloth, hearing nothing, went to one end of it—rather than disturb it trying to find its center parting—and slipped his head around it.

He found himself looking at a large, dust-dancing stairwell, with a railed landing joining it to his room and others out of sight beyond the wall that cradled the stairs.

"Nothing," a voice called suddenly. "Something disturbed the doves, right enough—a gorcraw, mayhap—but none of 'em had any messages. I checked every blessed one."

Rhauligan hastily drew back a breath or two before a bored servant-woman whose bosom resembled a large sack of potatoes trudged down the nearest stair and went along the landing.

"Well, that's all right, then," another, sharper voice said

from somewhere under Rhauligan's boots, presumably the next landing down. "So long as we miss nothing and catch no Lady-fury . . ."

"Huh," the large woman agreed, as she started down the next flight of steps and passed out of Rhauligan's view. "Can't be thieves, unless they can fl—" She stopped, stock-still and said in a different voice, "Hold, now! That was it—the window was shut! Shut and latched! One of them birds 'prolly came flying to get in and smacked right into the glass! Send Norn down to check for one lying in the gardens, and get the lantern—oh, and fire-pokers for the both of us! I'm not going back up there alone!"

"Aye," Sharp Voice agreed, her voice fading as she descended unseen stairs, "but what sort of thief shuts a window behind hisself?"

"An idiot thief, that's what sort!" Lumpy Bosom replied sourly, almost driving Rhauligan to chuckle.

You have *that* right, goodwoman, you do indeed . . . and I'm assigned to be her keeper, more's the pity. . . .

No, that was unfair. The Waterdhavian's only mistakes had been to blunder after a wizard to get here—and to run from half the gathered War Wizards and Harpers in the realm.

Well, she'd ended up with only one following her, hadn't she? So perhaps her lone hunter was the idiot. . . .

Rhauligan put away that wry thought and turned back to the task at hand. So the window had been left open to let doves in and out of their cote. Well, that explained the handy open window and the bird-dung . . . and if Lumpy there had gone up the stairs to answer whatever alarm Narnra had triggered in any sort of haste, the thief from Waterdeep had to still be somewhere above him.

Of course, he now had to keep watch over the stairs so she couldn't slip down past him and at the same time manage not to be seen by two wary she-servants when they came back up here—and walked right past his staring face—with pokers in their hands.

Perhaps the rooms on the far side of the stair . . .

Rhauligan was out along the landing and around the stair-head like a hurrying ghost, and into . . . more dark, shrouded rooms given over to dust. Smaller than the one he'd been in, one giving into another through archways, again. Must be hard to heat in winter, with no doors to close, and that was probably why this tower of the mansion had been the one chosen to languish as storage. Cold storage, ha ha.

Well, he'd best turn and find the best vantage p—hold! What was . . . another stair!

Rhauligan was across the room like a storm wind, already fearing he was too late. This stair was narrower and steeper—a servants' route, no doubt—and deserted. He peered at it then went chin-down to the dusty floor and squinted up at the steps. Aye, there! And there! She'd been down it, right enough, and not long ago.

* * * * *

Mask aid me, how big *was* this house? A grand pile indeed, from outside, yes—but to leave so much of it to the dark and dust! Was its owner a half-witted hermit, clinging to a few rooms and shuffling about mumbling about past glories? Or shut up in a sick-bed, with dwindling coins keeping fewer and fewer servants?

Or were there newer, grander wings and towers and entire rambling mansions beyond this, that she hadn't seen yet?

Somehow Narnra suspected the latter.

"Just go on being the Silken Shadow," she breathed to herself, hoping the Harper hound on her trail had given up or been caught . . . and knowing, somehow, that she was just dream-wishing.

Yet she felt—good. When her prowls were going well, she seemed almost to float along in the silence and the gloom, silence wrapped around her like a cloak.

She felt like that now.

Narnra gave the darkness a fierce grin and went on, wondering what lay ahead. Perhaps the stables, with a hay loft to hide in. And coaches. All nobles had coaches, and coaches betimes went out through city gates. . . .

* * * * *

Rhauligan followed the stair down as quietly as he could, which was quiet indeed. This was old, solid stonework and thick boards pegged into place, none of your slapdash modern gaudywork.

As he went down, the noises of work—servants, of course—began to be audible: people chattering, laughing, hurrying back and forth laden with things, someone chopping food on a wooden board or table, someone else making banging and scraping sounds.

"Where're them brooms, then?" The rough male voice was accompanied by a striding entry too sudden for Rhauligan to draw back. He froze on the stairs as sudden light spilled across a landing below, as a man with a long-ago broken nose and wheezing lungs snatched up a long-handled pushbroom from where it leaned against a wall, spun around without sparing a glance up the dark and dusty stairs where the Harper stood, and banged his door closed behind him again.

Rhauligan hurried, in case the habit was to return the broom the moment its job was done. He was past that door and on down the next flight ere the door opened again, but by then the growing hubbub and light around him, through various ill-fitting hatches in the stairwell walls—it seemed he was passing a large, multi-level kitchen where a small legion of servants were keeping quite busy—was considerable.

One hatch afforded him a gap large enough to peer through, and he put his eye to it. Shiny copper vats or tanks greeted his view, with men in aprons squatting at the taps filling great tankards as large as their torsos. Below them, several steps down on another level in the same vast room,

stood a great table covered with flour and dough, with
women swarming busily around it. Steam from cauldrons
was rising from a lower level yet, down out of sight to his
left. Rhauligan cast a glance right across the chamber and
froze again.

There, just visible through a forest of hanging pans
and pots and ladles, was another, open stair—and peering
through that kitchenmongery was Narnra Shalace, just for a
moment ere she melted back and away and went on down
those dark steps.

She must have passed through the rooms of the floor
above and found that matching servants' stair. So she was
below him, now, and he'd have to move like a man trying to
catch the morrow.

Rhauligan raced down steps with more haste than quiet.
Given all the racket in the kitchen, he'd probably have to
shout or bang one of those pans with a sword-hilt to be
noticed, anyway, and—

There was a door at the next landing, facing neither into
the kitchen nor away from it but north into the "blind end" of
the landing turn, and he plucked it open cautiously—in time
to see the heel of Narnra's boot flick past. He was out into
the cross-passage she'd been traversing as fast as he could
move, but she'd already stepped into a great room or gallery
beyond and darted to the right.

Rhauligan ran after her and froze, just before the archway where the passage opened out into this larger chamber
ahead.

It was a *very* large room, and lofty. This was almost
certainly the central hall of Haelithtorntowers, and he'd
probably be stepping out onto a promenade balcony part
way up its walls.

Torchlight flickered below, all along the front of the balcony. Across a vast ring of empty space he could see the far
sweep of them, beneath an archway that matched the one
he was standing in. They gave light enough to show the
Harper the walls of this huge room rising up out of sight and

curving inward, probably to a vaulted spire far overhead.

Painted coats of arms—wooden plaques as large as a stable door, each of them, and these were the old, fully-gilded sort with real helms and crossed spears affixed to them, not the simply carved false adornments more in favor, for some inexplicable reason, these days—adorned the walls above the balcony, and there were many tall, dark, closed doors between them. If Narnra didn't want to stay on display in this hall, she'd probably creep to one of them and try to open it.

For his part—he ducked low again, so as to be close to the floor when he thrust his head out to peer along the balcony in both directions, seeking guards—Rhauligan hoped she'd find them all locked. All but one that opened into a dead-end chamber where he could pounce on her, truss her up, and go and announce himself to the Lady Ambrur and request that he be allowed to remove his captive into the keeping of the Mage Royal. Enough of this chasing about through laundries and cookshops.

Even before the Harper had finished making sure there were no guards or servants within sight on this balcony, nor any signs that anyone often came up here, he caught sight of Narnra. Keeping low and out of sight below the balcony rail, she'd worked her way around the balcony to the far side, obviously intending to depart through that matching archway—but had now stopped to listen to the voices floating up from below.

And leaned daringly forward to hear everything.

Rhauligan frowned. He could hear only a few people engaged in private converse—with no link of cutlery nor bustle of servants. Out of long habit he cocked his head to listen, too.

A sentence or two later, he'd put aside all thoughts of trying to capture Narnra Shalace.

"You're in no pressing hurry, my Lord Starangh?"

"Not as yet, though I reserve the full disclosure of my

desired pace through the rest of this unfolding day until I learn the reason you ask such a thing," the Red Wizard replied calmly, inspecting the fingers of his own right hand as if he'd never quite noticed them before.

"Well, if we've the time and you've no objections on the grounds of, say, prudence considering our present company," the Lady Ambrur responded, "I'd prefer to unfold the information you seek in an ordered, chronological fashion—to tell it as a story, to use plain words. A brief tale, not deep history."

The Thayan raised his eyes to hers. "Why don't you begin that way? If things become overlong or drift far from what most interests us all, we can always cry warning and agree upon another manner of discourse, can we not?"

"Indeed, sir," his hostess agreed smoothly. "Let us begin, then, with the recent retirement of the Royal Magician."

Malakar Surth had been displaying some signs of irritation throughout the preceding discussion—his mouth drawing into a thin, disgusted line, his gaze beginning to wander around the hall, beginning with a glance at what her gown displayed to the watching world of the Lady Nouméa Cardellith's bosom—and so had his partner Bezrar, who'd slumped in his chair into a more sullen pose of boredom. Both leaned forward with renewed interest when the Lady Ambrur looked down into her empty tallglass for a moment then spoke to it gently.

"Vangerdahast ruled this kingdom for years. Azoun reigned, yes, dispensed justice, and rode to war when the need arose . . . but by his control of the Court, through manipulations of almost all of its officials, the Obarskyrs themselves, and many of the nobles who had dealings at Court, the Mage Royal held the day-to-day rule of this realm. Cormyr was ordered very much as he wanted it to be—until the coming of what most folk call 'the Devil Dragon.' We all know what befell Azoun and Tanalasta, but I also happen to know that Vangerdahast had some very trying adventures—alone—and almost met his death, too."

The Lady of Haelithtorntowers looked up from the depths of her tallglass to find the eyes of Harnrim Starangh dark and intent upon her. She looked into them and added, "Not a few folk at Court remarked that the Royal Magician looked more old and exhausted at Azoun's funeral than they'd ever seen him before. Most put it down to grief—for the friendship between the Mage Royal and the Purple Dragon was legendary—and the stresses of battle, but among the most senior Wizards of War there were murmurs of . . . deeper failings."

"Say more, Lady," the Red Wizard purred, leaning forward with his nonchalance forgotten.

"I believe it's safe to say that the death of Azoun forcibly reminded Vangerdahast that no man lives forever and that he hadn't much time left, He was growing steadily more frail. Yet we've all seen men enfeebled with age cling to what little they have left like a withering vine, hanging on grimly past all reason—until the hanging on prolongs existence past all enjoyment or a natural end. Faerûn knows legions of liches because of wizards who fiercely desire not to let go of life."

The Lady Ambrur rose and took an idle pace away from her seat. Out of habit all three of her male guests marked where she walked and laid hands to the hilts of daggers or wands, but their hostess took only one more idle step before turning about to face them again. "Vangerdahast feared one thing more than his failing body: his failing mind. Increasing forgetfulness is a deadly failure in any mage, the Mage Royal of Cormyr in particular, and his had become bad enough in matters large and small that War Wizards were noticing daily. The Mage Royal could no longer juggle dozens of intrigues and managed rumors and timings of events without dropping some of them—and could no longer deny this from himself. He hated it, but he feared for Cormyr with someone else at the helm—given the plentiful supply of traitor nobles, the headstrong Princess Alusair, and the defenseless babe that the fifth Azoun was and remains."

Lady Ambrur turned again to look at Lady Cardellith and
said gravely to Nouméa, "Finding his replacement could
have been an impossible job. He could well have died still
looking—but for the first time in his life, Vangerdahast was
truly lucky, or Mystra smiled upon him: He found his Caladnei, and though she's no wise old Vangerdahast, she'll do.
She has youth, vigor, and the ability to work as well with
Alusair as Vangey did with Alusair's father. That left Vangerdahast free to retire before he mishandled something into a
real disaster and let half the realm know that weakness now
walked the Royal Court. So he hastened to do so, seizing
on his long-held desire to be free of the petty, time-wasting
intrigues and demands of Court etiquette and routine, and
do something important ere he died."

Lady Joysil Ambrur spun around to face the wizard Darkspells and the two Marsemban merchants. "*That* is what
drives Vangerdahast, gentlesirs. That is what has driven
him for some years, ever since he judged himself successful
in schooling and guiding the great Azoun. He saw himself
as a successful guide, teacher, manipulator, and helmsman
of the realm . . . but other Royal Wizards of Cormyr have
been that. Vangerdahast wants more. He wants to leave
his mark in lore, so that men in centuries to come will say,
'Baerauble was the founding High Wizard of the realm,
aye, but Vangerdahast . . . Vangerdahast was probably the
greatest of them all.' It's not a hunger rare among mages,
I'm afraid."

Harnrim "Darkspells" Starangh did not smile at that observation, but Lady Ambrur was carefully looking now into the
round and startled eyes of the importer Aumun Bezrar and
no longer meeting the gaze of the Red Wizard.

"Vangerdahast is a builder of great ships of state and their
helmsman," she added, "so 'great things' to him doesn't
mean blasting cities flat or cracking open castles with their
archwizards and kings still in them. By *very* difficult and
expensive means I've been able to learn what two specific
things he does hold important. One is personal: to sire a

blood heir and enjoy romance and companionship, something he dared not allowed himself to do whilst serving as Mage Royal. One is his last gift to Cormyr, his legacy: to craft a great feat of magic, a webwork of spells that will defend and protect Cormyr after his death."

Abruptly Lady Ambrur sat down again and fell silent.

That silence stretched, almost echoing in the vast and largely empty hall, until at last the wizard Darkspells stirred and asked softly, "Have you any idea how this web of spells will defend the kingdom, Lady? Such a massive warding—if it is a warding—would drink deeply of the life of all things within it and could not help but be noticed. More than that: It could not help but change life in Cormyr, both through how magic works, and by what other properties it possesses. Such a thing would become a treasure to steal—or a barrier to test strength against—for many mages and could not last long. I doubt that even Vangerdahast could successfully create such a thing. So . . . a warding seems unlikely. Have your . . . sources . . . any hint as to what this great magic entails?"

The Lady of Haelithtorntowers nodded, unsmiling. "They believe it will involve binding heroes to defend the realm in place of the destroyed Lords Who Sleep."

"Heroes?" Starangh echoed, with a frown. "What great magic is needful in binding a few men, even against their will? Men can be compelled. Finding them need not take long—nor the crafting of magic to do the binding. The spells must be known to him as they are to me."

Joysil shook her head. "My information suggests that these are all new spells Vangerdahast is crafting—and having great difficulties doing so."

Starangh smiled. "So . . . he intends to bind more than mere heroes, then. And he's doing this *where?*"

"There's a forest village on the Starwater Road," Lady Joysil replied, "called Mouth o' Gargoyles. Magic goes wild when cast there. This curse has been known for centuries and is demonstrably real. Certain senior War Wizards, however, have been overheard telling particular Harpers that a hide-hold cavern was long ago established in the forest near the village by a Royal Magician of the realm and used by succeeding Royal Magicians. The magics they work are concealed from those who might otherwise come looking for explanations; any radiances or blasts or strange magical effects get blamed on the curse."

Harnrim Starangh's eyes narrowed. "So dozens of War Wizards know about this cavern and what goes on there—and have truly managed to keep it secret, for all these years?"

"No. Only a very few know of it, because the various Royal Magicians normally go there alone."

"So who lurks in the woods, keeping outlaws and nosy Harpers and blundering foresters away?"

"That," the Lady Ambrur replied, leaning forward to fix Darkspells with a very direct gaze, "is the most interesting thing about all of this. Folk who blunder too close without following exactly the right route—and no, I'm sorry, but I've not been able to learn the specifics of that trail—encounter creatures of Mystra: watchghosts and wizardly wraiths and the like, who turn them back with magic. Or they simply take one wrong step and are teleported halfway across Faerûn—seemingly to a different place every time. Most War Wizards who patrol the area are under orders only to observe who approaches and report such intruders to Laspeera or her most trusted senior mages. Most of them know only that something precious is located near Mouth o' Gargoyles and that the very existence of this unknown valuable thing is a state secret."

"So presumably a select few senior War Wizards do know the correct route to this sanctum," Starangh said softly, bobbing his chin onto his steepled fingertips. He suddenly broke into a wide smile, blinked, and added, "You shall be well paid, Lady Ambrur."

He opened a belt pouch, placed twenty thumb-sized rubies on the table in front of him, and added, "Consider

this but a first, trifling payment—a gift, if you will. The
worth of these is not be included in our agreed-upon price,
which shall be delivered to you on the morrow. For I deem
that you—*if* you forget all you've said tonight and speak
nothing of it to anyone else ever again or of the names and
faces of any of us three—have more than earned payment
in full."

He favored Nouméa Cardellith with a long, silent, thoughtful look but said nothing to her.

Starangh rose in a single smooth motion, nodded politely
to the Lady Ambrur, and asked, "Have you learned anything
more of interest, pertaining to this matter?"

"Not as yet," she replied gravely.

"No matter. You have rendered me great service, Lady. I
shall not intrude further upon your time."

He bowed, spun around, and made for the door. Wordlessly, the two merchants rose in his wake, sketched clumsy
bows of their own, and hastened to follow.

When the doors had closed behind them, Lady Ambrur
looked at her remaining guest with a smile. "Well? What
think you?"

Nouméa regarded her with large, dark eyes, shook her
head ever so slightly, and said softly, "I do not trust that
man."

"Nor should you," her hostess responded. "Are there
spells upon the rubies?"

Nouméa rose, went to stand over the stones, muttered
something, and passed her hand over them without touching
anything. "Yes," she said grimly, with no trace of surprise in
her voice.

Lady Ambrur nodded. "Touch them not nor send any
other magic at them. In fact, cast no more magic in this
room. Were I you, I'd use spells to disguise myself this very
night and lie low in some distant land for a month or so.
Red Wizards tend to have very long arms and sharply honed
senses of cruelty."

"But yourself?" Nouméa asked, waving her other hand

at the rubies. "What if he sends something deadly with his payment?"

"I can protect myself," the Lady of Haelithtorntowers said softly, acquiring a smile that was not at all dissimilar from that worn by the Red Wizard.

"Like Vangerdahast, I too have some important tasks I wish to accomplish before I die."

Eleven

A WIZARD IN EVERY SANCTUM

And so at last I was forced to put the world behind me and go and hide. I made myself a hole to hide in, pulled the hole in behind me, and there I was: nowhere.

> The character Greatghalont the Archwizard
> in Scene the First
> of the play *Endings In Innarlith*
> by Skamart "the Clever" Thallea
> first performed in the Year of Thunder

There was a moment of blue, endlessly falling mists, then solid stone under their boots, bright morning sunlight, and a smell of burnt sausage and scorched toast.

Caladnei blinked. "I've been here before. Just once, when Vangey was testing me—but then he cloaked it from me somehow. I've never been able to reach it again."

Myrmeen Lhal was shooting wary glances in all directions, her sword half-drawn. She gave Elminster an enthusiastically venomous look, so he smiled and blew her a kiss—which turned her glare stony.

They were standing in a flagstone-floored cellar, the cross-vaultings of its low, arched ceiling perhaps a handspan overhead. Ahead, beyond two littered tables and a hoopback chair be-draped with some rather dirty towels, was what looked like a kitchen: a scarred marble counter heaped high with dirty dishes and pans, flanking two sinks. Above the counter was a window, deep-set in a ferny bank and looking out through a few trailing vines over a pleasant deep-forest glade.

Standing at the counter with a bowl of almond butter in one hand, a fat loaf of bread under one arm, and his other hand wielding a knife that was scooping and slapping between bowl and the sliced-off, exposed end of the loaf, was an all-too-familiar man.

He was stooped and fat and wore dirty black robes and sandals. His wild gray-white beard flowed down over his chest and reached in every other direction, too. The mouth hidden somewhere in the midst of it was hard at work creating the reason he hadn't heard the ringing sound of Myrmeen half-drawing her blade, or Caladnei's softly wondering words.

Vangerdahast the wizard was singing a bawdy song about a lass from Arabel—Myrmeen's lips tightened—who'd fallen under his spell—Caladnei frowned—and was now begging for more . . . despite certain wizards growing sore . . .

Vangey's singing voice was atrocious—a flat, rough wreck of a tone cloaked in the exaggeratedly fruity stylings he'd no doubt heard the haughtiest bards offer at Court (though they'd probably kept to one key, something the former Mage Royal was in no danger of doing), and he kept breaking off his song to choke, cough, and spit enthusiastically into the sink.

His knife was layering a finger-thick and still growing deposit of almond butter onto the end of the bread-loaf. Its swirl of oily brown was already bedecked with sprinklings of parsley, chopped garlic, and dill . . . and Elminster grinned slyly as he looked sidelong at Caladnei's horrified face and watched it tighten in revolted anticipation of what her former mentor would most probably do next—which was, yes, to start to gnaw on the spread end of the loaf without bothering to slice it off or find a plate—though where a clean one might be lurking, in all the clutter, was itself a puzzling challenge—or, for that matter, make any sort of nodded offering to the gods.

What Vangerdahast did instead was launch into a second and filthier verse, through a mouthful of almond butter and bread while rocking on his heels and rhythmically conducting his imaginary wanton lass as he sang. In this manner, he turned away from the window just enough to catch sight of three visitors he'd certainly never expected to see standing in his empty pantry instead of the strongchests of provisions whose arrival he was expecting.

He blinked, rocked back to face the window while singing the next line, then turned again to frown at the pantry—perhaps in hopes the three were some sort of momentary mind-dream or the result of recently emptying the bottle he now plucked up from the sink to glare at.

The three figures did not go away—even after he spat the gooey remnants of almond-buttered bread at them in sudden fear and mortification, following these offerings with a roared, "How by all the Seven feldurking Sisters did *you* get here?"

"Magic," Elminster replied brightly with the broadest of impish grins.

Vangerdahast's eyes blazed. He flung bread in one direction and knife in the other, letting the empty wine bottle crash back down into the sink. In the next motion he raised trembling arms and took a step toward the Old Mage as if he were going to try to strangle Elminster. At last he let his arms fall, looked from the tip of Myrmeen Lhal's now-drawn sword, which came equipped with the face of the High Lady of Arabel glowering at him over it, to the frozen and disapproving face of Caladnei, the lass he'd picked to succeed him as Mage Royal . . . and shrank visibly, letting out his breath in a sigh.

Vangerdahast shook his head as if to clear it, crossed his arms across his chest to glare at all three of them as if they were common thieves he'd caught publicly in a personally embarrassing act, and growled, "This should *not* be possible. You arrived right atop my most powerful teleport trap and somehow bulled through it. You three should right now be standing bewildered in three separate and very distant spots on Toril. Far enough away to win me some time to myself, I *had* every reason to hope."

Elminster smiled again. "Remember, old friend, 'tis by Mystra's will such things work . . . and I myself continue to live and, ah, work by the same pleasure and divine power."

Vangerdahast shook his head in clear displeasure, and turned away. "You shouldn't have come here. You shouldn't be here now. I've retired from all the fawning and smiling and doing what's expected. My time is now my own."

"Very well spent, I see," Myrmeen said tartly.

The former Royal Magician rounded on her. "You, miss, would do better to hold and keep Arabel for the Crown, for a change! If you weren't so determined to out-swagger and out-swordswash every man in the realm, like a pale echo of proud little Alusair, perhaps you'd've settled down to being a very useful governor instead of governing one man at a time in your bedchamber! I—"

"My Lord *Vangerdahast!*" Caladnei snapped. "*No one* should speak so to any officer of the realm—nor to any lady! You—you disgust me! Your words lead me to wonder what were you really thinking about me when you praised me and named me your successor! 'Oh, here's some brown-skinned trollop who'll bed more noblemen than I could bring myself to do'?"

"*You be still,* little miss!" Vangerdahast roared, eyes catching fire. "I've had about enough—"

"So have I," Elminster announced pleasantly. "Ye used to be far more deft and sly in picking fights and making folk lose their tempers and forget their intentions, Vangey. Ye're losing it, ye are. Wherefore I'm going to be just as unpleasant to ye as ye've been to thy fellow folk of Cormyr for—oh, some six decades now, hey?"

He took a step forward, not appearing to cast any spell or awaken any ring, rod, wand, or gewgaw—but Vangerdahast floated up off the floor and hung rigid, limbs unmoving. "Now, speak. Unfold what ye're really up to here. Mystra wanted me to be a trifle more subtle about this, I'm sure, but I find myself not in the mood to be nearly so gentle with ye. Ye tried to enrage these two ladies so as to put their minds aside from prying some answers out of ye. Why?"

"I—I don't want to talk about what I'm at work on to . . . either of these two ladies," Vangerdahast replied gruffly, "whom I'm both sorry to have offended. I—no, I cannot. Caladnei and Myrmeen, forgive me, but your presence here ruins and reveals everything. I can't be honest with you. I daren't."

"Nay, Vangerdahast," Elminster said calmly, "Ye dare *not* fail to tell all and truly to these two: the Mage Royal of the realm, remember, and an officer of the Crown to bear witness."

"You are no longer my teacher, El," Vangerdahast said coldly. "I need no more of your lessons on obedience or moral authority. I would judge, as many in Faerûn do, that your own actions disqualify you from criticizing anyone else in this world on such matters."

"Vangey," Elminster replied gently, "I'm not asking ye. I'm telling ye."

He took another step forward and added, "We both fell into the 'might makes right, and I know this is right anyway, so just hold still whilst I do it to ye' trap long, long ago . . . and I daresay we've both found it easiest to remain there. I'm still there now. Ye *will* answer me."

"I will *not*," Vangerdahast snarled. "I—I . . ."

"Am disgusted with how cruel and tyrannical I can be?" Elminster asked, his voice almost a whisper. "So am I, old friend. So am I. Yet I long ago cast my lot with Mystra, and do what she needs me to do. Yet I've not yet reached the point of being so disgusted that I refuse to do it and defy her."

The Old Mage was aware of the two women backing instinctively away from him, awe warring with apprehension on their faces. "And like ye," he went on, his eyes never leaving those of his onetime pupil, "I feel the talons of time clawing at me at last. Like ye, I know not how much time I have left—but I know enough to feel 'tis not much any longer. So like ye, this drives me to do all I want to do, as swiftly as I can—and be damned to all these younger fools who stand in my way. I know *just* how ye feel, Vangey. Believe me."

He lifted one open hand, as if offering something invisible to the empty air. "So now, I'm going to ruthlessly compel ye—quite rudely, but 'tis necessary and this way 'twill at least be swift."

Vangerdahast glared at him, shuddering and going redfaced as he fought the invisible bonds of Elminster's magic. At last he barked out brief, wordless frustration and gave up, to slump and hang limply in midair. "Ask your questions," he said bitterly.

"I'm sorry, Vangerdahast," the Old Mage told him. "First then, precisely what creatures are you planning to bind, with these secret spells you're crafting?"

"*What* secret spel—"

"*Truth*, Vangey. The truth, if ye can still remember what that is after so many years at Court," Elminster ordered, his voice calm but implacable.

Vangerdahast glared at him then snapped, "Dragons. Neutral or benevolent dragonkind."

Both Caladnei and Myrmeen drew in breath so sharply that they almost gasped—but said nothing, their eyes burning at Vangerdahast. So it was true!

Elminster spared them not a glance. "Willingly or unwillingly bound?"

The former Royal Magician seemed to shrink, dwindling in the air. "Willingly, if possible," he murmured.

"To awaken at what triggers?"

"When called."

Elminster acquired a sour look. "Vangey," he murmured, "are we going to have to do this by dragging every last word out of ye like so many hooked sea-beasts being hauled ashore? No one in this room thinks ye're anything less than Cormyr's savior and staunch defender, the backbone of the realm. We *admire* thy intended legacy—so why not discuss it freely? None of us three wants to see Cormyr overrun by Red Wizards and Zhentarim—among many others—hunting for ye or for thy spells, so we're hardly likely to pass on what we hear to anyone else. I'll even mindshield these two ladies, if they desire it, so anyone who tries to read their thoughts or memories will get blasted by magic that should leave that anyone drooling-witless for a day or so. So why not just speak freely? Hey?"

Vangerdahast closed his eyes, sighed, and said, "Very well. I intend that the guardian wyrms will be awakened by any being who utters the right words of summoning. For the words to work, the speaker will have to find and stand in the active area of the right portal—there should be at least two 'right portals' per dragon—while holding an item of the correct substance."

"And that substance is?"

"I know not, yet. Most probably a particular sort of gem-stone. I haven't yet decided on that part of it. I'm leaning toward establishing two allowable substances in all cases, either one of which will 'work.' Of course, 'tis best if such substances will last down the years."

"Of course. Under what orders will these bound guardians operate when awakened?"

The former Royal Magician cast a quick glance at Caladnei—and just as quickly averted his eyes from her furious stare. "To defend and preserve the realm," he replied, almost sighing the words, "its government, and those of its folk who stand loyal. To strike at foes of the realm the guardian identifies or that are pointed out to it by its summoner and other beings it comes to trust."

"*It* comes to trust?"

"In the end, all things come down to trust," Vangey muttered quietly, looking at the floor. "They always do."

One of the two women drew in her breath sharply again, swallowing a tremulous sob that sounded the width of a sharp sword blade away from bursting forth as furious words.

Elminster smiled a mirthless smile, glanced at the two ladies—Myrmeen standing watchfully, sword out, ready to menace either of the two wizards, and Caladnei seething, her face white and her hands clenched around a chairback so tightly that it almost seemed her grip would crush the wood—and asked, "Whom would the guardians obey? Whom would they ally or cooperate with?"

"Their summoner would be their commander," Vangerdahast replied, "but they'd be freed of obedience to that being, instantly and forever, if ordered to harm any member of the Obarskyr ruling family, any castle or fortification of Cormyr, and . . . other conditions not yet specified."

"Left free for you to amend at any time?" Caladnei snapped.

The floating wizard kept silent for a moment, but before Elminster could order him to answer, he said heavily, "No. I . . . I'd not yet decided how long and precise a list of commands, and qualifications to those orders, to place upon the guardians."

"And if an Obarskyr threatens the realm?" the Mage Royal asked sharply. "What then?"

Vangerdahast turned his head to look at Caladnei. "I've been wrestling with that very concern for some months now, on and off, but still see no clear, correct conclusion."

Caladnei seemed about to say more—if her trembling was any indication, something intemperate—but instead waved a furiously dismissive hand and turned her face away.

"While in stasis," Elminster continued, as quietly and calmly as if Caladnei had never spoken, "these bound guardians will be kept where?"

"In an extra-dimensional space anchored to at least seven portals around Cormyr, only two of which will be made known to anyone but me," Vangerdahast replied promptly.

"Who'll know the location of their abiding?"

"No one, if I can keep it so."

Elminster nodded, took a step back, and let his former pupil descend a little. "How are the wyrms protected when in stasis?"

What might have been a smile touched Vangerdahast's lips for a moment. "Not at all, given how far my spells have progressed, thus far. Protections are something I must craft, however, if this scheme is to work at all."

Elminster nodded again. "Once loosed to serve, do the guardians return to their bindings?"

"No," Vangey replied reluctantly. "They'd be free, though someone who knew just which spells to cast could bind them again. The process will be lengthy and require the immediate presence of the guardian to be bound, so the dragon would have to be either subdued in some way . . . or willing to re-enter stasis."

"Mystra! Murderous mothering *Mystra!*" Caladnei shouted, boiling over at last. "Mage, I am appalled! Revolted! Disgusted at this treasonous betrayal of the kingdom we both love! How *could* you? After serving and stitching together this realm through years of strife and dire doom, you set forth to shatter it out of pure pride? O'erweening folly?"

"Oho," Elminster murmured. "Nice phrase."

The Mage Royal stalked past him to plant herself right under Vangerdahast's lined and unhappy face and shake a furious fist up at it. "I'm aghast that a Royal Magician of the realm—for you're still that, whether you wear the title or not—could play such a dangerous fool by contemplating forging this blade to strike at the very heart of Cormyr!

And to plot this without telling anyone—using *me* as your dupe!"

"Lass," the floating wizard told her sadly, "the very strength of this blade is its secrecy and always has been." He lifted his head, his voice growing stronger, and added, "You are the realm's hope and the realm's future, and I believe I chose rightly. Yet you're but young at this. In what is needful for Cormyr *I* know best, better than any man, maid, or beast living—like it or not."

Caladnei's mouth dropped open in astonishment, her jaw working in rage as she struggled through blazing fury to find the right words to hurl at him, and Vangerdahast gave her a wintry smile and said, "I'll admit this much, Cala: I've often hated what I've had to do in service to the kingdom . . . and what those doings have in turn done to me, down the years."

The Mage Royal stood with fists clenched at her sides, spitting and almost weeping in rage. "You—you! You! There—no—how . . ."

A long finger stroked gently down her cheek—and she spun around in surprise, eyes blazing and hands racing to shape a spell . . . only to freeze in mid-gesture as she found herself looking into the face of Elminster of Shadowdale. It was wearing a kindly expression.

"Easy, lass," he murmured. "Easy, now. Ye're right to be royally angered at being kept uninformed, but imagine now that the future of Cormyr depends upon thy wits and judgment being icily cool and calm, in the moments ahead . . . for—behold!—it does. Stop raging and show the same iron control that Alusair can manage for almost two breaths in a row when she has to . . . and hear me."

Caladnei was panting hard, eyes blazing at him, but she flung up her hands in an 'all right' flourish. Behind her, Myrmeen—who'd acquired a grim smile at El's mention of Alusair's self control—gave the Old Mage a nod and grounded her sword.

Elminster took hold of Caladnei's shoulders, facing her

squarely, and said, "There *is* some merit in the words Vangey's just spoken to ye, Mage Royal. No matter how much ye may personally dislike hearing so."

"Well, *you'd* think so!" Caladnei spat. "You've done just what he has—for centuries! High-handed, secretive, manipulative, deceitful—in every wise *precisely* the same way as this sly old *dog* here!"

Elminster smiled and clapped her shoulders cheerfully. "Of *course* I have! Ye strike right to the truth, exactly! If ye survive to serve Mystra for as long as I've done, ye'll probably behave in much the same way, too!"

"This is not," the Mage Royal hissed through clenched teeth, "any sort of laughing matter! And don't throw me glib words about Mystra's service driving you past sanity, either! If you can hurl 'right' and 'merit' and little judgments all over the place, you must admit to retaining the capacity to judge!"

Elminster smiled and embraced her, holding on like an imperviously smiling wraith through the storm of kicks and thrown elbows and raking fingernails and upthrust knees that followed. Through it all he crooned, like a favorite uncle to a small girl, "There, there. Let thy rage flow . . . let it out, there's a good lass. But ye can be so much more than that. Ye can be a good Mage Royal, too! For a *good* Mage Royal, now fully informed of Vangerdahast's secret scheme and thus warned, shouldn't waste more time tarrying here to rant and shout—when the daily crises of the kingdom face her uncaring back."

He let go of her and stepped back—a trifle hastily. Caladnei glared at him, bosom heaving, then set her jaw and said stonily, "Yes, you *are* right, Old Mage. So long as you make sure I'm not blocked or barred from reaching this place by spells, I should now take my leave, to consider and find calm, and look ahead."

She turned and shot a meaningful look at Myrmeen Lhal. Only Elminster had seen the grin that played along the mouth of the Lady Lord of Arabel moments before. There

was no trace of it now as Myrmeen nodded as if in reply
to an order, stepped forward to give both Elminster and
Vangerdahast level looks, and announced firmly, "I shall be
staying, for the good of the realm, to keep watch over Vangerdahast, here. Elminster, please set him down on his feet
again—and I must insist that you do one thing more for me:
Lay spell protections on me to keep me from being magically mind-meddled with by semi-retired Mages Royal."

Elminster smiled. "Of course."

In the background, Vangerdahast's sputtered protests
were firmly ignored. The Old Mage spread his hands and
took a long step toward Myrmeen—and an opaque shield
faded into existence out of nowhere to enclose them both.

Vangerdahast slammed to the ground as if he'd been
dropped off the end of a cart. Wincing and limping, he
approached the shield—only to come to a dead halt as Caladnei strode around its curve to stand in his path, two wands
raised in her hands and a cold, hard look in her eyes.

"Go ahead," she murmured grimly. "Take that next
step—and we'll both regret the battle that follows. If I must
die to defend Cormyr from the man who made her great, I'll
do so. If you wanted a spineless lap-slave, Vangerdahast, *you
shouldn't have chosen me.*"

"I wanted nothing of the kind and still do not," the
former Royal Magician growled. "But—but what's he up to,
in there?"

"Enspelling Myrmeen and her weapons, if he's thinking
anything like I am," Caladnei replied tartly. "You'll have to
do a lot to win back our trust, old man."

"Lass, lass," Elminster chided from behind her. "I'm going
to have to take ye away forthwith before ye can find anything
else cold and hurtful to say to the man who did ye such
honor by choosing ye."

Caladnei whirled around, but a grinning Elminster laid a
hand on her arm before she could say a word—and, just like
that, there was suddenly one less Mage Royal of Cormyr and
one less Chosen of Mystra in the littered kitchen.

Across suddenly empty space, Vangerdahast and Myrmeen stood gazing at each other.

Coldly he looked her up and down, from her drawn
sword to her patched and battered leathers, and a slow sneer
crawled across his face.

Myrmeen surveyed him from head to toe with raised eyebrows, shook her head, gave Vangerdahast a derisive grin,
and strode right past him.

"Don't *touch* anything," the wizard snarled, whirling
around to see where she went and what she did.

Which was three paces away, to stand with hands on
hips and slowly turn to witheringly survey the state of his
kitchen.

Swiveling slowly around to face him, the Lady Lord of
Arabel wrinkled her nose. "Is *this* what you've been eating?
No wonder your wits are so addled!"

Twelve

DRAGONFIRE

Come storms, great waves, earth-cleaving, god-smiting lightnings, and dragonfire, Faerûn shall abide. Us smaller creatures on it? I'm not so sure.

The character Blind Nars
in Scene the Second
of the play *Four Bloody Swords*
by Corsour Hamadder of Waterdeep
first performed in the Year of the Nightmaidens

The torches were guttering out now, one by one, leaving the great soaring hall of Haelithtorntowers noticeably darker. Two long-frozen figures in leather moved in sudden unison, both drawing back cautiously from the balcony rail—and lifting their heads to regard each other.

Narnra Shalace did not give her pursuer her usual angry glare. Like Rhauligan, she knew unfolding treason and disaster when she heard it. This was the sort of softly menacing talk she was sure went on inside the spires of the wealthy and nobility of Waterdeep all the time—though she'd never been foolish enough to try to enter and lurk in such places, with their alarm-magics, wardings, and enthusiastic guards.

No wonder nobles didn't want anyone close enough to hear what they were saying. Caethur the moneylender would have had to double-deal for years to reach the point of openly plotting ambitions like these.

She stared almost thoughtfully across the ring of emptiness at Rhauligan, knowing that she'd just gained one more reason to elude the Harper without being seen by others in this house. A very good reason.

Keeping herself alive at least a few nights longer.

* * * * *

It was a bright and breezy morning in Candlekeep. The sea-breeze blowing ashore could better have been called a strong wind. In front of the Lady Nouméa Cardellith, as she walked the last stretch of the Way of the Lion, the banners of a minor noble of Tethyr flapped and streamed in a constant fury. The rearguard of that personage—six riders in gleaming armor who rode with great spiked long-axes gripped in their gauntlets—were eyeing Nouméa narrowly, at least two of them always crossing to opposing sides of the noble party so as to keep full watch on her.

And no wonder. Through the wonders of magic Nouméa may have looked like a lone, bespectacled male merchant from Lantan, afoot and bearing only a leather carrysack slung over one shoulder—but she'd arrived out of nowhere, just suddenly *there*, in mid-step. And Tethyrian house guards who hadn't seen teleport spells in use before had certainly heard of them—and knew well enough to be wary in the presence of what must be an accomplished wizard or sorcerer.

Or something worse.

Wherefore they turned to present Nouméa with a leveled row of glittering spike-points when the party reached

Candlekeep proper and stopped to parley with the monks of the gate.

Nouméa came to a halt, nodded to them politely, and waited calmly enough. When it was her turn at the tall gates—spell-shrouded vertical bars as thick as her forearm, bearing the castle-and-flames device of Candlekeep and a guard of five purple-robed priests—she gave the expressionless monk who approached her a book from her sack and waited while he carefully stripped away its wrappings.

"The Life of the Sembian Woodworm," he read aloud, his voice devoid of judgment. With gentle fingers he opened the tome, glanced at a few pages, stopped to peer at what were unmistakably the glyphs of spells—minor wardings effective also against paper-worms, he noted with an audible sigh of excitement—then looked up and said, "A notable, valuable gift. You are most welcome within our walls, seeker of wisdom. What's your name, your land, and your intent within?"

"I am Roablar of Lantan, come from trading up and down the Sword Coast and most recently Sembia to examine certain texts. I'm most interested in Thelgul's *Do Metals Live?* and *Bracetar's Notes On Preservation of Foodstuffs and Oils.*"

The monk smiled for the first time. It transformed his face, leaving Nouméa with the impression that it was not an expression he assumed often. "Be welcome here, Roablar, so long as you treat books with the reverence they deserve, eschewing fire, damp, the torn page, and the removal of lore from the eyes of others. Cross the yard ahead of you to the green-hued door, and give your name to the Keeper of the Emerald Door. You'll be provided with food, a bath, quarters in which to sleep, and a moot with the monk who will escort you on your first visit to the rooms of the tomes."

"I thank you, sir," Roablar replied, bowing slightly and favoring all the monks with a beaming smile. He was waved in through the gap in the partly open gates and set off across the courtyard shifting his sack on his shoulder, as all travelers do.

"Well, Amanther?" the monk who'd dealt with him asked, glancing at the next supplicants—a large party of horsemen, still some way off down the Way of the Lion.

The oldest, tallest monk of the five smiled faintly. "A mage—human female, not old—wearing a very good spell-spun disguise. I daresay the books she mentioned are already familiar to her; I doubt she needs to peruse them again. Slyly learning spells is of course the aim of most who enter covertly, but she feels different to me, somehow. She'll bear close watching."

The other monks nodded. "Thaerabho already answers your signal," one of them said, pointing at a monk strolling across the courtyard to casually follow Roablar of Lantan up to the Emerald Door.

"Good," another grinned, rubbing his hands. "A new mystery to dissect at table this night. One can never have enough delving and prying. It keeps the soul young."

"A tongue more deft, Larth," Amanther admonished. "Say rather: Inquiry into all things keeps a mind bright."

"That too," Larth agreed with a chuckle, which was echoed by the other monks.

"Well, then, clever dissembler," Amanther said, waving at the approaching cloud of dust and sun-flashing armor. "Deal you with these next seekers!"

"With as much pleasure as humility," Larth replied cheerfully. "I'll wager they'll proffer a family history or perhaps a text on the genealogy or heraldry of their immediate region."

"Nay," said another monk, squinting at the banners. "I expect another copy of Navril's *History of the Parsnip*, with some obscure local collection of plays or minstrels' sayings to serve as their entrance-gift when we reject old Navril one more time."

The chorus of chuckles was hearty but brief, for it was not proper for monks of Candlekeep to be anything less than politely grave when first greeting supplicants.

Across the Court of Air, the monk Thaerabho gazed at the shoulders of the Lantanna talking to the doorkeeper and had to suppress an urge to stop, cross his arms, and rub his chin in eager anticipation.

This was going to be one of the interesting deceivers. He could feel it.

* * * * *

Lady Joysil Ambrur stood sipping wine and watching her servants reluctantly depart. Before ringing for them, she'd downed an entire bottle of potent vintage without any apparent effects at all and begun a second by the rather daintier means of filling (and refilling) her tallglass. Though she still stood by her high-backed seat behind the table, a new piece of furniture had made its appearance, in accordance with her orders, in the hall nearby: a broad, simple bed covered with luxurious linens, cozy-blankets, and pillows. Though it lacked a high headboard carved with her coat-of-arms, it was a bed for her.

Silence deepened in Haelithtorntowers around Lady Joysil as she sipped, regarding the rubies on the table—which lay undisturbed in their own little oval of light dust in the only part of the table that (again at her orders) had not been cleared and dusted.

The Lady of Haelithtorntowers was wearing a slight smile. She'd also ordered all the servants to take a day off from their duties, and the night to follow, in the luxurious guest apartments in the farthest tower of her mansion, Firewyrm Tower. They were not to disturb her or return until the next dawn for any reason.

Their obedience had been doubtful—wherefore, after their going, the Lady Ambrur had taken a scepter from the hollow leg of a particular piece of furniture and magically sealed the door that walled off the lone passage linking Firewyrm Tower to Great Tower.

At the heart of Great Tower was the hall in which she stood, and as the torches failed it was rapidly growing dark despite the brightening day outside. Appropriate for a weary noble lady taking to her bed alone—and Lady Ambrur did that now.

She took her glass and bottle with her, still showing no signs of being tipsy, and retained all her garments, from her jeweled slippers and glittering tiara to her rows of sparkling dangledrop earrings. In the deepening gloom she kept her eyes on the table and sat on the edge of her bed in calm silence, waiting.

Quite soon and suddenly ruby fire flashed from the gems—and four black-clad men appeared on the table above those stones, crouching with weapons ready as it groaned ominously under their weight.

Joysil daintily climbed up to stand in the center of her bed, spilling not a drop of wine—and as she did so, soft white-and-green radiance blossomed in the air around her, illuminating her bed, the table, and all points between.

"Greetings, unknown guests," she said calmly. "I didn't think your master would wait until nightfall. Red Wizards are *so* impatient."

The four hooded men in battle-leathers stiffened, beholding the calm noblewoman. She was tall, large-boned, and lush of figure in her magnificent gown, and a spectacular flood of slightly wavy, honey-hued hair descended her back, to that point where a back begins to swell out and become a behind. The nether tips of her tresses deepened to a coppery flame-hue. The calm eyes surveying her visitors were steel-gray, the slightest of age-wrinkles lurking at their corners. She held her goblet-sized tallglass in one hand—and a wand had now somehow appeared in the other.

The four snarled silently and hurled the daggers they held. The flashing steel spinning through the air bore vivid crazings of purple that cried "Poison!" to any astute observer.

They did not have to throw far, and their target showed

no signs of movement, but the whirling knives vanished a handspan from the Lady Ambrur.

A bare breath later, two of the men in black grunted, gasped, and pitched forward from the table, to crash down through a chair to the floor, and lie unmoving. Their own daggers stood out of their backs. Another knife spun past the ear of the man who'd hurled it and back toward the noblewoman again—only to vanish as before, snatched by the loop teleport she'd cast, and reappear behind its hurler again, sinking and spinning more slowly.

No one watched its next journey. The remaining pair of slayers burst forward from the table, racing to the attack. The Lady Ambrur's only reaction was to take another sip of wine.

One of her attackers plucked blades from all over his clothing as he came, snatching and hurling a storm of steel. Daggers bit at empty air, spinning over the bed to clatter and slide on the floor of the great hall—for the Lady Ambrur all of a sudden wasn't there.

She appeared by the table, glass still raised to her lips, and coolly triggered her wand. Its silvery beam lashed out to become a crimson blast of exploding head and brains where it touched the slayer who hadn't yet lightened his load of weaponry.

Headless and staggering, that black-garbed corpse wobbled forward to a loose-limbed collapse onto the floor.

The surviving slayer whirled with a snarl—and sprang aside as the wand fired again, leaping and rolling free of harm.

Swift and agile, he launched himself into an attack that dodged this way and that, avoiding another wand-blast. Like the wind he raced forward, to bring himself within reach of the noblewoman—

—Who blinked away once more. The black-hooded slayer did not freeze but kept running and dodging as he looked for her, and that saved him from the next bite of her wand, which blew apart a large wyrmtongue-leaf plant with its urn as he darted aside.

The wand spat again, striking aside a dagger he'd hurled in a flash of sparks. Tasmurand the Slayer put his entire shoulder and balance into another swift throw, right behind that first fang.

His reward was a burst of silver sparks. Lady Ambrur gave him a nod and a smile as she let the ruined wand tumble from her hand. She saluted him with her nearly empty tallglass and . . . blinked into nothingness again.

She reappeared on a landing of the ornate stair that swept up from beside the high table, linking the vast floor of the hall with—he glanced up—a promenade balcony that encircled the entire chamber high above where he stood.

"Shall we dance?" she asked archly, for all Faerûn as if she was the hunter and not the hunted. With a snarl Tasmurand leaped for the steps, still dodging and darting in case she snatched out another wand and sprayed the stair.

Lady Ambrur worked a spell instead, performing the gestures with flourishes like a cat at play. It bathed her slayer in purple flame when he was still four running strides from putting his blade through her.

Tasmurand roared in fear and frantic effort—but no pain came, and nothing seemed to happen except . . . she vanished again, leaving him rushing onto an empty landing. He slashed furiously at the empty air anyway, cleaving nothing with raging speed.

"I'm up here," she called pleasantly, as if guiding a guest who was a long-established friend, and the slayer looked up again to see the noblewoman smiling down at him over the balcony rail. He set his teeth and sprinted up the second flight of steps because it was all he could do, really. Tasmurand gasped for air as he sped upward, wondering fearfully what that purple glow magic had been and when he'd feel its effects.

The Lady of Haelithtorntowers watched his approach calmly, relaxing so far as to cross her arms on the balcony rail and lean forward to watch, like a Marsemban lass appraising the sweaty brawn of stripped-to-the-waist dock-loaders at work.

To Joysil's eyes, her last spell had worked just fine. Right now it was telling her that her visitor bore precisely three enchantments upon his person: two on daggers—one at belt, one in right boot—and a third within a metal vial inside his left boot. Almost certainly a potion of healing.

Fair enough. Unhurriedly Joysil Ambrur twisted one of the rings she wore and let its power sing out to enshroud her in a protective shield that could be heard—as the faint, high-pitched singing continued—more than it could be seen. She shifted around to sit at ease on and along the rail, bringing a shapely leg up and lounging back on one arm like an avid lass seeking to lure suitors, tossing her head to let her long hair tumble free.

Tasmurand's eyes widened at such craziness, but he neither hesitated nor slowed. Breathlessly, he reached the stair-head and burst onto the balcony, running hard around its promenade. Daggers flashed as he snatched them from their sheaths, never slowing as he bore down on the smiling lady.

He threw the first at just the right moment to spoil any spell she might be waiting to complete until his arrival—and she unconcernedly threw herself to one side, letting the dagger flash past . . . and pitching herself over the rail!

It would be a killing fall to the floor of the great chamber, but no doubt she'd magically whisk herself elsewhere again, ere striking the smooth stone below.

But no! The Lady Ambrur flung out her other hand to grasp the bottom of the rail as if frantically trying to catch herself from falling—but used that grip only to swing herself upright in the air . . . ere she let go and dropped.

Slowly, drifting down in a slow, gentle sinking that did not even lift the hem of her skirts.

Tasmurand's mouth tightened. Was the woman such a fool as to trust in a feather fall magic? Did she think he'd run out of blades yet? He flung a dagger at her throat, which if she went on gently descending would mean her mouth met it upon its arrival. It struck something unseen in the air before her flesh and clanged to one side, tumbling harmlessly away down to the floor below.

With a growl he plucked forth one of his enchanted daggers. The spell this one carried was designed for just one thing: to shatter wardings, shield spells, and similar barriers. An instant after it left his hand, another—non-magical—dagger followed it, so that when the first stripped away her defenses, the second would sink home in her breast. Done. He'd shortly be looking at the corpse of just one more noble who trusted overmuch in her expensive toys.

Tasmurand's hand was already on the hilt of his last enspelled dagger, just in case. This woman was, after all, in her home and seemed not fearful at all, though they'd been assured she was alone and no sort of mage nor sorcerer.

She'd been lucky thus far, that was all. Yes, nimble and overtrusting in her little tricks, possibly wearing yet another ring that commanded some minor magic or other. Tasmurand started back toward the stair he'd ascended, weaving from side to side of the deserted balcony and varying his pace out of sheer habit. If he could get down to the floor before she did and snatch down one of those tapestries, he could swing it beneath her and then jerk her from her feet and drag her helplessly to beneath his pounce—just one dagger-thrust would do such a one as this, if he could drive it home where he wanted . . .

There was a sudden shuddering of the air, a building thunder that shook his run into an unsteady sidestep and sent the smoking torches flaring back into last flames of life. In their sudden, bright tongues a silver-blue, scaled wall seemed to soar past his gaze, expanding up and out into—

Tasmurand the Slayer gaped up at the most splendid sight of his life—and his last.

Filling the great height of the hall above him was a slim, lithe dragon—if something the size of a Marsemban tall-house could be said to be slim. Most of that bulk was two great, batlike wings, spread in a great V-shape that raked sharply back to end in the curling tail they were rooted in, all down their lengths. Muscles akin to those of a great cat shifted under iridescent silver-blue scales as talons spread wide in the air, a long neck snaked down, and eyes of glowing turquoise gazed at Tasmurand the Slayer as if they could pierce his leathers and see him naked.

Above those deep, riveting eyes the dragon's head swept back in two great horns, and below them two cheek fins flared forth. Spiky, membranous "beards" beneath these fins quivered as the great jaws parted—and a great, glowing cloud of gas gushed forth, sweeping over Tasmurand with force enough to pluck him from his feet and hurl him back against the wall. He screamed, or thought he did, but the spicy, flickering gas was alive with darting, swirling bolts of lightning, so cold and yet so fiercely hot as they stabbed through and through him . . . the smell of his own cooked and blackening flesh like roast boar as darkness crowded in, his eyeballs sizzled, and he realized he could move nothing . . . had nothing left of his limbs to move anyway, as his fading, failing vision showed him crisped fingers crumbling away . . .

A blackened torso fell to the balcony, trailing thin plumes of smoke, and the cause of its owner's death towered over it.

"Tell the gods," a great hissing voice informed the ears that were no longer there to hear anything, "that you were slain by Ammaratha Cyndusk, a foolish dragon—but one not nearly so foolish as the humans who thought to slay her."

Thirteen

BUSINESS MEETINGS, BATHS,
AND SUBVERSIONS

*Looking back over all the years, I can't decide just which
memories are most important to me: the slayings, the
midnight meetings of plotting treasons and rule over all
the Realms, the few fumbling moments of lovemaking, or
the even fewer really hot, uninterrupted, contented baths.
I can still recall the little floating dragon bathtoy my aunt
gifted me with, one spring. . . .*

Thamdarl "the Wizard Unseen"
From *Tyrant's Throne to the Arms of a Goddess:
My Road To Mystra*
Year of the Broken Blade

The carpet was as soft as tomb-moss under her boots. The
tomb-moss of the City of the Dead . . . which was right where
Narnra Shalace would end up, or at least in the Marsemban
equivalent—one of the canals for all she knew!—if she didn't
get clean away from here.

By Mask and Tymora, of all the deadly foolish mistakes

. . . literally leaping into this unknown mansion, full of
nobles plotting treason and lady mages who spoke so casually of shattering spells laid covertly by others who'd just
left . . . or had they really left?

Flaming fury of Mask! She *had* to get away from here,
had to . . .

Narnra went down that dark and unfamiliar passage like
a racing wind, as stealthily as she could at full run, trusting in its straight, uncluttered path to keep from crashing
into anything. Statuettes and plants on marble pedestals
occurred often on both sides, but the central rug stretched
out clear and arrow-straight, on into the darkness, on to . . .
an ending.

The wall ahead was adorned with a huge statue, pale
white and gleaming. An elf female standing amid sculpted
ferns like a queen—if, that is, queens went outside wearing
nothing but their crowns and haughty expressions—with
various naked male elves entwined around her legs and
torso, long whipswords in their hands. Their faces, like
hers, stared endlessly down the passage in eternal challenge. To either side of this great carved group of elvenkind
was a closed door. Narnra drew in a deep breath and without hesitation opened the one to her right as quietly as she
could. It opened into—darkness, and steps leading down.
Thank you, gods!

As she crept down the unseen steps in a crouch, fingertips brushing one wall, Narnra shook her head. A Red Wizard
conspiring against the Crown of Cormyr with this Lady
Ambrur! Oh, there must be folk in Suzail who'd pay well to
learn about this! Why—

Something caught hold of Narnra's throat and slammed
her back against the wall. It was a hand, reaching brutal and
unseen out of the darkness below her—and a second hand
dug brutal fingers into her elbows and slammed them against
the wall too, one after the other, leaving her arms all fiery
numbness.

She couldn't snatch at her daggers, couldn't . . . The hands were at her throat and the scruff of her neck, now, dragging her leathers up in a grip that left her whistling and struggling for air.

"You, my little hare with long teeth," the voice of Glarasteer Rhauligan muttered in her ear, "are coming with me."

Narnra's head swam, and she struggled weakly as deeper darkness crept in . . . but the fingers never loosened.

* * * * *

The heavy, jarring fall woke her. She was hooded in something that smelled of sweaty man and jolted on Rhauligan's shoulders. The Harper grunted under Narnra's weight, stifled a curse then added in a curt whisper, "Sorry."

Apologizing? To me? A bit late, you bastard!

He broke into a run, hard and swift, bouncing and bruising her but somehow keeping his balance. His boots were on cobbles, now, with the sounds of Marsember all around. More echoes, the distant rumble of cartwheels, some chatter, and a growing din.

Rhauligan carried her into somewhere quieter that stank of dung, rotting fish, and other decaying things, turned a few corners, scraped her boots once against stone, and set Narnra down on what felt—and groaned—like a rickety wooden cart.

She sat still as he fastened something around her neck then set her on her feet and kicked away the cart. Its wheels set up a protesting squeal that ended in a crash of wood against stone. Narnra heard the familiar sound of a rat scuttling through refuse.

His hands were at a buckle, and . . . she was unhooded and blinking in the sudden light of day, gasping as none-too-fresh air was hers once more for the taking. Rhauligan shook out the hood, which proved to be a vest. His vest.

Narnra drew in deep breaths, looking around. She was in a garbage-strewn Marsemban alley, hobbled and with her thumbs and fingers wired together behind her back . . . and the cord around her waist and thighs led up to—she turned, lifting her head to look, and discovered she wore a choke-leash—the underside of a rusty iron outer staircase. The leash led there, too. It looked like the back stair of a warehouse that saw little use but presented an unfriendly, rotting fortress face to Faerûn anyway.

Rhauligan, of course, stood not far away—but out of any possible reach, no matter how furiously she might try to strangle herself reaching him.

"Important folk seem very interested in you," he said thoughtfully as their eyes met. "I wonder why."

Narnra shrugged at him through her tangled hair. "I know not," she snapped, "but I do know that I'm not yours nor your Mage Royal's to take and confine like some sort of pet or bauble—just as I was not Elminster's to give!"

"I can scarce believe, she-thief, that you've not yet learned that if anyone can do a thing to you, they've the right to do it—if they stand for law, and you do not."

Rhauligan cast quick glances up and down the deserted, refuse-heaped alley and added, "Brutal, yes, but outlanders like you who deal with the Lady Ambrur are buyers and sellers of information . . . and the whereabouts and doings of Vangerdahast is information that could make you very rich and doom Cormyr at the same stroke. Had the Mage Royal not commanded your capture, I'd be slaying you now, not bandying words with you. I dislike slaying young lasses, but if I must choose between spilling the blood of just one of them and saving a bright realm full of them, my choice is clear."

Narnra glared at him, straining against the wires until her fingers burned, and spat, "So you can sell the information yourself, no doubt, or we'd not be in this alley. *I* know Waterdeep, not Cormyr. I couldn't even find my way to a gate out of this city unless you let me search for a bit. Who'm I going to sell anything to? And how'm I supposed to know anything useful to sell to a realm full of folk I don't even *know?*"

Rhauligan's only reply was a wordless, crooked smile.

"So what's going to happen to me now?" she snarled. "Why'm I here?"

"Business meeting," Rhauligan said, looking up and down the alley again. "Important business."

"With?" Narnra demanded, staring around at the deserted, garbage-heaped alley with a skeptical eyebrow arched.

A sensation broke over her then, a creeping and tingling quite unlike anything she'd ever felt before. It was energetic, swift . . . and magical.

Narnra tried to curse, but her tongue seemed huge and heavy, and her suddenly slack mouth not her own. She tried to toss her head and—with a sudden leap of fear—found herself still standing motionless, still gazing just where she'd been looking before.

The invisible, paralyzing force was streaming into her from off to her left, about six paces away . . . where a heap of trash suddenly shifted and rose up with a little grunt of effort, falling away untidily to reveal a woman in trim dark robes, a gentle but noble face, and long flowing auburn hair—one lock of which had gone white.

"With me, as it happens," the woman said gently but firmly. "I believe we've seen each other recently. I'm Laspeera of the War Wizards."

Narnra glared at her, or tried to. War Wizards again, she thought, and I can't even move my mouth to ask, or protest, or . . .

Laspeera cast a smiling glance at the Harper. "I'd like to hear what's so urgent that the smooth and urbane Glarasteer Rhauligan races across Marsember like an overeager dog, toting smart-tongued street thieves."

"So you shall," Rhauligan replied and began to pant rapidly, his tongue hanging out.

Laspeera gave him a look. "What's got into you?"

"Revealing my innermost overeager dog, Lady Mage," he replied brightly.

Laspeera sighed, waved one graceful hand, and murmured, "Get on with it, faithful hound. I grow no younger."

* * * * *

Lord Vangerdahast of Cormyr leaned back contentedly from the table. His stomach promptly rumbled, sounding every bit as contented as he was.

The plate on the table in front of him was empty of all but a few smears of sauce, though it had been heaped high with rabbit stew not so very long ago. Good sauce, that . . .

The former Royal Magician of the Realm reached for the plate, leaning forward with tongue extended to lick it clean—but a grinning Myrmeen Lhal reached in under his arm with the speed of a striking adder and plucked the plate away. Vangey's fingertips thumped down on bare tabletop, leaving him blinking . . . then turning with a growl.

"You can thank me whenever you remember your manners," the Lady Lord of Arabel said impishly, heading for the washbasins beside the sink.

Vangerdahast scowled at her, which caused her to lift an eyebrow reprovingly at him, over her shoulder.

Under the force of her disapproving gaze he sighed, waved his fingers as if to banish what he'd just done, and muttered, "Have my thanks, Myrmeen Lhal. You . . . surprise me. I thought you were merely the best of Alusair's mud-spattered, eager she-blades, determined to outfight and outsnap any man."

"Oh my, and here I thought you were just a manipulative wizard driven by whimsy, a hunger for power, and a love of being mysterious and rude to everyone in sight," Myrmeen replied merrily, hurling herself into Vangerdahast's favorite lounge chair.

She bounced once amid its overstuffed, highbacked, and rather shabby comfort—and bent to sniff, frowning in appraisal. Then she shot him a scowl of her own. "Don't you ever *wash* things? Gods' grief, man! The lice are leaping all over me!"

She sprang up, growling in irritation, and clawed at buckles and straps, rapidly shucking armor in all directions.

It was Vangerdahast's turn to rise hastily. "Now *don't* you start throwing your skin at me! I knew—"

"You hoped," Myrmeen replied witheringly, bared to the waist with a bundle of leather and chain and armor plate in her hands. Her dangling suspenders, Vangey noticed with some surprise, looked very much like his own.

"Now," she asked briskly, "where do you bathe? You *do* bathe, don't you?"

"Huh-hahem. Ah, down that passage," he said, pointing. "There's a pool. The, uh, stars above it are a spell that mirrors the real sky, not a hole in the ceiling. The, ah, floating wooden duck is mine. I—"

Myrmeen strode forward, shifting her bundle against her bosom to free one hand—and used it to grab her host by one elbow. "Come," she ordered, starting to march him along.

"What? What're you—?"

"My hair was filthy this morning, and 'tis worse now. You can help me wash it."

"I don't—"

"Oh, yes, you do. Yours has been washed sometime this month, I'm sure of it. Come."

She half-led, half-propelled the feebly-protesting wizard down the passage.

Scarlet with embarrassment and breathless in his enforced haste, Vangerdahast vowed he would get his revenge on this ogre of a she-swordcaptain—and it would be a revenge that would last a long, long time and leave her begging for mercy.

*   *   *   *   *

The Harbortower turret was always cold and drafty, even at the muggy height of the warmest—and stinkiest—summer weather . . . wherefore this was not a popular duty-post among the War Wizards. When Huldyl Rauthur, a War Wizard of middling rank, had agreed to take it with slightly more eagerness than he'd ever shown before, old Rathandar had seen fit to grimly remind him that the old turret wouldn't stand up to any really spectacular experimental castings and that he'd personally lash some lasting stripes into Huldyl's backside if he found even the slightest sign of feminine companions teleporting or being teleported into or out of the turret during Huldyl's shifts. Steamy chapbooks and richly bad food, on the other hand, were quite understandable . . .

On this bright morning, however, Huldyl seemed unable to enjoy even one of his stack of daring chapbooks and had barely touched his amber-roast butterfowl—to say nothing of his sugarnuts. However, he was quite alone and had thrown no cloak over the bare cot by the back window to make it even uncomfortably suitable for dalliance . . . or slumber, for that matter.

Uneasily he strolled from room to room, peering out of the windows at bustling Marsember below more than he bothered to squint into the powerful farglasses aimed out to sea. "No pirates ho," he muttered, in mockery of the cry excited young War Wizards seemed to veritably itch to give tongue to . . . and restlessly went back into the room he'd just left.

Rauthur was a short, stout man who always seemed to some people to be nervous, because beneath his thinning brown hair, his temples were always beaded with sweat. Those who knew him better, however, judged him a good crafter of new spells and a sarcastic, often smug man whose green eyes would blaze wildly when he was really excited or fearful.

There was no one to take note of his eyes at this moment, however, as he stood alone in the turret, tapping fingers idly on the windowsill and listening to seabirds flap and scream. He sighed, turned, started back through the connecting archway once more—and came to a sudden halt.

The chair by the table bearing his books and food was no longer empty. A young, darkly handsome man clad in black and silver shimmerweave lounged there, an easy smile on his lips and *The Wanton Witch Said Yes* open in one hand.

He lifted an eyebrow and the tome together. "A coded spellbook, perhaps?"

Rauthur flushed, and glanced at the floor. His guest might look like a swaggering noble or idle merchant prince—but he'd met with Harnrim Starangh of the Red Wizards before.

"I—ah—no. Uh, to make my superiors think I lacked a woman to smuggle up here so they wouldn't scry us and see . . ."

"Me? Ah, but only you can see my proper self. To the rest of the overly curious world, I *am* a ravishing beauty in black silks—with the face of someone you prefer to privately refer to as the Crown Princess Wrathful, I believe."

"Princess *Alusair*—?"

"Oh, don't *gabble*, man! Be bold! Plenty of perfectly loyal folk of Cormyr say arch or even biting things about the royal family and live to repeat them more loudly at revels! Besides, you'll soon not have to worry overmuch about what others think of you."

The Red Wizard lowered the chapbook with a brittle smile to reveal a tight-rolled baton of parchment.

Huldyl Rauthur leaned forward eagerly, his eyes catching green fire, and the wizard best known in Thay as Darkspells unrolled the parchment to splay seven scrolls out in a fan array on the table. The sugarnuts were in the way, and without even looking up the Red Wizard sent them drifting smoothly through the air to hover by the War Wizard's face. The chapbooks descended only slightly less smoothly to a soft landing on the floor.

Hesitantly Rauthur plucked a sugarnut from the air and ate it.

Darkspells looked up at him, smiled again, and spread his hand in a flourish above the parchments. "So there you are: the seven spells, as agreed. The coins you've had already should be more than enough to buy you a handsome abode in Athkatla, Waterdeep, Sembia, or anywhere more distant, for that matter. These magics should enable you to slay with ease any War Wizards who come hunting you. Practice their use in private to ensure yourself of their stable and complete nature, power, and worth."

The scrolls rose in unison and drifted toward Huldyl in the wake of the sugarnuts, which the War Wizard gobbled more of hastily, wiping his sugar-coated fingers nervously on the front of his tunic.

Harnrim Starangh leaned forward over the table with an eagerness that matched his own. "I hereby reaffirm my earlier promise: the same amount of cash and seven more *very* useful spells will be yours when I've safely reached Vangerdahast and gotten away again."

Rauthur fielded the scrolls with a chuckle, eyes alight. "I'm your man, Lord Starangh, I am indeed. This is . . . princely."

"Prince," the Red Wizard purred. "Now there's a title to aspire to. You could, you know, if you time things right and use just the right spells to tame Alusair to your will and bed. After she delivers you an heir, there'd be no need to sit still for the searing of her tongue any longer. A little spell-blast, a lot of mourning, and you could then do as her father did: have your pick of all the women in the kingdom."

The War Wizard's chuckle was a weak one, this time, and he shook his head, shrugged, and said, "Lord, you've more boldness in you than I do." He shook his head again, in admiration. "Wouldn't that be something, though . . ."

Darkspells let him ponder for a moment or two then said gently, "To bind the trust between us, I'll now complete that linking spell . . . if you're agreed?"

"A-aye," Rauthur replied, in a low voice. He ran a hand through the thinning hair atop his head and blurted, "Remind me, Lord Starangh, of its specifics. I'd not want to put a foot wrong, if you understand me."

"Of course," the Red Wizard said gravely, watching the last of the sugarnuts hastily disappearing down Rauthur's gullet. "Things that befall one of us also befall the other, at the same time. These shared fates are drunkenness, injury, hostile—but not self-cast—enspellment, and death. We will not share thoughts, emotions, dreams, or other things I've not spoken of: these things and these only. The spell will fade in a year." Starangh locked gazes with the War Wizard and added in dry tones, "Which will give you plenty of time to disappear from both Cormyrean justice and Thayan regard."

Huldyl Rauthur smiled rather uncertainly and grunted, "My thanks, Lord. Do it."

Starangh nodded and beckoned the War Wizard over to him, rising from his chair to hold up both hands, palms outward and fingers together. Hesitantly Rauthur set aside the scrolls and held out his own hands to match.

Palms touched. The Thayan nodded approvingly and murmured a short incantation, awakening a tingling in them both that left their forearms shuddering as they stepped back from each other.

"I'm ready to proceed when you deem the time is right. Contact me at any time of day or night. I'll be pleased if you guide me through the defenses of Vangerdahast's sanctum to him sooner rather than later, if you take my meaning."

"I-I do," Rauthur assured him hastily.

Harnrim Starangh smiled thinly. "Just one thing more, Prince-to-be Huldyl. If this linking spell between us is broken, I'll instantly be aware of that and of your whereabouts at the time—and may well be forced, for reasons of prudent diplomacy, you understand, to strike out from afar with slaying magic to obliterate Huldyl Rauthur and whoever helped you remove the spell."

His smile widened and stayed broad and promising as the man called Darkspells silently faded away.

Leaving Huldyl Rauthur standing alone in the Harbortower turret, shivering in fear, with *The Wanton Witch Said Yes* lying fallen at his feet.

Fourteen

NARNRA TAKES A TASK

*Well, we all have to work at SOMEthing—even the gods.
So pick up that bucket, and let's have no more of your
backtalk.*

> The character Farmer Juth
> in Scene the Third
> of the play *Troubles In The Cellar*
> by Shanra Mereld of Murann
> first performed in the Year of the Griffon

A small, bright, and airy turret thrusts up from one corner
of the Palace of the Purple Dragon in Suzail: a lone chamber
whose four windows are open arches that breezes blow
through at will but no bird nor raindrop enters.

The door that links that turret room to a corner of the top
floor of the Palace stands open—and guarded by four veteran
Purple Dragons—at all times. The turret had for some years
been an abandoned dovecote before the coming of Caladnei
but was now a place much used by the Mage Royal to think

and pace and gaze out over courtyard and gardens, and think some more.

Caladnei of Cormyr (as she pointedly preferred to be spoken of) often teleported into and out of her turret room—but she'd never been known to do so in the company of anyone else before, and the guards were quite startled to suddenly hear the deep, hearty laugh of a fearless old man from behind them.

They whirled around, spearpoints glittering, and gaped at what they saw: the Mage Royal embracing a hawk-nosed, white-bearded old man in dirty robes. Caladnei was weeping softly, and the old wizard—whom more than one of the old warriors had seen before—cradled her shoulders with a protective arm, saying softly, "There, there, lass. 'Tis overwhelming, aye, but a sight all mages should see in their lives before they've too much time to do foolish things unmindful of the glory we all share."

"Uh . . . Lady Caladnei?" one of the guards asked uncertainly, lifting his spear to menace the old man.

"Lord *Elminster!*" the eldest of the guards said delightedly, clapping a hand to his breastplate in salute. The gesture was echoed by the guard beside him, as the other two Purple Dragons turned to gape at their fellows . . . then turned back in horrified slowness to gaze at the old man they were menacing.

Bright blue eyes gazed at them from under dark brows, and the Old Mage nodded, winked, and lifted a finger to his lips to request their silence ere gesturing down at the sobbing woman in his arms. The two guards who'd saluted him nodded and pushed aside the spears of their fellows, silently withdrawing a pace. Elminster gave them an approving nod.

"T-thank you, Lord Elm—"

"*El*, please, lass. Just 'El.' Or 'Old Mage' if ye want to scold me." He took hold of the Mage Royal's slender shoulders and stood her back a pace, to look gravely into her tear-bright face. "How do ye feel?"

Caladnei managed a smile, and then swiftly looked away
. . . then, deliberately, back up at him.

"Sobered. Shaken. And, may I say, vastly more respectful
of you and of Vangerdahast, too, damn him. I . . . thank you.
That was . . . magnificent."

"Much to think upon, eh?" Elminster reached out two
long fingers to touch her forehead. "This much I can do:
make sure nothing fades of this. Ye'll remember everything
we saw, vividly, whenever ye call it to mind. This shall be
with ye always."

Caladnei shook her head wonderingly. "What a . . . a . . ."

Elminster chuckled. "Storm called it a 'whirlwind tour,'
but I've shown ye but a handful of highlights from all this
vast and wonderful world of ours. 'Twas time for ye. Ye
needed it to set in perspective this fair land ye guard and
to temper thy rage with Vangey. Know ye this: When I took
him to see the same things, he wept even more than ye have,
begged forgiveness for his rudenesses, and told me he was
shamed."

"I—I feel I should do the same," Caladnei said with an
unsteady laugh, ducking her head and looking up at him
again.

Elminster recoiled. "What? And rob thyself of the chance
to get in some really good rudenesses to me, first?"

The sorceress burst into startled laughter and clung
to the old man's robes for support. He hugged her fondly
then—the eyes of the watching Purple Dragons narrowed—
reached down to his belt, fishing around in a pouch there
for something.

Cormyrean hands clapped dagger-hilts, tightened, and
. . . fell away unneeded, as Elminster's hand reappeared
holding a length of fine chain. He held it out where the
Mage Royal could see it, waited for her to notice it, and said
gruffly, "Yours, lass. An anklet. Nothing valuable, but—wear
it. Now and always. If ye feel the need, and say the word
'amulamystra' while wearing it, I will come."

Wondering, Caladnei closed her hand around the delicate

chain. The Old Mage bent his head and bestowed a fatherly kiss on the top of hers.

Then her arms were empty and she was staggering forward off-balance across a turret room that held no Elminster of Shadowdale. Caladnei looked around wildly and beheld only the four guards, staring at her.

She gave them a rueful half-smile like a child caught doing something naughty, and the guards drew themselves to attention and saluted. The eldest said politely, "Lady Mage, we've been requested to inform you that the Lady Laspeera, the Highknight Rhauligan, and a captive await you in the Dragonwing Chamber."

Caladnei drew herself up, suddenly every inch the brisk Mage Royal they knew so well, and snapped, "I thank you." She smiled like a young lass again, bent over and drew off her right boot, and clasped the chain around her ankle.

"Looks good," a guard said gruffly—then turned as swift as any whiplash to face away from her, at stiff attention. His fellows sprang to join him in the maneuver, so when Caladnei straightened, she'd have no idea which one of them had spoken.

She grinned at all four armored backs, parted two of them with firm hands, and murmured, "Old lechers," as she strode between them and marched off down the hall.

The guards saluted her in silent unison and went back to guarding the open door.

* * * * *

Roablar of Lantan sat back and sighed, rubbing the bridge of his nose where his glasses pinched—then rubbing the eyes behind them for good measure.

The everpresent hovering monk bent over the merchant. "Is there anything you're not finding, goodsir?"

"Ah," Thaerabho murmured, to the Keeper of that particular reading-room in Candlekeep. "It begins. 'Tis time for an unmasking." Silent in his soft slippers, he started to move purposefully toward the seated Lantanna.

"You can see what I'm seeking," the disguised Lady Nouméa Cardellith told her escort.

The tall, pockmarked monk ran a hand through his unruly, strawlike hair, bent closer, and replied in a low voice, "All you can about the Red Wizards of Thay, in particular recent writings. If you've come to Candlekeep in search of their spells, I fear you've wasted your journey. We keep those secure for very good reasons."

Without regarding them, Nouméa was well aware that several monks were silently drawing in around her. She smiled thinly.

"No, Esmer. What would a merchant of Lantan want with spells? I live and die by trade, and 'tis this new policy of establishing Thayan trade enclaves and who in the Thayan hierarchy is behind it that I seek to learn all about."

"I realize this is overbold, and you must feel perfectly comfortable in refusing to answer," an unfamiliar monk murmured from her other side, "but why?"

Nouméa looked up and gave him a smile.

"If we're being so blunt: I suspect this is but the first step in an elaborate plan to economically and then—covertly— politically dominate all realms of Faerûn."

"Of course," two of the monks said together, and at least another three in the ring that had silently formed around her nodded.

"Wherefore my fascination with recent reports and writings," Nouméa added, indicating the sheafs of parchment and stacked volumes on the slightly sloped reading-desk before her.

"I sense you're both well-traveled and worldly," a monk said from directly behind her. "Permit me, then, to mention something not to be found in these written records but only in the diaries we compile of the news and rumor that comes daily to our gates."

"Please do," Nouméa said politely, shifting slightly
and indicating the bench beside her. The monks smiled
as if she'd passed some sort of test, and the monk who'd
spoken from behind her stepped forward and sat down so
close beside her that his robe almost brushed her hip. A
white, puckered old sword-scar adorned one of his cheeks
diagonally, and his hair was as gray as a sword in need of
polishing.

"I'm Thaerabho," he said with a smile, "and my field is the
doings of those who wield magic in Faerûn outside temples
and priesthoods. You've heard of the Chosen of Mystra?"

Nouméa nodded eagerly, and Thaerabho's smile broadened.

"Then let me share this much: Some among them have
been working against the Red Wizards in a lovely manner.
With spells they 'twist' many of the portals established by
the Thayans in their enclaves so those who use such trans-
locations can have spells stolen from their minds en route,
suggestions planted, memories and information 'read,' and
so on."

"Sweet Mystra," Nouméa whispered, genuinely awed.

Thaerabho nodded. "If the Thayans ever grow too strong
in a particular place, if I may speak cynically, the portal in
that spot—or all of them, along with, of course, whoever's
using them at the time—could explode. Or perhaps a suggestion planted in the heads of all mages who've ever used
one of the Thayan portals could be awakened, all at once,
all over Faerun . . . a suggestion, say, to rush to a particular
Thayan city and attack Szass Tam or some other zulkir there,
before he accomplishes some dread goal that will sacrifice
them."

Nouméa shook her head and asked softly, "What if I am of
Thay or of the Chosen and want no one in Faerûn to suspect
any of this?"

The monk whose nose was almost brushing her own
replied, "No, Lady Nouméa Cardellith, you are of neither—
and are not a Harper, either. You're but a seeker after
knowledge, and we arm all who come here with the

weapons of fact and lore and reason-sorted rumor. What they do with such tools after they depart is not our affair. We but seek to arm those wise—or cunning—enough to come asking and looking."

"Who *are* you?" a shaken Nouméa whispered.

The ring of monks smiled.

"Simple folk of Faerûn who love old books, and learning, and reading the thoughts and hopes and records of beings now dust," Esmer replied.

Nouméa looked around at them all and shook her head. "I think you're among the most powerful and dangerous forces on all Toril."

The monks stopped smiling.

"That, too," Thaerabho agreed lightly. "Knowing that, what will you do now, Lady Nouméa Cardellith, sometime mage and unhappy wife?" More monks were in the reading-room now, drifting toward her from all sides.

Nouméa stared at him for a long time, ignoring the silent assembly of monks and the rods some of them held ready then lifted her shoulders in a shrug. "I . . . don't know."

The ring-wall of monks seemed to relax, and a few drifted away again. Thaerabho's smile returned.

"Ah, the truth. The right answer to give us, always."

Nouméa stared into his hazel eyes for a long time then drew in a deep breath and asked, "What do you think I should do?"

"Ah," the sword-scarred monk responded eagerly, as several of the closest monks drew in around her again, reaching in under the great reading-desk to unclip folded wooden stools from its underside, and sitting down on them. "Now you've done the next right thing. We'll not tell you what to do next. We never do. We shall, however, tell you all we can to help *you* decide where to go from here in life."

Lady Nouméa blinked at him. "Why didn't I come here years ago?"

"Why indeed?"

* * * * *

As the guards swung the great doors open for her, the Mage Royal of Cormyr looked in and up at the carved stone dragons frozen forever in the act of erupting from the ceiling of the room ahead of her. The scene was as magnificent as always, all scales, surging strength, and great sweeping curves of wings, catlike and serpentine both at once.

She found herself on the verge of tears again, and almost fondly muttered, "Damn you, Old Mage," as she entered the Dragonwing Chamber alone.

Three people stood in the center of its vast, empty polished floor awaiting her: Laspeera, Rhauligan, and the thief who'd fled from the cellars, captured at last. Narna Shalace.

Rhauligan was shrugging himself back into his vest, his belt still unbuckled at his waist. Caladnei smiled thinly. She must have led him a merry chase. The spell-thrall holding her now would be Speera's work.

She gave Laspeera and Rhauligan nods of thanks and approached their paralyzed but unbound captive, banishing Laspeera's magic as she came. "So we meet again, Narnra of Waterdeep," she began pleasantly.

The thief, who'd bent over to busily rub hands and ankles, shaking out her limbs as if her body felt unfamiliar to her, did not reply.

"Narnra," Caladnei continued, "you stand in the Palace of the Purple Dragon in Suzail, in the realm of Cormyr. As such, you're utterly within my power. Should not mere prudence lead you to some measure of polite cooperation, whatever your personal feelings toward us?"

The thief straightened up to give Caladnei a cold, considering look then glanced over at Laspeera and Rhauligan. They gazed patiently back at her, faces impassive.

Narnra tossed her head and glared at Caladnei. "You *have* an audience for your grand speeches," she said, nodding at the man who'd captured her and the woman whose spell had paralyzed her. "What d'you want of me?"

"Answers. A few civil, honest, and generous-with-what-you-know answers," the Mage Royal replied.

Narnra sighed. "I can't think what precious things I might know that could possibly be of any use to you. You're not planning to become the terror of purses in Trades Ward, are you?"

"No," Caladnei replied in a dry voice. "There! You see? An answer, and so easily and swiftly given, too. Try it for a short time, do well at it—and you'll be free to go."

"Go *where?*" Narnra snarled. "Out into the streets of your city, to starve? Or be pounced on by the next of your soldiers who doesn't like the look of me? 'Oh, sir, I'm just a thief from Waterdeep—that's right, a thief—and I've just been talking with your Mage Royal, and she'—oh, aye, I'm *sure* they'll believe me!"

"Do you love Waterdeep so much?"

"What? Is *this* one of your questions? Could you not have found a traveling merchant, and ask—"

"Do you love Waterdeep so much?"

Narnra flung up her hands. "I *know* Waterdeep," she snarled. " 'Tis my *home*, the only place I know, where I know how to get something to eat, where . . ."

She fell silent, eyes narrowing.

Caladnei was smiling. "You see? Honest answers are not so hard, once you begin. Do it twice or thrice, and you'll have found the habit."

Narnra gave her a dark look and hugged herself as if she were cold. "Wizards are *so* clever," she muttered. "I sometimes wonder how better off we'd all be without them."

That earned her wry smiles from all three Cormyreans, and Caladnei's voice was almost gentle as she asked, "Have you many friends in Waterdeep, with whom you talk? Share gossip with?"

Narnra hunched her head down and said nothing.

The Mage Royal frowned. "Enough of this," she murmured.

"'Time—and past time—for enforced truth." She muttered an incantation and traced a pattern with her fingertips.

There was a sudden flash of blue-white fire, and she drew her head back as if burned. "She's protected," Caladnei murmured, and cast a glance at Laspeera.

Who shrugged and asked softly, "Elminster?" as she raised her own hands and worked the same spell.

Seven blue-white stars flashed and spun very briefly around the young Waterdhavian, who seemed in a trance.

"Mystra," the Mage Royal whispered and looked at Laspeera again, almost helplessly this time.

The older War Wizard gave her another shrug. "So try the hard way, Cala. We can only try spells as they seem necessary . . . and see."

Caladnei nodded unhappily, drew in a deep breath, glanced at Rhauligan—who smiled grimly and gave her a nod of approval, and asked, "Narnra? How do you hear the news merchants bring, when they come to Waterdeep in their caravans? Do local wits cry news aloud in taverns in return for coins?"

Silence.

"Narnra?"

The thief's reply was to burst into a sudden sprint toward Caladnei, dodging twice. The Mage Royal flung up a hand to signal Rhauligan—who was already moving—to keep clear and worked a swift, muttered spell.

One blue-white star, whirling away . . . and winking out.

Narnra plucked for a dagger to hurl and ruin the casting but found her sheath empty and instead tried to duck around Caladnei—who politely stepped aside.

"The door," the sorceress told the hard-running thief firmly, "is not an option."

Narnra put her head down, growled, and ran. Invisible fingers were already plucking at her, and she knew that with *two* wizards of Cormyr in the room, her attempt at escape was doomed, yet . . . yet what else could she *do?*

She was running in midair, now, treading hard on nothing at all, as she floated backward toward where she'd been. She knew how comical she must look yet kept on running. Spells were mind-tiring—everyone knew that—and this Caladnei would have to set her back down sooner or later. If she was already moving fast and got a little lucky, she could—just mayhap—manage t—

"Narnra, answer me: How do you hear news and gossip in Waterdeep?"

Narnra spat out a wordless snarl of rising frustration and kept right on running.

"Narnra?"

"*Drown* you, mage! Blast and burn and rot you! I don't *care* about your questions or your nasty little plots or the oh-so-fair kingdom of Cormyr! Just *let me go!*"

"To steal in our streets," Caladnei said softly. "I think not."

"Perhaps worse than that," Rhauligan put in, holding up a handful of Narnra's daggers. At the sight of them the Waterdhavian shrieked in rage and darted a hand down the front of her breeches, to pluck forth a tiny knife from a sheath over her most private of places, and hurl it furiously at him.

Rhauligan sprang sideways, for her throw had been well-aimed—and Caladnei's mouth drew into a hard line.

The next thing Narnra knew, she was greeting the far wall of the chamber, hard enough to slam the breath out of her. She struggled, sobbing for air, and found herself pinned firmly against the dark paneling by nothing she could see at all.

Another blue-white star, winking and dying . . .

"How do you hear news and gossip in Waterdeep?" the Mage Royal asked again. Her magic relaxed just enough to let Narnra breathe, and the thief gulped in great shuddering lungfuls of air.

"Narnra?"

"Wizard, can't you tell I don't *care* about any of this? Go mount a dragon somewhere, and leave me be!"

"Narnra—"

"Caladnei," the Waterdhavian mimicked, in exactly the same tone the Mage Royal had used, "go stuff yourself. *If you please.*"

The Mage Royal's magic thrust Narna back against the wall again, pressing so hard on her that she couldn't lift her ribs to draw breath. She fought silently, twisting and writhing on the paneling, until all too soon the world started to go dim, and drift. . . .

The force eased, letting her gasp for air again. Narnra stared over the heads of her tormentors and panted, drawing in precious air.

In chill shadow, a blue-white star goes out. . . .

"Sweet wind," she murmured, quoting a Waterdhavian harbor song.

"What's that?" Caladnei asked sharply.

"Sweet wind, come again," Narnra recited the line between gasps, eyes meeting those of the Mage Royal. "Blow me away, far beyond pain."

The Mage Royal took a step closer, and Narnra noticed with surprise that she'd been crying. Recently. "Narna, please tell me this," she said softly. "How do you get to know rumors and what happens, all over Waterdeep and in Faerûn all around?"

"Caladnei," Narnra replied, just as softly, "I keep my mouth shut and my ears open. Even when tyrant mages slam me about with their spells."

In the sudden thunder of unseen force that plucked her from the wall then slammed her back against it again hard enough to rattle her bones and her back teeth, Narnra thought she heard Rhauligan make the briefest of chuckles.

Forlorn and drifting, another star flickers . . . and goes out. . . .

"Even then?" Caladnei asked softly. "How stubborn, thief, are you?"

Her magic snatched Narnra from the wall and slammed

her back against it again, hard enough to make a wood panel groan in protest. Narnra's limbs bounced helplessly against the wood. She whined like a dog for breath, fighting against the building pressure.

Silently, a fifth blue-white star flares—and is gone. . . .

Harder and harder the magic pressed her—only to relax when she was once more on the shuddering edge of sinking into insensibility and let her cough and choke and groan for breath.

"How, when in Waterdeep, do you get to hear gossip and news from afar?" Caladnei asked calmly.

Narnra shook her head. The Mage Royal repeated the question, and the Silken Shadow snapped, "*Away*, mage! Go and batter-bruise someone else! Kick a guard, slap a child, whatever pleases you!"

The magic slammed her against the chamber wall and pinned her once more, twice more, a third time.

Another star fading . . . leaving but one a-twinkle.

Caladnei repeated her last question in the same precise words every time she let Narnra breathe.

The last star wavers, trembles in the darkness . . . and winks out. . . .

At Caladnei's fourth patient repetition, Narnra replied sullenly, "I listen at windows and to folk muttering in alleys. I lie on rooftops hearing merchants plot and scheme—how else can I learn where they'll be, *and* their precious money?"

"Taverns, too?"

"When I'm thirsty and make it to South Ward or the docks, never my home streets."

"Nobles' windows?"

"Never. Too dangerous. Why walk there when I can hear more idling beside a street-seller unloading food after the highsun rush? Nobles are all high wind and preening, anyway, every third word a lie to impress or manipulate."

"This is much easier, Narnra. Thank you. I'll see that you get plenty to eat and drink when we're done. Now tell me: In all this daily chatter, do you ever hear talk of Cormyr?"

"No. I think I heard the name of your land a few times when merchants were talking hopeful prices. Sembia—mainly they talk about Sembians buying all the lace and jewels and scent-oils. . . ."

"More coins in Sembia," the Mage Royal agreed, almost soothingly.

There was other magic at work, now, across the room. Laspeera was casting something long and exacting. Narnra sighed and looked away from the woman, discovered she didn't want to look at Rhauligan's faintly smiling face just now, and brought her gaze back to Caladnei, who was just beginning another question.

"Wait," Narnra interrupted swiftly, "why don't you tell *me* one? What spell's she putting on me?" From the wall where she was still—lightly—held, she nodded toward Laspeera.

"One that will read the truth—or lack of it—in your words. It does no harm."

Narnra's dark eyes flamed for a moment. "And when you're done squeezing all the truth out of me? Will I be allowed to go on breathing then?"

"Narnra Shalace, know this: 'Tis not my habit to murder outlanders in the Royal Palace of Cormyr—or anywhere else, for that matter. Those who manage to refrain from hurling daggers at me or my fellow loyal Cormyreans, at least. So you tell me now, d'you belong to any guilds, brotherhoods, secret societies, trading costers, temple agent orders, nobles' 'fellowships' . . . or any other organization I've forgotten to list?"

"No. And I was never part of that conspiracy in the cellars."

"Have you any living kin? Friends? Particular foes?"

"No. Thrice no."

"Have you any outstanding debts, or agreements that bind you?"

"Nay."

"Are you under any threat at this time, facing reprisals if you do or don't do a certain thing?"

"No. Present company excepted."

"Fair enough. Why're you here in Cormyr?"

"Mischance and magic—and being too curious. I followed a wizard who spared my life. I knew not where 'here' was until after I arrived."

"What d'you lack most in life, beyond fame, high birth, and enough coins to do just as you please?"

"My freedom," Narnra snapped. "What answer did you expect?"

"If you were free and we'd never seen you and you were wandering Marsember unnoticed right now . . . what would matter most to you, if I met you, showed you I could slay you with magic on a whim, and asked you how you wanted to spend the rest of your life?"

Narnra smiled bitterly. "Getting away alive would matter most."

Caladnei sighed. "Could we move past fencing with tongues, Narnra? I've better things to do than hold you against the wall all day."

The Waterdhavian drew in a deep breath, eyed her captor, and said, "Mage Royal, I just want to get rich without working—unusual that, hey?—and to spend my days being free to do and go as I will—stealing what I can and doing just as I please."

"Sounds like several noble ladies of Sembia I've met," Laspeera muttered, an offering that earned her a silent 'Later' look from Caladnei.

The Mage Royal turned back to Narnra, relaxing her spell to let the thief down off the wall onto her feet again. "Let's end this all the sooner, if you're willing. Narnra, I think I know enough about who you are now. Now, I'd like very much to learn all you know, suspect, or have overheard as rumors in Waterdeep of any campaign to overthrow the Obarskyrs."

"The who? Oh . . . the ruling family here, hey?" Narnra looked at Laspeera then pointed to her own forehead. "Vouch for me in this, yes?" She turned and met Caladnei's eyes, and the moment she was staring into them said slowly and firmly, "Not . . . a . . . thing. I've heard nothing at all about anything political in Cormyr. Nothing until I got here, and all that Rightful Conspiracy gabble in the cellars—and I'm still not sure exactly what it was about. Discontent with the Crown, yes, but—" She shrugged.

"Keep to Waterdeep, Narnra. Purchases of swords, or the hire of warriors? Backed by merchants or nobles of Waterdeep? Warhorses? Hedge-wizards being hired for trips overland? The places might not be in Cormyr; they could be Westgate, or Saerloon and Selgaunt in Sembia, or Athkatla . . . or Iriaebor."

Narnra shook her head. "No, Mage Royal, I swear to you, nothing like that. A few horses and wagons between one merchant and another, yes, but nothing that could mean war—and no huge chests full of coins setting off anywhere, either. Not that anyone in Waterdeep would be fool enough to let word get around about something like that, anyway."

"Truth, Cala," Laspeera said softly. "Utter truth."

The Mage Royal smiled and nodded. "Well enough. We had to be sure." She took another step closer and asked quietly, "Do you know any magic, Narnra? How to cast spells?"

"No. If I did, would I be . . ." Narnra let her voice trail off instead of asking something bitter.

"I'm sorry, Narnra. Is the body we can see now your true shape?"

"Yes," Narnra replied, taken aback. "How could it not be?"

"How indeed." Caladnei did not take her eyes off Narnra as she asked over her shoulder, "Speera, has every answer given me by Narnra been completely true?"

"No, Mage Royal. There's one thing she wanted to be true, but stood in some doubt over."

"And that was?"

"Living kin. Until recently she was sure she had none . . . but now knows better. The knowledge does not please her."

In the silence that followed, Caladnei eyed Narnra thoughtfully, and then asked, "Are you going to tell me, Narnra, without greeting the wall again?"

The Waterdhavian clenched her teeth, looked at the floor, and burst out, "You've no *right* to do this. I don't want to spend the rest of my days being hunted by every gods-cursed wizard in Faerûn! Can't I keep this *one* secret? It's nothing to do with Cormyr!"

"I must be the judge of that," the Mage Royal replied softly. "Come, Narnra, what harm can saying a name or two do you? If 'tis nothing to do with Cormyr, as you say, then it can't be a lineage exiled from here, and so . . ."

Glarasteer Rhauligan cleared his throat loudly, and Caladnei looked over at him, stepping smoothly back from Narnra to do so.

"You thought your parents were dead, right?" the Harper asked Narnra.

She looked into his eyes and said, "Yes."

"You've never had siblings, aye?"

"Yes."

"So you've just learned your mother—or your father—was alive, hey?"

"Yes," Narnra said, shrinking back from him as if he was going to hurl something at her.

"You followed a wizard here, didn't you?"

Narnra glared at him and kept silence. Four people stared at each other in the vast and otherwise empty room before Laspeera asked, "You're the daughter of Elminster of Shadowdale, aren't you?"

Narnra shot her a look that had daggers in it and—reluctantly—nodded. Her voice, when it came, was barely a whisper: "I . . . fear so."

She looked up swiftly. Rhauligan was eyeing her with bright interest, while Laspeera's eyes had a strange expression that held several things, pity foremost among them. Caladnei was frowning.

"In the cellars of Marsember, Elminster certainly didn't

seem to be treating you as his daughter," she observed, stepping closer again.

Narnra drew in a deep breath and told the floor tonelessly, "I don't think Elminster knows he sired me."

The Mage Royal turned to Laspeera. "Does this seem likely to you?"

"The fathering? Very. The not knowing all of his offspring and their doings does surprise me, yes. I thought the Old Mage knew damned near every time any wizard in all Faerûn scratched himself."

Caladnei nodded and turned back to Narnra. "You realize the danger if word of your parentage spreads." Her words were not a question.

The thief from Waterdeep nodded and said bitterly, "All too well." She shrugged. "But as I seem doomed to spend whatever short remainder of life is left to me as a helpless captive, tossed from one ruthless wizard to another—present company very much included—it hardly seems to matter."

Caladnei's eyes were thoughtful. "What will you do if I release you?"

Narnra shrugged again. "Steal all I can, probably, until I've coins enough to buy caravan-passage back to Waterdeep . . . unless, while thieving here in Cormyr, I like what I see enough to stick around."

Caladnei smiled sourly. "As Mage Royal, I've a better idea: You can serve yourself best if you stay alive and serve Cormyr at the same time."

"Serve how?"

"As a paid spy while you thieve—with occasional offers of additional monies for more daring tasks of plundering or 'placing' items to be found . . . as Rhauligan, here, does for us."

"So it's agree or you'll kill me?"

"Oh, no," Caladnei said softly. "I need information about Cormyr's foes. It'll be much more useful to simply spread the news around Suzail that you're Elminster's daughter, and watch the wolves come out of hiding to get at you."

"I'll still *die!*"

The Mage Royal shrugged. "We all do, sooner or later—and you'll be free to die in your own way, just as you believe all of us overbearing sorts are." She waited. "Well?"

Narnra slid down the wall until she was sitting, sighed loudly, then told the carved dragon ceiling, "I'm furious at being at the mercy of any wizard." She turned her head to glare at Caladnei and added, "I think I'll tell you so."

Rhauligan's amused snort was echoed—in far more lady-like manners—by the two Cormyrean women.

"Moreover, before I agree to anything, I need to know not just the 'or else,' but also the 'what else' and the 'what about after,' too."

Caladnei was almost smiling. "And those things would be?"

"The bad things you're not yet telling me about this . . . and what happens to me when the Mage Royal of Cormyr deems me expendable."

Caladnei's smile appeared, wry but full. "Prudence at last. A bit late, but making an appearance nonetheless."

She knelt close to where Narnra was sitting and said, "To save Cormyr, we are *all* expendable. However, 'tis my hope that you'll become so useful to us all that you serve loyally for years to come—whereupon you might be rewarded with a 'way out.' A title, a nice mansion to live out your wrinkled years . . . a better 'after' than many can hope for. As for the 'what else,' I need to know your trustworthiness and so would begin by mind-reaming you directly."

"Turning me into some sort of brainless slug?"

"No. I'll *never* deal pain, mind-to-mind, as Elminster did. No, if you were found wanting, I'd put you through a portal back to Waterdeep."

Narnra almost sprang up from the wall. "You can *do* that?"

"Oh, yes. I must warn you that the portal I know will deliver you into a very public room of state in Peirgeiron's Palace. Have you a swift story ready?"

"Being the daughter of Elminster ought to do," Rhauligan murmured—earning him three glares at once.

Narnra bit her lip. "And . . . I'd just go back to Trades Ward? No one following me?"

Caladnei shrugged. "Not from Cormyr."

Narnra looked at her. "This mind-ream: What will it do to me?"

"Show me your thoughts and memories as I rummage. If you'd like to reassure yourself as to your fate at my hands, I can easily make the mind-ream a two-way affair so you can judge me while I do the same to you."

Narnra stared at the Mage Royal, awed and strangely excited—and suddenly angry again. She scrambled up, took a few stumbling steps away from Caladnei, waving at the Cormyreans to stay back from her, and leaned her head against the wall. "I . . . let me think."

"Of course," Laspeera said softly.

Breathing heavily, Narnra stared at the toes of her boots and thought hard. How did she feel?

Did she trust these folk? Laspeera seemed motherly, Rhauligan was—Rhauligan, dedicated to his task . . . and Caladnei had beaten her like a backstreet bully with magic—but not killed her when the slaying would have been easy and Narnra had been stupid enough to goad her. Repeatedly.

So how did she feel? Truth, now . . .

I'm more terrified than eager. And I'm angry. Angry at myself for being afraid, angrier still at Caladnei and Rhauligan for bringing me by force into this choice. I'm burn-the-gods furious with Elminster for siring me, just walking away, and luring me here from the streets I know.

"Truth," Laspeera said gently from behind Narnra. "Every word utter truth."

Gods, yes, she's been reading my every thought . . .

Narnra spun around with a frightened snarl, expecting to find all three Cormyreans closing in around her—but everyone was just where they'd been before, Caladnei still kneeling.

"If I agree to this . . . this madness," Narnra asked in a voice that was far from calm and steady, "when will this mind-ream take place?"

The Mage Royal of Cormyr rose slowly to her feet, smiling a little wryly. "In such matters, there's never any better time for boldly reckless action than . . . right now."

Fifteen

WHEN MARSEMBAN MERCHANTS GO WALKING

My son, it's not the standing merchants you need fear. It's when they get to walking somewhere that you'd best beware. It takes a heap of coming trouble for someone to get a merchant to walk anywhere.

The character Farmer Crommor
in Scene the First
of the play *Troubles In The Cellar*
by Shanra Mereld of Murann
first performed in the Year of the Griffon

The outermost of the ward-spells that cloaked the far corners of the room in roiling mists flared into coppery flames of warning, and a telltale chimed.

The darkly handsome young man clad all in black—open-fronted, flaring-sleeved shirt, tight leather breeches, and gleaming black boots—took his crossed feet down from the footstool, laid aside his book and his goblet, and rose from his chair.

He passed his hand over a dark sphere of crystal that shared its own upswept, teardrop-shaped duskwood plinth with an outer ring of smaller spheres. Another ring of roiling mists obediently wavered into emerald radiance and displayed an upright image in the air: a white-faced man in brown robes that matched his thinning hair was standing uncertainly in the midst of the emerald mists.

The man in black smiled and touched two of the smaller spheres. Two rings of mist fell away into nothingness, and the third took on that emerald hue. The Red Wizard then passed his hand over the largest sphere, and the scene of Huldyl Rauthur vanished.

"Enter the archway and proceed," he told the air calmly. "The way before you is quite safe."

The emerald mists at his feet flowed away to one wall in a purposeful flood and climbed it to outline an archway on the unbroken stone—which promptly split to reveal a long, rough tunnel through rock. A hesitant figure was advancing along it.

"Be welcome," the Red Wizard said quietly. "Importance brings you, I trust?"

"Y-yes," Huldyl Rauthur made reply, as he entered the chamber. "I believe 'tis time." The War Wizard was chalk-white with worry, and his face glistened with so much sweat that it dripped from his chin.

A weak reed, Master Rauthur, Darkspells thought. And weak reeds break.

"Good," Harnrim Starangh told the man he'd bought. "Return to the chamber you came from, and I'll follow in a matter of moments."

As soon as the fearful Rauthur started back down the passage, Starangh passed a hand over a crystal and sent mists billowing up between them once more. He drained his goblet in a long, unhurried quaff, plucked one of the crystals from the plinth and slipped it into his codpiece, and said words to the empty air.

Two men were promptly standing before him, blinking in startlement and alarm. They went pale when they saw who was standing facing them.

Starangh gave the merchants Bezrar and Surth a shark-like smile. "I hope you've eaten well. You're going on a journey."

"Eh? What j—" Bezrar began, but fell silent as Surth kicked his ankle savagely.

Starangh let them both see his smile turn soft and menacing and commanded, "Stand still and silent. Please."

They did so, and he cast an intricate spell that laid a fog of forgetfulness on them. Until it expired, they'd be compelled to seek the retired Mage Royal, being drawn always in his direction—but stripped from them was all remembrance of why they were seeking Vangerdahast or who'd enspelled and sent them. Anyone trying to break the spell before it ran out would reduce the two Marsembans to quivering mindlessness.

They stood like two gaping statues, no longer seeing the man who worked a second, minor spell to place images of the animated suits of armor known as helmed horrors in their minds. "When you see such a one," Harnrim Starangh told his two minions gently, "one of you will throw one of *these* at it, so as to strike it."

The black-clad wizard took the limp hands of the two oblivious men, and posed them so those of each man were cupped together. From a basket beneath his reclining chair, Starangh scooped many small, shiny, identical objects into those waiting palms: rune-graven ovals of metal that bulged plumply at their centers but thinned to the breadth of armor plate nigh all their edges.

He smiled at his two enchanted idiots, stepped around them to lay a hand on the backs of both of their necks at once, and pronounced another word that made them both vanish.

Humming a jaunty song, Harnrim Starangh made a last adjustment of his crystals and rode a plume of mist down the passage to join Rauthur. It was time to go hunting—for Vangerdahasts were suddenly very much in season.

* * * * *

Aumun Tholant Bezrar blinked, wiped his sweating face, and looked wildly in all directions with every evidence of utter bewilderment. Trees, aye, definitely trees.

As always, standing behind him like one more tree trunk, was his companion in so many crimes, Master Malakar Surth.

Surth was clutching a handful of something that looked like oversized silver coins, and frowning in puzzlement.

Bezrar looked down and discovered that his own fat, sweaty palm was cradling another handful of the same things: ovals of gleaming metal graven with intricate runes—nothing he could read or had ever seen before, but the same things on each one. These long-as-his-fingers gewgaws bulged in their middles like snail-cakes but were flattened out all around the edges like, well, again like snail-cakes.

So where by all the cozy Nine Hells had these come from—and where *was* here, anyhow? And how . . . how had he and Surth gotten here?

"Uh, Surth?" he asked, seeking some answers. "Surth?"

"Bite your tongue til it bleeds," Marsember's richest dealer in scents, wines, cordials, and drugs snapped, employing the standard polite port expression for what slightly more highborn Cormyreans usually rendered as "Belt up" or (if they were priests or elders) "Be silent."

Surth was glaring around at trees and vines and the deep damp green vista of more trees, that stretched away in all directions from the narrow trail they were standing on. His manner made it clear that he was blaming the trees themselves for being here—at least for the few moments it would take him to find someone nearby to blame.

"I don't know either," he muttered, as his face turned

slowly to regard his longtime partner. And darkened.

"What did you do to get us here, Bez? You must have done something! You're an idiot, you know that? An idiot! You must have fiddled with something enchanted or lit the fuse of that . . . that . . ." His face went clouded, almost frightened, and he waved a dismissive hand. "You know: that . . . man."

Bezrar drew himself up like an indignant walrus, puffing and sweating, and jabbed Surth's chest with one fat, hairy finger. "Now, you listen here, O mighty Malakar! *You're* the one who's always dabbling with Shar-magic, dark little toys and mumble-spells and all that untrustworthy idiocy! B'gads, you wound me, you do! 'Twasn't anything *I* did to get us here! 'Twas that smiling . . . some magic word . . . that green glow . . . him . . . he gave us these, didn't he?"

He thrust out his handful of shiny gewgaws and said, "He must've, because I sure by all the happy dancing gods haven't seen 'em before! You're holding some too!"

"I *know* that, you fat little dolt," Surth snarled. "I can see and feel, you know!"

"Odd's fish, but you can't *think* half as clever as you think you can, now, can you—hey?"

"Oh yes, I can," Surth snarled, reaching for the hilt of his knife.

"Well, then, use your thinking part, whatever 'tis, and tell me *how* we got here and *what* these things are and *how we get back to Marsember!*" the fat smuggler roared, his longknife already out and jabbing warningly at Surth's knife-hand. "Because sure as Shar's a dark lass, this ain't Marsember!"

His shout echoed a little way through the damp trees, and something unseen scuttled away from beside the trail nearby, leaving a trail of quivering leaves.

Malakar Surth drew in a deep breath, wrestling down his temper, and with a firm hand pushed the point of Bezrar's wavering knife aside. "Let me think," he snarled.

Bezrar gave him a sour expression and flourished his

hands in mimicry of a high-nosed Marsemban servant bidding a Marsemban noble to pass this way, or partake of this platter of viands, or do *something*.

Surth stroked at his chin as if its clean-shaven point was home to a handsome beard, stared around at the trees, and muttered, "Can't tell where the sun is, and we mustn't get off the trail. This forest is *big*." He shivered suddenly and muttered, "Mustn't be here when night comes."

Bezrar nodded, eyes widening in horror at the thought of long-taloned, creeping forest monsters, slithering closer. . . . He fought down a cry of alarm and started looking in all directions at once, crouching and waving his longknife wildly.

Surth gave him a sour look and murmured, "Fat, useless *idiot*." He held up a hand and said, "*This* way. I don't know why, but I'm sure this is the right way to head. Shar must be with me—*thank* you for invoking her, Bez. Come on."

The smuggler stood suspiciously looking in all directions, so Surth plucked him sharply by the elbow while passing, jerking him into a stumbling walk. No sooner had the fat wholesaler regained his balance when Surth took firm grip of his elbow once more and just as firmly propelled him into the lead.

Bezrar shot him a fearful look. Surth favored him with what was intended to be a reassuring smile and said, "Go on, but mind you go *quietly*. Don't worry. I'll be right behind you."

Bezrar's reply was a growl. The smuggler didn't quite dare to say that knowing Malakar Surth was right behind you was no cause for a lack of worry.

He needed Surth to do the thinking—and to be with him in this vast and rustling wood. The mere thought of—*what was that?*

"Mask and Tymora love me!" he cried, as a warrior in full armor rose up from behind some bushes, visor down and drawn sword in hand. "Surth?"

"I see him," Surth said in a strange voice. Bezrar cast a

very quick glance back over his shoulder to see why his partner's voice sounded like that—and saw that Surth had lifted one of his gewgaws in a trembling hand and was staring at it with a weird expression on his face.

"*Malakar!*" he snarled. "Help me here!"

His eyes back on the armored warrior, he moaned in fear as the silently menacing Purple Dragon drifted toward him. Aye, drifted—gods above, it was *floating!* Its feet were right off the ground, toes pointing downwards like a knight laid out for his tomb!

Yet that helmed head was turning to look at him then at Surth then back again, and the gauntleted hands were swinging that great naked sword up and back, ready to slash down and slay—

"*Surth!*" the smuggler almost wept, his longknife shaking in his hand. "Aid!"

Something bright flashed past his shoulder, tumbling end over end at the floating warrior. It struck that armored breast—and the world exploded in bright blue fire and ringing, tumbling shards of battle-steel that half-deafened Aumun Bezrar and flung him off his feet back past a tree or two and crashing down among bushes, very hard roots, and wet dead leaves, with pieces of riven armor pattering onto the ground all around him.

"Bezrar?" his partner cried in fear, stumbling blindly forward along the path and groping at the air. "Bez, where are you?"

Bezrar blinked at the leaf-shrouded sky overhead, deciding he was still alive and could hear things through a faint ringing in his ears and could feel all parts of his body with not much more than the usual pain. He rolled over hastily, driving his longknife into wet moss and earth as a handle, to puff his way to his knees and see . . . Malakar Surth stepping straight into a tree, shrieking in alarm, turning to run, and taking three wild, windmilling strides into—another tree.

Surth sat down hard, clutching at his head, and Bezrar,

surveying the now-empty path, found himself laughing wildly.

His chortles died away abruptly as he felt his free hand trembling. He looked down and discovered that he was clutching one of the gewgaws like a stone ready to throw and that it was glowing slightly, a blue radiance that pulsed and faded under his astonished gaze. More than that: somehow, in the moments of fear since he'd first seen that armored head rise into view, his free hand had opened two of his pouches, tossed away the palm-flasks of wine he carried there, and thrust all of the rest of the gewgaws into the emptied pouches.

"Mystra, Lady of Magic," he prayed hoarsely, watching the trembling in his hand grow stronger and realizing that *something* was urging him to return to the trail and take it ahead in *that* direction and to go nowhere else. "What by all your sacred mysteries is going on?"

Surth, he saw, was struggling to his feet, holding out another of the gewgaws in one hand as if it were towing him forward.

"We . . . we're being led like mules," he gasped, suddenly drenched in fear-sweat. "Oh, gods, we're going to die!"

As if in reply to his words, another silent armored warrior floated into view along the trail. It headed purposefully for Surth, raising its blade as it came.

Surth threw the gewgaw in his hand, and Bezrar hastily buried his face in the moss and leaves.

The blast was even bigger this time.

The tug of the thing in his hand grew insistent. He struggled to his feet and stumbled toward the trail. Surth was reeling among the trees—and there was already another gewgaw in his hand.

"Oh, Bane and black doom," Bezrar muttered helplessly, as he found himself heading for the trail as fast as his shaking limbs could take him.

* * * * *

"Wait," Rhauligan said suddenly. "What about that . . . protection?"

"The stars of Mystra did not bar me," Laspeera said, "and nothing steered me in my reading. I think."

"You truly think the goddess herself . . . ?"

"I don't know," Caladnei said firmly. "Narnra . . . did you see seven stars? Blue-white fire?"

The Silken Shadow stared at the three Cormyreans, sudden hope kindling. *I could play this as a shield, try to win free of this room and these three, and . . . and . . .*

As she discovered she didn't know what she'd want to do if she did win her freedom, Laspeera suddenly turned her back.

She's still reading my thoughts! She knows this would be a ruse.

"No," the senior War Wizard said firmly, turning around again to face Narnra. "Where the Mother of Mysteries is concerned, Narnra, none of us who work magic can be sure of anything. Your mind has already shown me that you saw seven stars go out, one by one, as the Mage Royal used spells on you. Yet Mystra's protection may still encloak you, whether you know it or not."

Caladnei nodded gravely. "I'd not like to proceed unless *you* say so, Narnra Shalace. Mystra may take note of your willingness or your refusal. So . . . what say you?"

My choice handed right back to me. Narnra stared at the three Cormyreans, wondering what other twists this day might hold . . . and what she should say now.

The three Cormyreans stared back at her, waiting.

* * * * *

"Well, Lady Joysil, I'm certain that everyone believes they have the misfortune to live in truly troubled times for Cormyr," Lady Honthreena Ravensgar observed, triumphantly taking the largest nut-cake with one hand and reaching for her just-refilled goblet with the other. "But truly

I think we *do*." She waved a profusely ring-adorned hand and added, "Oh, I know that dreadful Devil Dragon no longer menaces half the realm, gulping up knights and soldiers like snacks while orcs and goblins march, but . . . really, are things any better now?"

Lady Baerdra Monthor did not wait for the Lady Joysil Ambrur to answer but said darkly, "Well, unlike *some* at this table, I am truly a daughter of Marsember—and any misfortune to befall the Obarskyrs and the precious Royal Court in Suzail delights me! I'd be just as happy if they all fell down some dragon's gullet by nightfall today and let us regain rule of our own city! All these flirtations with Chauntea and boy kings and that *unspeakable* Alusair riding wild over half the kingdom—"

"The *male* half, dear," old Lady Hornsryl Wavegallant observed meaningfully—then tittered.

Lady Monthor waited for the ripple of catty mirth to die, and then resumed her verbal onslaught right where she'd left off. "—While some unknown little hussy of an *outlander* runs the War Wizards, and Obarskyrs trammel the rights of nobles here, there, and everywhere! Gods above look down, could they do *worse*?"

"Well," Lady Thornra Bracegauntlet said gently, "*my* sympathies lie with Filfaeril. A true Queen, of dignity and breeding, watching in silence all those years whilst Azoun bedded everyone who didn't flee in her skirts the moment his pennants were seen atop a distant hill—"

"Ah, *yes*," Lady Monthor sighed, looking at the ceiling in fond reverie and almost spilling her goblet.

But for the briefest of exasperated sighs, Lady Bracegauntlet ignored the interjection, and swept on. "—then watching her own daughter tear the codpiece off any young man to take her fancy, while the other daughter goes all foolish over a bad noble and goes and dies bearing his child—and how are all the rest of us to know it's legitimate and deserves to someday wear a crown?—and—"

"Years must pass before that little brat gets measured

for any crowns," Lady Ravensgar said darkly. "There's many a royal get that's been fitted for his coffin before his coronet!"

"Oh, stop *hinting*, Honthreena!" Lady Wavegallant said firmly. "If you've started or joined one of these little conspiracies, tell us! We want to hear all about it! As for Filfaeril, I hear she's doing quite well in the bedchamber herself these days with that old stuffy fool of a sage, Alaphondar!"

The Lady Joysil Ambrur had said little and continued to do so. She smiled over her favorite tallglass, watched her wine and cakes disappear with frightening rapidity, and deftly tugged out the choicest gossip. The nine noble ladies of Cormyr who'd been lucky enough to receive an invitation to this highsun-sup cooperated with enthusiasm—for they were only too eager to demonstrate how in the know they were. Little hard truth about conspiracies emerged, but Caladnei the Mage Royal, the Steel Regent, and the Dowager Queen Filfaeril and her antics with Alaphondar all came in for some colorful conversation.

After all, she thought with a smile—aside from occasional uncomfortable duties in the bedchamber regarding the provision of family heirs, and spending as much money on fripperies as possible, of course—that is what noble ladies are for.

* * * * *

Rauthur turned suddenly. "What was that?"

"My . . . diversion," the Red Wizard murmured. "Merely a few bewildered blunderers encountering the helmed horrors to snare the attention of your fellow War Wizards— just in case some of them are in the habit of spying on Vangerdahast."

Huldyl Rauthur mopped his pale face, sighed, and whispered, "Right. I see. Well, here we are. This is one of the 'back ways in' to Old Thun—er, Vangerdahast's sanctum."

"Old Thunderspells? I've heard that term before," Starangh

murmured. "Are we likely to encounter alarm spells, or guardians?"

"No, no, we're inside all that. Vangey can't do spellwork if his own castings keep setting off alarms and spell-backlashes. We just have to keep fairly quiet, because he has a guest."

"Who might that be?"

"I don't know, but he's talking to someone who's right here to move things for him, not someone at the other end of a farscrying spell or crystal." The War Wizard led the way cautiously along a dimly lit passage that smelled of damp earth. The tiles were damp underfoot, and the rough-block stone walls were pierced at intervals by closed doors. "Pantries and such—oh, there is one thing we have to watch out for!"

"Rauthur," the wizard called Darkspells said silkily, laying a hand on the War Wizard's shoulder, "I don't like surprises. You should know that by now."

"Uh, ah, *yes*, Lord! I-I-merely mean I forgot to mention something! Uh, tha-that Vangerdahast conjures pairs of floating eyes and flying hands that he uses as fetch-and-carry servitors . . . they won't be along here, but we mustn't go left up ahead or we may run into them—and of course, he sees through them, and . . ."

"Yes, that would be unfortunate. Is there anything *else* you're having difficulty remembering, friend Huldyl?"

"N-no, Lord Harnrim. I—uh, through here. There're steps up. You wanted to see Vangerdahast at work. . . ."

"Indeed," the Red Wizard breathed, his voice the merest of whispers and his hand remaining on Rauthur's shoulder. "Show me."

Unseen behind the trembling War Wizard, Starangh's other hand slipped the crystal out of his codpiece and held it ready in his hand—just in case.

The worn stone steps were a narrow, short flight that ascended into a sort of garden room, where benches held shallow trays of flourishing herbs and food plants beneath a ceiling of curving glass. Outside, a great ring of thickly grown trees surrounded the domed ceiling, which lay in its own little clearing—and among them, the Red Wizard could see the motionless forms of a dozen or more helmed horrors—so many empty suits of armor, floating tirelessly upright in the shade-gloom.

Rauthur had laid a hand on Starangh's arm, and he turned his head to glare—only to see the War Wizard pointing down.

Through a gap between two of the old bedding trays, more glass could be seen: a wall, this time, that overlooked an adjacent room whose floor was much lower. Starangh found himself looking down on the moving heads of a man and a woman.

Rauthur did something delicate with the air around them. There was a momentary flicker of magical radiance—the merest of ripples—and voices could be faintly heard, the words of the man and woman below.

The Red Wizard bent his head forward to listen intently.

A tiny whirlwind of flames circled in midair as Vangerdahast peered critically at it. "Not enough," he grunted, "Not enough."

Tiny threads of lightning spurted from his fingertips and crawled unsteadily through the air, flickering and darting to join the pinwheel of flames . . . which flared into greater life, wobbled—and promptly collapsed into winking sparks and fading smoke.

Vangey slammed one hand down on the table and rose on it to lean forward and watch every last instant of his spell dying.

"Not a success," Myrmeen Lhal observed gently from the chair across the room where she sat in full armor, her drawn sword across her knees.

Vangerdahast growled deep in his throat as she'd heard many a hunting-dog do and whirled around to glare at her. "I can't work with you *watching* me, curse it, woman! Why don't you take your sword and your armored self out into the woods and shred some small, furry things? *Leave me be!*"

"No," the Lady Lord of Arabel said sweetly, smiling at him with her chin cradled in her hands. Her gauntlets, he noted wearily, were perched on the great carved horns of the chairback. "I *like* small, furry things—even ones that wear wizards' robes and growl at me grumpily."

Vangerdahast growled again, more angrily this time, and brought his other hand down on the table with a crash.

"Patience in all things, Lord," she murmured. "If you expect to craft entirely new spells to bind dozens of dragons, you can't expect every spell to be a simple thing—or other mages would have done it already and bound every last one of them thousands of years ago."

"I've seen enough," the Red Wizard murmured in Rauthur's ear, "and shall take my leave of you. Conduct me to where it's safe to depart."

Huldyl Rauthur nodded and led the way quickly back down the steps to the passage, and along it the way they'd come. Halfway along the corridor he paused beside a door and muttered, "Lord Starangh, within are some of the floating eyes and flying hands that I know how to attune and activate. Would you like to use them to, ah, see farther through the sanctum than we've walked, thus far?"

The Red Wizard smiled. "How thoughtful—but no, thank you. Not this time. You've been very helpful and useful, Rauthur—and I trust shall remain so." He clapped the War Wizard warmly on the shoulder and added, "For of course, to betray me is . . . to die."

With that last whispered word ringing in Huldyl Rauthur's ears, the War Wizard found himself suddenly alone, staring at—the empty passage.

Mother Mystra, he's gone right through the wards! The wards it took Vangerdahast days of fighting just to modify!

Huldyl Rauthur shivered all over, like a wet dog, swallowed

with an effort, and hurried back to the garden room, to restore the silence shield.

So this is what true fear feels like—and everything up to now has been mere . . . apprehension.

Gods, deliver me.

Sixteen

A BUSY DAY FOR WAR WIZARDS

Then my spell burst among them, and—behold!—there
were flamebroiled WarWizards all over the place.

Morthrym of Selgaunt
Sixty Summers of Spellhurling:
My Career As A Mighty Wizard
Year of the Turret

The forest rocked again, and a flaming branch toppled
into the trail, bounced once, and rolled over. Malakar Surth
strode up to it, smiling confidently, and looked down at
a curved shard of war-helm that was slowly spinning to a
halt.

"This," he said, hefting the next gewgaw and admiring its
gleam, "is—transcendent. Simply transcendent."

"Easy, too," Aumun Bezrar agreed from right behind him.
"That's over a dozen now, hey?"

Surth looked up at the leaf-hidden heavens. "Fourteen,"
he said icily. "No thanks to you."

"Hey, now, b'gads! I blasted five of 'em!"

"Could you have done it had I not shown you how to vanquish these . . . these enchanted suits of armor? Bah, don't bother to parley and cavil—we must go forward."

"Uh, aye. Forward." Bezrar frowned as he watched Surth stride on down the trail into what seemed to be even deeper, gloomier stands of trees. Shadowtops and duskwoods, as old as realms and as large as cottages, soaring up into unseen gloom with moss-cloaked vines hanging here and there like gigantic spiderwebs . . .

"Uh, Surth, uh, just one thing: why?"

The tall, thin dealer in scents, wines, cordials, and drugs froze for a moment then said without turning, "I know not. We'll find out when we get there."

He walked on, and Bezrar hastily shuffled after him, wheezing along for a goodly way before he stopped and asked, "Uh, Mal?"

Surth rounded on him with a snarl. "*Don't* call me that!"

"Uh . . . ah, aye, of course, Mal. I—just one *more* thing."

"What?" Surth snapped icily, hefting his shining oval device in his hand as if he meant to hurl it at his longtime partner.

Bezrar held up his own gewgaw. "Uh . . . ah . . what happens to us when we run out of these things?"

Malakar Surth opened his mouth angrily—but when he saw Bezrar's stare go fearful and rise up over his shoulder, he shut it again and wheeled around.

Three helmed horrors were floating in menacing unison through the trees ahead, converging on him. They bore huge battleaxes rather than swords this time, and they were holding them raised and ready to strike.

"Tymora and Mystra both, be with us now!" he snarled, and flung a gewgaw desperately. Malakar Surth didn't know what would happen to one of the shiny ovals if he ever missed with one of his throws—and as he saw more armored forms drifting out of the treegloom, he told both goddesses fervently that he never wanted to find out.

The world burst apart in blue fire—he knew enough to duck down and shield his eyes now—and one of the helmed horrors was gone. The other two flew on toward him as if nothing had happened.

Which was when a distant voice said severely, "Brorm? You *know* Old Thunderspells doesn't want us hurling spells here, so close to him! I don't know what you're blasting, but stop it!"

An armored form loomed up over Surth, a battleaxe gleamed as it swept down, and—Bezrar snarled, "Eat flaming death, metal *pig!*"

The world burst bright blue again, tumbling Surth back head-over-heels into a tanglethorn bush, this time.

He blinked at the sight of his own blood, glistening in red droplets in a line across his thorn-torn hand, and heard that voice, a little nearer and a lot more furious now, shout, "Right, Brorm, *that does it!* I don't care how much the Old Man dotes on your spinach pie—I'm going to flail your backside for you! Don't you try to run now—I may be older, but I'm wise to your tricks, and 'twill take a lot to surprise old Pheldemar of the Fireballs!"

Bezrar promptly blew up the third armored sentinel, and in the wake of the blast, the two stunned Marsembans heard the unseen Pheldemar say something very rude.

There followed a crashing of foliage off behind the trees to the right of the trail, where the forest cloaked some gentle hills, a vigorous, hard-striding man in battle-leathers marched into view, wearing a long leather overcloak that flared out behind him with the haste of his approach. His face resembled an old boot, his hair was steel-gray, and a long black rod bristling with tiny spires and spikes that flashed with a spectrum of winking radiances was clutched in his left hand. His right hand wore a long, flaring-cut white glove, and a flickering radiance like white fire surrounded it.

"Brorm?" he barked as he came up to the trail, peering suspiciously in all directions. "Where by the brass breastplates of Alusair *are* you?"

His eyes fell upon the riven shards of a helmed horror on the narrow dirt path right in front of him.

Pheldemar of the Fireballs gaped down at them in astonishment—a dumbfoundedness that deepened as he glanced along the trail and saw more chunks and shards that had recently been the very best sort of Cormyrean coat-of-plate battle armor. He could see pieces of at least two helms without taking another step.

"*Mystra*," he swore, softly but with feeling—and hurriedly called forth a shielding-spell around himself from his rod. Whoever or whatever had done this must still be lurking nearby. That last blast had been only moments ago. Yes, there!—some of the shards were still rocking in the wake of the force that had hurled them to where they now lay. The War Wizard shook his head, went into an alert crouch, and advanced carefully along the trail.

Almost immediately he caught sight of a boot. The leg wearing it belonged to a man clad like a downcoast merchant—breeches, boots, the hip-length tunic so little seen in the King's Forest or the uplands where smocks were for field-work and belt-tunics for riding or stalking in the forest—who was lying beside a tanglethorn bush, eyes closed and one hand a-dew with fresh blood. He'd never seen the man before. His eyes fell to the belt—a longknife, of the sort used in Marsember. *Just* a longknife. Whoever this man was, he'd had something to do with the destruction of the helmed horrors . . . but he certainly didn't look like a brigand or a wizard or any prepared foe of Cormyr. As for whether he was really senseless or not . . .

Pheldemar leaned closer, pointing his rod at the man. A blast of conjured water sho—

There was a sudden crash and rustle from right behind the War Wizard. He whirled, rod rising—but was still halfway through his turn when something large, hairy, fat and sweating smashed into him and ran right over him, trampling hard.

"Reeeeaaaaaaaagh!" Aumun Tholant Bezrar screamed,

waving his arms wildly as he ran pell-mell through the forest, crashing into trees and saplings wherever the trail wandered and his frantic flight did not. "Rrrrruuhhhhh!"

He was trying to frame the word "run" with his mouth and call it out to Surth, somewhere behind him, but . . .

The War Wizard hit the ground with a grunt and bounced hard, rod flying away into the shrubs. His body settled and lay still, limp and silent, eyes closed.

Trembling with fear, Malakar Surth could see that much of the man through the slit of his almost-shut eyelids. Bezrar was still screaming through the trees, his cries echoing weirdly, and only the deaf could hope to avoid noticing the sound Bez was making. "No more wizards, ever! No more dealings with spellhurlers, oh no! I told Surth, I *told* him! No! No magic, not for any price! No no no *NO!*"

Surth grimaced. With that racket this "Brorm" and probably some other wizards couldn't fail to be here soon, all right—probably a *lot* of other wizards. He had to leave. He had to leave *now*.

The fallen War Wizard groaned and moved one hand, eyelids flickering. In sudden terror Surth burst to his feet and ran right over the man.

He might have made it cleanly over the Cormyrean, but the gray-haired wizard flung up one hand blindly, clawing the air for balance. Surth tripped on it and went sprawling.

Clawing at moss and dirt, never slowing, he found his feet again with a frantic mew of fear and ran on, pelting down the trail Bezrar was still shouting his distant way along.

Pheldemar of the Fireballs groaned again, shook his numbed hand, and rolled over. In the distance a head bobbed briefly in his field of view ere its fleeing owner raced around a bend in the trees and was gone behind a confusion of old, gnarled trunks.

Something gleamed on the trail in the mysterious man's wake, something that was winking back sunlight as it spun around and around, obviously just fallen.

Pheldemar got to his knees then up, took two unsteady

steps, and saw his rod. He retrieved it, wincing at the new aches he'd acquired—gods, that man had hit him harder that the pony that had run over him when he was but a lad!—and plucked up the gewgaw from the trail.

It more than filled his hand: an oval of shiny-smooth, polished silver metal, with an shine of blue where it caught reflections. Thick in the middle and thinning to its edges like a dainty-pastry, and graven with . . . runes of power, yes, but not ones he'd seen before. This looked like Eastern script.

His eyes narrowed. He turned it over in his fingers, finding nothing illuminating on the obverse, and—the light dimmed behind him.

Pheldemar of the Fireballs made sure he turned around fast enough this time, in a crouch and with his rod ready—

Two helmed horrors were floating along the trail toward him. They came to smooth halts, their enchantments recognizing him as a commander rather than a foe. Pheldemar frowned down at the gewgaw in his hand, lifted his gaze to the nearest helmed horror—and on an impulse tossed the oval lazily at the chest of the armored sentinel.

The singing of his shielding, still in place around him, flared into a high shriek as the helmed horror blew apart, tumbling its still-intact fellow end-over-end through the air for an impressive distance. Shards of twisted silver-blue battle armor crashed and rattled off branches in all directions, pattering down through dancing leaves. Several pieces sped into his shield and were slowed to a snail-drift by it. Pheldemar stepped out of the way of the only one of these that was proceeding into a collision with him and peered at it with interest as it ghosted past.

The surviving helmed horror was upright again, flying impassively back toward the trail with its sword raised. Pheldemar looked at it then down at the wreckage at his feet, and lifted both of his eyebrows aloft in earnest.

"Well, now," he said thoughtfully, hand straying to the alarm-horn at his belt. "Well, now . . ."

* * * * *

Ah, Great Mystra? Goddess? Are you here, in my mind?

If so, what should I do?

Narnra smiled wryly. *And if you're there, WHY are you lurking in my mind, without telling me? Are you a Cormyrean, perhaps?*

She expected nothing but silence in reply to that.

Silence she got, but also a stirring in the darkness of her mind.

Seven sparks winked, just for a moment, as if amused . . . and that was all.

* * * * *

Something like a wavering shadow appeared in the air of the room Rauthur had first brought him to, thickened, and grew an arm and an alertly peering head.

"I come from Suzail with urgent news for the Lord Vangerdahast," it announced excitedly, and then waited. Silence was the reply.

The head smiled, and surged forward, growing a body. It did not look like the customary handsome form Harnrim Starangh was wont to wear, but then he wasn't called Darkspells for nothing.

Aside from himself, the dim room was deserted. He cast a swift spell and nodded in satisfaction. "Off that way, where the shield-spells grow strongest," he murmured, "I must not go . . . but here, these shields I can work with. . . ."

That fool Rauthur's mind had been fearfully a-bubble with rushing memories during their visit together, wherefore the boldest Red Wizard in Cormyr now knew there were scrolls in plenty beyond *that* door down this passage and also *that* one, which also led to a closet that held some wands and a rod or two better left undisturbed because hidden tracer-enchantments could well have been built into them. The really powerful—and experimental—magics Vangerdahast kept hidden behind shields that could slay, shields attuned only to him, but there'd be chances enough to gain those later. First, the—

"Blaedron? Is that you?"

Starangh sent a slaying-snake spell through the air even before he melted his body back into a shadow flickering among the pulsing shields. The War Wizard coming around with the corner with a frown on his face and a wand in his hand walked right into the fangserpent and managed only the choked beginnings of a scream before his face was sucked away by the magic—eyes, breath, flesh, and all.

Blood-drenched bone stared with empty sockets at Starangh for a moment ere the man toppled.

Darkspells smiled and cast another magic that made the body a flickering shield-shadow like himself. It'd reappear when the shields were banished, of course, but until then . . .

He left the wand lying right where it had fallen and hastened on.

There was a flash of blue-white fire, and Vangerdahast laughed aloud.

"Yes!" he spat in delight, hands spread wide in the last flourish of his casting. "Done—and perfect!"

He chuckled in triumph, scribbled a note on his parchments with some panache, and rolled his eyes when Myrmeen asked from behind him, "Time for a break, Master of All Magic? Just a few moments to sip water, stretch, and wipe noses?"

Vangerdahast whirled around, robe swirling grandly, and made a very rude gesture he'd seen Purple Dragons present enthusiastically to each other on several occasions.

Myrmeen decided it was her turn to roll *her* eyes.

Rauthur's mind held very clear directions on how to open the armory shields for someone not keyed to them. Merely mutter the right phrase, make the correct gesture, and step forward.

Into a chamber where two War Wizards turned startled faces toward him.

"Laspeera sent me!" Starangh told them anxiously. "There's—"

By then he was close enough to touch one of the men, releasing a spell that twisted the man's only active enchantment—a personal shield; by the kisses of Loviatar and of Shar, these Cormyrean mages lived like scared rabbits!—into a quivering paralysis field.

The other man gaped at him, hands flashing up to shape a spell. The Red Wizard reached into his sleeve, plucked a poisoned dart from a forearm sheath that held two of them, and tossed it into the man's face.

The man shouted and clutched at his eye. Starangh lunged forward and punched him hard in the throat. The War Wizard went down gargling, and by the time he hit the floor the foam was coming to his mouth and the spasms had begun.

Starangh stepped clear and let him thrash. He'd deal with these two after he'd snatched what he'd come for.

The closet door had no lock. He used a daggerpoint to draw it open and moved aside with it, just in case, but no doom lashed out. Inside were dozens of pigeonholes labelled with unfamiliar glyphs, stuffed with scrolls. He selected three at random, peered at them, then pulled out a sack from his belt, shook it open, and started to fill it. There'd be time to find out what magics he'd gained later. Tarrying here would not be wise. He took the rolled parchments from the niches that held the smallest number of scrolls, stuffed the sack until it was full then—paused in mid-reach.

Something was winking in an empty niche: a tiny star of activation. The Red Wizard stepped back. He'd seen the most powerful of zulkirs use such things. Unless touched by the right being or counterspelled in precisely the right way they visited disaster on anyone disturbing them. Its presence meant that Vangerdahast had a second array of scrolls behind this first one—and that he was far more powerful in his Art than Starangh had thought.

The Thayan frowned, whirled, and carefully cast the spells that would burn out the brains of the two War Wizards from within and take with them all remembrance of his own appearance. He plucked his dart from the bubbling flames and took it with him, just in case. It had taken two years of retching weakness to build up a resistance to killing doses of staeradder, but he could now employ it without fear of dying from a casual scratch.

The man War Wizards called Old Thunderspells was not a doddering old fool but a graybeard magically much stronger than anyone in Thay gave him credit for. Defying him with taunts and a flourish of spells would be the act of a fool—and Harnrim Starangh would not leap into the recklessness that had taken so many ambitious young Red Wizards to their deaths.

It was time for the velvet glove, not the fist of fireballs. He'd arrange for Joysil to learn about Vangerdahast's scheme. In her dragon shape, her enraged attack should destroy or weaken the old wizard. Whatever befell in battle, more magic should be uncovered for Harnrim Starangh to oh-so-casually find.

Darkspells of Thay departed the sanctum as hastily and stealthily as he knew how.

The whirling flames collapsed again, taking a small and inoffensive three-legged stool with them this time. It was flaming kindling in an instant and drifting ashes the next.

"Blast! Damn and blast!" Vangerdahast said wearily, leaning on his worktable. "There's something wrong with this last bit." He tapped two lines of runes then brightened. "Hey, now! If I change—"

"Into a pumpkin? Perhaps, but tomorrow'll be soon enough for that," Myrmeen Lhal said firmly, springing up from her chair and sheathing her blade with a flourish.

She took the former Royal Magician firmly by one elbow and turned him from the table, the pain causing him to blink at her, scrabble wildly to keep hold of his notes then give up and stumble along as she towed him, snapping gruffly, "You don't have to treat me like some witless sack of grain, lass!"

"No, of course not," she replied fondly, leaning close to him with her eyes dancing, "and I'll soon stop doing so just as soon as you stop behaving like one!"

"Lass! Uh, *lass!* Myrmeen, damn you, girl! I've just a few tweaks more to work with it and 'twill be *done*, damn it!"

"Of course—as you work right through the night and the next morning and much of the day that follows it, doing those few little tweaks!"

Vangerdahast blinked at her as they went out into the passage. "But of course, lass. 'Tis *magic.*"

"Indeed," the Lady Lord of Arabel agreed, still towing him firmly along. "And magic of a different sort will soon unfold in the kitchen, once you're sitting there resting with a good stiff drink and I get started on the cooking. Gods above, man, you've waited decades to play with your spells—this one can wait for a single night longer."

"Oh, but . . ."

"Oh, but you're almost falling-down weary. Take a seat." The ranger practically shoved Vangerdahast into a chair, clunked his best drinking-horn down in front of him, and filled it to the flaring brim with—

"Gods, woman! Old Amberfire! Where did you *get* this?"

"From your cellars," Myrmeen told him sweetly. " 'Twon't keep forever, you know—and neither will you. When you're dead, you'll wish you'd opened a few more bottles of it instead of always leaving them for 'the right time.' The right time is always now."

The mighty innermost shields of the sanctum hummed and pulsed around them as she unconcernedly started unbuckling straps and shucking armor in all directions.

Vangerdahast blinked at the sight and swiftly looked

away. He cleared his throat loudly, took another swig . . . and slyly looked back at her again.

Ignoring him, Myrmeen plucked out the towel that all wise Cormyrean warriors keep strapped inside their breast-plates beside the spare dagger, towelled herself dry, and reached for the largest skillet.

"It astonishes me," she observed as she murmured the word he used to ignite whatever she'd left ready in the firebox, and went to the pantry cold-shelf for the crock of hog-fat and the string-sack hanging near it for some onions, "how you managed to keep such a round little belly on you, eating as you did."

"Well, lass," Vangerdahast grunted amiably over his drinking-horn, "I was alone and therefore relaxed. However tardily I thought of victuals and clumsily I prepared them, I could dine at leisure. No stress, see you?"

Myrmeen plucked down one of the kitchen knives she'd sharpened and commenced to do deft murder upon the onions. One thing for the old windbeard's magic: His cantrip made the stove hot in a hurry. She cast a glance at the wood ready at hand, judged it wasn't time to add any yet, and made busy greasing the pan. "How often did you end up groan-ing your guts out over the sink or yon bucket? Thrice I've scrubbed it and still can't get rid of the sick smell! No stress then, I suppose?"

Vangey sipped, cast a surprised eye at how little remained in his horn, and observed to the low-beamed ceiling, "The trouble with overclever lasses is their tongues. Sharp like swords, and always jabbing jabbing jabbing at a man."

Myrmeen snorted as the first onions hit the pan with a loud hiss and replied, "The trouble with overclever wizards is their hogheaded-stubborn insistence on always being right, which really means the world must do everything their way. Now, if they were really brilliant enough to choose the right way as their way, those tongues of their lasses could get a rest, and there'd be no jab jab jabbery at all!"

Vangerdahast chuckled and brought his booted feet up on

the footstool. It had been months since it had been handy to do that with. Someone—Mreen here—must have cleared all those old scrolls off it, taken it out of the corner, and put it ready for him. Thoughtful lass.

He leaned back at ease and toyed with thoughts of what barbed comments he could make next to hear her laugh again and bring another thrust back his way. He hadn't chatted this way for years.

The retired Royal Magician of Cormyr sighed with contentment and drained the last of his amberfire, as the warm smell of frying onions rose around him.

* * * * *

The blind-shield behind him flickered as someone passed through it, and an anxious voice asked quickly, "Huldyl?"

For the briefest of instants, Huldyl Rauthur froze in fear—then clenched his fists, drew in breath, and turned, face serene and eyes widening in unruffled inquiry. "Yes?"

Pheldemar Daunthrae stood in the guardroom, slightly out of breath and sporting the beginnings of what would soon be splendid bruises. He held his rod ready in his hand as if expecting a fight.

Huldyl eyed it then looked up at its bearer. "Some sort of fight?"

"We've lost about eight of the sentinel horrors, as far as I can tell," the older War Wizard reported tersely. "Intruders— at least two, though I saw only one of them. Didn't look like warriors or mages or—or anything except Marsemban merchants, actually. They were carrying some sort of enchanted blast-bombs."

"Bombs?"

"Throw one, hit helmed horror, horror blows apart. Little circular silver disc-things, with runes on them in Thayan or some other Eastern script. No fuse, no trigger words, just throw, hit, and—boom!"

"They got away, these intruders, without leaving any of these, ah, bombs behind?"

"I found one, tried it out, cost us a horror. One of them got stunned by his own blast, I think—I heard the explosions, came looking, found him, and was just bending closer when another one burst out of hiding and ran me over from behind. By the time I had my wits again, the stunned one was gone too."

"*Eight* sentinels? Gods forfend."

Pheldemar nodded grimly. "Possibly just a foray to damage as many sentinels as possible, but if they'd been carrying sacks of these bomb-things and I hadn't come to see, they might have blasted their way right to Lord Vangerdahast's front door."

Rauthur nodded. "Certainly seems a determined attempt to reach the sanctum. The Highknights must be told."

"Aye. Shall I—?"

"If you would, yes—and have Thaerma take a look at you before you seek rest, just in case they did you some harm you haven't noticed yet. Those bruises look nasty."

"Thaerma? Go back to the Court?"

"Oh, yes, I think so," Rauthur replied, in tones that made it clear he was issuing an order. "Tamadanther took over your duty-guard as usual?"

"Aye," Pheldemar growled, departing with a none-too-pleased look on his face.

"Come, come!" Huldyl said jokingly. "In a short time the gentle hands of Thaerma will be . . ."

"We go way back, lad, she'n'me. 'Tis not the joy for me you imagine it to be." Pheldemar turned the corner and was gone.

Huldyl shrugged, half-smiled, and turned back to his game of plundercastle. The cards that showed the attacking Witch-Lord wyvern-riders had struck him with damnable luck, and most of his turret-warriors were dead already. Gloomily he moved one of the survivors along the ring of turrets.

I'm just choosing which one he'll die in.

He stared at the board with more foreboding than he'd

felt since just before the last battle with the Devil Dragon.

Very much like the choice I've just made for myself.

Which is when he heard the running footsteps. Someone frantic, coming fast and crashing into things along the way in his haste.

"Huldyl? *Huldyl?*"

Darthym was one of the few half-elf War Wizards, and he prided himself on being pleasant, soft-spoken, unassuming, and a mage of no gossip and few idle words. Now, however, he was wild-eyed and panting.

"Huldyl, Jandur and Throckyl are dead! *Dead*, blasted down with spells!"

Rauthur erupted from his seat, spilling pieces and cards in all directions. This must be Starangh's work—but he had to make his reaction look right, and he'd been losing the damned game anyway. "*What?*" he roared, trying to match Darthym's fire-eyed look.

"I-in the armory! Blown apart! Throckyl's head is just *sitting* there, all by itself, looking out the door at me! I—"

"*Thank* you, Darthym. No sign of who did it, I suppose? Look you: Go and wake Sarmeir and tell him in my name that he's to stand duty-guard with you here. Tell him all you want about what you found, but direct the sanctum defenses if any of the outside guards report troubles to you. *You're* in charge. I *must* report this to Laspeera without delay!"

"Y-*yes*, Rauthur!" The half-elf leaped away down the passage, glad of something to do and direct orders letting him do it. Huldyl shook his head and smiled grimly. Ah, such troubled times. . . .

He ran a hand through his thinning hair, wiped his sweating brows with a knuckle, stood still, and cleared his mind.

It was still in place, as strong as ever. The mindcloak spell Starangh had given him was whispering ever so faintly at the back of his mind, a ready wall to block all probing magics.

Even those of a suspicious second-in-command of all the War Wizards of Cormyr. He was ready to go and make his report.

Seventeen

MINDPLUNGE

The most punishing spell I can think of is one that hurls you into your enemy's mind, and he into yours. Minds rubbing raw on each other—now there's true agony.

Skandanther of Saerloon
Spells Are The Wings That Carry Me High
Year of the Lion

Narnra looked up at the magnificent ceiling of the Dragonwing Chamber. Huge sinuous scaled bodies, swirling and rolling over, frozen forever on the verge of bursting forth in full and terrible glory . . .

Someone—probably several someones—with skill enough to sculpt something much, much larger than they could see all at once had carved those awesomely beautiful, *real* dragons. Someone who must have felt very safe and secure here in Cormyr to spend the months, nay, *years* it must have taken up on ladders in this room, sculpting such a masterwork. Safe, secure, and paid well enough to eat. By a king

or queen of Cormyr who loved beauty enough to pay for
the making and leave this chamber unused for the sculptors
to work. It would take a strong realm, a stable realm, and a
flourishing realm to permit that.

Narnra clung to that thought and let her eyes fall from
the magnificence to the emptiness of the vast room. That
took confidence and wealth, too, to leave such a large and
therefore useful room empty of distraction and so leave the
carved ceiling that much more striking to the eye—and the
three people standing patiently facing her.

Rhauligan, the watchful hands-on-weapons agent of the
Crown of Cormyr . . . what she might become. Might.

Laspeera, the kindly yet powerful wizard. Regal and yet
motherly, the sort of person who's "always there," a solid
part of the furniture trusted by many, who'd be shocked
when death finally took her because they'd come to think of
her as a pillar of Faerûn. Like folk here had thought of this
Vangerdahast . . . like someone, somewhere, had presumably once thought of Elminster—probably in a land now
dust, in a time long ago.

Caladnei. Her tormentor and the one in command
here. The Mage Royal of Cormyr, outranking the older
two Cormyreans—and at a glance an outlander, her skin
dusky. Probably resented by many at Court, who wanted no
stranger seizing power that should rightfully have drifted
into their hands.

Narnra's eyes narrowed. Laspeera should be one of those,
yet she seemed not to be. Wherefore this Caladnei was a
witch who ruled minds by magic or . . . someone worthy of
respect, loyalty, even love.

She stared into the dark eyes of the Mage Royal, who
gazed gravely back. Dark brows, stern—but not quite
imperious—manner. A little frightening.

The woman who wanted to invade her mind.

Narnra found herself breathing faster, almost panting.
Part of her wanted to shout in revulsion, part wanted to hit
out and run . . . and part was sneakily eager and excited,

wanting to see what would happen. That was the spark in her that had taken her to greater and greater boldnesses on the rooftops, and she loved it—though it was a lure into trouble. There was something else rising in her, too . . . slow and hesitant, deeply submerged for too long. She could taste it, catching at the back of her throat.

Loneliness.

She'd been friendless and alone for far too long, Narnra against all the world . . . a world that was to her an endless collection of dupes, unseen passing folk, the rich and powerful best avoided, a few sharks cruising as she was, and—authority. The Watch, the Guard, the Watchful Order, the Lords of Waterdeep: the folk who could slay and flog and imprison and maim with impunity.

Narnra hated, feared, and despised all authority. These three people all held it, Caladnei the most. How much of her fear and defiance was rooted in her own hatred of authority? How—

Never mind. My choices are rough, and I've taken the best one. Mystra even smiled at me. I hope. Let's get this over with.

"Well," she announced quietly, lifting her chin, "I'm waiting."

None of the Cormyreans laughed. The two women both took a step toward her—and the Mage Royal stopped, obviously surprised by Laspeera's advance.

Laspeera kept on coming.

"Narnra," she said gently, "this will go best if you lie down. Right here, on the floor."

Narnra blinked at Laspeera then doubled up and sat. The War Wizard sank down with her as if she was some sort of delicate invalid. When she was lying on her back on the floor—staring up at that splendid ceiling again—Laspeera turned and called Caladnei over. Then she stood up and calmly undid her robe, hauled it off—revealing a gown-like underrobe of red satin—and rolled it.

Silently, she pointed Caladnei to the floor beside Narnra

then slid her rolled-up robe under the backs of their heads.

"A pillow?" Narnra asked incredulously.

"Something to keep you both from splitting heads open on the hard floor," Laspeera replied rather severely, "if emotions surge. Now, hold hands and begin."

"Yes, Mother," Caladnei replied in a gently mocking voice. Narnra found herself smiling. The Mage Royal murmured a long, complicated rising and falling incantation, and . . . the dragons overhead went away.

Warm and dark, descending, the darkness around flashing with a bewildering whirl of half-glimpsed bright scenes, bursts of sound, surges of anger, amusement, even weariness . . .

[Narnra.]

[Narnra, hide not.]

Surge of energy, darkness going rubyshine, lights and noise coming fast . . .

[Narnra Shalace!]

I'm here. What do you want of me?

[Show me your mother.]

Raven-black hair and kind emerald eyes, bent over her in a face as white as bleached bone, cheekbones that made her look as exotic as she was beautiful, tender deft hands cradling her so firmly and yet gently. Maerj, the apprentices called her . . . Mother Maerj, comforting her in a dark room, her sniveling still loud around them. "There, there, my little one. Dreams can be bright as well as terrible. Like meals, some are good and some bad, but we need them all, just the same. . . ."

As always, Narnra found herself aching to reach out and clutch her mother's fingers, to cry her name, to speak her love and loneliness so Mother Maerj would hear and smile and tell it was all right, everything was all right.

[Of course. Come away, and see something of mine that will hurt less.]

Sudden raucous laughter, and thick smoke in a low-beamed, crowded, candlelit inn common-room. Swaggering men with bright goblets in their hands and weapons strapped all over them, striding past and then—noticing her, and leaning close to peer.

"What's this? Caladnei of the Scrolls, eh? You read scrolls for fees? What idiot can't read a scroll?"

"One who has a *magic* scroll, sir, but can't work spells," Caladnei's young but firm voice said quietly, tight with the fear of coming trouble.

Three young, bristle-bearded, red-with-drink faces were leaning over her now, peering—and breathing the fumes of golden Sarthdew she hadn't coin enough for even a finger-flagon of, all over her.

"You a mage? Who'd you study with?"

"No one, sirs. I . . . my spells come from within."

"Well, now. What say your parents about that?"

No lass restlessly chafing under the rule of parents and afire to see the wider world likes to be thought of as a child out on the sly, and Caladnei's voice was stiff as she replied, "My parents let me find myself and make my own dealings with Faerûn. Do yours?"

There were snorts and roars and guffaws of mirth, and one of the men bawled, "I *like* you, lass! Want to ride with us?"

"Where is it you ride, sir, and for what?"

"Across all wide and splendid Faerûn, Lady Caladnei—in search of adventure and lots of *these!*"

An eager hand un-throated a purse and spilled dozens of heavy gold coins across Caladnei's little table with a flourish, leaving her gaping at more money than she'd ever seen in her life before. Some of the coins rolled, folk everywhere leaned to see—and a shorter man in the group, almost a boy by his looks, plucked up one rolling coin and tossed it idly with two fingers . . . right down the front of her dress.

There was another roar of laughter, and Caladnei knew her face was burning. The mirth spread around *The Old Cracked Flagon*, and she clenched her fists, wishing she were anywhere but here.

"Yours, lass," the first man roared. "Yours to keep—and plenty more like it if you come with us! We need more magic to back up our blades!"

"Oh, but . . ."

"Hold, now," the oldest face among the men looming above her table said quietly. "We'd best talk to her parents. I don't want to be hounded as a slaver, snatching young lasses . . ."

"Gods, Thloram, anyone can see we're not *slavers!* Nor lechers, neither—we've got Vonda for that!"

"Aye," a buxom woman whose lush curves were spilling out of a loosely laced bodice purred, sidling past the men to appraise Caladnei with an almost contemptuous eye. "And I can handle the lot of you! Don't worry, dear, I'll see that they're too weary to come pawing you. Oh, stop *laughing*, you hogs! Here, dear, take a handful of these coins, and pr'haps Marcon will stop leering at you quite so overeagerly!" She turned. "Stop pestering locals, you louts, or we'll have more trouble! She's barely old enough to—"

"I'm coming with you," Caladnei announced suddenly, standing up and hearing the stillness of utter astonishment spread across the common-room in an instant. "Keep your coins—I'll win my own."

[Enough. Now . . . what's this? Something hidden, not just from me, but from yourself . . . something old. Let's see. . . .]

Cowering in her cot late on a dark night, as angry voices soar up the stairs. A man with a fluting, patrician accent— some noble on the city, she knows not who—is shouting at her mother.

Too far away to hear, too scared to slip out into the chill to hear better.

Her mother's replies, too faint to make out the words, but cold and angry and sharp-edged.

The voices building, louder and faster, slashing and snapping like crossed swords—then suddenly a mighty roar that shakes cot, room, stairs, and all. A startled shout amid its thunder and . . . silence.

No! No, I don't want to see this! I never wanted to see this again! It never happened! Never never NEVER!

[*Easy*, Narnra. See something else of mine, now. Something happier.]

Laughter and warm firelight, and Marcon pouring a river of gold coins down onto her body while Bertro and Thloram Flambaertyn grin and clink goblets with her, all of them bare and a-tangle amid the furs. Rimardo hooting with laughter across the room and springing from the top of an ornate wardrobe—newly purchased, every bit as fine in its carving as her father's best work and priced accordingly, too—onto an unseen Vonda, who shrieks with laughter and mock pain and slaps him energetically. Umbero intoning solemnly through the midst of all the merriment: "Truly Tymora smiles upon we of the Brightstar Sash! I make the count to be a full six *thousand* full-weight gold coins, not counting what you're playing with in here, and the odd ones!"

[But enough of my good times. Let's see something of like excitement from you . . . yes.]

A warm summer night, all the roofs of Waterdeep flooded in full moonlight, and Narnra in her shift gazing out at it all from her high bedroom window. A ghost of a breeze from inland, warm and dry and banishing the smells of salt and dead fish. The stirring excitement of putting one leg over the windowsill—something forbidden, something daring. . . .

The roof-slates rough underfoot but reassuring and

standing now right out under the moon and glorious vault of stars, only a few tiny clouds torn and tattered off to the north. Nothing between her soft skin and all the warm night but light, gauzy fabric. Boldly striding down the sloping roof to the edge to get a better view of great Waterdeep spread out before her and dark Faerûn beyond. Looking idly over the edge, seeing that it was a long, killing way down to the garden but being utterly unafraid.

Suddenly, in the distance, across the silver vista of roofs, a lone dark figure darting and leaping—a thief? Someone hurrying on the rooftops. Heart suddenly in throat, Narnra looking around at the roofs nearby, that one so close . . . a quick run in bare feet, a leap, the warm wind in her hair, and landing catlike with a gentle thump that might just have awakened a servant if the Maurlithkurs forced one to sleep in their attic. On across their larger, sagging roof—tiles starting to go in one place, sliding askew—to the one beyond and perching there amid on an unfamiliar dormer hidden from her own window by the peak of the roof.

Perching like a carved gargoyle or an owl looking for prey, long legs doubled up, feeling truly *alive*, and laughing at the excitement. Castle Waterdeep soaring just over there and the great dark shoulder of the mountain beyond, with the tiny winking lights of lanterns where guards were at their lofty posts, looking down on . . . *her*.

Rush of fear, heart hammer-beating, laughter, springing aloft, and turning a cartwheel on a flat bit of roof ere landing to strike a wide-armed, defiant pose. "Yes! Here I am! Come and get me!"

Excitement like fire in her veins, leaping from roof to roof, and finally back home to her waiting sill and in—in to wash filthy feet so she'd not be caught come morning. Looking back at the window knowing a whole new world— *her* world—lay waiting now, every night she wanted it.

[Ah. See then my moment of bold venture.]

Dimmer moonlight and Thloram murmuring, "Easy, now. The rest of us have come this way before, and returned. 'Tis safe."

Caladnei's hand trembling with fear as she holds it out to him then turns to face the cold, steady blue fire that bides so impossibly between the two ancient stone pillars. Cracked and vine-covered, nothing like the splendor she'd envisaged: no glowing runes on gleaming metal nor sinister guardians . . .

The first portal she'd ever seen, and merely being this close to it left her wet and shaking in terror.

"Where's our Caladnei of the Scrolls?" Thloram murmurs.

From somewhere she finds just enough will to force out a laugh and stride forward into waiting blue fire, biting her own tongue in terror to keep from sobbing. . . .

[Now, d'you recall your first theft? Show me.]

The next summer, a night just as warm, Narnra better at tumbling, bolder now. Often perching gargoyle-like on gables and around corner-spires, watching folk of Waterdeep through their bedchamber windows—and learning much more than some young lasses do.

Brawls and drunken fights and hurried little deals in dark streets and alleys, a knifing or two, many snatch-and-run thefts . . . and this night, one such that leaves a fat merchant on his backside grunting in pain and a fleet-footed, desperate loader-of-wagons pelting down an alley, heavy purse in hand . . . turning right beneath Narnra's perch and racing up a rickety, groaning outside stair, gasping raggedly for breath, snatching out a hand to a door-catch—and freezing to peer in the narrow lit sliver of window, stand uncertainly for a moment with a whispered curse at someone recognized within, and strain up on tiptoe to perch the stolen purse up on the edge of the roof overhead. Going inside, door banging closed, to raised voices and Narnra so excited she thinks she's going to be sick.

Dare she? Watch-lanterns down below and armed men tramping, clouds blotting the moon . . . and like a night-viper, Narnra crawling chin-first down the steep roof, grazing the tiles with her body as she keeps low, Watch officers calling closer . . . down to where she can put her hand on the purse, heavy and excitingly solid. And draw it oh-so-slowly back and up to where she turns and steals away with it. Opening it on another rooftop a safe distance away, when a cloud rolls on to let the moon stab down and show her coins galore between her hands!

[But things have gone darker for us both, haven't they?]

Great batlike wings and loose brown scales bristling from a gigantic bulk, shoulders like shifting boulders as the wings spread in a banking glide down . . .

Down toward her, great jaws gaping wide, stinging tail lashing the air.

"Help! Help!" Bertro calling weakly, blinded by his own blood, Umbero sprawled senseless or dead over him.

Caladnei cursing just for something despairing to say as she starts to run right at the swooping wyvern with no spells left and only a broken sword in her hand, running like a mad thing into the jaws of doom because her friends need aid. . . .

[No, I'll spare you those deaths. Every bloodletting leaves a stain on those who see it. What of the death that overturned your world?]

No! No, damn you, mage! I don't WANT to—don't—

Her mother working late that last night, before the great blast that left her broken and burned amid the shattered shell of her front parlor. Magic killed her, of course, but whose? A wizard who hated her? No, someone hired to slay—but by the House of Artemel, or the Lathkules, or another?

Bresnoss Artemel himself had brought the tiara to her

shop, ringed by eight bodyguards openly wearing Artemel
livery. Its glory-rubies had been the size of Narnra's fist,
even the smallest ones were as large as her thumb. They
were to be recut and set in matched pairs into a navel-length
pectoral.

Maerjanthra had pinned the fine chain of the pectoral up
on a cloth-covered dummy to begin the task, even as word
had raced through the streets that a tiara worth millions in
gold had been stolen from the bechamber of House Lath-
kule, the finest jewelers among the nobility of Waterdeep.
Then—

No! {furious turmoil, claw thrust shake} *NO! I won't see
this! I WON'T!*

—Later, wandering alone and despairing across the piti-
less rooftops, weeping and raging. The rubies gone from the
shop before Narnra, flung out her windowsill by the heaving
shuddering of the explosion, could even climb back inside
to . . . to . . .

*Get out of my head, Caladnei! Get back go away leave
me!*

On the rooftops months later, as that winter came stealing
in with ever-colder breezes, still heartsick, still wondering:
Had it been the Artemels, wanting to silence Lady Maerjanthra of the Gems so she could never reveal that the rubies
had come to her in a tiara? Or the Lathkules, wanting to
obliberate a long-time rival at gemcutting, perhaps thinking
her the tiara-thief? Had an apprentice betrayed her mother,
whispering to the Lathkules, or . . . ?

Caladnei! {sobbing anguish, blind clawing and fighting}

[My apologies, Narnra. I've known sorrow too.]

Hurrying home to Turmish on a borrowed horse after hearing the dark news, along winding upland lanes to the tiny Turmish village of Tharnadar Edge. Her mother had been born there and now was gone, lost at sea, not even any bones to bury.

Her father Thabrant, still tall but now dark-eyed, grim, uncaring. A hollow shell of a man with no vigor left in him, not even any tears. She'd cried for the both of them, arms fierce around him. He'd stood like a statue, quietly telling her he'd never trust gods again.

He told her he was going to go home to Cormyr to die. "On the smallest ship I can find, Cala, with the worst crew. I hope Talos and Umberlee take me when we're on the waves, as they did her. I'll go to their altars and curse them both before I go aboard."

No chance for either of them to say goodbye to the swift-tempered, passionate bird of a woman who'd been the hearthstone for both their lives: Maela Rynduvyn, slender, deft, and quiet-footed. Her hair russet, the same strange eyes she'd given Caladnei, dusky-skinned, most comfortable barefoot in old clothes. Drowned in a storm off Starmantle on her way to Westgate to see a long-lost sister.

Her father had held his gnarled woodcarver's hands awkwardly that day, the first time Caladnei had ever seen him do so. He'd cradled empty air as if he were carrying something precious or hoped to catch it by never looking at it but keeping always ready. He hadn't looked at the meal Caladnei had made for them both or at anything but her. She'd shivered often that night as she lay unsleeping in the dark watching him sitting by the window staring back at her—because she knew he wasn't seeing her but her mother. Only her mother.

Mage, I don't CARE about your dead mother or anything of your life! I just want this to be over and you to be out of my mind, my—my—

[Easy, Narnra. Easy. Show me the first thing that comes into your mind.]

Alone and hungry, that first winter, being passed a flagon by a man with an easy smile, slouched outside the open door of his hut in Dock Ward. It was more than wine, a fire in her belly that soothed and drove off the chill and helped her laugh. They told jokes and tales and snorted at each other's mimicry of the street merchants, and after a time Urrusk had taken her inside to swipe the flies from a half-gnawed roast goat-leg and hand it to her.

Her empty stomach had made her pounce on it and gnaw like a panther, and he'd laughed all the more, refilling her flagon often and just laughing when he fumbled with her lacings and couldn't find her belt and fell on his face against her shins.

Another man had lurched in the door and backhanded Urrusk away. "Dolt!" he'd snapped. "I hire you to lure the slaves, not ruin them!"

With a growl he'd reached up into the crowded tangle of oddments in the rafter and brought down some jangling manacles, advancing on Narnra with a glint in his eye that suggested he might continue where Urrusk had been hauled off, after he—

She fought weakly as he snatched at her wrists. His fingers were as cold and hard as stone when he caught her, and he'd lifted her like a doll toward a ring set into one wall, chuckling. Then up from behind him Urrusk had lurched, face twisted in rage, and thrust the chain of the second manacle around the larger man's throat, ere hauling hard.

The big man's eyes had bulged as he roared and tugged. Narnra had put her shoulders to the wall and kicked him between the legs, as high and as hard as she could, ending up bruisingly on her behind on the littered floor as he staggered, found a wall with his face . . . and she was out into the night like a rushing wind, running blindly with a Watch-patrol soon after her. . . .

{Fear disgust rage helpless rage revulsion}

[Narnra, be *easy*. You're not the only one who knew trouble in Waterdeep.]

Sweating and panting in that upper room in the house off Soothsayer's Way, where old Nathdarr ran his school of the sword better with one eye than many men can fight with two. Caladnei the only lass in the room, her desperate leaps and nimble bladework slowly turning his contempt into grudging admiration, until the night when Marcon and Thloram burst in breathless to shout at her to flee with them—now!

While she worked to become better with steel, her companions of the Sash had run riot spending their coins in the City of Splendors. Rimardo and Vonda had foolishly tried to rob a noble, and his men had captured them and tortured them to death, forcing from them the names of all in the Brightstar Sash . . . as the noble's guards had jeeringly told Marcon whilst trying to impale him in a tavern, less than an hour ago.

He and Thloram had fought their way clear, with a mob on their heels and four guardsmen in livery dead, and now the Watch had joined the hounding. If she still had most of her gold, they knew where they could buy room together inside a crate being loaded onto a wagon for transport out of the city this night.

Nathdarr's look of admiration had melted back into sour disgust. He was shaking his head as they ran out the back way into the night—but when the mob came howling up to the front door of his training-room, he'd calmly put his sword through one, two, and three of them before drawing breath.

Such fun. So did you outlive all the others then come running to Cormyr to hide?

[Cruel, Narnra. I'll show you why I parted ways with the Sash. You deserve that much.]

With Thloram dead and buried in the Rift, Marcon was the only one left of the jovial band who'd plucked her up from her table at the Cracked Flagon. Oh, he'd found replacements—more blades and wizards than ever, younger and even more apt to swagger than Bertro had been—but the *fun* was gone. Too many sad memories, too many absent smiling faces.

Wherefore she hadn't bothered to tell Marcon when Meleghost Telchaedrin had sent word that she should come to him in private. If some decadent Halruaan wanted to make an end of her, so be it. We all greet the gods sometime, and Caladnei was past caring when her time would come.

The Sash was here in the Telchaedrin family towers to accept a commission. Sarde Telchaedrin wanted them to hunt down a renegade heir before the bloodtaint spell he'd crafted spread death to every corner of Halruaa. It was a task Caladnei mistrusted, but the coin being offered was staggering—another mark of suspicion that her younger comrades in the Sash didn't seem to see . . . and Marcon obviously didn't want to notice.

Lord Meleghost was an older uncle of Lord Sarde, considered "an odd one" by the few Halruaans Caladnei had been able to mention his name to. In his younger days he'd gone adventuring outside the Walls, bringing back strange tales of colorful Faerûn beyond the mountains. He was alone when she arrived in the high-vaulted, empty marble hall, standing on a high dais by a great oval window as tall as six tall men. Even beside it, Lord Meleghost was a very tall man.

"Welcome," he murmured without the usual elaborate courtesies, extending a hand to her. "Thank you very much for coming, and please accept my assurances that I mean you no harm and intend no deceit."

Caladnei blinked in surprise then gave him a smile and

her hand together. "You seem in haste, Lord—a pace and a plain manner I must admit I find pleasing. Please unfold your will to me without delay."

Meleghost nodded, peering at her over his long nose like an old and weary bird of prey, and said, "As you wish. This commission is a ruse that will lead you into disaster. Sarde is steering you into unwittingly attacking a rival family of our realm. You should depart Halruaa—alone—now."

Caladnei nodded slowly. "I've been uneasy about this from the first." She took a step forward and asked, "Why are you telling me this?"

Meleghost also stepped forward until their faces were almost touching—his breath smelt pleasantly of old spices— and murmured, "I once adventured with your father, and I mindscry him from season to season so we can chat together. Child, Thabrant is dying. He dwells in a hut in the hills north of Immersea in upland Cormyr and fails slowly—but he's grown desperate to see you. He said to tell you that his pride is all gone now and he needs you."

Caladnei stood trembling on the edge of tears, swallowing hard. The old Halruaan folded comforting arms around her and bent his forehead to hers.

A moment later, grieving and confused, she felt a fire flooding into her mind, bright white and irresistible. . . .

She gasped, or thought she did, and suddenly the thrill of a new spell was in her mind, laid out clear as crystal for her to see: a translocation spell that could snatch her from place to place. Teleport! This was the magic wizards called teleport.

This should help you to flee Halruaa, so long as you never try to use it inside one of our buildings—including this one.

His voice was like soft thunder in her mind. Impulsively she said back to him, *I cannot thank you enough, but I insist that this not be a gift, but a trade. This is the best magic I know. Please take it.*

The spell of flight? I have it, but gladly I'll accept yours.

A true daughter of Thabrant Swordsilver to deal thus in honor. Fare you well, Caladnei, and have a good life.

Weeping, she kissed his cheek, whirled away, and fled. It took a good few teleports to reach upland Cormyr.

[Do we understand each other enough, yet?]

Yes. Damn you, yes.

[That's good. I like you, Narnra Shalace. I hope you can come to like me. But all is going dim around us because this is . . . tiring. Very tiring. You've been thrashing like a hooked fish.]

Caladnei, I FEEL like a hooked fish!

Up from the rushing darkness, like a fish swimming up to sunlight, up to the brightness and noise and—

Flash of silver, crash of cascading swirling water, bells and horns and bright burning . . .

Narnra found herself staring into the eyes of Caladnei—which were a deep brown-red, and royal blue at the center, she saw suddenly—and the Mage Royal was looking back at her.

They were both weeping silently, faces wet with tears, as they lay together on their sides, locked in a fierce embrace.

Over Caladnei's curves Narnra could see Laspeera and Rhauligan standing watchfully near, she holding a wand ready, he a drawn sword.

Trapped. Trapped and bound and cheated.

In sudden red rage Narnra tore herself free of Caladnei in a welter of shoves, slaps, and thrusting knees and hurled herself back into the air and away.

The Mage Royal's shielding spells flared into life like white flames, enshrouding Caladnei from view.

Narnra landed, rolled, and came up running. Laspeera

and Rhauligan were moving—keeping between her and the doors!

She swerved away from them both, sobbing bitterly, and ran to the farthest empty corner of the chamber—where she slammed her fists against the unyielding wall until they hurt too much to go on pounding.

She sagged, forehead against a smooth and uncaring wall, and sobbed until she was empty. Empty and . . . alone.

"Well?" the Mage Royal asked softly, from behind her. "Not the usual training I give agents, but are you a mite more . . . content?"

Narnra whirled around to glare back at her. "Where's my *freedom?*" she snarled. "Mind-chains, you give me! What you choose to show of your past and what you want to take of mine! Content—*bah!*"

Caladnei's face looked as unhappy as her own. As Narna watched, a fresh tear welled out of her eye and ran down her pale cheek.

"And your choice?" the Mage Royal whispered, holding out her hand like a beseeching beggar.

Narnra looked at it and whirled to look away, breathing heavily.

What choice have I? Where in all Faerûn can I run to?

What will she do to me if I refuse?

Her mind whirled an image back to her once more: that glimpse of Caladnei trembling with fear before the first portal she'd ever seen—then forcing a laugh and striding forward into its blue fire biting her own tongue in terror . . .

Caladnei, running toward a swooping wyvern with no spells left and only a broken sword in her hand, because her friends needed her . . .

Friends. Someone to laugh with. That brought a new scene: Caladnei laughing by a fire, laughing to cover her embarrassment and pain as old tuft-bearded Thloram gave her warm spiced wine and pulled back the sleeping furs to lay her bare for all to see and sew up the sword-gash she'd taken in their victory that day . . .

Thloram, lying broken and dead after a fall in the Great Rift, his jests and his comforting hands and his splendid hotspice stews gone forever in an instant . . .

She would have liked to have known Thloram.

This woman had *lived* so much more than she had.

Like the legends said Elminster had, and still did, after a thousand years of battles and monsters and fell wizard-foes.

It was a long, silent time before Narnra said slowly, not looking up, "I believe, Mage Royal, you've found yourself a new—and, gods curse you, loyal—agent."

Eighteen

REVELATIONS AND MISSIONS

Know thy traitors and who's the kin of whom, and that's half the deaths delayed. Averted, one more optimistic might say, but I've never been one of those. I'm the other sort of fool.

Szarpatann of Tashluta
Advice to the Doomed:
A Chapbook for Would-Be Rulers
Year of the Twelverule

In a high, narrow, and deserted hallway outside the Dragonwing Chamber, Huldyl Rauthur frowned thoughtfully. If the echoing spillover of the Mage Royal's mind-ream hadn't been wrinkling his face in pain, he'd have been grinning.

The backlash outpourings were making both the High-knight Rhauligan and Mother Laspeera herself wince. Huldyl could feel their pain, too. Between them, Caladnei and this sorceress Narnra must have minds to overmatch any twenty War Wizards of the realm combined. Mother

Mystra, make that any *twoscore* mages of Cormyr.

So this little thief-lass was the daughter of the Great High Elminster himself, eh? Small wonder Caladnei had rushed to make her an unwilling agent of the Mage Royal, a sort of "Highknight on probation." Well, well.

It would be best to tell no one, not even Starangh. Just in case Huldyl Rauthur needed something important to bargain with for his own life someday.

He'd better wait a few breaths and let everything settle down in there before knocking. Reporting the trouble at the sanctum to Laspeera was urgent, of course, but as the sayings went, prudence was prudence, and an overbold War Wizard is a swiftly dead War Wizard.

*　*　*　*　*

"Gods bless you, Narnra," Rhauligan said roughly from somewhere behind her.

They'd waited for her and kept silence while she made her choice.

Narnra drew in a deep breath, spread both of her hands on the cold wall, and pushed hard, forcing herself to turn around and face them without taking however long she might have needed to muster up enough courage.

Her choice was made, the first bend of her road ahead clear before her.

"Command me, Mage Royal," she forced herself to say. She even managed a smile.

*　*　*　*　*

Suddenly, Huldyl Rauthur was no longer alone in the corridor. A Purple Dragon winked into existence, gave him a smile, and raised one hand beckoningly.

The warrior's face melted—just for a moment—into that of the wizard Darkspells.

Huldyl considered fainting for a moment then settled for

just swallowing hard and obediently walking toward the Red
Wizard, who smiled, became a Purple Dragon again, and led
the way through another door.

* * * * *

The anklet was doing its work perfectly. Even better,
Caladnei thus far suspected nothing. A trifle too slow and
trusting still, our Mage Royal . . .

Elminster smiled wryly. To say nothing of the increasingly
slow wits of one Elminster of Shadowdale.

Caladnei's thoughts had certainly been in turmoil this last
little while, as she kept a hostile mind sane within her own,
but the anklet's light prying had been more than clear on one
matter: Narnra Shalace *was* his daughter.

"Bless ye, Mystra," he murmured. "This now calls for
bolder action."

He called to mind her likeness there in his paper-littered
study and with a soft-spoken spell built it from a vivid mental
image to an apparently solid figure in leathers, glaring at him
through dark hair. Its pose was frozen as he strolled around
it, peering critically and adjusting hips there and height of
shoulder *there*. . . .

He frowned, beckoned with his finger, and told the
curved pipe that answered his summons, "I can't remember
how she *walked* and held her hands when she moved. Time
to go and take a peek."

Leaving the pipe floating mutely in front of a fading
Narnra, he turned, took a step, and vanished.

* * * * *

The bard wore leathers that were gray with age and thick
with road-dust. His face was largely hidden behind a pewter
tankard as tall as a short warrior's breastplate, and he sat
hunched over a table in the gloom in the back corner of this
particular taproom in Suzail because this—specifically, the

broom-closet door behind him—was where the portal-link to Marsember was.

Roldro Tattershar didn't think too many folk of Cormyr, even Highknights and War Wizards, knew about this particular portal anymore. Not even most of his fellow Harpers had heard of it. Wherefore Roldro took care to affix a villainous false mustache onto his upper lip whenever he visited The Green Wyvern and employ garb far different from his customary floridly flamboyant dress.

However, as he set down his tankard on this particular occasion, he choked and almost swallowed his mustache when the air right in front of him wavered and suddenly produced two men, standing with their backs to him where there'd been nothing but empty air before. Swiftly and silently Roldro put his head down on his arm and let his tankard loll and lean in his thumb, looking every inch the passed-out drunkard.

"I can't stay long!" the shorter man hissed, running a nervous hand through the few strands of brown hair that were left across his balding pate. "I was about to report the ah, troubles at the sanctum to Laspeera. A lot of palace duty-guards saw me pass!"

"How much do you think the Mage Royal and Laspeera know about the details of Vangerdahast's work?"

Rauthur frowned. "Almost all of it. He trained both of them."

"No, no! His grand scheme—the one he's working on right now! Binding dragons to be defenders of Cormyr!"

"Oh! Ah, *that* plan. Is that really what he's . . . ? Gods! Uh, I'm—I'm not sure. I can try to find out, but . . . well, I'm not a very sly questioner."

"*That's* stone cold truth, Rauthur. Why not say you heard Vangerdahast muttering something to himself like 'these dragon bindings will never work!' when his shields went down for a moment, as part of these 'troubles,' and mark their reactions?"

"Ah—yes, yes, of course!"

"Good!" The taller, thinner man muttered something else—and the room was suddenly empty again of all but three tables, their chairs, and a Harper feigning a drunken stupor.

Roldro Tattershar promptly sprang up from his chair like a bolt of lightning in a hurry, yanked open the broom-closet door, and drained his tankard in one long pull ere setting it down carefully on the table and backing through the closet door.

Vangerdahast planned to bind dragons to protect Cormyr? Well, well! It was certainly time to stir the cauldron and see who bubbled to the top first!

Besides, being a Harper was hungry and thirsty work, and the Lady Joysil Ambrur would be sure to pay handsomely for *this* information.

* * * * *

Caladnei smiled. "Well, I'm sure you're in need of food, drink, a long soak, and some sleep. We daren't give you those here lest someone see you and take note that our hunted prisoner is now more of an honored guest, but we can give you ample coins to get such necessities at an inn. Rhauligan?"

The Harper rolled his eyes, told the ceiling in a mutter, "Always me! Always! Have you noticed?" and from a pouch poured out an ample handful of coins into his palm. He put all of them carefully into Narnra's hand.

"Hear then," Caladnei continued, "your first task: Find the traitor I know is among my War Wizards—*not* by magic or by confrontation but rather by observing the doings of certain War Wizards in Suzail from the background, trying to stay unnoticed as much as possible."

Narnra raised an eyebrow. "You can't just mind-ream them?"

"Many have trap-magics bound into their shield-spells . . . moreover, they do much better work for me when they think their little sideline activies go unobserved."

" 'Little sideline activities'? Illict and corrupt this and that?"

"Some of them, yes. Others merely have undignified hobbies or socially awkward liaisons, and I don't want them unhappily peering over their shoulders expecting my cold eye on their backsides for the rest of their careers—or those careers will end up being worth very little to me."

"Caladnei, I'm the stranger here. How am I supposed to know when a surreptitious visit to a bedchamber or a murmured name traded for a few coins is a little sideline and when it's high treason to Cormyr?"

The Mage Royal sighed. "A good point. Look, Narnra, I don't care—Speera here doesn't care, Vangey in his day didn't care, and all the Wizards of War knew it—if this or that hairy male War Wizard likes to put on rouge and lady-gowns or roll in nutbutter honey behind closed doors. Or tries to seduce every last noble lady—or lord, for that matter—in the realm. I also don't care if they mutter future trade opportunities to every merchant in the kingdom."

She waved an emphatic finger. "I *do* care if they go behind closed doors to talk to rich Sembians, Red Wizards of Thay, Zhentarim, anyone from Westgate, or nobles who seem to be using false names or who never leave dockside inns in Suzail. I care if they go anywhere to meet alone with independent mages or disappear for days on end into the mansions, hunting lodges, or castles of our nobles."

She sighed and added in calmer tones, "If they do, *don't* try to confront, harm, or follow them. Just come and tell me who went where. I'll know, of course, if they're supposed to be doing something sly for me wherever you saw them."

"And if I'm arrested as an outlander spy?"

"Demand to be interrogated by a senior War Wizard—something so feared by most Cormyreans that they'll be impressed and won't think you're bluffing. When you end up facing any War Wizard, tell them to contact Laspeera or myself 'in the name of both Azouns.' They dare not ignore that phrase. We'll tell them we've cast a spell on your mind as an experiment and you may therefore do all sorts of odd things . . . and aren't to be prevented from doing so."

"Well, *that's* true enough."

Caladnei looked hurt for the moment it took her to see Narnra's crooked smile.

"I'm sorry," the Mage Royal said gently. "I know none of this has been easy for you. Think of it as a long, grand theft and us as your fellow gang members."

Narnra rolled her eyes and said briskly, "This is going to proceed much better if I know who these War Wizards are, what they look like, and where in Suzail I might have the slightest hope of finding them."

Caladnei nodded and reached out a finger to touch Narnra's forehead. "Hold still. This is the easiest way, believe it or not."

There was a moment of icy tingling then images burst into Narnra's mind, unfolding from momentary confusion into the faces of a dozen War Wizards. Two women and ten men, all moving slightly, just as they'd been doing when captured by Caladnei's magic. Names appeared in her head with each one, reappearing whenever she turned her attention back to an image already seen. "Thaeram Duskwinter, Bathtar Flamegallow, Calaethe Hallowthorn, Iymeera Juthbuck, Helvaunt Lanternlar, Bowsar Ostramarr, Huldyl Rauthur, Storntar Redmantle . . ."

Narnra frowned, closed her eyes, and sat back, shaking her head slightly.

"Got those?" Rhauligan asked. When she nodded, he added, "Good," and drew a much-folded square of vellum from his sleeve. It opened out into an incredibly detailed map of Suzail that made Narnra lean forward in awe to peer at the little dots that denoted every last building in the city. The Harper put a finger on one dot and said, "This is a tavern called The Downed Falcon, a favorite haunt of Flamegallow and Ostramarr. And this down here is the—"

Narnra chuckled despite herself, looked slyly over at

Caladnei, and asked lightly, "No mental images of taprooms and ladies' privy-chambers? You disappoint me!"

Laspeera closed the door of the Dragonwing Chamber and turned to give Caladnei an expressionless nod. Narnra had departed, presumably soon to creep about on local balconies and rooftops, listening and peering at certain War Wizards.

Caladnei gave Rhauligan a mirthless smile. "You know your task?"

"Shadow her."

The Mage Royal nodded. "Let yourself be seen only to prevent Crown treason on her part or to save her life. Otherwise . . . just watch. Unless we've been *very* lax, none of those twelve is a traitor, but they've all met with Rightful Conspirators recently. I want to see how some of them react if they happen to notice a stranger lurking and watching *them*. If Narnra does spot you, tell her we decided we were unfairly sending her forth without a proper grounding in our politics—and offer to tell and show her more."

"Of course," the Highknight replied, rising.

"Some of those coins bear tracer-spells?" she asked him, nodding at the door Narnra had left by.

He smiled. "All of them." With a wave of his hand to Laspeera and Caladnei that was more of a salute than a farewell, Glarasteer Rhauligan strode to the nearest wall, did something deft to its paneling, and departed through a secret door neither woman had thought he knew anything about.

"There goes a good man," Laspeera murmured.

The Mage Royal nodded. "Let's hope I don't get him killed," she sighed bitterly. "I . . . I truly wish Vangerdahast was still irritating half of Cormyr by running things in his usual capable fashion. He'd handle things *so* much better than I do."

Laspeera smiled and hugged Caladnei. "Keep feeling that way and I'll know you're doing a gods-damned good job of being Mage Royal. It's folk who think they're doing just fine because they're so brilliant and masterly at magecraft who scare the backbone out of me!"

* * * * *

Rauthur blinked in surprise and peered in all directions. By the sunlight and the smells, he was still in Suzail—but in some narrow alleyway in the poorer, westerly part of the city, not in a passage outside the Dragonwing Chamber.

"*This* isn't the Palace!" he protested.

"Indeed it's not," Harnrim Starangh agreed—in the instant before something boiled up inside the War Wizard and blew apart.

"*Such* a suspicious War Wizard," he murmured as he surveyed the bloody bones and smoke that had been Huldyl Rauthur a moment earlier. "Gone missing just after so many deaths and disruptions at the sanctum—who would have thought *he* was a traitor? It just goes to show . . ."

He smiled as the plume of bloody smoke wafted away, leaving only a messy pile of dog-gnaw bones for the next cur—or starving citizen of Suzail looking for something to fill a stewpot—to find.

"I'm so sorry, Rauthur," he addressed them. "I fear I may have neglected to mention a few details of that linking spell. Or this other magic, for that matter."

He made a swift gesture. The skull rose, dripping, from the rest of the tangle and floated in the air facing him, cloaked in the very faint, flickering aura of his magic. The spell he'd just cast would preserve the brain behind those now-eyeless sockets long enough for him to read Rauthur's fading mind.

The wizard best known as Darkspells looked up and down the alley to make sure he was unobserved—he'd chosen this narrow, bending way carefully, noting this stretch between two large heaps of rotting, discarded crates some days ago; there was no one coming now to see—and carefully cast yet another spell.

Rauthur's mind was screaming at him.

"Why why why why *why*?"

"Never leave witnesses and co-conspirators," he replied softly, "and they can never drag you down with them. Trust, my weak friend Rauthur, is a weakness. A fatal weakness."

He bore down on the dying mind, forcing his way in through the shock and pain and tattered memories, seeking first any contingency magics that might be set to awaken against him. He didn't think Rauthur had the power or skill to craft any such magics, nor access to those Vangerdahast undoubtedly commanded.

As he probed deeper, it seemed he'd been right about contingencies . . . but it also appeared Rauthur had really known nothing of much interest, beyond the nicknames of a few fellow War Wizards that might prove briefly useful as lures.

Oh, and one other thing, glowing here in the most recent 'must remember' elements: One Narnra Shalace, currently a guest of the Mage Royal of Cormyr, is the daughter of . . . Elminster of Shadowdale.

Starangh's eyes lit up with excitement. "Well, well," he murmured. "Larger fish frying right in my lap."

* * * * *

The doorguard sneered.

"The Lady Joysil will have nothing to do with street beggars," he said curtly. "Be off with you, or I'll summon the Watch!"

The man in dusty, filthy leathers who stood facing him, an obviously false moustache askew on his upper lip, gave him a rather cold glare and said, "Joysil and I have done business together before and parted quite amicably, I might add. *Quite* amicably. I'd not be here now if I didn't have something urgent and of the gravest importance to impart to her, and I'm *not* leaving until she's heard it—in private and from my lips alone!"

The doorguard used the bracer on his wrist to rap a small, unseen gong inside the doorframe, and stood his ground.

"And *I* am not allowing some stranger at this gate who could be any sort of murderer, kidnapper, blackmailer, or common thief to reach the Lady Ambrur *alone!* I'm paid to see to the safety of her person and property, not allow any swift-tongued rogue in from the streets to wreak whatever havoc whim moves him to!"

"So call the Watch," the man in dusty leathers said softly, "and we'll all go in to see her together. I'll lay you a large wager that she'll be most displeased, when she hears my news, that she has any sort of audience to see her reaction."

The doorguard raised his eyebrows. "*That* makes me even more determined not to let you pass. News of that sort should not be—"

"Yes, Melarvyn? What's the trouble here?"

The steward of Haelithtorntowers was a brusque and efficient man. He was not disposed to look kindly on any wastage of his time, trivial matters, or unnecessary distractions. The doorguard knew this well and stepped back with a tight smile as he indicated the dusty man standing on the threshold.

"This—ruffian—is demanding an audience with the Lady Ambrur. He won't go away, even when threatened with the Watch, and insists that his business is urgent and that he has a personal relationship of some sort with the Lady. I believe him not, but in fairness—"

"Fairness? Melarvyn, since when did *fairness* play any part in life, beyond nursery tales? Since when have I allowed any hint of 'fairness' into the daily governance of Haelithtorntowers?"

Without waiting for a reply, the steward looked coldly down his nose at the aforementioned ruffian on the threshold and began, "As for you, sir—"

The dusty man peeled off his mustache and said quietly, "Enough foolery, Elward. Take me to Joysil *now* or I'll inform the Watch of the fate of Iliskar Northwind. And the matter of the missing Selgauntan crab shipment last month. To say nothing of your part in the disagreement between the Seven Traders and the port tax-takers here two months before that. Or the new Marsemban trade-agent of the slaver Ooaurtann of Westgate who goes by the name 'Varsoond.' But then, Elward Varsoond Emmellero Daunthideir would know nothing about a buyer of slaves, would he not?"

The steward had gone the hue of old cracked ivory during the stranger's soft little speech, and he'd begun to swallow repeatedly, his left eye twitching as if there was something in it.

The doorguard had slowly stepped back from Steward Elward Daunthideir as his own face had slid from annoyance to rage to astonishment to dumbfoundedness. His facial expression was now veering toward something akin to amazement.

"Uh, wha . . . whuh . . . ahem," the Steward began then suddenly smiled, stepped forward to offer the stranger his hand and asked brightly, "Why, Lord sir! Whyever didn't you mention all of this *before?* Of *course* the Lady Ambrur will be happy to see you—immediately, I might add, and it would give me the *greatest* pleasure, it would indeed, to escort you to see her myself!"

He ushered the dusty stranger across the threshold and in through the thick outer wall of Haelithtorntowers with swift, florid gestures, almost sweeping him along the short, curving path to the nearest grand door of the mansion. The doorguard stared after them with an amazed whistle on his lips and wonderment in his mind.

He broke off whistling to remark, "I'll bet it would, I do indeed—and I'll bet yon stranger had best look sharp, or he'll never reach the Lady alive." His face darkened. "Whereupon *my* hide will be next, as old Elward knows I heard all of that, too. Wherefore I'd best confide in the Lady myself, and soon, too. Hmmm . . . what if she knows about all of these matters? What if he fronts for her in them? Oh, *gods* . . ."

The Lady Joysil Ambrur was in her retiring-room, reclining in a vast couch strewn with a waterfall of pillows. Her gown was of a rose-pink silk, her feet bare, and her hair unbound to spill and swirl across the pillows.

Tomes were piled all around her, some of them larger than the tops of her small, ornate side-tables. It was a wonder how her slender, languid limbs could lift them—but perhaps servants assisted with the larger ones. Some of them looked magical and dangerous.

One such was spread open on her lap as she looked up, more surprise than annoyance in her gaze. The servants knew she was not to be disturbed when . . .

Her steward bowed lower than she'd ever seen him do before and raised pleading eyes to her. "Ah, Lady, a very *special* guest has come to us in some urgency, with a private message for your ears alone! He says you know him well."

A shapely eyebrow arched, long fingers closed the book and set it aside, and a hand extended in a beckoning gesture.

"So bring him to us."

The steward bowed again, his manner fawning rather than its usual careful, slightly disdainful dignity, and turned to the door he'd entered by behind the hanging tapestry at the foot of the great couch.

Roldro Tattershar strode in wearing a grave expression. At the first sight of him the Lady Joysil said sharply, "Elward, you may withdraw. To the south pond, where the rainbow-fins are in need of feeding."

The steward nodded stiffly, face frozen impassively, and departed. The bard in dusty leathers waited, his hand raised to signal silence, and after a few breaths went quietly back to the door, opened it, and peered out. Elward was gone.

He returned, nodding in satisfaction, and the Lady Joysil rose to embrace him fondly and murmured, "What is it, Roldro? No good news, I can tell."

"Ammaratha, I've just come from Suzail, where I overheard

two War Wizards talking about the retired Lord Vangerdahast's current work."

"Yes, he's crafting new spells at his sanctum—difficult magics, it would seem. Powerful ones, without a doubt. Binding spells to establish new guardians for Cormyr to replace the Lords Who Sleep, who were all destroyed. Some of his early ones had to do with finding and calming the guardians he intended to hunt for, I believe."

The Harper nodded. "Indeed. So much We Who Harp also believe. However, I doubt you've discovered just whom he intends to bind."

"I'll pay you what I did last time, Roldro, to learn this," the Lady Ambrur said calmly.

"That much coin will be quite acceptable."

The noblewoman looked at him sidelong. "Why are you backing away from me?"

"To give you room," the bard replied calmly.

Her eyes narrowed. "What do you mean?"

"Ammaratha, hear this: For his new guardians of the realm, Vangerdahast intends to bind—dragons."

"*What?*" The air shuddered with a furiously rising thunder, and Roldro Tattershar winced then scrambled back to the foot of the couch.

Silver blue scales flashed and shone, mighty wings spread and flapped heedless of the cracking, groaning ceiling, and the glare of those piercing turquoise eyes froze the cowering Harper where he crouched.

The great tail lashed, long legs sprang—and the ceiling was crashing and falling in huge chunks of plaster, riven wood, dust and tumbling stone all around Roldro. The room rocked, and its pretty oval skylight vanished forever into tinkling shards. A much larger window was left behind in its place: The entire top of the chamber gaped open to the misty Marsemban sky.

The song dragon was soaring up into the blueness above the city-stink and heading northward, flying fast and furiously.

Roldro stopped holding his breath, gasped for air—and promptly started coughing furiously. He was covered in thick dust and could hear faint shouts from below as guards and servants wondered aloud of the gods what had happened.

Ammaratha Cyndusk was already no more than a tiny, dwindling dot. Roldro struggled across the room, scooped up one of her jewel-coffers as the first installment of his payment, and started searching for the way into the secret passage he knew departed this room from the westernmost closet. Crooked stewards he could handle—but crooked stewards commanding a dozen or more furious and well-armed guards might well be another matter.

"May you find fair fortune, Ammaratha," he whispered, between coughs. "If I could turn into a dragon, I'd not go roaring openly down on Vangerdahast unless I was seeking my own swift death."

There was a decanter of wine on a shelf in the closet, and the last of the Tattershars decided to take it with him and banish his coughing the enjoyable way. The panel gave him some trouble, for the wall above it was buckled and sagging . . . but he got it closed behind him a good two hearty swigs before the furious pounding on the retiring-room door began.

"How *dare* he!" the song dragon roared into the wind of her own furious flight. "How dare he!"

She ducked one shoulder and turned a little westward without slowing, cleaving the air so fast that breathing was hard and her wings hummed and hissed in their battle with the air.

"Such an insult to all dragonkind! Such colossal arrogance! Even if some wyrms submit willingly to ages-long slumber and eventual perilous service, the wizard's plan endangers us all! Once Vangerdahast has developed binding spells that work on dragons, anyone who steals them or acquires them after his passing can use them against any dragon!"

Her voice was ear-splitting, but the heedless skies made no reply. With a snarl of seething fury she ducked her head and beat her wings in earnest, darting furiously on toward the green vastness of the King's Forest.

On to the sanctum where the villain Vangerdahast was lurking.

Nineteen

DRAGONRAGE AND DECEPTION

Deceit and falsehood wound me more deeply than mere daggers—poisoned or not. Thy tolerance may, of course, differ.

> Selemvarr of Pyarados,
> "The Old Red Wizard"
> *My Century of Might and Folly:*
> *A Career In Robes of Red*
> Year of the Gauntlet

Outside the kitchen there was a mighty crash, and someone screamed. The ground shook, setting the lanterns to swinging, and Myrmeen started for the window in a wary crouch, blade drawn.

Vangerdahast did not look up from his spell. "Not *now*," he snapped. "How am I ever goin—"

"*Vangerdahast*," the Lady Lord of Arabel snapped, "get over here! There's a *dragon* digging out your sanctum like a dog hunting for bones!"

"Eh? A wyrm? Excellent! I can try my—"

"I doubt either of the two War Wizards it's just flung away over the trees would agree with that 'excellent' of yours," Myrmeen interrupted crisply. "And I doubt this sword of mine will do much more than amuse our unexpected guest! I've never seen this sort of dragon—silver blue, but with the shape of a copper wyrm. . . ."

Vangerdahast made a small sound of exasperated annoyance, abandoned his spell with a dismissive wave of his hands, and strode to the window.

"A song dragon! Well, now!" He rubbed his hands together. "I wonder how her human form strikes the eye?"

Myrmeen gave him a strange look at about the same time as the massive tail outside swung toward the window in a suddenly looming slap. The windows crashed in, riven spells bursting into crawling fingers of lightning that wrestled with the glass, splinters of frame, and dislodged stone blocks—then stabbed out in all directions. The Lady Lord shrieked as one bolt found her armor and writhed briefly up and down her, and Vangerdahast grunted as another made one of his rings burst apart without triggering its magics, almost casually flinging him across the room as it did so. The north end of the kitchen groaned as unseen pantries beyond it collapsed, the chambers beyond them dug open and flung apart.

"Wizard!" a great, roaring voice hammered at them. "Where are you, wizard?"

Vangerdahast's answer was three carefully enunciated words that called up the defenses of the sanctum.

The shields all around him flared white and *flowed* forward, in a gathering charge that flung the song dragon back across the glade. Helmed horrors came racing through the shattered trees like arrows, converging on the thrashing wyrm. A pale green radiance began to gather around Vangerdahast, leaking out of the empty air like so many humming sparks to settle around him, cloaking him in rising power.

"Lass," he growled, in obvious discomfort, "see yon stone? The one with the rune on it?"

Myrmeen looked up at him from where she lay sprawled and gasping on the floor, face white and hair scorched . . . then turned her head to look where he was pointing.

"Pluck it up, and drink all you need of the healing potions beneath," the former Royal Magician of Cormyr grunted, striding past her with green radiance surging and building around him. "For once have a little sense and crawl away somewhere to lie quiet and keep out of the way. In all that battle-steel, you're nothing but dragonbait: Yon wyrm breathes lightning-gas!"

The Lady Lord of Arabel stared after him . . . and with trembling hands, as she lay on the floor, tried to unbuckle and shake off her armor. Vangerdahast cast a glance back at her, shook his head in disgust, and flexed his hands.

Green radiances flashed, and all over the sanctum wands, rods, rings, and odd diadems and orbs flashed, quivered, and grew green haloes of their own.

Outside, the helmed horrors were hacking and stabbing at the rolling, tail-lashing dragon, unaffected by the cloud of gas that gouted from its jaws. Scaled claws snatched and flung them often, and from time to time tore one apart in a flare of white radiances, the pieces of armor tumbling separately to earth.

Vangerdahast calmly watched the song dragon writhe and roll its way through the forest, toppling trees in all directions. If it started working magic, he'd smite it with the whelmed power of the sanctum, but until then, as long as his horrors held out . . .

These guardians didn't last very long, anyway. The flight enchantments he gave them gnawed endlessly at the magics that animated and bound them together, so they were a loss he could bear. The imprisoned criminals who'd elected to be put into dreamsleep so their sentiences could be used for these horrors would have sudden awakenings and probably an unpleasant burst of nightmares, scaring their jailers and adding to the meal preparation burden in the few remote keeps of the realm that had been turned into jails . . . but they'd be there again when new horrors were needed.

The horrors were swarming like angry hornets around the coiling and rolling wyrm, smashed away in their dozens when it slashed out with wings or tail, only to dart right back in and jab, jab, and hack again. There came a brief shimmering in the heart of that fray, and Vangerdahast lifted a hand, eyes narrowing.

In the next instant, the dragon collapsed, that great sleek scaled body in the heart of the darting, armored cloud suddenly falling away to being . . . not there.

And a staggering, panting woman clad in a few tatters of rose-pink gown suddenly stood before the shattered windows, calling, "Vangerdahast? Wizard? Where are you? We must have words together!"

"I am here," Vangerdahast replied calmly, the green radiance rising up in front of him like a wall. "Had I known you were coming, I *might* have been more welcoming. As it is, I'd prefer that your next words to me be your name and your business. Unless, of course, you'd like them to be your *last* words."

The woman put a hand on the shattered window-frame and ducked gracefully to climb down into the kitchen. Her state of dress made her lack of weapons plain to any eye, but Myrmeen, still sprawled on the floor, laid down the potion vial she'd just emptied and reached for her blade again.

"My name, Lord Vangerdahast, is Ammaratha Cyndusk," the woman replied, stepping down onto the counter between two plate-racks in a catlike crouch. She was tall, well-built, and wise-eyed. "In human shape I dwell in Marsember, and folk there know me as Lady Joysil Ambrur."

"Ah, the lass who likes to know all secrets," the wizard replied, nodding. "And must now have learned this one of mine. Who told you, may I ask?"

"A Harper whose name you'll not learn from me—who

told me a War Wizard spoke of it to another War Wizard. Before I throw my life away trying to end yours, I'd like to make sure I understand correctly: You're developing spells to hunt, lure, and control dragons, intending to accumulate a collection of dragons whom you'll bind—with other spells you're also working on—as sleeping defenders of Cormyr, in much the same way as the Lords Who Sleep formerly guarded the realm?"

"That is correct, yes."

"And you'll not be swayed from this scheme? Into using, say, *willing* War Wizards or Purple Dragons or other humans of Cormyr?"

"Human participation is likely, but I firmly intend to use dragons for most of the realm's defenders. Are you interested?"

The woman suddenly vanished from the countertop—and reappeared with her legs scissored around Vangerdahast's head. She twisted them sideways in an attempt to break his neck as her body arched over backwards down his front, and slapped both her arms out behind her to strike down his own and ruin any castings he might try.

"In your death, wizard!" she gasped as they crashed together, her back slamming into his ankles.

Vangerdahast still stood upright, his neck unmoved, so she threw herself from side to side, whipping her legs back and forth—but she seemed to be pivoting on something rigid, immobile, and as hard as stone. Something shrouded in more brightly pulsing green radiance.

"Interesting view," the wizard managed to say, in the moments before Myrmeen Lhal crashed into Joysil, tore her free from Vangerdahast, and bore her to the kitchen floor.

They skidded along together as Vangerdahast frowned down at them both. "Lass, I can fight my own battles, thank you. See this field around me, this green glow? It both protects my neck and keeps this song dragon from regaining its real shape and crushing the both of us against the walls and floor. It should also prevent her from teleporting again, now that she's this close. Get clear, now. I want to talk to her."

Myrmeen gave him an 'are you sure?' look, and he nodded. She rose off Joysil, springing clear to keep from being tripped or having any of her daggers stripped from her, and Vangerdahast laid a hand on her arm and said gruffly, "Oh, and lass, thank you."

Myrmeen gave him another strange look and backed away to the sink.

"You might as well kill me," Joysil panted, from where she lay bruised and winded on the floor. "Unless you renounce this plan of yours—and I can somehow believe you—I'll just keep trying to slay you. No dragon in all Faerûn is safe once those spells of yours work and are written down."

Vangerdahast nodded, and green radiance flowed from his fingers. In a room far away across the sanctum, two wands flickered and flashed. "I fear you'll now discover that you can't move, Lady Cyndusk—or Ambrur, if you prefer. I'd rather not be slain, thank you very much . . . and yet there's truth in what you say. These spells shall be my legacy to Cormyr. Others must be able to cast them after I am gone to augment the ranks of defenders or replace those fallen in battle. Some wizards may well use them less . . . judiciously than I shall. So, yes, I *am* a danger to dragonkind."

He sighed. "I've spent my life wrestling down my own desires—and dreams, and sympathies—to cleave always to one guiding and supreme pursuit: the betterment and defense of Cormyr. I will do *anything* to keep this realm strong—and its character much as it is now and has always been. I believe it to be among the best achievements of *my* kind, dragon, and want to keep it so . . . whatever the cost to anyone."

He went to a drawer, pulled forth a clean tablecloth, and laid it carefully over Joysil's frozen form. "I've no robes your size, but if you don't mind some of my winter weathercloaks . . . the moths always get at them, but . . ."

"*Wizard*," the helpless song dragon on the floor hissed,

"you promote the worst sort of slavery for dragons. Even if you find some willing slaves to be your guards, these spells will get out, and there'll come a day when the only wyrms *not* under the command of someone will be those who die fighting after your other spells find them, lure them, and hook them!"

Vangerdahast nodded a little sadly. "I had foreseen this consequence, yes. Have you any bright solutions for me that I've thus far missed?"

"You—you *monster!*" Joysil stormed, trembling against the paralyzing magics that held her. "Youuu—"

She tried to turn her head away as he bent near, and when she found she could not, she shut her eyes and screamed—a cry that soon faded, warbled, and died away.

"Sleep," the old wizard told her gently. "If Mystra smiles on me for once, I'll have thought of something before I have to wake you."

He turned away with a sigh and added bitterly, "Or more likely not."

Myrmeen Lhal regarded him gravely. Her sword was sheathed, and there was a strange look in her eyes, a different strange look than before. "You could have slain her—easily—and did not. Why so?"

Vangerdahast regarded her a little sourly. "I've seen too many problems in life to enjoy disposing of them by working murder any longer, lass. I need some time to decide what best to do to calm and heal her."

The Lady Lord of Arabel nodded, folded her arms across her chest, and said, "Yet the ruthless defender of the realm might say the best thing for Cormyr would be to eliminate this dragon now—mercifully, while she sleeps, helpless. One less foe, one danger gone, the realm thus that small measure stronger."

"This is not the Devil Dragon," the former Royal Magician sighed, "and truth to tell, lass, I've seen and done more than enough killing."

He shook out another tablecloth, spread it on the floor,

and did something that made the green radiance brighten all around them and raise Joysil's rigid body into the air. Unseen forces lifted the tablecloth up to her from beneath. Thus sandwiched in cloth, the body floated toward the kitchen door.

"I believe," Vangerdahast added as he started after it, "I've finally grown up enough to hold the view that folk whose views differ from mine are not necessarily foes I should slay."

There was clear respect in Myrmeen's eyes as she looked at him, smiled, and suddenly reached out to take his arm.

He patted her hand with his own, suddenly conscious of her hip brushing against his, and looked back at her. As their eyes met, Vangerdahast felt—with no small surprise—long-suppressed feelings stirring within him once more.

* * * * *

Narnra rolled her eyes as she dropped down from yet another window. Gods, what a lot of petty little bickering, arrogance, and rivalries! These War Wizards were almost as bad as Waterdhavian nobles!

Almost. Bane come striding, if this was what the law-keepers were like, what might the nobles of Cormyr have to offer?

"Who was that idiot who said, 'Always more treasure beyond the next hill'?" she muttered aloud—then froze again on all fours on a potted-fern-crowded balcony as two War Wizards strolled out to stand at the rail not four paces away, laughing cynically.

"Well, I always knew Old Thundersides wouldn't let go his grip on the throne all *that* easily!"

"Dragons! After all the blood elves shed to snatch this land away from being the private hunting-ground of various wyrms! I can't believe it!"

"*I* can. Who else sleeps for centuries, anyway? Who else can last so long and still be alive instead of undead and hating the living? Who else in Cormyr could he trust? Our *nobles*?"

The two shared a bitter, derisive crow of laughter. The second robed mage shook his head and replied, "Who can truly trust a dragon? What must they think of us humans who butcher, steal from them, take their eggs, and . . . sweep them aside, where once they ruled all Faerûn?"

The taller, older wizard shrugged. " 'Twas the elves did that to them—oh, and that cult among the hobgoblins that thought eating dragonflesh would make them into a larger, stronger breed . . . they used to take more eggs than humans ever have."

"D'you think old Vangey will snatch some eggs and try to hatch wyrmlings he's bound and brainwashed with spells?"

"Mayhap," the older War Wizard replied, turning away from the rail to walk back inside, "but he needs grown ones, too. Wyrmlings are like ignorant but recklessly overconfident youths—and can do about as much unintended damage to themselves, as well as to whatever they're *supposed* to be protecting."

Miraculously, the two mages didn't notice the rock-still thief crouched on her fingertips. Narnra let out a long, slow breath as quietly as she could, gathered in air, and sprang forward and over the balcony rail.

Vangerdahast's secret was out. Spellbound dragons to guard Cormyr! So she'd found Duskwinter, and that jovial trim-bearded one in the bath earlier had been Bathtar Flamegallow—more interested in floating carved little wooden ships than anything else, that one, but his jokes had certainly been amusing. Calaethe Hallowthorn was out near some place called Jester's Green—and was being out and about in the countryside suspicious? She knew too little about these War Wizards to judge—but the other woman she was to watch over, Iymeera Juthbuck, was a bit of a wildcat when it came to strong adventurers, if the rather catty War Wizard gossip could be believed—and what did the Harpers think of all this, anyway? Had Rhauligan told any of them?

Ah, this was the place. Dark My Harp Yet Flaming. Gods, what a name!

Narnra paused on a rooftop, peering down at the old, ramshackle club. It had once been a grand mansion, by the looks of it, before later owners had grown it wooden side-wings in all directions. Well, at least no din of bad minstrelsy was clawing her ears from this distance, at least.

With a shock she realized that no less than three sentinels were watching her—one from a tiny moon-window in the club roof and the others from different buildings on either side of her.

To her relief, the one on the nearest building gave her a curt nod as their eyes met. She responded with a grave wave of her hand and proceeded down to the street to enter the club openly. If she'd been seen anyway, it'd be best not to risk any bowfire.

The wig she'd "borrowed" through an open window a few frantic hours back was slipping again, but she needn't have bothered with any attempt at stealth. Dark My Harp Yet Flaming was dimly lit, crowded, casually cozy, and—no music, thankfully—a-bubble with talk of nothing else but Vangerdahast's plan.

"Gods, man, we'll be crotch-deep in slinking and grandly mysterious mages with fireballs up both their unwashed sleeves the moment word of Vangey's grand plan gets about!" one man with a lute strapped across his back and daggers sheathed everywhere else all over his well-worn leathers growled, slamming down a tankard as big as Narnra's head. "All sorts of mages'll want his spells and kill to get them! Who controls the most dragons, and first, will be able to settle a *lot* of old scores before the rest of us can unite to try—and I say *try*—to rescue all the Realms from him!"

"What if a dragon gets those spells and builds himself into

a new Dragon King?" a shortish man with a wildly bristling mustache responded. "That's what I want to know!"

Narnra listened to this and similar loudly enthusiastic speculations as she drifted through the club, playing the old game of feigning looking for someone she knew.

When she recognized two of the Harpers who'd been part of that grim line down in the cellars when Mystra herself had been awing the squitters out of everyone, she sidled in their direction. They headed grimly up a flight of stairs, listening to the chatter and exchanging sour glances about it as they went.

Narnra walked away from the stair, around a corner, and raced up another staircase she'd spotted earlier. The floor above would have a linking passage, she was sure, and if not . . .

The creature at the top of the stair was the largest, ugliest half-orc she'd ever seen—all pimples and open, weeping sores and yellow, roughly broken-off tusks. Steady eyes that held promises of both humor and casually swift death peered down at her as one claw-like hand drew aside a fold of cloak to reveal the first six-bolt-at-once handbow Narnra had ever gazed upon.

The glittering-headed bolts looked very sharp, and they were all trained on her. Lips drew back from the great reeking mouth above them to mutter, "And on your deathbed, little rat, you will—?"

Narnra swallowed, drew in a deep breath, and managed to say the word "Harp" confidently enough that it didn't—quite—seem like a guess.

The cloak drew back over the bow, the head nodded grudgingly, and with astonishing speed that mountain of flesh drew aside to let her reach the head of the stair and pass.

She gave the—the *thing*—an expressionless nod as she did so and strode down the passage confronting her as if she knew quite well where she was going.

A door was open halfway along it, and a voice from just inside was saying, "I care not. Let every sneak-thief and fat merchant in all Suzail hear us debate, Sareene! I want them all aware and alert and mindful of the danger we all face—because we *all* face it, no matter who or where we are!"

"Naetheless, Brammagar, you're proposing a *very* dangerous double game!"

"What choice have we?"

The backs of the two men standing just inside the door looked very familiar, so Narnra dared not ask what Brammagar's proposal had been. Thankfully, someone else did it for her.

"I dare not leave Dragondusk right at this moment," said a strangely remote, echoing voice, "and my magic was not working in time to hear Brammagar speak. What proposal, please?"

"That We Who Harp protect Vangerdahast by lying in wait for all mages, so as to have a chance at taking them down as they arrive to attack Vangey . . . then, when the time's just right, we turn around and ruin the old wizard's spell-work, to make sure he *never* manages to bind a dragon by any new, more powerful magical means."

"And who among us gets to decide which mages we slay and which we let live? You're tossing maggots into all our soup, I say!"

"Kill as many as we can, regardless, and give some shred of power in Faerûn back to all of us who aren't spellslingers!" someone else grunted, and a burst of argumentative voices began.

Narnra went on down the passage to the other stair as swiftly as she quietly could. Traitor-wizards would have to wait. She had to get to Caladnei in all haste. *This* must be reported to the Mage Royal without delay!

Harnrim Starangh smiled down at the lithe figure in leathers as his careful casting came to an end—and the building looming beside the rooftop she'd just landed on started to topple.

No matter how swiftly she leaped, she couldn't hope to

avoid its thundering, crushing flood of stones. They'd bury the entire roof and probably smash flat the building beneath it . . .

The rolling crash shook his own perch, here atop one of newer and loftier buildings in Suzail. The dust rolled up . . . and with a groan like a dying dragon, the building the thief had been trotting across collapsed under its load of fallen stone, to the accompaniment of a few fresh screams.

Yes. Exit Narnra Shalace, and enter—her impostor.

Trying to bargain for the life of his daughter with Elminster and all the Chosen the Old Mage could call on was sheer foolishness . . . to say nothing of what such an . . . ah, *active* captive might do on her own, whilst he was busy bargaining . . . but *being* Elminster's daughter himself, now—yes! Even if the Old Mage caught up to him, the old goat could be warned away from mind-thrusts and meddlings by claiming Mystra's protection.

Yes. Risky, but everything to do with magic held risk. And if a certain Darkspells could stay ahead of the Old Mage of Shadowdale and snatch War Wizard magic by being Caladnei's little agent on the one hand and Elminster's daughter on the other, he could gain much ere it became necessary for Narnra to forever disappear.

The Red Wizard smiled thinly and waved his hand. The air beside him obediently wavered into an image of the Waterdhavian thief he'd just slain.

He studied it carefully, peering and crouching to do so, before beginning the spell that would give him Narnra's likeness.

Across a forest of rooftops, Glarasteer Rhauligan stared at the rising dust in horror, his last glimpse of the frantically leaping Narnra as the stones came down etched into his mind.

"*Narnra!*" he shouted, knowing that his cry was in vain. Nothing could have survived that smashing blow from above, even if . . .

A movement caught his eye on another rooftop, and he found himself gazing at a robed man who was just gaining a companion—as Narnra's image appeared out of thin air before him. The man studied it, frowning and ducking about to peer intently, and started to work a spell. His shape rippled and started to change—even as the conjured Narnra rippled and started to fade.

Rhauligan burst into a run, leaping and racing across rooftops, jerking out daggers to hurl and spitting furious curses non-stop, trying to get close enough to . . .

Harnrim Starangh struck a pose and looked down at the hand-mirror he'd propped against the husk of a long-dead pigeon earlier. Yes, he now looked like that pouty, hawk-nosed lass.

He retrieved his mirror, stowed it in an unfamiliar pocket, and gave Suzail a farewell smile. It was time to see Shadow-dale again, cozy up to the oh-so-great Elminster, and learn a few of his secrets at last.

The figure atop the roof vanished abruptly, and Rhauligan's first dagger flashed through empty air to clink and rattle to a tumbling stop at the far end of an empty roof. The Harper's roar of rage followed it.

* * * * *

The street full of rubble and running, shouting men suddenly gained another occupant. This one was tall, gaunt, and dressed in shabby robes that vied with their wearer's long white beard in looking old and the worse for wear.

Elminster raised one bristling brow and peered around, humming thoughtfully as War Wizards and Purple Dragons came pelting up from all directions.

Barring spell barriers, his tracing spell should deliver him to a spot mere feet away from Narnra, and that could only mean she was . . .

Oh, Mystra. Oh, bleeding merciful Mystra.

Heedless of shouts calling on him to surrender or identify himself and to lay aside all weapons, the Old Mage knelt by the great pile of shattered and tumbled stone that reached to the very toes of his worn old boots and muttered a very old spell. Some of the rocks right in front of him glowed, and he spat out a curse that made the Purple Dragon running up to him with drawn sword at the ready gape in surprise.

The old man planted his feet, shook back his sleeves, and raised both hands to begin a casting—so the onrushing warrior did what he was trained to do: bellowed to try and disrupt the wizard's concentration and reached out with his blade to try to strike aside one of those hands and so ruin any spellcasting.

The old man promptly surprised the Purple Dragon again—by dropping into a crouch and whirling to face his attacker. The blade passed harmlessly over one robed shoulder. The old man turned, taking hold of the warrior's swordarm by wrist and elbow, and flung him at the rockpile with a sudden shout of his own: "*Start digging*, you motherless dog!"

"There's the one who caused it!" a War Wizard howled, aiming his wand. Elminster flung himself aside without bothering to turn and see who his accuser was, and the wand-blast seared stones and sent the staggering Purple Dragon into a shouting scramble for cover.

Elminster rolled behind a heap of tumbled rubble and snarled out a spell that lofted most of the stones around him—plus the lone and by now thoroughly astonished Purple Dragon—down the street in a bone-shattering hail that left the advancing Cormyreans strewn on their backs, cursing and groaning.

Ignoring them, the Old Mage scrambled to his feet and peered at the front edge of the rockpile, now much reduced by the scouring of his spell. *There!* A bloody, leather-clad arm protruded from under two large, wedged rocks. Elminster dug his hands in under one of them, heaved with all his might—and succeeded only in making it wobble a few inches to one side.

Gasping in defeat, he grimly cast another spell, this time plucking stones straight up so as to not to allow the slightest possibility of harming Narnra further.

She lay sprawled and senseless beneath a thick coating of dust, one leg obviously broken, one arm a flopping and many-times-shattered thing, and . . .

He winced, dragged that broken body as gently as he could out from under the stones hanging menacingly aloft, and called up Mystra's silver fire.

Wielding it slowly and gently was always hard, healing doubly so, and he persisted only long enough to discover that she was still alive and not faltering. To do this properly, he'd have to devote all of his concentration to the task, leaving himself defenseless and pressed against his daughter—not a wise thing when more angry defenders of Cormyr could arrive at any moment.

So instead, he shifted his outward appearance to exactly match Narnra's—farewell, bearded old lawbreaking wizard—and got down beside her to let out the silver fire slowly and carefully.

When a company of Purple Dragons arrived in a thundering of boots, it was the work of but a moment to let the hanging stones fall with a crash among them, while he lay still alongside the obviously injured Narnra.

Knitting and mending, drawing back blood here and teasing aside shattered ends of bone there . . . Slowly he worked his way through her broken body until he was satisfied she'd live. He could do the rest better at his tower, where he could nurse and coddle properly instead of fighting off War Wizards every few breaths.

Someone who was whooping for breath and whose footfalls crashed down in hasty weariness burst onto the scene. Elminster turned his head and saw Glarasteer Rhauligan lurching toward him over the rubble-strewn street in as much haste as possible.

With a sigh, the mage got to his feet, picked up Narnra—ignoring Rhauligan's sudden shout—and whisked himself and his daughter away to Shadowdale.

Rhauligan staggered to a halt, staring in dumbfounded rage at the spot where *two* Narnra Shalaces had just vanished, right under his nose.

"Bloody brazen hinges!" he gasped wearily, staring around in wild frustration. "*Blistering* bloody . . . brazen . . . hinges!"

*   *   *   *   *

Florin Falconhand was whistling softly as he traversed the well-worn flagstones that led to Elminster's tower. In his dripping left hand he held no less than nine large greenfins, fresh from the river. The Old Mage had a weakness for pan-fried greenfin.

It was time and past time for one of the Knights to invite Elminster to dine, and—

The ranger came to a sudden halt, hand flashing to the hilt of his blade.

On the path ahead—right at the halfway bend, on a gentle slope that had been utterly empty a moment earlier—stood two figures.

Two identical figures, one of them carrying a limp, senseless third duplicate who was shrouded in dust and blood and whose clothes were much torn.

Florin stared. Aye, all three were the same slender, muscled woman in tattered leathers and boots, with tousled, hacked-off-short black hair, dark eyes, and a strong nose like a gentler version of Elminster's hawk-beak.

Both of the upright women were staring at each other in obvious surprise—unwelcome surprise.

Then the one carrying the third knelt quickly, snapped, "Stay back, Florin!" and set down her burden. She started casting a spell while still on her knees.

The other one was casting a spell too, obviously intending to blast her double.

Florin's sword sang out as he broke into a trot, asking himself, *What NOW?*

Twenty

TO WAR

So it comes down to what it always does, when men swagger and dragons fly: red war, and much death, and a lot of things ruined and cast down broken. Little decided, much lost, many left to weep. Yet for the rest of us, it seems to entertain.

Amundreth, Sage of Secomber
Thoughts on the Folly of Kings
Year of the Highmantle

Halfway along the passage, Ondreth stopped still.

"By the Dragon Throne," he gasped, putting out a hand to Telarantra's arm, "what's that?"

His fellow duty-guard War Wizard followed his gaze down the longest passage in the sanctum to what was traversing a cross-passage in the distance and murmured in her usual deadpan manner, "Vangerdahast, the Lady Lord of Arabel, and a woman in the thrall of his magic, I'd say—how else would she end up floating along on her back in midair, with her eyes closed?"

"No, no," Ondreth said excitedly, "I saw her change, in the battle! *That's* the dragon that did us so much damage!"

"Is it indeed?" Telarantra asked softly.

The spell that clutched Ondreth Malkrivyn in an icy grip was as sudden as it was unexpected. It was draining his life-force before he could speak or even lift a hand.

The last thing he saw as the world dimmed for him was Telarantra's triumphantly smiling face above him, as she gently lowered his withering body to the floor.

"Farewell, fool," she told him almost affectionately. "Know that the Rightful Conspiracy values your sacrifice. My next spell will break the stasis on yon song dragon—and we'll see how old Lord Windy Royal Magician fares in battle *without* the risen defenses of the sanctum ready in his hands."

She turned and did something, but Ondreth Malkrivyn was too dead to see it—or feel the mighty blast that followed. It hurled the husk of his body at the ceiling as the entire passage rocked, ceiling-tiles fell like rain, and the sanctum tried to leap upward and join the sky.

* * * * *

Though he stood like a statue, Rhauligan was inwardly almost dancing in impatience, but one did not interrupt the Dowager Queen of Cormyr in mid-word . . . not when the Steel Regent was by her side, glaring pointedly at impatient Harpers. Alusair even put an imperious finger to her lips as Filfaeril bade Laspeera answer.

"The evidence of Amnian and Sembian backing is now clear," the most senior War Wizard began, "and the nobles of this 'Rightful Conspiracy' grow ever bolder. We would have seen swords out openly long ago, I think, were it not for the wits of the wisest along them. One of our Highknights died to inform us of this much: An elaborate scheme is building, to slay all Obarskyrs in an orchestrated manner that will allow the conspirators to win control of the realm while avoiding both a ruinous ground war or—much—civil war after all of the Blood Royal have been eliminated, by also slaughtering all other blood claimants to the throne but one: their chosen, mind-controlled puppet. We're not sure just which of the Crownsilvers, Huntsilvers, or Truesilvers is their selected—and willing—dupe, but rest assured that—"

"We're doing all we can," Caladnei took over smoothly. "Of course." She sighed, spread her hands as if to clear an imaginary table—or her mind—and added, "One of the bolder moves Speera just referred to was a clever attempt to snatch the young Azoun—an attempt aided by hired wizards. It was foiled by some alert knights and by our most trusted mages, who constantly spell-scry the King from afar, 'watching the watchers' who protect the king, for signs of treachery."

She sighed again. "If all that truly protected Azoun was his visible bodyguard, that attack could hardly have failed."

The Mage Royal turned to look at Laspeera, and—gasped and reeled in pain.

Laspeera was similarly stricken, an involuntary moan of anguish bursting from her lips as she stumbled forward. From across the room, among the handful of War Wizards and Highknights guarding the inside of the doors, came more outbursts of pain. One mage toppled to the tiles in a dead faint.

Rhauligan and the two royals reached out to steady the two, Alusair the swiftest to speak. *"What's happened?"* she snapped.

"The sanctum," Caladnei gasped, clutching at her temples. "A violent—very large—release of magic! We're attuned to its defenses. They must have . . ."

"Gone down," Laspeera said, from her knees. She struggled to her feet, pale and sweating, and added, "We must—"

The door-gong rang. Alusair and Filfaeril spun around and assumed regal poses and expressions in an instant, and Rhauligan moved quickly to take Caladnei's arm and turn her. The gong signified that the guards outside had intercepted someone having a rightful need to enter.

Raised shield-spells flickered as the Highknights and War Wizards guarding the inside of the doors opened one of them a trifle. The most senior mage of that guard then murmured a message that his magic took straight to Caladnei, for everyone standing with her to hear: *A herald. Alone. We've stripped and spell-read him. He wears only a tabard of our proffering.*

Alusair put a hand on the hilt of her sword. "Bid him enter," she ordered curtly.

The herald came barefoot, obviously naked under his tabard. He was tight-lipped and pale, though whether his pallor was born of fear or anger those in the room could not tell.

Only Caladnei did not recognize him. The man was a professional Sembian herald-for-hire of long career and exacting correctness.

Stopping a careful six paces away, he bowed deeply to the Dowager Queen and then to the Steel Regent before raising his hand in the "cupping empty air" gesture that requests peaceful parley.

"Speak," Alusair said.

"I am asked," the grand voice rolled out in response, "to request the presence of Queen Filfaeril Obarskyr of Cormyr and Regent Princess Alusair Nacacia Obarskyr at Thundaerlyn Hall in Marsember on the morrow, at First Candlelight, to discuss the bright future of this kingdom with certain noble-born Cormyreans loyal to the realm who are concerned about Cormyr—and represent those who are now the careful hosts of both the infant King Azoun and the retired Royal Magician."

Filfaeril and Alusair both cast swift glances at Caladnei, who shook her head to tell them that the claim—about Vangey, at least—must be a lie.

She mindspoke the two royals: *I believe we can protect you if you accept.*

"It shall be our pleasure to attend in Thundaerlyn Hall, at the time proposed," the Dowager Queen replied serenely, adding a nod of dismissal.

The herald seemed about to say something else, just for a moment, but instead nodded, made his bows again, and departed. The Obarskyr women stood watching him like grave statues until the doors closed behind him.

Caladnei turned her head. "Speera?"

Laspeera was still pale, but her mind-probe had been as deft as ever. "He knows nothing but the words he memorized and cares for their implications accordingly. He was given that message in writing in Saerloon by someone unfamiliar to him—a hired Sembian intermediary, by his looks in the herald's memory—and paid very well to hasten here to deliver it."

"It's a trap," Alusair snapped.

"Of course," Filfaeril agreed quietly.

"So we send some spell-disguised War Wizards in your places?" Rhauligan suggested.

Alusair shook her head. "No. We attend. In person. I'm more than weary of perils unfolding in Cormyr behind my back or when I'm busy dealing with something else—I'm *never* going to cling to the title of Regent whilst sending others to sweat or die in my place. If the realm means anything to me, I *must* be there."

Filfaeril nodded. "Well said. All of your well-chosen words apply equally to me."

"Your Majesties," Rhauligan protested, "though my heart leaps to hear you speak so, is it wise for the realm to risk both of you in one place? Hazarding the loss of all Obarskyr wisdom and influence, should you—watching gods forfend—be stricken down together?"

He laid one hand on a vial at his belt, and asked, "Though I risk treason and my own death, dare I allow you to so endanger the realm while I have power left to prevent you?"

The Dowager Queen put a swift hand on Alusair's sword-darm to forestall any word or action and smiled.

"Rhauligan, the loyalty and service of you and men who act and feel as you do is Cormyr's backbone and its splendor, not the surname shared by we two. Yet in truth my daughter and I are both now expendable so long as Azoun lives, is kept safe, and is guided and instructed well. You must trust us that he is."

She impulsively stepped forward and wrapped her regal arms around Rhauligan in a fierce hug.

As he blinked in astonishment, she snapped into his ear, "I, too, am sick unto death of standing *watching* when I could be—should be—doing! If Thundaerlyn Hall be a trap, so much the better! *My* Azoun would not have wanted me to sit idle as the passing days carry me ever closer to the grave . . . as he never did!"

Filfaeril thrust him away to stare into his eyes and added, "If it makes you feel better, Rhauligan, you may hide ready in Thundaerlyn and run to my rescue if needful—but you may *not* stand in front of me like a shield, or bundle me into some cloak-closet 'for my own good'! Do we understand each other?"

Rhauligan went to one knee, brought her fingertips to his lips, and said huskily, "Lady, we do."

* * * * *

"I said *back*, Florin!" the young lass snapped again, as the ranger charged forward, blade raised. Her fingers never slowed in their deft weaving—but mere paces away, her double ended the swifter casting of a spell with a flourish and a cry of triumph.

Reddish-purple light burst into being in that one's hands and raced forth in thin, arrow-straight beams from every one of her fingers, stabbing at the lass who'd warned Florin off . . . only to strike something unseen in front of her target, claw at that barrier, and rise skywards in a building, trembling wave.

Florin Falconhand decided it was prudent to obey that warning and sprang hastily away to the side and rear of the lass who'd hurled the spell—and who was now grimly pouring her will and perhaps other magics into it, drawing lips back from teeth in a soundless snarl and trembling to match the arcing fires of her spell.

A thin sheen of sweat sprang into being all over her as Florin watched. He took a step toward the lass who was hurling fire—and the other identical young lass repeated her warning, in a waspish, somehow familiar tone that made Florin's eyes narrow.

Could this be . . . Elminster?

His gaze went to the straining, warring magics overhead, where those fires were being thrust over and around, curling back toward their creator from above.

The sweating lass knew her danger and was already eyeing the roiling power above her. Abruptly she sprang aside with a curse, ending her flow of fire—but the over-hanging doom followed her like a great gliding dragon as she scrambled . . . and suddenly fell from above with a crash that shook the meadow.

Florin was hurled from his feet as the ground heaved and the stricken, desperately shouting lass vanished from view in the flames. Her double, who'd sent this doom against her, stood still and firm.

Something confusing happened in the rolling, swirling inferno, and the lass engulfed in it was abruptly some twenty paces off, sobbing on the ground . . . still caught in fading, flickering coils of her own flame that had clung to—and made the journey with—her.

Florin cast a quick glance at the lass standing calmly then started toward the fire-wreathed one, looking back for a warning that did not come.

The spell-flames were dying away swiftly, now, and the lass within them was beating at the ground in pain, writhing and weeping, raising a sooty and tear-wet face to Florin that was—no longer feminine at all!

Florin pounced on the wounded man, ignoring the threads of smoke rising from the blackened and ashen rem-nants of robes. A pain-twisted face tried to shape a word, so he slapped that mouth with the wet greenfins still in his

hand. By the time the smoldering man had finished sputtering and spitting, his wrists were pinned to the scorched turf
under the ranger's knees.

"Elminster?" Florin called back at the other lass.

"Indeed," a familiar voice replied. "None can hope to
deceive ye, gallant Florin!"

The ranger's reply was a swift, rude snort of derision, followed by the words, "This dog has the look of a rogue mage.
Should I be slaying him about now?"

"Nay. I've a use or two for him yet. Hold him still, will
ye?"

As he spoke, the likeness of the young, hawk-nosed lass
melted away from him, revealing an older, hawk-nosed,
weatherbeaten, and very familiar Old Mage of Shadowdale—
who promptly bent and, with a grunt, picked up the stricken
lass he'd been carrying when he appeared.

Florin shook his head slightly and asked, "Are you going to
tell me why all three of you arrived wearing the same shape?
And who it really belongs to?"

"No," Elminster replied serenely, "to thy first, but as
to thy second, this in my arms is truly herself: a lass from
Waterdeep—a thief, so watch thy pockets—hight Narnra
Shalace. *That* beneath ye is a Red Wizard of Thay."

The handsomest man in Shadowdale received this news
with no evidence of surprise, merely asking, "Will any of you
be staying for a nice fish fry?"

"I'm afraid I know not, yet. We wait upon the temper of
a woman."

"A—?" Florin looked down at the broken, white-faced
body that Elminster was laying tenderly beside him. "This
Narnra?"

"Indeed. Hold the Thayan securely, now. Defeating his
spell was a simple matter of calling on the defensive enchantments of my tower, but now I must work a rather exacting
magic."

"I should hope so," the ranger murmured. "Sloppy spells
give mages a bad reputation—when the wrong castle gets

blasted to dust, the wrong thousand folk slain, and so on."

Elminster gave Florin a sour look. "Aren't there some ladies somewhere ye could be causing to swoon about now?"

Florin raised both his eyebrows and the still-dripping bunch of fish. "With these?"

The Old Mage sighed, gestured for silence, and cast his spell. In the creeping silence that followed, both men watched as Narnra's broken body slowly became whole again . . . and that of the Red Wizard took on her injuries, sinking and twisting under Florin. As the Thayan began to gasp and moan in pain, Narnra's eyes fluttered open, and she stared up at them and felt her limbs—and sudden lack of pain—in wonder . . . and growing apprehension.

"W-where am I *now?*" she murmured. "There was a rooftop . . . something falling . . ."

Elminster took her shoulders and gently helped her to sit up. "That was just magic, lass. Bad magic."

As Narnra got a good look at the unfamiliar green trees and meadows of Shadowdale, and the pinched, pain-wracked face of the Red Wizard beside her, all the color drained out of her face—and she flinched away from the hands on her shoulders.

"Will you send him back like this?" Florin asked quietly, eyeing Narnra's shaken face.

"Nay," Elminster said quietly. "I'll teach him some magic, show him why I made some of the moral choices I did, then set him loose . . . and he'll choose his own fate, for good or ill. The world needs Red Wizards just as it needs carrion-worms. Let's see if I can steer this one. My Lady The Simbul herself cannot slay them all. However . . ."

He looked at his daughter, and said, "This wizard tried to slay ye with his spells just now, back in Marsember. I place his fate in thy hands."

He put a hand on Florin's arm to signal the ranger to rise and step back. Together they withdrew, leaving Narnra sitting facing the Red Wizard. Hastily, she scrambled to her feet, and backed out of his reach, snarling, "Keep back!"

With an obvious effort, the Thayan started to speak. "I am too . . . maimed to work spells or offer you violence."

"You tried to kill me!"

"I did."

"Why?"

"I needed you gone to impersonate you. To learn the secrets of Elminster."

She glared at him, then at the Old Mage, then back at him and spat bitterly, "You're no better than he is!"

"True," Starangh whispered. "Right now, I'm much worse."

"What good are his secrets to you?"

"Power," the Thayan husked. "All mages crave power."

Narnra's eyes blazed. "To make slaves of the rest of us!"

Starangh tried to shrug, but the movement brought such pain that he ended up writhing and groaning.

"Why don't you apprentice yourself to him or some other mage?" Narnra asked. "Why kill and deceive?"

"Trust someone else as my master? Leave myself so vulnerable? That road is the way of the fool," the Thayan told her, his voice a little stronger.

"Trust," Narnra told him furiously, leaning forward to drive her words home with slow, soft emphasis, "is a strength."

"You *are* a fool," he replied.

"And you're a cruel idiot," she replied scornfully. "Are all Red Wizards of Thay like you? Preening villains?"

Starangh shook his head. "Just kill me and have done taunting."

"Why? Do words of sense truly hurt you more than wounding magic?"

"Kill me," he pleaded, furious and ashamed.

"No," Narnra snapped, turning away. "My father shall have his chance to twist and shape you, as he does to so many. Why should you escape my fate?"

* * * * *

The flash and flare of magic in their faces sent Vangerda-hast staggering back into Myrmeen even before the great silver-blue, scaled bulk burst into being, shattering the low passage ceiling with a roar of mingled exultation and pain then bursting forth skywards, flooding the sanctum with sunlight.

With a surge of wings and claws, the song dragon turned and pounced on the War Wizard Telarantra, rending her limb from limb before she could even shriek—to turn and hand the dripping result to Vangerdahast.

"Here's your traitor," she said, in a soft and vast echo of her human voice.

Back on his feet, Vangerdahast stood facing her calmly, as Myrmeen scrambled to her feet to defend him with her blade.

However, the song dragon did not strike. "Why," she asked the former Royal Magician, "did you spare me?"

"Lady," Vangerdahast replied gruffly, "you fought for your cause as I fight for mine. You've long dwelt among folk of Cormyr and must enjoy our company somewise to have per-sisted so long in doing so. I bear you no malice—and hope to turn you to support my plans."

"So I might become one of your willing defenders," she replied, a touch of bitterness in that great voice. "Exhibiting the grand destiny of . . . a useful tool."

Vangerdahast sighed. "Of course you'll see dragon-binding as evil. In truth, I'd avoid it if I could find a better way—but for me, all other things fall before my devotion to Cormyr."

"What has Cormyr done for you to deserve this devotion?"

The old wizard sighed. "Lady, defending this fair realm is what I *do*. There is no higher calling, no greater task, no brighter boon to all Faerûn than this."

The great dragon head shook in resignation, those burn-ing turquoise eyes never leaving those of Vangerdahast—yet searing also into Myrmeen's wary gaze. "What will you do now, Vangerdahast, if I fly away, gather a dozen dragons, and return to destroy you—and your precious sanctum—utterly?"

The old wizard shrugged. "Try me."

"Are you not afraid?"

"No," the retired Mage Royal replied. "I'm growing too old to fear for this wrinkled old hide."

"Do you not fear for your precious realm?"

Vangerdahast raised both of his empty hands in expressionless silence—and spell-links shone forth in the air like silver spiderwebs, spanning emptiness between the rings on his fingers and the winking radiances of risen spells and a dozen revealed wands. They formed a vast and glowing ring around Joysil and pulsed powerfully enough that she did not—could not—doubt that they could destroy her in an instant.

The song dragon regarded them . . . and shivered. "Will you use these? If I try to fly away now?"

Vangerdahast shook his head. "Nay. Sworn to defend Cormyr I am, but in her defense I'll stand and fight those who come against her and me. I'll *not* lash out and become a tyrant over those who *may* menace her or rival me. I will *never* make Cormyr into the likes of Thay, or Zhentil Keep, or Mulmaster, just to keep its name on maps."

He started to pace, as if forgetting how close and powerful she was, and added, "I've far more to worry over than dragons—I've the usual treachery among nobles, traitors among the War Wizards, and more than one eager Red Wizard all seeking the downfall of the Forest Kingdom. Any of them is apt to do more harm to Cormyr just now than dragonkind of any sort."

He stopped and turned to face Joysil again. "I don't intend to bind any unwilling dragon—and now I must take steps to link the spells you so fear to my own life, so that if I'm slain they'll destroy themselves and leave no mage empowered to bind you or your ilk."

The dragon's turquoise eyes studied him thoughtfully. Joysil sprang into the air, swooped low and away behind some trees, and flew away, her wingbeats fast and furious.

Myrmeen and Vangerdahast stood in the sunlight watching her distant form dwindle, until the old wizard sighed, shook his head, and peered about to see if there still was a passage he could traverse ahead of him. At his shoulder, Myrmeen said softly, "You're either the greatest fool I've ever met—or the greatest man."

Vangerdahast looked at her. "The former, I fear—yet I'll cling to some pride in not trying to be the greatest villain, when the power to be so has come into my hands, time and time again. 'Tis why I admire Elminster, my sometime teacher, even though he infuriates me more often than not. Temptation snatches at him and finds him wanting, over and over."

Myrmeen nodded. "I've met Elminster . . . long enough to come to know him better than some high ladies of Cormyr know their husbands. A very great rogue. We parted with swords drawn on each other—respectful, but wary."

Vangerdahast lifted one bristling eyebrow. "That," he told her, "is a tale I must hear in full someday."

He spun around to stride briskly down another passage back to his spellchambers. "But not now. Now I must do as I promised Joysil and bind my spells to my life."

"How swiftly can that be done, and at what risk to you?"

The retired Mage Royal shrugged. "In the space of a grand fool's speech akin to the one I just uttered. The risk is no more than the one you both apprehend: Slaying me ends this danger to dragonkind."

"What do you expect the dragons and the other foes you mentioned to do now?"

"Come here with all speed and slay us," Vangerdahast replied gruffly, throwing wide the door to reveal a glimmer of lantern-light and walls cloaked in a latticework of full scroll-shelves. "So I must get you safely gone ere I must go down fighting. 'Twill be interesting to see who gets here first."

"My lord, I'll not leave you," Myrmeen said, lifting her sword.

Vangey chuckled. "Lass, I can have you deep in dreams-lumber and halfway across Faerun before you can blink."

"But you won't," Myrmeen replied, diving forward to lie across a desk of spell-scrolls challengingly, clasping the lit lantern to her breast. "I've but to smash this, and let the flaming oil spill . . ."

Vangerdahast sighed. "All right, lass—what do *you* want?"

"To stand with you and die fighting at your side. I, too, am sworn to defend Cormyr."

"Right then, so you shall. Now put that damned lamp aside—carefully!—and get your distracting self up and off my writings so I can fulfill my promise!"

The binding took a long time, and Vangerdahast was trembling with weariness when he finished. They exchanged glances, and Myrmeen put a steadying hand on the mage's shoulder. "And now?"

The former Royal Magician shrugged. "And now we wait for someone to attack. My spells are ready, each set to unleash when certain conditions are met. We wait to die, I suppose."

Myrmeen gave him a dark-eyed look then set down her sword. "Well, then, I'm going to dare to bed the greatest man Cormyr has ever known," she said firmly, grasping at the front of his robe.

"I'm—Lady, I'm centuries too old for you," Vangerdahast protested, "and ugly, besides. I—"

Her lips found his.

When he could speak again, it was to cough, shake his head, and whisper, "Lass? Would you?"

* * * * *

The fang dragon hissed in rage and fear when no less than a dozen wyrms suddenly alighted on the edge of the great rock-cauldron mountaintop that was its lair—but the song dragon that approached from among them did so murmuring words of polite supplication in a soft thunder that held no malice.

In truth, the fang dragon was gigantic among its kind and bore the scars of many battles won, including a vast, rainbow-hued swath of scales on one flank where a great old wound had healed imperfectly. Had the song dragon been alone, it would have pounced and torn apart the overbold intruder very swiftly.

"I need you," Joysil said gently. It had been a very long time since Aeglyl Dreadclaw had heard such a sentiment. He laid aside his wild schemes of escape and revenge in an instant to listen . . . and when she was done speaking and laid bare the bald truth of her words with a spell that Aeglyl had last seen cast in his youth an age ago, the great fang dragon drew itself up and hissed, "Lead me, and I shall fight wing to wing with you. This peril must be swept away for all our sakes."

The song dragon turned, flapped her wings, and all of the wyrms took wing, climbing and drawing apart to let her and the newly recruited Dreadclaw soar into their midst.

"We must hasten," Joysil called and hurled herself through the air toward Cormyr—with a dozen dragons in her wake, a scaled host going to war.

Twenty-One

NO SWORD SHARPER THAN HER TONGUE

The din of battle can be deafening, even to dying ears—but give me twenty such deafenings over one bitter dispute with my wife.

Sarseth Thald, Merchant of Amn
Musings On Being A Merchant Prince
Year of the Turret

"B'gads, Surth! How much longer must we sit here in the dark starving, eh?" Aumun Bezrar wiped his sweating brow with one plump and hairy forearm, and waved at the window with his knife. "The rest of Marsember grows richer by the passing hour, while here we sit!"

The tall, lean figure leaning on the windowframe straightened and said icily, "We're *not* starving, Bezrar. You've sliced open a good dozen cheeses since I started keeping count—and emptied an entire hand-keg of Sembian jack, too! I chose this warehouse for two good reasons and the plentiful supply of food was one of them. Mind you don't 'starve' too much or you won't fit through the door when the time comes to go!"

"When will *that* be? Stop me vitals, Surth, they can't care enough to spell-hunt us forever—just as I can't eat cheese forever!"

"I *know*," Surth said darkly. "The *other* reason I chose this place, dolt, is that crate you're sitting on. 'Tis full of Selgauntan glowstones, and their enchantments—duly registered and duty-paid—should hide us from any seeking spell that's not cast from right inside this building. I hope."

"Odd's fish, Surth—don't you *know*? For sure? We could be cowering here for *nothing*?"

"Stop waving that fish-gutter of yours and sputtering at me, *Master* Importer Aumun Bezrar, and—"

Malakar Surth fell silent in mid-sarcasm and threw up a hand for silence. With a warning hiss, he slapped a finger to his lips and took two swift steps toward his fat, sweating business-partner to drive home the urgency of his warning. With his other hand, he pointed repeatedly at the floor-boards below. Someone had entered the vast, cavernous ground floor of their warehouse.

"You're sure this place is safe?" a cultured male voice asked doubtfully, bringing a whiff of strong musk with it. Surth bared his teeth in a silent sneer. A noble, for all the coins in Marsember.

"As safe as anywhere in this rotting fishgrave of a city," another man replied in amused tones. "The rogues who own this cargo-barn haven't been seen for some days—and small wonder, with the Watch looking everywhere for them!"

"All the better reason to be wary," the perfumed noble said angrily. "Who's to say there isn't a purple-noses patrol in here now or heading here for a regular peer-about?"

A sudden glow flared below, shining up through gaps in the floorboards to show Bezrar and Surth each other's tense faces.

"Behold," the amused noble said, "my glowstone. We can take a good look about as we talk and be gone before anyone's the wiser. If the Watch does burst in, saw you the 'storage for reasonable coin' sign outside? Well, we're two empty-handed nobles inspecting the place to see if it's dry enough to store the next incoming shipment of the wardrobes of Eastern silk our wives have gone mad for, hmm?"

"All right," the perfumed noble said grudgingly. "Shine it over there—I thought I saw something moving."

"You did."

"Tymora's sweet tea—!"

"A big one, yes. No, let it go. A rat that big is the main nightfeast for some dockers' families in this city."

"Thandro, you're *sick!*"

"So my mistresses often say—but they never refuse my gifts nor company, I've noticed. Enough of this. Satisfied?"

"I suppose. Thundaerlyn Hall, yes, and I've found five minor baubles my kin won't miss—a comb that slays lice, the head of a walking-stick that knows north, that sort of thing."

"Good. How many blades can you muster?"

"Seven at least, three trained to the blade, and two experienced hireswords. When and where?"

"Under the broken lantern on Thelvarspike Lane—you know it?—by five-toll at the latest. We have to be in our places well before First Candlelight, when the royals are supposed to arrive."

"They'll bring dozens of War Wizards and Purple Dragons, Thandro!"

"Of course. We of the Rightful Conspiracy shall be ready for them. Act like you're out for a night of scouring the taverns, get to that lantern-post, and all will be well. We've blades and wizards enough to take care of any army the Obarskyrs bring—and yes, we expect to have to deal with the Mage Royal and her bully-spells, too."

"I don't like it."

"Your sort never do, Sauvrurn. If it wasn't for men like me, you'd be muttering darkly about Obarskyr misrule from now until doddering to your grave seventy summers hence—doing nothing all that time but fuming. You want a new Cormyr? Well, we'll give it to you *and* the 'true power' you crave so loudly. You can use it to order Alusair—or whatever's left of her—brought bound to your bed by morning and stop boring our ears with *that* oft-repeated demand, too. Who knows? You might even get to father the next King of all Cormyr, you lucky dog!"

"My family beast," the perfumed noble replied icily, "is the winged lion—*not* some mongrel hound."

"Well, my Winged Lion," Thandro replied, his voice fading as he moved toward the door, "just you be there under the Lightless Lamp before five-toll, and you'll get your chance to leave the Steel Regent gasping. If you don't have to slice her up like sausage-meat in the fray, that is."

"She'll be no match for me in swordplay, so keep your men well back. . . ."

Sauvrurn's voice faded entirely, and the two men in the loft heard the door-bar crash back into place.

"B'gads, Surth!" Bezrar hissed, sweat streaming down his face like a waterfall. "What have we gotten ourselves into?"

"*Nothing*," Marsember's wealthiest dealer in scents, wines, cordials, and drugs snarled, "if you shut your loose jaws for once and help me get the roof-trap open. We have to stay quiet, and move quick—and get as far away as the walls of Marsember let us from all the bloodshed that's going to erupt ere dusk! Whatever happens in Thundaerlyn Hall, this city is going to be scoured out and turned upside down by every War Wizard the realm can muster by highsun tomorrow!"

* * * * *

Florin Falconhand stood with his fish dripping forgotten in one hand and his blade ready in the other, warily watching the sprawled Red Wizard. Helpless at his feet, Starangh stared back. If glares alone could slay, the ranger would have been done for—but as it was, the real battle was taking place a pace or two beyond them both.

Narnra Shalace stood facing her father, her anger boiling over. "You're no better than this grasping, evil Thayan!" she snapped. "You do just as you please and have done for years! Years of meddling in the lives of many, more for your own satisfaction and amusement than anything else!"

Elminster shook his head. "I've done most of my deeds and misdeeds in the service of Mystra, the most powerful goddess of all," he replied quietly. "For good or ill, I've been a finger or two of her hand and acted as she commanded me."

Narnra waved away his words with a sneer of disgust. "You could've refused! You could've renounced it all—if you hadn't wanted all that *power!*"

El shrugged. "Want it or not, I have it—why should I not use it? Who better than myself can I trust to use it well?"

"It's not about power and control," Narnra snarled furiously, "it's about doing the right thing."

"Ah, and what *is* that 'right thing'?"

Narnra drew herself up scornfully. "If you can't tell—"

Elminster said a single cold word that echoed across the meadow like a thunderclap, freezing everyone. Narnra's face went bone-white and terror flamed in her eyes as she found herself unable to move or speak.

Her father took a step forward and suddenly seemed a shade less old and ridiculous. Contempt flared in his blue-gray eyes as he met her gaze and said softly, "My daughter—just one more young hothead with all the answers. The 'right thing' is whatever ye think it is . . . but unfortunately ye've seen so little of the world and are capable of understanding so little beyond what's right at the end of thy nose for thine eyes to fall upon easily that ye only see one 'right thing.' "

He walked right up to that nose and began to circle her, keeping close, hands clasped behind his back, voice soft but fierce. "*Listen* to me, lass: I'm guilty of whimsy and vengefulness and standing in judgment and bad temper, willful meddling, and even loss of my wits, often—but before I try to shape the world around me I also try to do something ye've not yet learned to do: I try to look at things from all sides, to understand disagreements and rivalries through the eyes of all involved . . . more than that, to look ahead to the probable consequences of what I might do."

He stopped in front of her and said more gently, "Sometimes I may appear heartless to ye, young Shining Eyes with thy heart ruling ye—but I *think* about what I do, before, during, and after, and turn right around to try to right my mistakes instead of striding on and dismissing yesterday's misdeeds as gone and past, beyond recalling. If ye don't grow enough to do that, *ye* are no better than this grasp-all, evil Thayan."

He waved his hand, and Narnra found herself free to walk and speak. She trembled, wondering if she dared say anything but found herself whispering, "And you expect me to see all your manipulating as right? And wise? Benevolent, following some master plan I'm too stupid or impatient to see? You think manipulating folk isn't the greatest evil there *is?*"

"Lass, lass," Elminster replied wearily, "manipulating folk is what humans *do.* If ye knew of my youth, ye'd know just how much I hate mages who rule, and being manipulated . . . but I learned down the centuries that 'tis best to do some steering of folk before the steering is done to ye. Because, rest assured, 'twill be. I can at least be sure of my own motives, and that I've thought about them, though whether they be 'good' or 'evil' is for others to judge. The motives of others, I can never be so sure about—until I see the glee in their eyes reflecting off the bright blade aimed at my heart . . . as they swing it down."

"You . . . you're maddening," Narnra snarled, fists clenched. "You—you heartless *monster!*"

"That's right, hurl back views that force ye to think by

namecalling—'tis the grand old tradition, let it not down! Anything to keep from having to think, or—Mystra forfend— change thy own views!"

Narnra glowered at her father. "Just how am I to learn how to think? By being taught by *you?*"

"Some folk in the Realms would give their lives for the chance to learn at my feet," Elminster said mildly. "Several already have."

He turned away. "However, I think ye're not ready for that, yet. I'm too useful to ye as the villain who sired then spurned ye, Old Lord Walking Blame For All Things Dark. No, I think ye must find thy own teachers in thy own way, taking no hint from me. See how well ye've received the few words of advice I've offered here and now?"

Narnra took a deep breath and wrestled down her rage. "So what advice would you give me, Old Lord, about where to go now and what to do? *Not* how to govern my own wits and what views to hold—but what to do next?"

Elminster met her gaze again and said, "Come into my Tower and have a cup of tea. Let thy anger fade, and we'll talk. I'll give ye some baubles of magic and mutter a lot of stale old advice then whisk ye with my Art to wherever ye desire to be—and hand thy choice right back to ye. As I see it, ye can travel and adventure and broaden thyself right away . . . or reward Caladnei's trust by serving her as a loyal agent—then, when ye grow restless, steer her into giving ye tasks that let ye travel Faerûn and see as much of it as possible. Ye'll always be welcome here, and one of the trifles I'll hand ye will enable ye to call on me from afar should ye need aid . . . or even, make the gods gasp, advice."

Narnra stared at him and snapped, "The tea, I'll accept." She looked down at the Red Wizard. "And him?"

"He lies in pain, awaiting thy judgment. Were ye very cruel, ye could just leave him, or tell me to carry him off across the field to yonder anthill, to itch and burn whilst we sip. Or I could restore him to full vigor and give him a wand to smite us all with. The choice is thine."

"And if I said healing and the wand?" Narnra asked, her whisper a challenge.

"I'll do it . . . but have ye given thought to the consequences?"

"Yes," she snapped fiercely, setting her jaw. "Yes, I have. Do that for him. Do it for *me*."

Elminster muttered something, made a shape in the air, then stared at a spot above the Thayan. A smooth, tapering stick of wood promptly appeared there and floated serenely above the twisted Red Wizard as the Old Mage cast a more elaborate spell.

Harnrim Starangh gasped once, writhed and arched briefly, shuddered all over—and sprang up, pale and sweating. He faced Elminster with wild eyes, but the Old Mage stood like a statue.

The Red Wizard cast a quick glance at Florin, whose sword was now drawn back for a deadly throw, then gave both Narnra and Elminster odd looks, snatched the floating wand out of the air—and vanished.

Elminster calmly muttered something, waved at the place Starangh had been, and turned away, offering Narnra his hand.

She did not take it, but followed him up the flagstone path to his squat, leaning rough-stone Tower.

"Not much of a grand fortress, is it?" she asked tartly.

He shrugged. "We heartless monsters must make do."

Not quite hiding a smile, Florin opened the door for them, waving them within with a grand gesture that was only slightly spoiled by being made with a handful of still-dripping fish.

"Enter within," he said. "Old Lord Walking Blame and guest. I'll stand guard here for returning Red Wizards, whilst you . . ."

"Try to learn to speak civil words to each other," Narnra replied a little wearily, stepping past him into the dusty gloom.

Behind her back, the two men exchanged glances.

Elminster nodded to the ranger, said gently, "Do that," and went inside.

* * * * *

In a high window not far away across Shadowdale, Storm Silverhand lounged with harp in hand, singing softly to herself. Her farm chores were done, and it was time and past time to take some ease, even for daughters of Mystra . . .

In mid-song she became aware of a shimmering below as her wards sprang to life. She stilled her strings to call, "Yes?"

Standing in her courtyard, ringed with crawling blue fire, was a gaunt, trim-bearded man holding something under his cloak. "Good lady," he greeted her gravely, "I am Alaphondar Emmarask, High Royal Sage of Cormyr, and I bring a thing most precious with me. Pray banish your fires."

Storm set aside her harp and swung herself through the window, floating gently down to join her unexpected guest. She made an intricate one-handed gesture as she descended, awakening an unseen magic that seemed to satisfy her. Her next gesture made the flames sink away to nothingness.

"Be welcome, Lord Sage," she said politely. "Will you stay, take shelter, and dine? I've pheasant roasting over one hearth and a cauldron of rabbit stew a-building in the other."

"Thank you, Lady Silverhand. I cannot say what my reply to your kind offer will be until I have your decision as to my . . . burden."

"The king you're hiding under your cloak? He's right welcome, too," Storm said dryly. "I'll endeavour to keep you both safe—and unseen. No doubt some in Cormyr would be quite upset to learn you're here, and others . . . would become all too eager."

Alaphondar's smile was rueful. "Lady, you state matters very well. I'll stay if you'll have me. How strong are your wards?"

Storm's smile was broader than his. "I *am* a Chosen of

Mystra," she reminded him gently. "Take off your boots, soak your feet in yonder oil, and let me have a good look at the next scourge of womanhood in the Heartlands."

Alaphondar winced. "Lady . . ." he started to protest then fell silent.

"I have my own reputation," Storm replied, "remember? Which reminds me: How is Fee?"

Alaphondar winced again. "Harpers see all, indeed. My royal lady was well and happy when we parted some hours ago. I hope—oh, gods, I hope—that I shall see her so again, soon."

"You," Storm said, sliding an arm around his shoulders, "need a drink. Sit you down, and I'll get a scrying-crystal— and you can watch over Filfaeril whenever you desire. Now, off with those boots, and haul forth young Azoun before he suffocates under that dirty old cloak of yours!"

* * * * *

Narnra shook her head at the dusty stacks of parchment and books crowding all around her and seemed eager to escape to the spartan, less-cluttered kitchen, where a pass of Elminster's hand made the hearthfire rise under a kettle. The Old Mage pointed at a shelf. "Teas. Choose."

Narnra dubiously examined the jars thereon. "Dragon-skull?"

"Just a little," Elminster replied. "Powdered fine, of course."

Narnra gave him an incredulous look. "So what," she asked challengingly, "dare I assume is in tea labelled 'Finest Thayan She-Slave Skin'—as this jar is?"

"One of Lhaeo's little jests. I'm sure it's far from the 'finest' skin."

Narnra sighed, shook her head and defiantly held out the Thayan jar to Elminster. He took it without a word.

Silence stretched between them—enlivened by the climbing cry of the kettle—until Narnra became restless.

"So impart," she said, peering around the little kitchen, "some of that dusty old advice you spoke of."

"We all have to die and can take nothing of mortal riches or power with us," Elminster replied promptly. "I've died several times already—and on at least two occasions started over with nothing, not even my name. So unless the cold decay of undeath beckons ye, remember, it ends for us all. What matters is what we do with the brief time we have."

"*Your* time hasn't been so brief," Narnra flared.

Elminster bowed his head. "*That* is my curse."

Narnra stared at him then folded her arms and asked, "Why did you leave my mother?"

Elminster stepped forward to take hold of her shoulders. They stared into each other's eyes, noses only inches apart.

"Lass," he said gently, "just being near me gets folk killed. I speak now not of foes I smite or fools who make reckless attempts to exploit my power or presence to further their own dangerous causes, but folk who simply get in the way or come to the notice of those who love me not. I know of—and knew well—over two hundred 'hes' and 'shes' of all the lands and races ye could think of who died in torment because some more powerful foe thought I might have given something or told something of importance to them . . . or just to lure me within reach or cause me distress when I learned of the torture later. And so—"

"And so you wrap this sorrowful 'I must do thus and so for the protection of others' explanation around yourself like a cloak and prance through life wenching and using everyone who comes within reach as if they were your personal chambermaids, hmm?"

"Fair enough," Elminster said calmly, stepping back to pour two large tankards of tea, "I suppose I do. Armed with this knowledge, ye'll do—what?"

Narnra stared at him, chin balanced on her knuckles, and said, "Ask you again: Why did you leave Maerjanthra Shalace, after wooing and bedding her?"

"To answer ye properly," the Old Mage replied gravely,

"I must know the answer to a question of my own. Have ye ever seen this before?" He dipped a finger into his steaming tea, drew a complicated symbol on the table between them with its wetness, let her gaze at it for a moment, and swiftly wiped it away.

Narnra sat back, strangely excited. "No-no," she said, frowning, "I don't think so. Wait. A jewel Mother crafted . . . and wore as a pendant, for a time. Why?"

"'Tis a symbol of the goddess Shar," Elminster murmured, "who among other things works against She whom I serve."

"Mystra. You mean . . . what do you mean?"

"All gods and goddesses work through mortals. Shar is one whose manipulations are legendary. Deservedly legendary."

Narnra frowned. "You think Shar was using my mother to influence you?"

El nodded.

"But that's ridiculous! That's—"

"What happened. I was in thy mother's arms, tongue to tongue, eye to eye. I felt the darkness slide into her and reach for me. So did she and whimpered and clung to me the tighter. I thrust her away and departed out the window, glass and frame and all, as fast as I could move. Had I remained, I'd have been taken or Maerjanthra would have been consumed in Shar's hunger to corrupt me. Rather than bearing ye, thy mother would have been left a crumbling husk."

Narnra stared at him. "So you went away, and my mother had me. Are you saying I'm consecrated to Shar—a creature of the Mistress of the Night from birth?"

"No," Elminster replied gravely, "or I'd have blasted ye to ash when first I read thy mind. Only created creatures and those born of the gods or their avatars or beings the gods spend much time mind-meddling with while yet unborn come from the womb 'belonging' to this deity or that. All the rest of us are free to choose our faith—influenced by any who may try to sway us, of course. Ye are Narnra Shalace, free to choose. Shar—or Mystra, for that matter—

could possess and control thy body but would burn it out in hours or days by the very might of their manifestation. Failing that, ye're free to choose as ye will. I am not free. Bound to Mystra am I—but Mystra desires all mortal creatures to possess the freedom given them by personally wielding magic."

"A sword in every hand," Narnra muttered. "Which inevitably leads to much spilled blood."

El bowed his head. "The highest price of freedom is always its misuse by many."

Narnra turned away. "Mother seldom wore that pendant," she murmured to the tea-shelf, running her fingers along it as if answers were going to sprout helpfully among the jars.

Elminster kept silent, waiting.

His daughter turned around and looked at him in clear challenge. "What if I tell you now that I defy your moral claptrap, Father, and go my own way, stealing and thieving and never speaking to you again?"

"That's thy choice, and by Mystra's grace ye're free to make it. I'll still give ye those baubles I spoke of, my promise of welcome here whenever ye desire it, my friendship if ye'll have it, and my fond regard even if ye don't."

"And if I fling all that in your teeth, meddling old wizard?"

"That will be my loss and sorrow," Elminster told his tankard quietly.

"*Damn* you, old man!" Narnra said, hurling what was left of her tea into his face as she sprang up. "Damn you!"

Elminster sat with tea dripping off his nose and beard, and replied calmly, "My damnation happened centuries ago the first time—and again some dozen times since."

"Save such words for someone who'll be *impressed!*" Narnra snarled and strode back through the dusty gloom to the door, snatching it open.

Florin stood just outside, arms folded, blocking her way.

She put her head down and charged right into him, punching viciously.

The ranger stood like immovable stone, absorbing her punishment, and called calmly, "Elminster?"

"Let her go her way," came the calm reply. "She's discovering that growing up is painful—when she thought she'd finished with growing up some time ago."

Florin nodded and bowed to the furious, now-weeping Narnra, indicating that her way was clear with a wave of his hand.

She stormed past him in tears, striding angrily out to where the flagstone path forked. Ahead was the road—where a few carts were creaking past, bearing farmers of Shadowdale who glanced her way curiously—and to her right was a placid pool. She stood trembling for a moment . . . then turned right.

At the water's edge was a large, flat rock. Narnra threw herself down on it and gazed at the water, muttering soft curses.

He went away and left me. He just went away. And Mother died.

All this alone, all this clawing for coins and food, all this risking my neck for years *in Waterdeep . . .*

And now I'm snatched away from home, and halfway across Faerûn with no way back, bound to another *meddling wizard. All because of him.*

And he sits there like an old stone gargoyle, looking down from the ramparts of his years and being sad that I don't make the same mistakes he did. Bah!

Narnra sprang to her feet and kicked at the earth, seeking to drive a stone—any stone—into the water. The pond was like glass, her reflection as clear as any mirror. She struck a pose. Huh; the Silken Shadow indeed.

Furiously she kicked at the earth again. Grass and dirt fountained, and one tiny pebble flew, bounced, and found the water.

She watched its spreading rings for a time, and sat down to do so. This place was beautiful. She lifted her gaze and looked around. A castle keep—built with a strange twist to it—across this meadow, a cart-road off to her left with a few mule-carts being led out onto it, a rock twice the height of Waterdeep Castle rising right up out of the grass to her right, behind *his* tower . . .

Atop it, helmed heads and a few spears. She was being watched. Even here.

You bastard, old man. You suspicious old . . . but no. Banners are flapping up there, no one's moving—except there, to point down at the road. They're watching the road.

I suppose someone will always be watching, wherever I go.

A gentle breeze arose, fresh and fragrant with wildflowers, and Narnra lifted her face to catch it, and looked around at the rustling trees and waving grass.

This was a fair place. It must be nice to live here. Wherever "here" was.

Some time later, Elminster quietly sat down beside Narnra and steered a fresh mug of tea into her hand. "Ye, ahem, threw away the chance to finish yours," he said gently.

Narnra gave him a red-eyed glance and—after a long moment—took the tea.

Saying nothing, she quickly looked away, and sat cradling it and staring at the pool.

After a time, she absently sipped it.

A little later, she risked a glance to her right. Elminster was sitting silently beside her, looking out over the pool rather than at her, his unlit pipe floating in the air near at hand.

Is he just going to *sit* there? Waiting for me to beg his forgiveness, cry for his acceptance, say I love him? Knowing I can't run from him, don't even know where to run to, and that he can blast me whenever he wants?

I threw my tea in his face, shouted at him—why hasn't he blasted me already?

What's he afraid of?

Narnra shot a glance at her father. He didn't look afraid of anything. He was smelling the breeze, nose lifted, a half-smile on his face.

He doesn't look afraid, he looks smug. Damn him.

Oh, yes, too late for that. Such big words, such calm claims. Smug old man.

She drew in a ragged breath, looked away, and sipped from her tankard again.

It was getting cold—but grew warmer, even as she drew back and made a face at it.

Narnra glared at Elminster. "Are you using your magic on this?"

"Of course," he said gently. "Ye prefer it warm, d'ye not?"

She regarded him, hefting the tankard in her hand as if she might throw it at him. Again. "And you always use your magic to do what other people prefer?"

"Nay. Most folk don't even know what they prefer. Most never stop to think." He turned his head to watch some flower petals drift by. "Do they?"

You mean that as some sort of a thrust at me, old man? You think clever words can change everything?

Narnra turned her back on her father again.

Every time she turned around again, however, he was still there. He smiled at her once or twice, but she gave him stony silence. After a while, she started watching *him*.

He sat and looked around at Shadowdale, not seeming to mind.

Later, her tankard empty, Narnra murmured, "This place is beautiful."

"Aye. I sit here often. Dawn, sunrise, sunset, and dusk offer the best views, of course. If ye want to bathe, soap-flakes and hair-scent are under yon rock."

Narnra gave him a startled look. "You expect me to stay?"

Elminster shook his head. "I expect nothing—but I offered ye welcome at any time ye might care to claim it, and ye might arrive some day desiring to get cool or clean or wash the blood of someone ye disagreed with off ye, so 'tis handy to know where the soap is."

"I suppose you have drying robes waiting under some other rock?"

"No, but if ye go and lie on yonder stone, ye'll find it both heats and sucks away the damp. The black velvet butterfly hanging on the shrub beside it is one of Jhessail Silvertree's hair-slides. She comes here often to lay her hair out in a fan to get it properly dry."

It was Narnra's turn for head-shaking. "I—I don't understand you. You seem tender and kind, you protest your noble reasons and causes, insist you look at everything from all sorts of viewpoints . . . yet you use people as if they were farm-beasts, love women and leave them as casually as you change your socks, and–and—*why?*"

"Because I'm a mere mortal, twisted beyond sanity by what I've seen and done, and by holding a goddess in my arms, and by living for far too long," Elminster whispered. "I'm a crazed villain and a proudly enthusiastic meddler as well as thy father . . . but I'd also like to be thy friend. I take folk as I find them and leave judgments to the young; I hope ye can learn to do that, too."

"Old Mage," Narnra told him firmly, "young people *have* to learn to judge others or they never survive to become older. Yet I'll grant that you . . . are more than I thought you were."

She turned to look directly into his eyes and added, "If I'd never known you'd sired me, we'd already be friends. I'm . . . I'm trying to set aside my anger over growing up fatherless then being left alone to fend for myself after my mother died. I may be just one of uncounted thousands of forgotten, abandoned orphans in Faerûn, but I'm *me*, the only person I've ever had to worry about, and—"

"Precisely. Ye're the only person ye've ever had to worry about. Go get thyself a few friends—*real* friends—and ye'll have that many more folk to worry over."

"And you worry about thousands, is that it?"

"Worry and do something—lots of things, endlessly—for them. Grieve for all those I failed and those the passing years have taken from me. Whole realms I loved are now gone," Elminster replied and added calmly, "Boo hoo."

Narnra snorted in surprised mirth and set her tankard down. "I could learn to love this place," she said almost wistfully—and then turned her head to look into her father's eyes and added slowly, almost struggling with the words, "To accept you too, I think, with all your lies and meddling. Someday."

"I'd like that," he said gently. " 'Twould mean much to me."

She nodded, and they looked calmly into each other's eyes for what seemed a very long time.

Abruptly Narnra became aware, as she stared through it at her father, of how tangled and sweat-soiled her hair was. Her gaze fell longingly to the pool, and after a few breaths of silence she asked, "Would you mind going away whilst I bathe if I promise to work no mischief?"

Elminster chuckled, took up her tankard, and laid a hand on her shoulder. "I'll be up in the Tower preparing evenfeast when ye're done. Florin has probably worn his sword-edge dull slicing edibles by now. I'm not much of a family, lass, but ye're welcome, whenever."

Narnra gave him a strange look and waved at the pool. "There aren't—snakes or biting turtles or anything like that, are there?"

"Nay," Elminster told her, as he conjured up a fluffy robe,

towels, and slippers, and bent with a grunt to lay them out
on a handy rock. "I asked the beast that eats them to depart
when ye arrived, and it did."

She gave him a longer look, until he turned and added,
"Trust me."

"I'm learning to," she said with a lopsided smile. "Don't
make me regret it. Please."

"Well, if ye'd like to toss your clothes onto yon rock, I'll
snatch them away with a spell and give them a wash whilst
ye're soaking—because they certainly need it. Knives and
all, mind. I'll be careful not to let things rust. Oh, and the
little blades ye keep hidden in thy hair, too they're starting
to tarnish."

Narnra gave her father quite another look and said, "If
you trick me . . ."

"I'll be overcome with remorse," he said with a grin and
strolled off, his pipe floating after him.

Narnra watched him go, shaking her head. Well, at least
she had an *interesting* father. When she heard the Tower
door close, she disrobed, carefully putting her gear where
he'd indicated—all but one knife with its sheath, which she
laid ready at the water's edge.

She lifted the stone Elminster had pointed out, scooped
up some flakes of soap, and waded in.

The water was wonderful.

* * * * *

"B'gads, what if they find us here?" Bezrar muttered.
"What tale do we tell them *then?*"

"That we're thinking of importing some new sort of
shingles from—from Alaghôn, and had to see if the barracks
roofs would ever be a market for us," his partner Surth
hissed. "If you *shut up* for once, perhaps they *won't* find us
here!"

They both froze, there on the roof of the largest
Purple Dragon barracks in Marsember, as at least a dozen

dragons—each larger than any barracks, and far more impressive—swooped past, in a mighty hurry to get to somewhere in the city!

The great wyrms passed over the barracks so low that Malakar Surth, the taller of the two swindlers, could almost have touched one of those vast and scaled underbellies by standing tall and leaping upward.

He chose not to do so. It seemed more sensible to faint instead.

Twenty-Two

A LITTLE VICTORY

Sometimes, all you can do is take what little victory you can.

Sorbraun Swordmantle
*Seventy Summers A Purple Dragon:
One Loyal Warrior's Tale*
Year of the Prince

"Stand easy," Laspeera murmured. "Whatever happens, we've War Wizards enough to keep you both safe."

Filfaeril and Alusair gave her identical sighs. "Speera, it's not that," the Steel Regent exclaimed, armor gleaming. "It's how many loyal folk this will cost us—and how many noble families who lose their young hotheads here will turn against us. When will Cormyr stop *bleeding?*"

"Here they come," Caladnei muttered, stepping back, as many men stalked into the dimly lit hall, drawn swords glittering in the light of her conjured light.

"Hail, Ladies Obarskyr," one of them called in a grand

and cultured voice. "Your attendance—even with so many
of your mages—gratifies us. We desire to discuss the future
of our fair real—"

The noble staggered forward to fall on his face with a
cough and lie still, sword ringing on the tiles. His fellows
whirled around with shouts of anger.

Many men in robes were fading into visibility out of
empty air—Thayans! Harnrim Starangh glared coldly around
Thundaerlyn Hall and commanded his fellow Red Wizards,
"Kill them all—yon women first. Let no one leave alive!"

* * * * *

Bezrar and Surth came back to Marsember at about the
same time, with damp and misty air singing past their ears
as a grand rooftop—all spires and skylights—rushed up to
meet them. They were . . . oh, gods . . . in the grip of great
talons.

Talons that were attached to a huge and iridescent silver-
blue dragon. Turquoise eyes burned into theirs with force
enough to keep them blinkingly, tremblingly awake. When
both Surth and Bezrar would quite happily have fainted
again great jaws hissed in a soft thunder, "Open those skylights so we can see and hear who's within. I've no desire
to provoke all the War Wizards and whatever other mages
happen to be in Marsember by tearing apart a few buildings
at random and slaughtering folk heedlessly."

"B-b-but—" Bezrar managed to splutter.

"However," Joysil told him, "I *can* make a few exceptions
when it comes to slaughtering if you provoke *me*. Yes, this is
the roof of Thundaerlyn Hall, and yes, I'm a dragon, just as
you are Aumun Tholant Bezrar and *you* are Malakar Surth.
Get those open!"

The two smugglers leaped to the panes with frantic eagerness, fumbling at catches that hadn't been oiled or thrown
open in decades—decades of sea-mists and incontinent birds
and nesting fowl that . . . that . . .

"Oh, *gods!*" Surth hissed, his fingers trembling helplessly. "We'll never—"

Beside him, Bezrar drew his longknife, puffing like a walrus and sweating a river, and brought its pommel down firmly through the dirty pane in front of him.

There was a shout from within, and a roaring gout of flame burst up out of the shattered skylight. A dragon banked sharply overhead, thrust out its neck, and breathed something back.

Bezrar emitted a sort of frightened mew as he tumbled over backward. Spells were bursting out of skylights up and down the roof now, shards of glass tumbling in all directions, and dragons were diving down and breathing death of their own.

It was, yes, a *luminescent* time to faint, Bezrar and Surth decided in unison—and did so.

* * * * *

Caladnei and Laspeera did nothing but hold up shimmering shielding-spells around Alusair and Filfaeril as they all rushed together to the east end of the hall—which saved them, even as Red Wizards by the dozens vanished in dragon-spew.

The very floor-tiles of the central open hall exploded, heaved, and melted where the full fury of dragon-magic struck, and the roof started to come down in great crashing chunks.

The two highest-ranking War Wizards reeled, moaning in pain and clutching their heads, as their shieldings were torn asunder. Somewhere down there, the Obarskyrs were on their own, now . . .

Doors burst open in the darkness all over the hall as Rhauligan and the other Highknights decided that with War Wizards screaming and fainting and igniting like torches all around them they might already be too late to rush forth and perform a rescue.

The Red Wizards Starangh had been able to assemble were the youngest and most ambitious Thayans handy in Sembia, but they neither trusted each other nor had much experience in working carefully together in spell-battle . . . so in the flashing, bursting confusion of swooping dragons and men running about with swords, they soon started hurling death at anyone and everyone they saw, including each other.

Harnrim Darkspells looked around from a high balcony in disbelief as War Wizards and his fellow Thayans hurled spells, chairs, and knives at each other with equally blind fury. This was a swiftly unfolding disaster! He had to—

Something made him duck and turn, and the point of Rhauligan's thrusting blade flashed harmlessly past his arm. With a curse, Starangh teleported away, leaving the Highknight slashing empty air and airing a few curses of his own.

Down below, terrified nobles were swording everyone in their haste to escape what they correctly saw as a deathtrap. The ring and clang of sword-steel rose deafeningly in the hall.

Rhauligan whirled around and raced down the nearest stair. He had to get to Alusair and Filfaeril and keep them safe, whatever happened.

* * * * *

"Get *down*, Mother!" Alusair snarled, hacking a man to the floor viciously and stamping on his throat. "That gown won't stop a child's knife! I've got to set aside having to defend and worry about you! Too many of these dogs are getting away!"

"Look—unnh!—to your own back, dear!" Filfaeril called, whirling her overgown around a man's head and rushing past him to drag him off-balance. Wildly slashing nothing, he went down, and she leaped in to land knees-together on his chest, and drive her little jeweled dagger into a face she couldn't see. "I'm Cormyr's past, daughter—*you're* its future!"

Alusair laughed bitterly as two swords reached for her. "Yes, but for how long?"

* * * * *

"Cala, we've got to get back to Luse and Fee," Laspeera panted. "They'll get *butchered!*"

"If we don't drive off these dragons," the Mage Royal of Cormyr spat back, "we'll *all* wind up fried, crushed, and entombed before six-toll!"

"They're drawing off!" Laspeera gasped, pointing. "Look! They're flying away!"

* * * * *

"ENOUGH!" Joysil roared, in a voice that shook every spire in Marsember. "We can do no more without destroying every human down there! Come—to the sanctum!"

"To the dragonbinder!" dragon voices thundered in chorus, and wings flapped and wheeled in the sky.

* * * * *

"Shields!" Caladnei cried, clutching at Laspeera. "Find them! We must raise the shields around them again!"

Laspeera peered helplessly around the darkened confusion of the hall, made a sound of exasperation, and cast a bright radiance spell out into the chaos.

Everywhere, knots of men were fighting, their swords flashing. Bodies lay huddled in their blood everywhere, too, and robed War Wizards waving daggers were rushing down stairs and along balconies, shouting.

"There!" she cried, pointing to where she'd seen Alusair's familiar hair swirl, just for a moment, amid a glimmer of clashing blades.

Hip to hip the two mages worked a casting, then collapsed with a groan.

"I worked an ironguard on them," Caladnei gasped. "Rhauligan's coming—see?—and he should be able . . . to take care of . . . men who can only punch . . . and gouge and strangle."

"Wait, what's that?" Laspeera snapped. Where they'd thrown their shield, something flared like a momentary star.

"Fee's teleport gem," Caladnei said with a grin. "She's taken them back to the Palace. Find that portal, and let's get there before Luse tries to bring every last Purple Dragon in the place back here!"

* * * * *

"What was *that*, Mother?"

"My teleport gem," Filfaeril gasped. "This dolt of a Dracohorn brought his blade down on it, before I . . . before I . . ."

"Mother!" Alusair cried in alarm, whirling back to the queen. Filfaeril was clutching at her side. She sat down against a heap of bodies, managed a little smile, and said rather triumphantly, "Before I put my little knife through his eye." She waved a hand. "Don't worry, I'm just winded, not cut. I trust."

The singing of a shielding-spell—at least, Alusair hoped it was a shielding-spell—rose around them, and she waded through the dead and dying to get to her mother.

She was still two paces away when the balcony above, smoldering in the aftermath of a spell, tore loose and crashed down on them.

* * * * *

"Hah!" Darndreth Goldsword cried triumphantly, as something splintered and the door sagged open. "Out, lads! Out!"

The dozen or so nobles of the Rightful Conspiracy surged forward as one, panting in fear and weariness. This had all gone so wrong—*dragons*, by the gods!—wizards everywhere! More grim men with swords than they'd been able to muster in the first place! And all the doors spell-sealed, too!

This was the only one they'd been able to get open, and now they'd have to run far and fast before the Obarskyrs set the hounds of the realm on—

Darndreth staggered back with a cry, almost spitting himself on half a dozen swords. "Who—?"

"No one important," the lady who stood outside replied calmly, her eyes large and dark in the glow of the conjured dagger and whip-sword in her hands. "Just someone who grew bored in Candlekeep and looked in a scrying-stone to see what was happening back in Marsember. Not that I found anything surprising."

"Stand back!" one noble shouted.

"Make way or we'll kill you!" the youngest Goldsword added, in a snarl.

The lady slashed his thrusting sword aside with her own, the meeting of blades numbing his arm as if he'd touched lightning. "You may try," she commented pleasantly.

"Who are you?"

"The Lady Nouméa Cardellith," she answered, parrying his furious attack, "of Sembia. Stay within, traitors, and face justice."

"Justice! You're not even of Cormyr!" a noble panted furiously, trying to reach his sword past Darndreth's shoulder to stab her.

"No matter. I stand for peace and honesty, whenever possible . . . to slaughter a ruling house always plunges a land into strife and outlawry and suffering, and the lurking monsters and dark cabals alike come prowling . . . or have you so swiftly forgotten what befell in Tethyr?"

"Hah! You can't stand against us! One woman, alone?"

"I don't have to," Nouméa gasped, as a blade drove her own sword aside and two others thrust into her. "I only have to delay you, until—"

Glarasteer Rhauligan struck the knot of nobles from behind like a deadly storm, four Highknights with him—and only five of the traitors had time to start pleading. Their frantic attempts to make deals went unanswered.

*   *   *   *   *

Vangerdahast gently parted Myrmeen's arms and set her aside. "'Tis done, lady," he said gently. "Our time together. They've come."

He waved above the wide expanse where Joysil had felled so many trees—and the Lady Lord of Arabel found herself looking up at a sky full of dragons.

The song dragon arrowed down into a wing-fluttering landing in front of their shattered window, the other wyrms wheeling and banking watchfully above.

"Mage," Joysil said, "we flew to war—and this threat to Cormyr from Red Wizards and traitor-nobles, at least, has been ended."

"In return," the former Royal Magician replied, silver and green fires briefly shining forth in a visible web that made more than one dragon hiss and rear back, "look, and see the truth of my words: I've bound my dragonbindings to my own life. If I perish, they go with me."

"And so?"

"And so I'm ready," he said roughly, using a chair to climb up onto the kitchen counter. From there he walked out onto what had recently been his gardens and a pleasant glade, adding, "for you to slay me."

Behind him, Myrmeen clutched a kitchen chair so hard with trembling-white hands that the wood groaned. Silent tears spilled from her eyes as she watched Vangerdahast walk to his death.

An amethyst-scaled wyrm glided down, jaws opening to breathe on the lone, trudging man—but Joysil threw out a wing to shield the retired Mage Royal, and cried, "*Cease!*"

Vangerdahast stood very still beneath that vast wing, as

dragon after dragon thudded to earth, landing in a great ring around Joysil.

"We fought well together," she said in her voice of gentle thunder, "but this human has ended the threat we gathered to destroy. He need not die. I offer you my hoard, to divide among you if you now disperse and never return to harm this Vangerdahast."

Myrmeen had heard a dragon rumble in thought once before, but when a dozen of them were at it, the field shook to their purring din. Then the great head of Aeglyl Dreadclaw nodded, and the fang dragon growled, "The fray was . . . good, yes. I am content."

That set head after head to nodding, until all the wyrms had agreed.

"Seek you then the spire of the ruined keep atop Claw Peak," the song dragon told them all, "and shatter it. Within it is a cavern stuffed full of speaking gems."

"*Speaking gems!*" several wyrms echoed eagerly—and there was a general rush into the skies.

"What," Vangerdahast asked, watching dragons dwindle into tiny specks among distant clouds, "are speaking gems?"

Joysil snorted. "Magical things, wizard—nothing *you* should be meddling with. Some four thousand-odd I had from the Church of Shar years ago . . . when I saw the world somewhat differently." Those turquoise eyes stared into the old wizard's for a moment longer before she asked, "What is it you *really* want to ask me?"

Vangerdahast sighed. "My life. Why did you spare it?"

"I went to confer with the oldest, wisest dragon of my kind, who took me to someone you know all too well: Elminster of Shadowdale. He offered a solution."

It was Vangerdahast's turn to sigh. "I might have known. And that would be?"

Myrmeen saw something out of the corner of her eye. She let out a little cry of alarm as she whirled around, snatching for her sword—and the Old Mage rising from the hitherto-empty seat of Vangerdahast's favorite chair obligingly offered it to her.

"Old friend," he said to the retired Royal Magician, stepping past Myrmeen, "why not this: Use thy own spells to bind *thyself* as thy kingdom's guardian? Become a dragon. We Chosen can aid thee in that aim with spells to do so that will transform thee, lengthen thy years, and enhance thy vigor."

Vangerdahast frowned. "One dragon, to defend a realm? Not even the Devil Dragon could stand against . . ."

"No," Joysil said in her soft thunder. "Not one. I've long sought a purpose to go on living, and I believe I've found it. I'll willingly join you in stasis, as your consort."

Vangerdahast gaped at her. Then, very slowly, he turned to peer back into the ruined kitchen of his sanctum, at the tearful woman standing there.

"No," Myrmeen whispered, face white and working. "No, I cannot give up being human. I—I . . . Vangey, forgive me!"

"There's naught to forgive, lass," two old wizards said in unison. Then they stopped and traded uneasy grins.

Myrmeen burst into tears, and groped for Elminster's arm. When he proffered it, she clung to him, dragged herself upright, and fought down her weeping until she managed to gulp, "Yet it would g-give me g-great pride and pleasure to bear and raise your heir, Lord Vangerdahast, to be trained as a wizard loyal to Cormyr."

Elminster lifted an eyebrow. "Mystra smile, but ye work swifter than I do, Vangey!"

Out across the trampled grass, Vangerdahast made reply—with a very old and very rude gesture.

* * * * *

A blood-drenched, battered figure rose from a heap of the dead in the shattered ruins of Thundaerlyn Hall, shook aside some ashen, still-smoking splinters of balcony, and limped across the rubble-strewn floor, a notched and bent sword in hand.

"Mother?"

Another figure arose serenely out of heaped bodies not far away.

"I'm not dead yet," the Dowager Queen replied with a weak smile, wiping blood from the sword in her own hand with the hem of her jeweled gown. She surveyed Alusair critically. "Which is more than I can say for you. You always *did* like getting dirty, didn't you?"

"Indeed," Alusair said with a sudden laugh, embracing her mother. "And I still do."

Purple Dragons, Highknights, and War Wizards were eyeing them from a discreet distance and shuffling closer. Filfaeril chuckled and told her daughter, "Come, find us that portal back to Suzail, or we'll have to spend the rest of the night answering questions!"

* * * * *

"Come, lass," Elminster said to Myrmeen, "ye need to eat. There'll be naught to see now for some days, until all our castings are done."

He turned away to lead the weary and saddened Lady Lord of Arabel to a chair—only to freeze as a voice thundered behind him. Joysil's voice.

"Mage, I've learned of your recent wranglings with a certain young lass of Waterdeep—where is she right now?"

Something in that grim tone made Elminster spin around, letting go of Myrmeen's hand and stepping away from her in haste.

"Ah," Elminster replied with a grin, "ye know the saying about wizards never letting slip their secrets?"

"Almost as well as I know the one about how tasty wizards can be," the song dragon growled. "So I'll amend my question into two lesser ones: Do you know where she is, and is she safe?"

"Aye, and I hope so. Thy interest in her proceeds from—?"

"Dragons eat *their* secrets, man. Let me unfold this my way. There's one more thing to be said. We know each other rather better than you realize."

"Oh?" El asked, spreading his fingers to display the rings on them—rings that winked with the light of awakened magic. "Is there an old score ye need settled? Some share of *my* hoards, perhaps? Or is it my skin ye seek?"

"Once we sought each other's skin, Elminster of Shadowdale—ardently and often."

The Old Mage's eyes narrowed. "What name and shape did ye wear then?"

"For some years I was the sorceress and jeweler Maerjanthra Shalace of Waterdeep."

Myrmeen gave Elminster an incredulous look and found the Old Mage's face every bit as astonished as her own.

He managed a pale smile then bowed deeply to the looming dragon. "Well, well—ahem—my apologies for knowing ye not, Joysil. So ye're Narnra's mother!" He shook his head, adding hastily, "Well, now. I . . . I'll tell her only much later, I think, when the lass is ready for such news."

"Wise choice," Joysil said in dry tones.

Elminster cast a swift glance at Myrmeen. Fresh tears were streaming down her face, but she waved him away as she sat in a chair. Not just away. She was waving him toward the dragon.

The Old Mage looked up, swallowed, and asked, "Wha . . . ah, how d'ye feel toward me now, ah, Lady?"

"Joysil. Call me Joysil." The great dragon head lowered, those burning eyes seemed to sear through him, and the jaws beneath slowly . . . smiled.

"I must confess I'm—pleased—to see you so taken aback. You're learning, El . . . learning doubt at last. Archmages who know *just* how to rule the world scare me, and you were worse than most. One bed one night, another the next, no thought for the ruin you left behind or what *I* went through, tearing free from Shar. Too many realms to conquer, liches to blast, other wizards to humble—all stars in your eyes and rushing to save Faerûn, that was you. And yet I . . . I love you still."

"Ye . . ."

"I loved you then for the same reason I'm still fond of you, Old Mage. Your tenderness. Your gentleness, your understanding. Never lose that, El, or I might just awaken, leave Cormyr undefended, and come looking for you." Joysil sprang aloft.

"I—I still care for thee, Maer—Joysil," Elminster called quickly, stepping forward.

"I know, El. I know. So keep yourself alive for years to come, hold that madness at bay, be happy with the Queen of Aglarond—and look after our Narnra well—*without* smothering her."

"I . . . of course. Her safety shall be—"

"The pleasure you endure now," Joysil said in a voice as dry as the desert, "in return for the pleasure we shared then."

She flapped her wings once, circled so low over the Old Mage that Myrmeen cried out in alarm, and whispered, "Farewell, El. I *do* love you." She soared away, silver-blue in the lowering sun.

Elminster went to his knees as his spell flung his thought after her: *I love thee, Joysil, and I love our Narnra. Trust in me.*

He got back of flare of amusement. *Trust. Of course.*

Elminster stayed on his knees, watching the sky where Joysil had gone for some time.

"Well, now," he said finally, getting up with a wince and a hand on a stiffening hip. He didn't look at the Lady Lord of Arabel, and she watched him in silence.

"Well, now," Elminster muttered again, several times, as he peered into larders, drew forth tureens, and gathered kindling for the hearthfire.

"He hasn't taken very good care of the place," a familiar voice floated out of the distance.

Myrmeen's head jerked up. "Laspeera!"

"Well, you know Vangey," another voice agreed wryly, and Caladnei led three rather battered-looking women down a rubble-strewn passage into the kitchen. "Aha," she said as Elminster straightened up from the growing fire. "He had help destroying things. I might have known."

The Crown Princess asked sharply, "So what happened, Mreen? Is the realm now at war with Elminster of Shadowdale?"

The Dowager Queen Filfaeril stood with her, both of them stained with blood and looking as if they'd been in a battle.

Myrmeen shook her head, fresh tears glimmering in her eyes. "No," she quavered, "but I'm not sure what to tell you first. I . . ."

"What befell in Marsember?" a new voice asked from behind the two highest-ranking War Wizards, causing them in turn to whirl around. "Am I now holding the last living Obarskyr?"

The glow of a spell was just fading around the ankles of Storm Silverhand, who stood with the infant Azoun cradled in her arms, the sage Alaphondar at her side, Florin Falconhand standing watchfully by with two swords drawn—and Narnra flanking him, drawn daggers in both hands.

Of course, everyone started talking at once.

* * * * *

Storm, Florin, and, surprisingly, Alaphondar and Filfaeril all pitched in with the cooking, and the resulting feast was wonderful. Much later—magic being a wonderfully useful thing—the shattered kitchen had become a haven of warmth and softly leaping firelight, wherein all sat at ease with boots up and glasses to hand—save for the snoring King of Cormyr.

It was the first time in years that Narnra Shalace could remember being truly happy.

"Forgive me," Myrmeen asked her politely across the table, "but I hear the swifter, harsher speech of Waterdeep on your tongue. What brought you to Cormyr?"

Narnra smiled. "I was thieving and followed a man I failed to rob, who intrigued me." She nodded across the room, to where a white-bearded wizard was gently spell-rocking a conjured cradle for Azoun Obarskyr and humming a nameless tune, while rubbing the feet of a bootless Storm Silverhand as she groaned in contentment. "Elminster of Shadowdale," Narnra explained, "who turned out to be my father."

"Elminster?" Myrmeen asked. "Your father?"

"Yes. Wherefore I happen," Narnra added, "to be one of the two or maybe three women in all Waterdeep who *aren't* breathtakingly beautiful."

"Well, luckily the gods didn't give you the worst of his hawk-nose—or his beard," Myrmeen chuckled. "I remember from my younger days that being stunningly gorgeous was more bother than it was fun—being as I wasn't an empty-headed, spiteful little bitch of a noble, looking to spend my days marrying one nobleman and bedding all the others after revels."

Narnra nodded, drew in a deep breath, and turned to Caladnei. "So now that you know all about me, will you still have me in your service? Or slay me?"

"Of course I'll still have you," Caladnei replied warmly, and turned her head to look at the Lady Laspeera. "As for why, you're the best one to make answer, Speera."

Laspeera nodded. "Narnra," she said gently, "I, too, am a daughter of Elminster. Welcome, sister. Truly, I am. . . . and there are a lot of us."

"Myself, for instance," Queen Filfaeril said calmly, causing Cormyrean jaws to drop all over the room. "Though neither of us knew it for some years."

"Gods," Myrmeen said, turning to gaze at the bearded man by the cradle. "You *have* been busy, haven't you?"

EPILOGUE

Humans like to mark endings—but such events are seldom the real end of any tale.

Amaelree Windhover
One Elf in Minstrels' Robes
Year of the Splendid Stag

Brine. This leaking cog was loaded with sides of pickled beef—bound for Sembia. *Witch of the Dragon Waves*, indeed. Harnrim Starangh sighed and hastened down the companionway. His spell would wear off in moments—if some vengeful War Wizard didn't trace him by it before then—and none of the other ships in Marsember were showing any signs of leaving soon.

He had to get out of Cormyr. With but three spells left to him—and certain superiors among the Red Wizards certain to be looking for him with even more fury than these law-mages of the Forest Kingdom—the mighty Darkspells was going to have to vanish for a while. Perhaps for a long while.

He had been close. So close . . .

Harnrim Starangh permitted himself a single soft but heartfelt curse before he worked the magic that would turn him into a ballast-stone . . . and toppled into the filthy water of the bilges.

* * * * *

Glarasteer Rhauligan was in no mood for delay. His burden had fainted as he'd carried her along dark and secret tunnels from the portal. The palace room they were in now was off limits to all but War Wizards, who were lazyrobes all, which meant that instead of a lantern that had to be lit, there'd be a hooded glowstone right about—*here*.

In the revealed radiance the Highknight selected a row of steel vials from one of the crammed shelves and started biting off their corks. Why they couldn't make these so they were easy to open one-handed, he'd never know.

He forced three of them down Nouméa's lovely throat before her eyes fluttered open and her flank ceased to feel like . . . well, like some butcher of a nobleman with a sharp sword had slit it open.

"T-Thank you, sir," she murmured, staring at him. "You're . . . Rhauligan. A Highknight of Cormyr, I believe. I owe you my life. Why? What do you intend for me now?"

Rhauligan shook his head. Quick-tongued, these Sembian nobles, even while weary and weak with half their life-blood spilled. "Bed rest in one of the state guestchambers yonder," he told her, "a meal if you're up to it—and *I'm* certainly going to feast, even if you want nothing—and we'll talk in the morning. Cormyr has a certain shortage of nobles the realm can trust, right now."

"And one cast-aside highskirts woman from Sembia can make a difference?"

"Lady, one person can *always* make a difference—and their name need not be Azoun Obarskyr, Vangerdahast, or even Glarasteer Rhauligan, for that matter. What's Cormyr—

or any fair realm—but a lot of lone persons, who believe in the same thing?"

"This is the dream you believe in?" Nouméa murmured, as Rhauligan picked her off her feet and carried her into the next chamber.

"Lady fair," Rhauligan told her, as he laid Nouméa gently on a bed and started to arrange pillows behind her head, "'tis what gets me up in the morning."

* * * * *

Bezrar made a choking sound and lurched toward the rail. The *Witch of the Dragon Waves* was starting to roll and wallow already, with the harbor barely astern.

"Nine blazing Hells," Surth hissed, swallowing hard to keep his own gorge down, "are you going to do *that* all the way to Yhaunn?"

His fat business partner's reply was a whirl of impressive alacrity to grip Malakar Surth's throat with fingers that were as hard as their arrival was sudden.

"*You* shut up, for once, Cleversneer," Aumun Tholant Bezrar snarled furiously, "or by all the gods I'll—"

He fell silent to gape up into the sky and shrank away from Surth to cower.

Surth whirled around to see what had frightened his partner, knowing as he did so that it was an action he was going to regret.

He was right. Out of the mists something was gliding past, slow and low and menacing. Something larger than the *Witch of the Dragon Waves*, and far more graceful: a gigantic fang dragon with a rainbow-hued swath of scales on one flank.

When it was quite gone, Bezrar and Surth swallowed in white-faced unison, there as they cowered on the deck of the creaking, wallowing merchant cog.

"We can't reach Sembia swift enough for me," Surth whispered, though in truth he cared not if the rolling ship beneath him was bound for Yhaunn or the Pirate Isles, or Westgate, or anyplace else in all wide Faerûn that wasn't controlled by Red Wizards. Yet.

"Well," Bezrar growled, from beside him, "at least we're well away from Darkspells, and all his schemes. *That* one made me shiver, I can tell you!"